Beside Two Rivers

What do you get when you combine authentic history, picturesque settings, dynamic characters and a feels-like-you're-there storyline? You get a Rita Gerlach novel, and in *Beside Two Rivers*, Book 2 in her Daughters of the Potomac series, she delivers all that and more. My advice to readers: Make room for this one on your "keepers shelf." My advice to Rita: save space on your "awards wall," because this tale is sure to earn a bunch!
—Loree Lough, best-selling author of more than 85 award-winning books, including *Honor Redeemed*, Book 2 in the First Responders series

Rita Gerlach has penned another engrossing historical with a spirited heroine, this one about a long-hidden secret and how it threatens lives and love.
—Julie L. Cannon, author of *Truelove & Homegrown Tomatoes* and *Twang*

Other books by Rita Gerlach

Surrender the Wind

The Daughters of the Potomac Series

Before the Scarlet Dawn, book 1

Beyond the Valley, book 3, coming February 2013

Beside Two Rivers

Book 2

The Daughters of the Potomac Series

Rita Gerlach

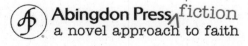

Abingdon Press fiction
a novel approach to faith

Nashville, Tennessee

Beside Two Rivers

Copyright © 2012 Rita Gerlach

ISBN: 978-1-4267-1415-3

Published by Abingdon Press, P.O. Box 801, Nashville, TN 37202

www.abingdonpress.com

The persons and events portrayed in this work of fiction
are the creations of the author, and any resemblance
to persons living or dead is purely coincidental.

Published in association with Hartline Literary Agency

Library of Congress Cataloging-in-Publication Data

Gerlach, Rita.
    Beside two rivers / Rita Gerlach.
       p. cm. — (Daughters of the Potomac ; bk. 2)
    ISBN 978-1-4267-1415-3 (book - pbk. /trade pbk. : alk. paper)
    I. Title.
    PS3607.E755B47 2012
    813'.6—dc23

                                                                2011051567

Printed in the United States of America

1 2 3 4 5 6 7 8 9 10 / 17 16 15 14 13 12

To all those who seek the Truth

Acknowledgment

Thanks to Barbara Scott, my agent, whose gentle nudge forward made me realize one book should turn into a series.

Part 1

Peace I ask of thee, O River
Peace, peace, peace
When I learn to live serenely
Cares will cease.
From the hills I gather courage
Visions of days to be
Strength to lead and faith to follow
All are given unto me
Peace I ask of thee, O River
Peace, peace, peace.
—Attributed to Janet E. Tobitt

1

The Potomac Heights, Maryland

1797

She'd been warned not to venture far from the house, nor go near the river, nor climb the dark shale bluffs above it. But Darcy Morgan had inherited an adventurous spirit that could not be bridled. It had been her favorite place to retreat since the age of nine, when she had discovered it one morning while trekking with her cousins over the ridge that shadowed the Potomac River.

Bathed in sunlight, she stood at the bluff's edge and gazed down at the water as she had done a hundred times before. She looked at the sky. Pink and pearled, speckled with white summer clouds, it looked heaven-like in the glow of a golden dusk.

Mottle-winged caddis flies danced in hordes at the brink and Darcy paused to study them. How could such delicate wings flit so high without turning to dust in the breeze? It caressed her face, blew back her dark hair, and eased through her cotton dress. She breathed deep the scent of wild honeysuckle that traveled with it. Drowsy warmth hung everywhere, while the birds sang evening vespers.

With closed eyes, Darcy listened to the water tumble over the boulders and rocks below. Stretching out her arms, she turned in a circle and soaked in the majesty of creation.

"Darcy . . . Darcy Morgan . . . Where are you, you adventuresome pixie?"

Turning, she spied her uncle, William Breese, as he lumbered along the ridge toward her. With caution, he stepped over rocks and between roots of great trees, a barrel-chested man with stocky legs. His eyes were pale green against his swarthy face, his head framed in a nimbus of white hair. Darcy's father, Hayward Morgan, had been his half-brother, and Darcy wondered if her father's eyes had been like her uncle's, for she could not remember his face. Breathless, her uncle glanced up to see her, and she skipped down the path toward him.

When she reached her uncle, he put his hands upon his knees to catch his breath. "Your aunt has been fretting all afternoon, wondering where you had gone off to."

Regretting she had caused her aunt such uneasiness, Darcy brushed back her hair and halted before him. "I am sorry, Uncle Will. I should have told her. I did not mean to cause Aunt Mari to fret."

"Ah, the woman has had a nervous constitution from birth to forty and two. She fears that one of her girls, and you, Darcy, could be *injured or lost, fall from the bluffs, or be swept into the river and drowned.* She goes so far as to believe that one of you could be carried all the way to the Chesapeake and then out to sea."

Darcy giggled. "It would be an adventure to survive such an ordeal, to perhaps be rescued by our Navy."

He shrugged. "Only you would think so. Your aunt wrings her hands and paces the floor every time one of you ventures out-of-doors. Think of me, dear girl, what I've had to endure."

Darcy smiled and put her arm around him. "Are you angry with me?"

He smiled and wiggled his head. "I could never be angry with you, Darcy. I like your drive for exploration. Just look at that patch of sky. Only God can paint a picture like that."

She raised her face to meet the sunlight. "I've been watching it for hours, how the light mellows the clouds."

"I wish your aunt were more attentive to the things of nature."

"To console you, Uncle, I have seen her pause to admire the flowers she brings into the house."

"Indeed, and now she has news and is eager for you to come home." Mr. Breese looped Darcy's arm through his and proceeded to walk with her down the hill. "She has the girls gathered in the sitting room and refuses to read a letter until I bring you back and we are both present."

"I imagine she is cross," Darcy said.

"She would have forbidden you at this late hour. Next time tell me." He threw his free arm out wide. "I don't mind, and most likely will join you."

The house belonging to Mr. Breese was modest by well-to-do standards, but affluent for a Marylander living miles away from the cities of Annapolis and Baltimore. Darcy loved it, with its broad porch and dark green shutters. Its meadows filled with Queen Anne's lace. Its forests thick with ancient trees and wild lady slippers. Above all, she loved the river and the creeks that flowed into it.

She stepped down the path between rows of locust trees, aiding her uncle along, for he was not strong in the legs at his time of life. The windows glowed with evening sunlight. The front door sat open, allowing the breeze to flow free. A shaggy brown dog slumbered on the threshold with his head between muddy paws, and when he heard her whistle, he lifted his head and bounded up to her and her uncle.

When Darcy entered the cool narrow hallway of the house, she pulled off her broad-brimmed hat and shook back her hair. Even with a bright sun that day, she had not worn it on her head, but let it hang behind her shoulders. She set it on a hook beside the door and paused when she heard her aunt's voice in the sitting room.

"Darcy," Mari Breese called.

She stepped inside with a smile. "I am here, Aunt Mari."

"Where on earth have you been? I have worried." Mrs. Breese fanned her face with the letter, set it on her lap, and fell back against her chair. Accustomed to her aunt's melodrama, Darcy dismissed her troubled tone of voice.

"I was out walking." She kissed her aunt's cheek.

"Walking, walking. What is so grand about walking? On my word, I do believe there are still Indians roaming about who would be pleased to snatch away a beauty like you. They might lust for that lovely hair of yours, I dread to think."

Proud of her locks, Mari Breese tucked her mouse-brown hair, peppered with gray, further into her mobcap. Her eyes were dark blue, close to the shade of ink that stained the letter she held. The rose in her cheeks heightened, not from the heat in the room, but from the excitement. Darcy wished she could calm her. Everyone would be better off.

"Uncle Will said you have news, Aunt. May we hear it?" Darcy sat next to her cousins, who were seated with perfect posture in a row upon a faded settee.

"Yes, Mama. You said you would read it once everyone was here," said Darcy's cousin Martha.

Her eldest cousin possessed a flawless row of pearl-white teeth and eyes like her papa's. She and Darcy were the same age, and their resemblance to each other caused people to think they were sisters. She wore her hair in a loose chignon today, silky and dark brown, accenting her fair skin. Darcy could not tolerate the style, and each time Martha urged her to try it she exclaimed it gave her a headache.

"We have been patient," Martha reminded her mother. The other girls—Lizzy, Abigail, Rachel, and Dolley—chimed in.

"If your father would be so good as to sit down, I will begin. It involves all of us."

Mr. Breese drew his pipe out from between his teeth. He sat in a chair beneath the window, picked up the newspaper, and proceeded to look it over.

"Will, your attention please." Mrs. Breese slapped her hands together.

"Here's an interesting article, girls," he said. "In March, a gentleman by the name of Whitney invented a machine that removes the seeds from cotton. Calls it the cotton gin. Fancy that!"

"More than likely it will add to the South's sinful institution of slavery," Darcy said.

"I hope not, Darcy. But with an invention of this kind . . ."

Mrs. Breese stamped her foot. "Husband, do you wish to hear this or not?"

He set the paper down on his lap. "What is so important, my dear?"

"We've received an invitation. I must say, I have been anticipating this, and now we have something to break the boredom we endure in this wilderness."

"Boredom, my dearest? With this lot, how can you be bored? And it's hardly a wilderness anymore, not with towns and villages springing up everywhere. It is no different here than in New York."

Mrs. Breese huffed. "New York indeed. New York is a city. This is the end of the earth as far as I am concerned."

"No different from where you were raised, then."

"Indeed that is true. This invitation reminds me of when I was young. You girls shall benefit from this."

Darcy's cousins pleaded for her aunt to reveal the facts. She sat quiet, her mind summing up all the things this invitation could be. A ball? A dinner party or picnic? She thought of the few neighbors they had, and not a one seemed given to hold such events. But on the other side of the river were large plantations, and the Virginians were noted for gatherings of all sorts. She'd never been to the other side of the Potomac, and the chance excited her.

Mr. Breese lifted his paper and glanced over it. "Are you going to keep us in suspense, my dear?"

"I shall read it when I am ready . . . I am ready now."

"I am glad to hear it, my dear."

"Which do you wish to know first, who it is from or where it is from?"

"I suppose you will tell us both, whether I want to know or not."

"It comes from Twin Oaks. A country picnic and dance is to be held this Saturday in celebration of Captain and Mrs. Rhendon's son's homecoming." She wiggled and her mobcap went awry. The girls were bursting with smiles and exclamations.

"How thrilling." Mr. Breese yawned.

"It says here that Daniel Rhendon has returned from a long stay in England and wishes to celebrate. I imagine every-one has been invited. Meaning those of good social standing like us."

"Why do you suppose that, Mother?" Rachel winked at her sisters, her blonde curls, amid a wide blue ribbon, toppling over her slim shoulders.

"Because, my dear, we are people of quality, and it is only proper the Rhendons would invite us."

Darcy wondered, *Why now?* "They never have before, not in all the years we have lived here."

"That is true. Perhaps an acquaintance mentioned us."

Mr. Breese blew out a breath. "It would displease your dear departed mother to know you approve of the Rhendons, my sweet."

Mrs. Breese arched her brows. "How so, my dear?"

"Have you forgotten, she was a loyalist during the Revolution?" Darcy's cousins turned their heads in unison and looked at him with wide-eyed interest. "Their neighbors convinced your papa to join the militia at a ripe old age. Remember?"

Mrs. Breese shrugged. "I do. And Mama said rebellion was an evil thing. She grieved that Papa thought differently and took up arms against the King. I recall her wails that he'd be hung by the neck along with the rest of the traitors—which meant the Patriots."

This sparked Darcy's interest. Her aunt shared so little about her family. "Did their difference of opinion cause them to love each other less, Aunt?"

Mari Breese shook her head. "Not one whit. Mama swore she would not abandon Papa for his misguided politics, and she never did. His stint in the militia did not last long. He was too old to cope."

It pleased Darcy to hear that love had won out over all odds. If only it had been that way for her parents. She knew something dark had happened between them, with the little she could remember, but she had never dared to force the information from her aunt and uncle. They never offered to reveal anything. And so, she left well enough alone.

Darcy shut her eyes and forced back one memory—that of her mother lying still and pale. She could not see Eliza's face, only a flow of dark hair. She remembered the firm touch of her father's hands, the sound of his voice, and the words—*You've heard of Hell, haven't you? Well, that's where your mama will be.*

She had vague memories of her father, some that were nightmarish that she kept to herself, others of a loving parent who pampered her. Her heart ached recalling him and her mother, whose faces were a blur in her mind.

"This gives me pause to think of your own parents, Darcy," her aunt said. "Such negligence by your father to have left for the West the way he did, leaving you with us without a forwarding address of any kind. But I should not have been surprised."

"I do not remember him well enough to know, Aunt. And I doubt there are forwarding addresses into the Western territories."

"I would say it was more that he did not wish the responsibility of raising a girl," said her aunt.

You see, if you are a bad person and sin—that is where you will go. That is where your mother is going . . . forever.

Those words came back again, causing her heart to sink. She gazed at the evening light pouring through the window and wished it could erase them from her memory.

Night was falling and the crickets in the garden were chirping. Aunt Mari stood and pushed the window wider to allow the breeze to pass into the room. Then she sat back down and looked over at Darcy. "Oh, it has troubled you for me to mention them. Would it help if I told you that your papa loved your mother? That much I can say with certainty, Darcy."

Darcy raised her eyes to meet her aunt's. "Do not worry yourself, Aunt Mari. I was so young and do not remember them. You and Uncle Will have been my parents, and I thank God for it."

"I believe the truth is when Eliza died, Hayward went West to lose himself in his grief," her uncle said.

"Oh, how romantic!" cried Dolley. Her winsome blue eyes glowed as she clutched her hands to her heart. Dolley heaved the next two breaths while she brushed back her light brown hair from her forehead.

"Romantic?" Mrs. Breese clicked her tongue. "A sad turn of events, shrouded in mystery is hardly romantic, Dolley. There were things said and done we will never know . . . never."

Darcy grew silent, for she had nothing she wanted to say that would reveal her own thoughts and feelings on the subject. But within her, emptiness remained.

Her aunt reached over and patted her hand. "Never mind, Darcy. You should not think on such sad things. I'm sorry for mentioning them. Let us return to the Rhendons' invitation instead. I wager you will catch the eye of many a young man at this event. Perhaps even find a husband."

Darcy shook her head. "Oh, not me, Aunt."

"Why not? You are just as pretty as Lizzy and Martha, and I dare say even Abby and Rachel. Dolley is yet too young."

Darcy disagreed. She thought her cousins were far more attractive. They were enamored with fashion, wore their hair in the latest styles, and always wore stockings and shoes; whereas she cared little for what was in and what was out, wore her hair loose about her shoulders, refused to wear stockings in hot weather, and loved going barefoot in summer.

She stood up and, going to the window seat, leaned on the sill and drew in the air. "If you could have your way, Aunt, you would have us all married by Saturday eve."

Her aunt sighed. "Well you should have married a year ago. Lizzy and Martha should be married by the year's end. I was sixteen when I married Mr. Breese."

Mr. Breese looked over the rim of his spectacles. "Thank you for the reminder, my dear."

She gave him a coy look in response. "Now, girls," she went on. "We should look at each one of your dresses to see if they are in acceptable condition for this affair. If they are not we shall see if we can make subtle repairs or changes to them, perhaps add or subtract where needed."

"Can we not make new dresses? Or go into town and buy new ones?" Lizzy gazed over at Mr. Breese with a demure smile and batted her large blue eyes. Darcy had seen it many times—Lizzy's attempt to twist him around her finger.

"For all six of you?" Stunned, Mr. Breese lifted his brows. "I am not a rich man, Lizzy. You must make do with what you have."

The girls pouted in unison, but Darcy rose to her feet and swung her arms around her uncle's neck. "We shall make you proud of us. Our clothes are just as good as any others, and we should not be judged by what we wear. French fashion is out, since their gentry are wearing sackcloth and ashes these days."

Mrs. Breese brushed her handkerchief over her neck. "Oh, Darcy. I hope you keep opinions like that to yourself while at Twin Oaks. Many people judge a young lady by the clothes she wears. It says where you fit in."

"Yes, Aunt." Darcy wrapped a strand of her hair around her finger. "I hear they have fine horses at Twin Oaks. Do you suppose they shall let us ride?"

Astonishment spread over her aunt's face. "Certainly not. It would be unbecoming."

"But ladies ride all the time, Mother," said Abby. She had not spoken until now, and Darcy smiled. Lately, Abby strove to break out of her shy nature and join in the conversation. She was the politest of young ladies, and in appearance the image of her mother. Horses were her passion, and the idea of possibly riding one at Twin Oaks caused her eyes to light up.

"I do hope the Rhendons allow it, for you especially, Abby," Darcy said.

"Ladies should not ride horses at country picnics," said Mrs. Breese. "I will not have my girls racing about the grounds like backwoods bumpkins."

Lizzy had to inject. "What do you suggest we do, Mother? Sit all day fanning ourselves, melting in the heat, making eyes at the boys?" Each girl giggled, except for Darcy, who smiled.

"There will be other things to do," said Mrs. Breese. "You older girls must strive to be noticed, dance with those who ask, and do all you can to win a heart or two."

"Sounds boring to me," Rachel moaned, "and too hot to do anything."

"Then be sure to wear plenty of powder, and stay in the shade," said Mrs. Breese.

"Anything else we should know?" Mr. Breese folded his paper again.

"Well, I have not finished reading the invitation." Mrs. Breese held the letter up to her eyes. "It says young Mr. Rhendon has brought a party with him from England. It does not list the names, but it says he brings two ladies and a gentleman."

"The English cannot keep themselves away, can they?" Darcy said.

Mrs. Breese gave her a sidelong glance. "It says here, the gentleman is an exceptional rider and will make inquiry into Captain Rhendon's thoroughbreds." Again, she set the letter down on her lap and sighed with delight. "How interesting is that, my girls? Two ladies and an English gentleman."

Mrs. Breese folded the invitation and set it on the side table next to her.

Darcy went from the room out into the hallway. She stepped out the door, sat down on the stone stoop, and stroked the dog's ears. What would happen if she caught the eye of some gentleman at this gathering? He would have to have excellent qualities for her to like him, and she doubted if there was such a man alive, for her expectations were much too high.

She wanted a man like her uncle, kind, generous, with a sense of humor that matched his sense of duty. Could there be such a man searching for a girl like her?

She listened to the chatter coming from upstairs where the girls had gone to sort through their clothes. Missy, their housemaid, came down the stairs with an armload of frocks, stockings, and laces, all in need of washing and repair.

Her aunt appeared on the upstairs landing. "Darcy, come look at your gown. It is important."

She did as she was asked, and when she drew out the best dress she owned from the armoire, she held it out before her and looked it over. Her aunt stared at it, tapped her forefinger against her chin, and huffed, "It will have to be made over."

The gown in question opened down the back and closed with hooks and eyes. The bodice seams were piped with narrow cording of matching fabric, and the deep hem was faced with heavier fabric to protect it from wear.

"I think it is fine the way it is, Aunt. But if you think it needs altering . . ."

"Oh, indeed it does. We will alter the sleeves and add ribbon and trim. And we should remove the lace. It is so out of fashion."

"Seems like too much work for one day's outing."

Mrs. Breese took a step back and squared her shoulders. "I dare say, Darcy, I have never known you to have a lazy bone in your body. Believe me, altering this gown shall be well worth your time. Besides, the cloth was too dearly acquired to abandon, and too many hours went into the original stitching to cast it off."

Darcy agreed. She was not in the least bit slothful, but sewing made her fingers sore. Yet, she would follow through. "I did not mean we should cast it off, Aunt. I just happen to like it the way it is."

"Then keep it as it is, if it pleases you." Slapping her hands together, her aunt let out a little giggle. "I am so happy that full skirts and tight bodices are out of fashion, as well as high-dressed hair and painted faces."

Darcy smiled at the image in her mind. "I cannot picture you with your hair piled high and powdered, or your face painted."

"Never!" said her aunt. "A tight bodice yes. But the rest, I cared not. For it was so vain and made a woman look clownish."

Expecting such an answer, Darcy laughed. "Then I, too, am happy."

Her aunt leaned toward her. "Now, we have four days to complete our tasks. Saturday shall be here before we know it."

"Yes, Aunt."

"Missy shall take care of the rest of the chores so you girls can work without interruption. Now you should be glad for that. No feeding the chickens. No collecting eggs. Isn't that grand?"

"I like feeding the hens and collecting eggs." She glanced at her aunt with insistence. "I can still do my work and finish my dress."

"Let us not put that to the test, Darcy." And off her aunt went through the door, leaving Darcy to stand in the middle of the room with her dress in hand. She held it against her body and gazed into the mirror.

"It will do just as it is."

With that resolved, she put it away and headed downstairs. She took up a willow basket from beside the kitchen door and went off to the hen house.

2

Along the country road, summer thrived, and the breeze blew dogwood petals onto the ground. Wild raspberry bushes drooped with succulent blood-red fruit along dusty hedgerows, and the songs of goldfinches echoed through the woods.

The Breeses owned one wagon, which doubled for family transport when needed. Mr. Breese had applied a fresh coat of black lacquer to it and painted the wheel spokes bright red.

"I wish we owned a carriage." Mrs. Breese frowned. "People will stare and think very low of us."

Darcy moved closer to speak to her aunt. "Just think, Aunt Mari, no wagon of this kind has ever rolled down the lane at Twin Oaks before, or along the river road for that matter. People will admire it, you'll see."

Darcy and her cousins sat together in the rear, while her aunt and uncle sat in front on cushions. A hat made of tightly woven straw shaded Darcy's face. Her plain gown paled among the pink and blue calicos her cousins wore. Their hats were trimmed with matching ribbons, and each girl wore tan gloves and pale yellow shoes.

"Gloves are out of the question on such a hot day." Darcy slipped them off and set them beside her. Her aunt turned with pursed lips.

"Dear me, Darcy. No gloves? What will Mrs. Rhendon think? At least keep your hat on until we enter the house."

Darcy smiled and adjusted the wide ribbon under her chin. She brushed away a few petals that had found their way into the folds of her gown and settled back. Pulled by two dappled horses, the wagon rolled over the river road under a canopy of tall trees and then crossed the creaky bridge into Virginia. Crossing the bridge frightened Mrs. Breese, and she looped her arm through her husband's and shut her eyes the whole way over.

When Twin Oaks came into view, Darcy put her hand above her eyes to study the large house with white porticoes and a wide porch. Embowered in wisteria, it stood at the end of a broad drive lined with sugar maples, with two oak trees out front. Farther back in the rear stood a stable, a smoke-house, and an icehouse constructed of whitewashed stone.

Locusts trilled, and warm air drifted through the trees. To the right waved wheat fields, to the left an apple orchard. At first glance, Twin Oaks appeared a pretty picture, but Darcy wondered how appealing were the lives that dwelt within its massive walls.

Out front were a number of carriages and saddled horses. "Many guests have already arrived," commented Mrs. Breese, nodding back to the girls. "I'm glad we are not the first. I just hope we are not the last."

"I *hope* they have lemonade." Dolley fanned her face with her hand.

"And cake," Rachel chimed in. "I adore cake."

Martha nudged Rachel's shoulder. "How can you think of food on a day like today?"

Abigail and Lizzy joined in to chastise their sisters, each chattering away at the same time. Darcy sighed and gazed up at the lush umbrella of limbs overhead. How misty the streams of light looked as they filtered through the trees. It made her heart swell. Why could her aunt and cousins not see such beauty and soak it in the way she did?

Dolley and Rachel sat on each side of Darcy and she looped their arms within hers. "Just look at the light coming through the branches above us. Is it not lovely?"

Dolley huffed. "Oh, Darcy. Must you grow poetic? We'd rather see tables full of cakes and pies and . . ."

"I am certain they shall have food and lemonade in abundance for you and Rachel to enjoy, Dolley. Your sisters are older and have no interest in the food at such a gathering as this. For there are other distractions."

"Darcy is right," Martha said. "Just look at the men gathered on the porch. Have you ever seen such gallants as these?"

"Are they not fine?" Abigail sighed.

"We are not close enough to tell," Darcy said. "Besides, they may all be taken."

"Still there are plenty to dance with," finished Lizzy.

After they alighted from their wagon, a carriage rumbled toward the plantation house along its shady drive. Clouds of rust-colored dust whirled about its wheels. When it came to a halt at the front of the veranda, swarms of people gathered around.

"Look, it is Daniel Rhendon and his party." Martha said. Darcy's cousins straightened their backs and lifted their heads to get a better glimpse of the English guests.

Lizzy sighed. "He's handsome."

"Yes, but too young," Martha said. "I prefer an older man."

Lizzy laughed. "Very well for me then, for I like him. Unless you are interested, Darcy."

Darcy glanced over at her cousin and smiled. "I will not interfere with your pursuits, Lizzy. But prepare yourself, for one can see he has designs on the lady he is helping down."

Darcy watched on as the ladies were handed down. Two were lovely, their posture regal, and their clothes the finest summer gauze. The third woman was older and dressed like a servant. Her matronly attire matched her figure, her posture stiff as starch. Darcy's gaze shifted to the man who had given his hand to a lady. He held her fingers firm until her pink satin shoe reached level ground. Then he let go.

Her first impression of him rang of prejudice, he being British. But she liked how he dropped the lady's hand and moved back. Perhaps such a woman had no power over him. The lady glided away and at that moment, his gaze turned toward Darcy. Their eyes met and held. Darcy looked away.

Mr. Breese placed his lady's hand over his arm and proceeded toward the veranda. Arms linked, the girls followed. Anxious young men gathered on the porch fixed their eyes upon them.

"Why do they stare at us?" Martha whispered to Darcy.

"They are looking at you and Lizzy, because you are so beautiful."

"You leave yourself out, Darcy?"

"I do. I am plain next to you."

"That is not true. You are so lovely, especially your hair. You know I've always envied it."

"You are sweet to say so, cousin."

"You caught the Englishman's eye."

A corner of Darcy's mouth lifted. "I doubt it."

"He is very handsome."

Darcy hugged her cousin closer. "Do not be deceived by the outward appearance, Martha. There is no telling what kind of rogue is beneath that skin."

She looked back over her shoulder. The English gentleman turned his eyes and held Darcy's gaze, then turned away, his brow gathered. Had she intruded upon him?

His dark brown hair touched the edge of his collar. The cut of his coat, his black leather boots, and his white linen neck-cloth were simple attire compared to some of the other men's. Either he was rich and preferred not to flaunt his position, or he was a man of modest means.

Martha pulled her along, and as they reached the top step, Captain Rhendon and his wife welcomed them. His neck-cloth, snowy-white and looped about his neck, looked too snug. His hair, gray and brown, whisked forward along his forehead and temples. Mrs. Rhendon, a head shorter than her husband, stood beside him.

A glimmer of envy was noted in her aunt's eyes when she laid eyes on their hostess's gown. Darcy did not care in the least what Mrs. Rhendon wore, but she did admire the color of the fabric. Pale yellow looked striking against her flawless skin.

"My dear Mr. and Mrs. Breese, so good of your family to come." Mrs. Rhendon held out her hand. "We're all about to gather out on the lawn. I hope the food meets the taste of Marylanders."

Mrs. Breese smiled. "I'm sure it will. My, what a beautiful home you have here."

"These are your daughters?" Mrs. Rhendon glanced over at the girls. Each curtsied prettily and smiled.

"Indeed they are. This is Martha our firstborn, hopefully the first to wed. And this is Lizzy. Her artistic talents are unsurpassed. And Abigail here has the voice of a nightingale."

Appearing intrigued, Mrs. Rhendon's brows arched. "Oh really? Perhaps she will entertain us with a song later."

"She'd be glad to. Won't you, Abby?" Mrs. Breese squeezed Abby's elbow, and Abby nodded. "Rachel is an accomplished musician and plays the pianoforte very well. She and our youngest, Dolley, are with the other girls their ages. So you must excuse them."

Darcy was last to be introduced. Her uncle, looking assertive, drew her forward. "And this is our niece, Darcy Morgan."

Captain Rhendon lifted his chin. "Morgan? Not of River Run, I hope."

His reaction to her hurt, but she tried not to show it by maintaining her smile. "I was born there, sir."

Captain Rhendon spoke something beneath his breath, so quiet, no one caught his words. But Darcy had no doubt it was an expletive. River Run had not been lived in since she left it. The last time she ventured near it, thistles and pokeweed smothered what had once been a green lawn.

"We had no idea, Mr. Breese, you were related to that particular family," said Mrs. Rhendon.

Mr. Breese made no effort to explain, but simply said, "My half-brother, ma'am, was Hayward Morgan, a true patriot of our cause."

Mrs. Rhendon snapped her fan shut and turned to Darcy. "Your mother was a beauty, Darcy."

"You knew her, ma'am?"

"Yes. When your father returned here with her, they attended a similar affair here at Twin Oaks. I recall her gown was deep amber, which set her apart from all the other ladies. But I dare say you take after your father's good looks." There was a faint ring of sarcasm in her voice, but her eyes, so well trained, did not show it.

Darcy extended a polite smile. "Thank you for your kind words, ma'am."

Mrs. Breese squeezed Darcy's hand. "Is your son well, now that he is home?"

Darcy breathed a sigh of relief that her aunt was astute enough to change the subject. For a moment, she dwelt on why the Rhendons seemed repelled by her last name.

Mrs. Rhendon replied. "He is well, thank you. You'll meet him shortly."

"We have met him already," Darcy said.

"Where? When?"

"It was long ago. We were down at the river one Sunday, and he . . ."

Mrs. Rhendon stiffened. Darcy realized she did not wish to hear anymore about her son's treks to the river—or hers. Her aunt touched her sleeve, a sign for her to rein in. "The English ladies and their gentleman companion must find Twin Oaks a rival to what they are used to back home, Mrs. Rhendon," said Mrs. Breese. "I do not doubt they envy it."

Mrs. Rhendon fluttered her fan near her chin. "No doubt they do."

Mrs. Breese's eyes blinked. "Are the ladies beautiful? I was unable to see them clearly from a distance. My eyesight is poor."

Darcy drew in a slow breath and looked away. It was embarrassing to have her aunt dig for information, and she hoped Mrs. Rhendon would answer her in such a way that her mind would be satisfied. Their hostess craned her neck to look out among her guests. "Miss Byrd is a lovely girl with pretty eyes. But Miss Roth rivals her in beauty. I do believe she is Mr. Brennan's intended, although he did not introduce her in that way. One would assume there is an understanding between them since she never leaves his side."

"I imagine Mr. Brennan is a fine gentleman," Mrs. Breese was so bold to say.

"He is, Mrs. Breese. You must excuse me. I have other guests." And Mrs. Rhendon stepped away with a sweep of her gown.

Moving to the lawn, the girls sat under the shade of an enormous oak. Darcy looked out across the green that stretched to the top of a hill. Her romantic nature carried her away to it, and she wondered what beauty lay beyond.

She stood and put her hand over her eyes. "I wish to walk the grounds. The ride over stiffened my legs."

"You're always walking about, Darcy." Lizzy sighed. "Can't you sit still for five minutes?"

Darcy smiled down at her cousin. "No, not when there is such beauty to see."

She stepped away, with her gown clinging to her limbs because of the breeze. With a graceful, yet eager stride, she strolled up the green expanse bordered by forest. When she reached the summit, she gazed down into a valley. In the meadow, deer grazed. They lifted their heads, sensing her presence. A stream curved through the vale and flashed in the sunlight.

Such beauty poured into Darcy with romantic passion. The land seemed to be a great barrier between her and some place that she would be called to someday. Where and when she did not know, but she yearned for it, for the adventure of it, the love that awaited her, and even the hardship and peril that would bring her closer to finding her heart's desire.

She stood beneath a solitary maple so large she could not imagine how long ago the Ancient of Days had sprouted it from the earth. Heavy branches stretched high above her, and the cool shade fell over her. She shook back her hair and raised her face. Shutting her eyes, she drank in the world around her. Beneath her feet, she felt a vibration, soft at first, then stronger as if a hundred drums beat beneath the sod. The hard gallop of a horse grew louder, and before she could move from the rider's path, he crested the hill. Startled, she turned and threw her back against the tree. The horse, black and large, reared and curvetted, having too been startled by her presence and the violent pull of its rider. It whinnied, blew out its nostrils, and pawed the mossy earth.

The rider swung down from the saddle and approached her. A thump in her chest snatched her breath and she placed her hands behind her to feel the safety of the tree.

"Are you all right?" Standing but a yard away, he breathed hard.

She nodded. "I believe so."

"I was unaware anyone would be here."

"I was unaware anyone would be riding so fiercely toward me."

The regret in his eyes deepened. "Please forgive me. You could have been hurt."

Darcy gazed at him, and then checked her winsome expression. "You did not know, sir."

"That is no excuse for me not to have been more careful. At least allow me to take you back down. The horse may look fierce, but he is harmless."

She glanced at the fearsome stallion. "By the size of him, and the way he behaves, I doubt your word."

"Doubt it, but just the same, he is gentle. I am considering buying him from the Rhendons to take back to England."

"His gentleness is not proven by how unsettled he appears. I hear they have a fine gray in the stable which would give no trouble."

The gentleman's countenance eased and he inclined his head. She knew what he interpreted in her comment—that his judgment was weak—and felt her face flush.

"I have plans to buy a mare as well. You could give me your opinion."

"I am not that astute when it comes to buying horses."

"Well, at least let me take you back."

"I am able to find the way myself." She smiled and walked away knowing he watched her go. She glanced back at him over her shoulder. "Thank you for not running me over." She hurried away, down the hill, skipping at places.

"But what is your name?" he called.

Forcing herself not to look back at him again, she did not answer. A smile brightened her face and laughter rose in her throat. He would have to make inquiries to discover who she was.

Taken off guard by the opinionated female, Ethan stared after Darcy as she descended the grassy field toward the house. His eyes followed the twists of her hair, how it tumbled about her shoulders down to her waist, how it caught the sunlight. Miss Roth wore her hair parted in the center in tight cork-screw curls. He found it stiff and unnatural, something a man dare not reach out and touch. She would not permit it. He did not desire it.

As for this girl, he could run his fingers through her hair if she permitted him. "Who are you, that God would put you straight into my path?" A brave and spirited one, for she had not screamed nor fainted when he came upon her.

He thrust his boot into the stirrup and swung into the saddle. The girl with the high spirits and flowing hair disquieted Ethan, and as he moved the horse on, he watched her walking in the distance. She bent down, her gown clinging to her well-formed legs as she plucked a dandelion from the ground.

3

"*D*ar—cy! Mar—tha!" Mari Breese waved her handkerchief as if she were swatting a fly. "Come away from there at once and join us."

If only her aunt would not call to her, wave to her in such a flustered way, then people would not be staring and drawing conclusions. A few more paces down the hill and Darcy met Martha.

"I wish Mother would be more reserved," Martha said, walking alongside Darcy. "Everyone is looking at us."

"She means well. She's a mother hen who likes her chicks around her, you know. Besides, not everyone is looking. Just that group of ladies and gentlemen within earshot."

"Well, that is enough, I'd say. I am glad you are back. My sisters left me alone, and I grew worried about you."

Darcy smiled as she recalled the rider's astonished look when he happened upon her. "I returned as I left you—even though the Englishman nearly ran me over with one of Twin Oaks' horses."

Martha gasped. "The English gentleman?"

Darcy nodded. "Yes, the *English gentleman*."

"He is reckless, Darcy, and obviously has no mind to be aware of young ladies strolling the grounds. You should have nothing more to do with him."

The sun strengthened through the trees and she stepped into a shady spot. The cool caress of the breeze and the scent of lilacs and roses filled the air. For a moment, it distracted Darcy from thinking about Mr. Brennan.

"I think it's time we show Miss Roth how fast our thoroughbreds are," she heard Daniel Rhendon say to the guests gathered on the porch.

"Surely, sir, our Virginia horses are superior to what they breed in England," said one gentleman in a gray suit. "What proof do they need?"

"Since you have no English stallions in your stable, Mr. Rhendon, I do anticipate your competition between riders," said Miss Roth, while fanning her face with an ivory fan. Her eyes glanced sideways toward Darcy, and then moved back to the circle of men. Then from out on the lawn, a man shouted, "Here they come!"

The guests rushed to the porch rail, and some hurried out onto the lawn. Down the hill came two riders. They jumped their mounts over a hedge, gained control, and galloped at a breakneck speed past the crowd. Cheers rang out as they skidded to a halt, the horses rearing under their firm hands. Ethan dismounted along with his competitor and they shook hands.

Captain Rhendon threw up his arms with a broad smile. "I'm afraid it is a tie, ladies and gentlemen. Both gentlemen have shown exceptional horsemanship. And my horses? Well, it goes without saying how superior they are."

Cheers and handshakes all around, the crowd dispersed back to the veranda or the shade of the trees. Darcy turned away. "We cannot judge Mr. Brennan too harshly," she told her cousin. "He is a bold rider and that says something about his character."

Martha guffawed. "Hmm. I'd like to know what."

Darcy took her cousin's hand and moved with her to a bench beneath the veranda. "I have a stone in my shoe." At once, she drew it off and shook free a tiny pebble. She hesitated when, just above her, she heard voices and the stomp of boots across the porch. She slipped her shoe back on and looked up through the lattice above her.

With his back turned, Ethan could not see her below. She noticed flecks of mud on his boots. Sunlight alighted over the earthy color of his hair and across his broad shoulders. How would it turn the color of his eyes? Would they lighten, or be averse to the glare?

She heard him say, "Who is the young woman with the glorious hair?"

Daniel replied, "Which one? There are several—and all so pretty."

"The one who does not wear it up, but loose down her back. Do you know her name?"

"Ah, yes. I know whom you mean."

Martha's mouth fell open, and Darcy pressed her finger against her cousin's lips to silence her.

"I believe her name is Darcy. Her aunt and uncle are over there, Mr. and Mrs. Breese. I saw her once down at the river. She and her cousins were wading . . . a wondrous sight for any young man to behold. *Hair Glorious* had her dress looped up above her pretty calves."

Ethan leaned back against the banister. "I imagine the rest of her is just as lovely."

Darcy widened her eyes and a flutter seized her. Never had she heard a man speak of her in that fashion. *How dare he say such a thing aloud, or think of me in that way.*

Martha cupped her hand and whispered in Darcy's ear. "He must be a libertine and a hedonist. Did you hear what he said about you just now?"

"I could not help hearing it." If their paths crossed again, she determined she would get the best of him. Were not the English more reserved than this?

"Come on," Daniel said. "We shall hunt her and that fetching cousin of hers down, and I'll introduce you."

Then from the corner of her eye, Darcy watched Ethan turn away. "Later."

A coy smile tugged at her mouth, and a tinge of insult caused her eyes to narrow. "Later?" she whispered back to Martha. "I shall avoid him at all costs."

"Girls!" Her aunt tapped her fan against the railing and leaned over another inch or two. She made a most severe motion for them to make their way above.

Martha walked ahead of Darcy, with her head erect and her gait graceful. Darcy followed her up the stairs, and as she turned to the left to join her aunt and cousin, a shadow fell over her. She stopped short, glanced up, almost bumping straight into the man who seemed bent on meeting with an accident that would embarrass them both.

His eyes fixed on her face. "Excuse me."

"Again I am in your way, sir. I should not rush so."

"Nor should I . . ."

"I am to join my aunt and cousin, so if you will excuse me."

He turned and looked over at the lady fast approaching them. "Would you be so kind as to introduce me? After all, I may need to do some explaining to your aunt if word gets out that I almost trampled you."

Darcy shook her head. "No, you cannot say a word of it to my aunt. You have no idea how fast she can spread a story and how twisted it will be in the end."

He inclined his head and spoke low. "You spare me, Miss . . ."

The warmth of his breath caressed her cheek and the tone of his voice captivated her. He stood near and a strange sensation filled Darcy, as if he were meant to be so close, a kind of sentinel over her.

"Dear me." Mrs. Breese put her fan between them and Darcy stepped back.

"I found one, Ethan." Daniel Rhendon drew Martha forward, smiling. "And you the other. Mr. Ethan Brennan, may I introduce Mrs. Breese?" Darcy's aunt dipped with her eyes lowered. "Miss Martha Breese." Martha mimicked her mother. "And finally, Miss Darcy Morgan."

✍❦

A muscle in Ethan's chest constricted when Daniel pronounced her name. He could not help staring at her face, at its delicate shape; could not help gazing into her vivacious eyes, and comparing them to another pair he knew. "Morgan, you say?"

Daniel gave him a slight nod. "Yes. A fine name for a fine lady."

The twists of hair that fell over her head and along her throat were tantalizing, and Ethan found himself soaking her in with his eyes, drawing in the essence of her with each breath. Her mouth parted to speak, but faltered. An impression he had no word for suddenly swelled within him as dusky pink swept into her cheeks. He knew then that she was not accustomed to a man's eyes being so intent upon her.

The temptation to reveal to her the secret he held tittered on his lips. But the oath he had made kept him in check. "The surname of patriots," Ethan said.

Mrs. Breese sighed with approval. "You know our history, Mr. Brennan?"

"Only what I have read, ma'am."

When Mrs. Breese extended her hand to him, she bumped into her charge, which caused Darcy to stand closer to Ethan. His hand touched her forearm to steady her.

"I beg your pardon, sir." Mrs. Breese waved her hand at Darcy. "Darcy, you are too close to the gentleman. Step aside and give him room. You must excuse my niece, Mr. Brennan. She has a tendency to be in places where she should not be. Not that being in your presence is wrong, mind you. It is hot and crowded here on the porch and not suitable for lengthy conversation."

Darcy's lips parted when Mrs. Breese took her hand. She turned Martha by the shoulder with the other and slipped off with them into the crowd, to a less populated part of the veranda. When Darcy glanced back, something warm charged through Ethan's heart. The year before, he had met Miss Roth on a cool summer evening at a social gathering. What he thought he felt was an attachment. But never had his heart pounded like this, nor had his blood raced so heatedly. He'd been wrong that a man could not love a woman at first sight.

She bent her head against the girl beside her. He hoped she was not telling her cousin about the near accident on the hilltop. Was she laughing at him? Forced to linger behind, he looked away, still wondering what this girl thought of him. And now that he had seen her, he could say she was in good health and happy, despite her past.

"Ethan?" Daniel Rhendon stepped alongside him. "You haven't heard a word I've said."

Ethan looked at him with a shake of his head. "You must forgive me. I was distracted. Yes, your horse is fine, but does not suit me."

"What's wrong with him? He's spirited enough."

"I'm not the right one to own him."

"Why?" Daniel looked in the direction of Ethan's glance. "Oh, is it because of Darcy? That would be nonsense."

"The horse would remind me of how I almost killed a woman."

"Ridiculous, Ethan. The horse is yours and at a good price. Sanchet does not belong in Virginia, but with you."

"He'd be too good of a sire for me to take him away from your mares."

"My mares want nothing do to with him. They prefer Allegheny, the one I call Old Al. You'll offend me if you turn down my offer."

Ethan hesitated and held out his hand to shake Daniel's. "You are right. I would regret it later."

4

$\mathcal{D}$arcy thought she should, perhaps for a time, rebel against the attraction she had for Ethan Brennan. "I imagine the stable-hand has removed the saddle from that beast of a horse and locked him in a stall," Darcy said to Martha as they sat together on a quilt spread out beneath a tree.

"After much thought on the matter, I think you should forgive Mr. Brennan for being so distressed and concerned."

"Certainly I forgive him," said Darcy. "It was my fault as well, I suppose."

"You like him, don't you?" Martha nudged her.

"No. He is British and I am a proud Marylander."

"Proud to have a heritage that rebelled against the monarchy."

Her other cousins rushed over. "Have you seen the tables on the porch?" said Dolley. "They are all covered in white tablecloths and loaded down with so much food one would think they'd collapse."

China plates edged in gold leaf, diamond-cut glassware, and silver sparkled. A joint of beef and an enormous ham were on the center table, flanked by roasted fowl and bowls of bright green pole beans and cucumbers. Loaves of homemade bread and rolls were heaped in baskets, accompanied by pots of butter. Yellow cakes dripped with sugar icing among platters of nuts and fruits. At each table, a sentry was positioned. Negro youths as young as eight years held large wicker fans in their hands to shoo the flies away from the bounty.

"Just look at that," Darcy said to her cousins, annoyed. "Children should not be forced to stand by a table and swat flies all day."

Martha tapped Darcy's hand with her fingertips. "But they are slaves, Darcy."

"Yes, that is the problem."

"You think too hard on such things."

Darcy looked in disbelief at her cousin. "And what is wrong with that?"

"Our brains were not made to ponder so deeply such strenuous issues."

Darcy balked. "Where did you hear such nonsense, Martha? Uncle Will never taught us such a lie. And a lie it is, for God made us just as smart as men, if we desire to be so. And I do not mind saying that slavery is an evil we must not abide."

Martha looked back at the boys fanning the tables. "You are right to say so. I imagine those boys would rather be swimming or fishing on a day like today."

Darcy sighed. "Instead they are enslaved and will stay that way until the day they die. Let us be kind to them."

"Well, I shall find the cake," said Abigail rising, "before Rachel devours every last crumb."

They all hurried off and left Darcy alone. Above her, the oak spread out in a parasol of green to shade her. She opened her eyes and gazed up at the waxy leaves that twisted in the breeze.

"Your opinion of slavery is much different from that of some others in your country. Are you permitted to voice it to people other than your own family?"

She jerked her head around to see Ethan leaning up against the tree, the sole of his right boot pressed against the trunk. She gathered her dress about her knees and glanced up at him. She could not help feeling the flutter in her chest upon seeing him. His eyes were warm as they met hers.

"Forgive me," he said, pulling away from the tree. "I've startled you again."

She turned her head away with a lift of her chin. "Not at all."

"And my question?"

She smiled back at him. "My uncle encourages us to speak our minds."

She looked away toward the porch. Her cousins were busy, along with the other guests, filling their plates with the milk and honey of Virginian hospitality.

"My family welcomes my opinions. As for strangers," Darcy said, "I did not know anyone else would overhear my comments."

He inclined his head. "I beg your pardon. I was walking this way without the intention of eavesdropping. Will you not follow your cousins to the tables?" He put out his hand hoping she would take it.

She ignored his offer. "I am not hungry. And it is too hot to eat."

"I agree . . ."

She gave him a haughty look. "I believe you are a lady's escort."

"How did you know?"

"We saw the carriage drive in, and you gave your hand to one. Won't she be angry that you are speaking to me? It is rude of you to leave her alone."

"She hasn't even noticed I've gone. She has a swarm of men surrounding her and is getting plenty of attention."

"Is she not engaged to you?"

"No, only assumed to be."

"I see. She is beautiful."

"Yes, but beauty fades." With his eyes fixed upon Miss Roth, Ethan's voice fell into a tone that hinted upon disappointment. In those large blue eyes belonging to Miss Roth thrived no sign of love, only possession and disapproval that he spoke with Darcy. She headed in Ethan's direction once she broke free of the men around her.

"Pray, Ethan, present me," she said.

"Miss Roth, may I present Miss Darcy . . ." and he hesitated.

Miss Roth leaned against Ethan. "Perhaps she hasn't a last name of any importance. Shall we join the others? I have an appetite now."

Then, with a regal lift of her head, she held her hand out to him.

Darcy glanced at Ethan, watched the anger bank in his eyes. She wondered if Miss Roth saw it too. If she did, she cared not a whit. "Will you walk back with us, Miss Darcy?"

"Yes, I think I will. But I will have to join my aunt. She is motioning to me."

Giving his arm to Miss Roth, Ethan led her across the grass to the stairs, to the cool shade of the veranda. Darcy was mortified by how the snobbish Englishwoman had treated her. She detested the sanctimonious smile, the critical eye that Miss Roth had cast upon her, as if she were one of her servants.

Yet, I feel sorry for her. How exhausting it must be, demanding the attention of others, striving to be something she is not.

When she glanced at Ethan and saw his eyes turn in her direction, but never catching them, her breath held and she looked at him with a yearning to make him think better of her than what Miss Roth had made certain to plant within his mind. Or had she?

The sun dipped low along the horizon, and a butler dressed in scarlet stepped out among the guests gathered on the porch. With an elegance that matched that of an English herald, he lifted his head, his white-gloved hands motioning to all before him.

"Ladies and gentlemen, attention if you please." His voice rang mellow and deep, and it caught Darcy's ears. A memory forced its way to the surface. She had once before heard a voice such as this—long ago as a child. A face she could not see, but she remembered a pair of hands, calloused and sinewy, picking her up, placing her on a swing, and pushing her with gentleness on a midsummer day.

She blinked the memory back and watched the butler bow low to the assembly and sweep his hand toward the door. "The musicians have tuned their instruments, rosined their bows, and gathered around their sheets of music, and they await your pleasure. If you please, follow me into the great hall, where your host and hostess bid you to dance."

With an elegant turn, he proceeded through the entryway. The guests followed him with excitement in their steps. Mrs. Breese drew Darcy and her older cousins close to her. "Come, girls. Remember what I taught you. A graceful figure gathers attention."

Once inside the house, Darcy glanced over the trappings. The entrance to the dance hall was a carved frame painted pale yellow, with a bower of blood-red roses set above it to scent the room. Paintings hung on the walls. Chairs of blue velvet lined the perimeter. Tall French doors stood open.

Darcy's heart raced at the sound of violins. The music struck up and gallants gathered up girls and drew them out onto the floor. A long row formed, gentlemen on one side, ladies on the other. They weaved up and down the line, ending with their hands touching a partner's.

Pulled into the fray of dancers, she scanned the room for Ethan. A moment more, and there he was, standing near the entrance. Miss Roth opened her fan and sat down in the chair near him, followed by Miss Byrd. Their heads were held high, and they sat with their backs straight as broom handles.

Darcy thought it a shame to live day in and day out with a face covered in powder and rouge, to be confined to a life of boredom, of social gatherings where one's rank ruled supreme. She felt sorry for Miss Roth. But then their eyes met, and Miss Roth gave Darcy a cold stare.

The slow turn of her body, her hair loose about her shoulders, the elegant music seeping through her pores, brought Darcy back and made her feel happy to have lived the life God gave her. She smiled as she glided, going from one gentleman's hand to another's.

But never Ethan Brennan's.

5

$\mathscr{E}$than looked out into the crowd of dancers. Amid the laughter and happy voices, one would think he would have joined in the merriment. But Miss Roth held him near and refused to partake in the *Americans'* country-dance. She pleaded he not leave her side, but allow her to sit awhile until an old-fashioned gavotte played.

"It is vulgar the way Americans strut and whirl," she said. "These are the cream of their society, yet they glide and trip like the lower classes back home. There is no grace, no elegance. It must be due to their bloodline."

It did not show on his face, but Ethan was annoyed at her narrow-minded remark. "Why should bloodline have anything to do with dancing, Miss Roth?"

"A talent for dance is inbred, sir. I doubt any of these people descended from English nobility but rather from indentured servants and headstrong rebels." She then snapped her fan shut and sighed. "Therein lies the answer, I believe."

"Your prejudice fails to flatter you, Miss Roth," Ethan told her.

"Oh, it is not prejudice, Mr. Brennan, but simple observation of what is true."

"Observation is jaded by prejudice."

"Is it? Well, you shan't catch me whirling and leaping about like a common herd-girl."

"No doubt I shall not. You are too tightly wound."

Miss Roth's mouth fell open. "I hope you meant that as a compliment, sir. Or shall I think otherwise?" She leaned over to her friend seated beside her. "Miss Byrd, you heard what Mr. Brennan said. Have you an opinion on the matter?"

"I am sure Mr. Brennan means to be kind, Miss Roth," Miss Byrd replied. "To be *tightly wound*, as he put it, means you are dignified."

Miss Roth sucked in her cheeks. "You think so?"

"I know so. That is how it has been explained to me." She smiled, her teeth the color of old ivory, her lips thinning out as she spoke.

Ethan took in a breath, bored with their shallow assumptions and senseless comments. He gazed over at Darcy, and then looked back at the snobbish Miss Roth. Why people ever thought he had considered the lady as a potential mate was beyond all reason. She was dull, critical, and slighted the religious—qualities he scorned in a woman. His father would not have approved. "Consider the words of Solomon, my son," he would say. "Find a wife whose price is far above rubies."

Now his eyes beheld a girl with both virtue and spirit. Her passion for life sparkled in her eyes, illuminated her face, and echoed in her laughter.

"It is shameful," Miss Roth went on. "The girls here expose their ankles on every turn."

Ethan refused to comment. Why should he? If he were to voice to Miss Roth what he really thought, it would give her more reasons to insult each and every girl in the room, for she had a jealous nature.

"Ethan?" Miss Roth stood and tapped his arm with her fan. "Ethan, why do you continue to stare at that girl? What is she to you?"

He leaned close to her ear and said, "You are overly jealous when you are not the center of attention. A trait that is unbecoming in a woman. Try to behave yourself."

Affronted, she pressed her lips together. "It slipped my mind, sir, that some of your ancestors were rebels. Is that why you show such favoritism?"

He smiled. "I thank you for the reminder. I am not ashamed."

"Perhaps that is why you are attracted to Miss Darcy."

"She is different, I will admit." He would not be surprised if Darcy were to kick off her shoes and dance barefooted. In a way, he hoped she would.

"I cannot understand why you are attracted to her."

"Whether or not I am, it should not alarm you."

"It does, for I thought we had an understanding."

"If my interest in others has offended you, or breached any inkling of an understanding, have I stepped over the line? Your envy is unseemly."

"And you are blinded by a pretty face, sir. I must open your eyes."

Miss Byrd, along with their chaperone that sat behind them, sucked in a breath. "Miss Roth, you will remember your manners," whispered her chaperone. "You will be seated." And she yanked at her sleeve.

"Leave me be." With a lift of her head, Miss Roth moved closer to the line of dancers. Darcy stood close enough to hear Miss Roth. "I would not doubt that every man in the room has already exhausted Miss Darcy's mysteries."

Ethan twisted his mouth. "That is too low even for you."

The lady's face flushed. Her eyes glistened with self-pity. She stared at him, raised her face, and then lowered herself with a sweep of her gown to the chair. Ethan stepped away and removed himself as far as possible from a woman whose mouth was like a continuing dropping of rain upon his brow. He strode toward Darcy when he saw how pale her face had gone, and how sad her expression.

After hearing what Miss Roth said, Darcy's hands dropped from the man who held them and she stood stunned. She lifted her eyes to the gentleman and excused herself. Then she caught the venomous glance of Miss Roth and the proud look that spread over her face. Darcy wanted to confront her, but no good would come of it. She would not lower herself to Miss Roth's level.

She should not care what Miss Roth thought of her. What did her opinion matter? The lady had nothing to do with what course her life took. Ah, and she was freer than Miss Roth to be who and what she was. She would wear her locks as it pleased her, dress in simple clothing, wear hats that she and her cousins made from the reeds cut from the riverside. She would wear what she wished even if it were secondhand, speak to whom she liked whether rich or poor, and not take anything Miss Roth said to heart.

If only it were so easy.

The heat in the room grew as oppressive as Miss Roth's words. Whispers rose and she heard the name *Morgan* pass from person to person. People stared—some with disdain, others with curiosity. She questioned why. Had she done something to deserve such looks? Why had her last name drawn this kind of attention, along with Miss Roth's rude comments?

And so, Darcy slipped between the dancers and headed toward the door leading to the terrace outside. Before she could pass through it, Ethan stepped in front of her.

"It is too fine an evening to leave, Miss Morgan."

"You will excuse me, sir." Her voice trembled and the tears that swelled in her eyes burned.

"Once again, I have intruded. I only want to help."

She gathered her gown in her hands. At every turn, Ethan met her. "I am in need of air, sir."

"It is stuffy in here . . . much like my traveling companion Miss Roth." He moved her to the open door where it was cooler. "I can tell you heard what she said. She was sure to say it loud enough. I am sorry. It was uncalled for."

His words caused her to smile. "I must praise her that she is not afraid to voice her opinion. But for her rudeness, for speaking what she thinks of me in public, that I condemn."

"And justly so."

"I was told Englishwomen are reserved and take care of what they say and to whom they say it. So untrue this must be if Miss Roth is any kind of example of an English lady."

"She is snobbish. It was wrong of her to insult you the way she did."

"Indeed, for she does not know me at all."

"Whether she knew you well or not, it is not her place to pass judgment."

"She judges me solely upon appearance . . ."

"Which is lovely, if you do not mind my saying so."

"Oh, not true, sir, for I am plain. I have not the elegance of your Miss Roth."

"She is not mine."

"Oh, yes. As you said before."

"If you would observe her, Miss Roth's beauty is pretentious." He leaned down. "Lots of powder and rouge."

Darcy's palms grew moist and she wished she had worn her gloves. The caller announced the next dance. "Please form the set, ladies and gentlemen, for 'The Flight.'"

She knew the tune, the romance of it. "May I have the honor?" Ethan held his hand out to her. And when hers became lost in his, he drew her beside him out onto the floor. Once they faced each other they stood a few feet apart, his eyes resting upon hers. The music drew them near and their hands reached out. His fingers touched hers, and then slid into her hand.

Darcy picked up where they had left off. "I suppose you think flattery will make me forget Miss Roth's cruelty."

"Not at all. Flattery does not cure the sting of false words."

"Then you need not strive for it, sir."

"Surely an honest compliment helps in some way."

"I suppose it does. I am grateful God looks upon my heart, and not my outward appearance, and will do so even when I am old and wrinkled from head to toe."

He faced her smiling, released her hands, and bowed in time with the other male dancers. "I admire your faith. But is it so wrong for a man to marvel at a pretty woman? Are we not to regard God's creations with awe?"

Darcy fixed her eyes on Ethan with wonder and did not reply. A sensation prickled over her skin and something whispered into her mind, *he is the one*. "I do not know what to think of you, sir."

Ethan's stare warmed. "I hope you will think of me as your friend."

They were silent after that, and when "The Flight" came to an end, Darcy's aunt came through and bumped into her—again.

"Darcy, we are leaving. I can no longer abide the heat." Mrs. Breese turned to Ethan. "It was a pleasure to have met you, Mr. Brennan, though I must say Miss Roth was very rude to our Darcy, and I pray she eats her words one day soon, and that you change your mind about her."

Ethan nodded in agreement. "May I pay a call upon your family before I leave for England? I promise to come alone."

Mrs. Breese gave him a broad smile. "We'd be pleased if you paid us a visit."

He looked at Darcy. "And you will be there?"

"Perhaps." She gave him a coy look and left him in the stuffy, crowded room.

6

A week went by after the gathering at Twin Oaks. The day dawned warm, and by late noon the honeybees played over the zinnias in the garden. So absorbed in the small book of poems she was reading, it wasn't until Martha's shadow fell over the grass beside her, that Darcy closed the book and looked up.

Martha sat beside her in the shade. "Darcy, have you wondered if Mr. Brennan will keep his word and visit us?"

With a sigh, Darcy leaned back against the tree. "I have not given it much thought."

"I do not believe you," Martha laughed.

"I mean not much thought today." Darcy ran her hands through her locks with a smile. "I want him to visit us—out of curiosity."

"I dare not ask for an explanation," Martha said. "I know he said he'd come alone."

"I doubt he shall."

"Surely he will not bring Miss Roth and her little entourage?"

"Miss Roth would not stoop so low as to pay us a call. It is obvious she feels she is too good for us, too blue-blooded to grace us with her imperious self."

"Perhaps he will bring Daniel Rhendon with him." Martha looked hopeful.

Darcy reached over and cupped her cousin's chin in her hand. "Yes, perhaps he will. We shall have to wait and see, won't we?" She stood and stretched her arms. "I need a walk. Care to come along?"

"Not I. Mother wishes me to wash Dolley's hair. She got into the honey earlier and how she managed to get it into her hair, the Lord only knows. Do not venture too far. You know how my mother worries."

"Say nothing to her. But if she asks, tell her I have gone to fetch lady slippers for Uncle Will."

When she reached the Potomac's stony shore, she raised her hand above her eyes to spy out the opposite side. She slipped off her shoes, lifted her dress, and stepped into the water. The muddy bottom seeped between her toes. The swirl of water moved around her ankles in time with the sighing breeze.

In the middle of the river, a stretch of boulders gleamed in the sunlight smooth as a ship's deck. Where she stepped the river was shallow, and she decided she would wade out to the stone ledge, sit upon it and watch the swallows and herons. Reaching it, she pulled up her legs and sat with her arms hugging her knees. The river flashed and murmured, and the sun grew into a great orange orb, surrounded by white thunderclouds.

"Lord, I wish I had someone to share this with." She dipped her hand into the water and drew it back when a bass nibbled her fingertips. "I suppose the fish and birds will have to do."

She was over twenty and Darcy wondered if men thought she was homely. Perhaps it was her spirited nature, her love for the outdoors, for trekking the countryside that put them off. She had no dowry to bring to a marriage, and she was orphaned. Those two things alone would make most men look the other way. Whatever caused them not to pursue her was troublesome, for her heart yearned to be loved. Her desires surprised her, for they were as raging as the rapids ahead. Then she smiled and shook back her hair. This is how it is supposed to feel, she told herself, when a woman wants to be a wife and a mother someday.

She dropped her knees and slapped the water with her hand. The confusion that Ethan had brought her was overpowering. Standing, she walked to the edge of the rock. Others were before her, stretching toward the Virginia side but not without a span of water to cross. She put out her arms for balance and then went forward. Here the river flowed deeper than she thought, up to her knees, but no threat. Then it reached her hips, and she pulled her feet up and swam toward the great rock ahead. The river was calm at first but unpredictable. It pulled at her from beneath and she went under.

Panic seized her as the river dragged her down. She jerked her legs free and swam to the surface. She gasped for air and thrashed forward while the current moved her along. She reached the rock and hauled herself up to the edge, gasping for air. It was slick and she lost her grip. The water claimed her and took her into a plane of deeper currents that ran swift. Ahead she saw a fallen tree, and stretching her fingers as wide as she could, she reached for it, grabbed a branch, and hauled herself up against it for dear life. Frightened, she wondered if her time had come, if angels would lift her from the water. Would it be over quickly and painlessly?

She had no fear of entering eternity, but the fear of drowning so young seized her so violently that she railed against it and rallied the fight within her. She gripped the old tree. Her fingers turned as white as the foam in the surge. Her hands shook and her nails dug deep. Shocked by the cold rushing water, she held tighter and looked up at heaven above her.

"You know, God, if you spare me, Aunt Mari is going to kill me."

❧

Down the river path and under a canopy of trees, Ethan galloped Sanchet. To the right the trees opened and he could see the river clearly. The Potomac flowed in the sunlight, reflecting forest and cliff and seams of an azure sky. Mallards skimmed the shallows, and a blue heron opened its wings and flew from the bank to the opposite side.

Now, to see it for himself, he understood why the river received such high praise, and why those who loved it longed to see it again. Its beauty and peace touched his inner man, and he wondered if he, too, could leave it.

A sudden movement in the trees caused his horse to side-step. From a willow, a brown hawk mounted the sky like a wind-blown leaf. Ethan watched it soar higher and then dive with folded wings to an outcropping of rock in the middle of the river.

Sanchet's mane snapped back in the rising breeze, and Ethan's eyes traveled from the hawk to a woman clinging to an anchor that could only keep her safe for a few moments. Alarm seized him. Digging his heels into the horse's sides, he spurred it down the slope to the river's edge, leaped from the saddle, and yanked off his coat. Without a moment to lose, he hailed her as he rushed to the water's edge. She turned her head and gave him a weak smile, looking embarrassed and frightened.

"Is that you, Darcy?" he called, a serious panic in his voice.

"It is, sir." Her soaked dress clung to her shivering body, and she sank further into the water so he would not see. The bronze tresses of her hair floated and swirled around her shoulders.

"What are you doing out there in the middle of the river? You must be a very good swimmer." Ethan unbuttoned his waistcoat, tossed it down on top of his coat.

"Indeed I am."

"I sincerely doubt it." Ethan pulled off his boots.

Darcy thrust her head upright. "I can swim back with no difficulty, Mr. Brennan. If you please, I would prefer that you ride on."

"Would you?" He hurried out into the water. "I'm coming out to get you."

"I am capable . . ."

"Of drowning. I have no doubt this same stubbornness got you in this fix."

With haste, he plunged into the water toward her, fighting the currents, hoping to reach her in time.

The timber inched away and risked taking Darcy along with it. Fear tightened her throat and shot through her chest. She dug her fingers into the bark not caring how it tore her skin. As soon as the tree broke loose from the rock that moored it, it moved slowly at first. Then the river pulled at her and she slid under the water after her hands lost their grip and the tree floated away.

For her life, Darcy kicked and twisted to gain ground, her lungs ready to burst out the air she held within them. Her head surfaced and she let out a gasp. Ethan called to her and she reached for him against the flow of water. She watched him drag himself head down through the current, his arms battling the river's power. The moment he reached her, she sank under the water and felt his hands drag her up to the surface. His arm went around her waist and held tight.

"Hold on to my neck and do not let go." He swam with her beneath his chest held by his arm, her cheek in the curve of his neck. When they reached the shallows, he set his feet into the riverbed. His breathing hurried and his hair clung to his shoulders as he trudged from the river to the shore. He set her down and unlocked Darcy's arms from around his neck. Her lips trembled, and kneeling in front of her, he rubbed her hands within his.

"Mr. Brennan," she murmured. "Thank you."

He picked up the clothing he had cast off, and put his coat over her shoulders. Then he reached for his boots and slipped them back on. She had no idea what he was thinking—that she looked a waif, a creature of the river and woods.

He glanced up at the sky. "Come, I will take you home." He extended his hand and when she placed hers within his, and he closed his fingers over hers, he lifted her up into his arms.

"You need not carry me," Darcy said.

He looked into her eyes and laughed. "You have been through a trial. You are shivering. In fact your lips are blue."

She touched them. "Really?"

"Blue as the sky above." He carried her up the bank to his horse. "When there are no clouds gathering. Looks like rain, Darcy."

She stared out at the river. Grave silence fell over her, so suddenly snatched out of Death's hand that the sense of awe that she was saved washed over her. The fine thread that was life grew more precious. It was a miracle Ethan had come and had seen her in the water when he did. Shutting her eyes, she breathed out, then in again, and whispered thanks to the One who made her. Life had become more precious, and she would cherish every breath from that moment on.

She held tight to Ethan as he guided his horse. The pale light of day slanted through the forest. In the branches overhead, a mockingbird sang. Chickadees chirped and fluttered from tree to tree.

Ethan looked back over his shoulder. "Which way is home?"

"To the right. We mustn't stray from this road, else we will be lost."

His eyes glowed at her words, as if they had some double meaning. He looked away, ahead to where the road curved. Then he walked the horse on.

"Will you grant me one more favor?" she asked.

"What is it?"

"Please do not tell my aunt I nearly drowned. She is so fearful of such things."

"She will ask what happened, and your uncle will demand to know."

"You are right. There is no getting out of this."

Soft rain fell from the clouds and drenched the earth, sparkling on leaves and vine. Thunder cracked overhead, frightening the horse and causing it to rear. Darcy held tight. Gaining control, Ethan galloped Sanchet down the river road toward the Breese house and the anxious family that waited there.

7

$\mathscr{M}$ari Breese wrung her hands and paced in front of her sitting-room window. Her instincts told her something awful was about to happen when storm clouds swept over her rooftop, when rain glazed the trees and filled the holes in the drive. Darcy had been gone for hours, and Mrs. Breese feared her niece would come home dripping wet, at risk for pneumonia.

"I hope to heaven Darcy did not get lost in the woods or wander close to the river and fall in." She wiped the window with her handkerchief, gripped the windowsill and looked out. "It is Darcy with Mr. Brennan! Dear me, what was she thinking to be out in this weather?"

Mr. Breese leaned toward the window. "I don't believe she knew it was to rain, my dear. It was a fine sky earlier."

"I could have told her differently. The aching in my joints is a clear sign of inclement weather. Now she's soaked through and liable to catch her death of cold." Turning on her heels, Mrs. Breese whirled out of the room into the hallway. "Missy! Boil hot water for Miss Darcy, and put a brick in the hearth upstairs. There is clean flannel in the cupboard to wrap it in."

Missy looked down from the upstairs landing. "But we've no fire in the hearths this time of year, madam."

"Well then, make one—a small one, mind you. She's soaking wet. You attend to her, Missy, as soon as Mr. Brennan gets her indoors." Rushing forward, Mrs. Breese opened the front door. A brisk wind drove in a mist of rain.

The Breese girls gathered in the hallway. As one, they moved to the window beside the door to watch Ethan dismount and help Darcy down. He lifted her within his arms, hurried to the door, and stepped inside with his burden close against his chest.

"Thank the good Lord, sir." Mrs. Breese sighed in relief. "You have brought Darcy back to us, though wet to the bone, I see." She shot Darcy a stern look of disapproval. She would deal with her later, as soon as she could think of some kind of punishment to fit the crime of being so thoughtless—so reckless.

"It is nothing, Aunt." Darcy brushed back her hair from her cheek.

Dolley, the youngest, began to cry. "Darcy is going to catch pneumonia and die." She rubbed her eyes and slumped onto the first staircase step.

Groaning, Mrs. Breese hauled her daughter up by the shoulders. "Darcy is not going to die, Dolley. Now stop that crying, else your papa will give you something to cry about." Blinking back her tears, Dolley sniffed and wiped her nose. Mrs. Breese turned to Ethan with a toothy smile. "Girls can be so emotional in these instances."

$\mathcal{L}$❤

Upon Mrs. Breese's direction, Ethan carried Darcy upstairs to her room and set her down at the threshold. It did not feel right going further inside. She looked over at him and her eyes flooded with gratitude. He enjoyed the feeling she gave him, but disliked the pain. If she knew the true reason he had come to America, how would she react? How swift would that knowledge turn the current of her life? The temptation to reveal his mission overwhelmed him. Again, he reminded himself of his oath to the one who sent him.

"You must forgive us if it is warm in here, Mr. Brennan," Mrs. Breese said. "I had Missy set a small fire to chase away any chill that Darcy might have, and to warm a brick for her feet. Are you chilled, sir?"

Ethan shook back his hair. "Not at all, madam."

"You have suffered to bring her home." Mrs. Breese scanned Ethan's wet attire. "Dear me, it appears as if you swam to get here."

"You need not worry about me, Mrs. Breese."

"My husband shall provide you with a set of dry clothes, while yours dry." She threw Mr. Breese a nod when he appeared behind Ethan. Then she closed the door.

A firm hand landed on Ethan's shoulder. "What happened, Mr. Brennan? My niece does not appear to be herself. I can see past her soaking."

Ethan shifted on his feet. "She is unscathed, sir."

Mr. Breese set his mouth in what Ethan thought was a distrustful expression. When the girls poked their heads around the corner, he ushered Ethan downstairs to his study and closed the door. A square room, shelves hugged one wall loaded with books. Near the window stood a stool and a drawing table. Ethan observed a watercolor of thistles, paints and brushes, an inkwell, and a large notebook and portfolio. Bottles filled with flora specimens cluttered a table.

The older gentleman's brows rumpled above his wary eyes. "What exactly happened to Darcy? Spare me no details."

Ethan looked down at the puddle of water made from his boots and frowned. "She begged me not to say, sir."

"That is just like her. She may withhold from my wife, but from me, Darcy can hide nothing."

"I imagine, sir, she has given you reason to be concerned."

Mr. Breese drew Ethan to the window. "She started climbing those trees at six, hiked in the forests when she was seven on to this very day. Sometimes she does not come home until after dark. She says the stars are too lovely to abandon."

Paternal love glowed within the old man's eyes. The way he described Darcy gave Ethan more reason to like her.

"I wonder how such an adventurous spirit was born within a girl."

Will Breese shrugged. "I have no doubt it was passed down to her from her mother."

Ethan fastened his eyes on the trees outside and imagined her sitting on one of the large limbs, her bare feet dangling beneath her. "So, Darcy reminds you of her?"

"Only from what I've been told about Eliza. I never had the chance to know her personally."

"For a girl to be so curious holds some danger."

Mr. Breese nodded. "Alluring, is it not, for a young man?"

Ethan, taken aback by the comment, did not reply. But he agreed. Darcy Morgan had a way of drawing him to her.

"Well, I imagine two things may have taken place this day." Mr. Breese picked up his pipe from off his desk. "Either she lost her way and was caught in the rain, or she fell into the river. I beg the latter be not so, sir, but if it is, you have my profound thanks for rescuing her."

"You have guessed right, sir. It was the river. Do not tell your wife. Darcy was worried she would be upset."

"Believe me, I know how ill my wife can be over such things. Was it very bad?"

"If I had not come along when I did, I have no doubt she would have been swept away. Yet I doubt Darcy would have allowed the river to get the best of her. She is very determined."

Letting out a long breath, Mr. Breese lowered himself into a chair. "Thank the Lord. He saved her once again. I am indebted to God more times than I can count, Mr. Brennan. Having six young ladies under my roof, with a nerve-stricken wife, is most taxing at times. I do not know what I would have done if they had all been born boys."

Ethan shook his head. "I can only imagine yours is a lively household, sir."

"It is that, Mr. Brennan. How to keep Darcy from the river I do not know. Marry her off I suppose, to some man that shall take her far from it."

A strange, but vague, feeling stabbed Ethan. For Darcy to be married off to a man who would remove her from the place she loved seemed unnatural. Yet, he romanticized the idea, wondering if he could make her love him enough to leave the river and cross a vast ocean to England. But that would complicate matters.

He shifted on his feet and looked Mr. Breese in the eye. "I would imagine that would make Darcy unhappy, no matter how in love she might be with a man of your liking. The river and this valley seem to seep into every inch of her, sir."

"You are correct to say so, Mr. Brennan. Why were you riding on this side of the river anyway, if you do not mind my asking?"

"There is a pretty stretch of land not far from here that caught my eye."

"You are thinking of buying it?"

"I wish I could."

Mr. Breese twisted his mouth showing his curiosity. "What would you, being an Englishman, do with such a piece of property?"

"To own even one acre of God's green earth in America might give me incentive to settle here."

Mr. Breese put his hand over Ethan's shoulder. "Then you must dine with us tonight and see how the average family manages to live in this wilderness. The Rhendons, the good people they are, mirror the aristocrats. It is the least I can do to express my gratitude for your saving Darcy. She is a daughter to me."

"You have my thanks, but I am expected back at Twin Oaks—business, you see. If I have your permission, I would like to call tomorrow."

"You have it, Mr. Brennan. You will disappoint my wife, however. I know when she is counting on a thing, and she wanted you to save your wet clothes from ruin."

"The clothes are of no matter, sir, and the rain has lessened."

As Mr. Breese strode to the door with Ethan, his look was contemplative, and Ethan knew much was on the older man's mind. "I must know, are you and Miss Roth engaged?" he asked.

Ethan paused on the threshold not at all surprised by such a question. "No, sir. But Miss Roth thinks differently in that regard."

Mr. Breese cocked his head to one side. "It is usually the case when a man travels a great distance across the sea with a woman and her companion."

"I have given that impression, I know. But Miss Roth is the kind of woman I could never marry, let alone love. Her behavior has shed some light on what I'd be in for if I did."

Mr. Breese agreed with a light laugh. "I asked the question for good reason, for my niece is dear to me. I would not want her heart to become fixed upon a man who has an understanding elsewhere. You are returning home soon, and if there should be any feelings within her toward you, it would break her heart."

Ethan could not help but press his brow in a worrisome way. "I would never do anything to hurt Darcy, sir. In the brief time I have known her, we have become friends."

"Your father—what does he expect from you regarding a bride?"

"My father is deceased. It is Miss Roth's father who pressed the issue. But I have not bent to his wishes."

"I have no doubt in due time you shall if she has a handsome dowry. I ask you, do not give Darcy any room to love you, Mr. Brennan, if it is possible you and Miss Roth would eventually marry."

"The chances of that are slim, sir." Ethan held out his hand; and Mr. Breese, looking down at it, took it within his and bid him a good day.

On the floor above, Ethan heard the patter of feet crossing the floorboards. Before he turned out the front door, he looked back, seeing Mrs. Breese and her girls at the top of the staircase. In unison, they gave him a dip. He nodded and strode out. His horse sidestepped when he put his foot in the stirrup, and he soothed it with a calm word as he climbed into the saddle.

Heavy and dull beat his heart, as an old longing rose there, sharper now as he lifted his eyes to the window above and saw Darcy come to the sill and lean out on folded arms. Upon seeing him below, she gave him a gentle smile and lifted her hand. He took in the beauty of her face, the way her hair fell loose over her shoulders, the firelight from within the room catching each silken strand.

"You are leaving, Mr. Brennan?" A sound of hushed disappointment etched her voice.

"Indeed, for your aunt fears you are ill and I've stayed long enough."

"If anything, I might inherit a slight cold, nothing more."

"Should you be sitting at the window then?"

"Of course. I would sit here every day if I had the leisure." She leaned a little lower. "I am a firm believer, sir, that fresh air and a beautiful view benefit the health."

Ethan's hands held the reins. "Beautiful—yes. And there are other things that do the same, that I had not known until recently."

"What could they be?"

He hesitated, drew nearer, and kept his eyes on hers. "The warmth of your eyes and face for a start."

She looked down at him stunned. "Your words should be saved for another, Mr. Brennan."

Ethan steadied his restless horse. "You speak of Miss Roth. I have no more affection for her, or interest in wedding the lady, than a wolf has for a snare."

Darcy lifted her head from her folded arms and looked down at him with her face flushed, her eyes looking into his. "I hope she is aware of your true feelings, for she seems very attached to you." Then she reached for the latch. "The wind blows too cool for me now. I must go."

Before he could say more, she closed the window and moved from it.

Ethan made for the road, down to the bridge that led across the river. He laid the reins hard against the horse and pushed it to a gallop. Mud splashed his boots. His mind raced, thinking over the incidents that had occurred, over his commission by another, and the secret he must guard. His pulse pounded in rhythm to the horse's pace. Could it be possible to love Darcy so soon? He had journeyed thousands of miles across ocean and land to see her, and now his heart lay within her hands.

It was up to her whether she would treat it gently—or break it.

8

The following day, Darcy watched streamers of sunlight cross the walls and paint them a shade lighter than the marigolds that bloomed in her window box. A pair of goldfinches fluttered close to the blossoms, then darted away. But the sparrows remained perched on the edge of the sill where she had placed some breadcrumbs.

From her dresser drawer she took out her journal, opened it, and drew away the scarlet cord that marked the last page where she had made an entry. She wrote: *Last night, I dreamt black water swirled around me, sucking me down, pulling me into the current as a dark wanton hand reached up through the water and grabbed my limbs in a frantic effort to own me. I could not breathe. My lungs felt as if they would burst, then I woke and sat up gasping. Once I had quieted, seeing I was safe at home, I lay back down and thought of Ethan, how he had redeemed me from the demanding river and risked his life for mine.*

She closed her journal and stepped over to the window. Toward the house rode Ethan on the same horse on which he had carried her home. She stepped back from the window, smoothed her dress and hair, and hurried downstairs to the sitting room.

She peeked around the edge of the curtain and watched him dismount and step up to the door. As she waited, she heard the door open and Missy greet him. Then his footsteps echoed out in the hallway and she turned when he was announced.

His eyes were warm upon her. "Are you well?" he said, stepping closer.

"Yes, I am well, thank you."

"I am pleased to hear it."

She invited him to sit, but he preferred to stand. She sat in the chair and looking up at him said, "It is a long ride from Twin Oaks, two days in a row."

He shifted on his feet. "The Rhendons send their regards and hope that you are recovered from your accident."

A flash of heat coupled with dread rose within her. "You told them? Everyone knows?"

"I only told Daniel, and at dinner he let it out. I am sorry."

"You have no reason to apologize. But I imagine they must think I am reckless."

"What you did was careless, going out as far as you did."

"Yes, I suppose it was."

"There is no need to treat yourself harshly for it. A person cannot always predict danger." He moved to a chair across from her, sat down and gazed at her with eyes that showed grave concern. "Swear to me you won't do it again."

She looked back at him. "I shall keep to the riverbank from now on."

"You wouldn't want it to happen twice."

"No, I would not, but you do not know the river like I do."

"You could have drowned, and you think you know the river so well. Think of the pain that would have caused your family and friends."

She glanced away, biting her lower lip. "The river draws me. It is the one place I can go to be alone, to think, to dream, to pray."

Without smiling, he said, "Well, Miss Morgan, the river might have ended all that."

She brushed back a curl that tickled her cheek. "If you had not come along when you did, I fear to think what would have happened to me."

"You must be more careful. At least do not go there alone."

"I have learned my lesson, I assure you."

He turned his hat between his hands. "Have you any plans today?"

"Yes. My uncle wishes me to collect wildflower heads."

"For what purpose?"

"His book. He paints them, you see, and writes about them. He is a botanist by profession, and is documenting the flowers that grow along the river."

"May I accompany you?"

"If you do not find such a venture boring."

She stood and went out into the hallway. Ethan followed. She sat on the bottom step of the staircase and pulled on her walking boots. "My aunt is busy in the kitchen with my cousins. They are making jams today."

"And your uncle?"

"In his study working." She grabbed her hat from the hook beside the door and drew it on, then picked up the jar kept in a cloth bag on the table under the window. This she attached to her waist. Once outside, she took a deep breath of the morning air. "Try it, Mr. Brennan."

A corner of his mouth lifted. "Your meaning, Darcy?"

"Breathe in the air." He did as she bid and she laughed at him. "Deeper. There, do you not feel how pure it is? It comes down from the mountains into the valley, gathering every scent God has blessed in nature."

They walked side-by-side along the path and trudged up a hillside. Once they reached the top of the bluff, they looked down at the place where the Potomac and Shenandoah gathered. Across the way, a peaceful village stood in the gorge. Darcy drew in another breath, turned, and headed back down the hill with Ethan.

After walking a mile or so downriver, they came to a clearing rife with wild fleabane and red clover. She chose a few dry heads and put them inside the jar. "I fear the rain has gotten the best of the old blooms," she said, tossing away some moldy ones.

Ethan observed her. "Yes, and your shoes and dress as well."

She laughed. "That you would care to notice, sir."

"I cannot help it," he told her. "You must allow me to do the work."

"I am fine," said Darcy. "Let us walk on to a drier place."

After the span of a few yards, Ethan lifted his eyes to see the old house situated in the distance upon a plane of overgrown grass peppered with thistles.

"I rode here yesterday," Ethan said. "It must have been a fine house at one time."

"Yes." Darcy put her hand above her eyes to block the glare. "But River Run is long forgotten."

"Perhaps it still lives in the memories of those who once lived there."

Darcy gazed ahead at its brokenness, its sadness not escaping her, seeping into her as if an old wound had been made to open and weep. Inside the window casements, shards of broken glass sparkled in the sunlight. A dirty film glazed them and gave the decaying structure a forbidding atmosphere. The roof had rotted away in patches and many shingles were long gone. The front porch stretched across the front and dipped to one side, the simple columns covered in poison ivy. It was a lonely place, a place of the past, ravished by winters and summer storms, a skeleton of its former existence. They drew closer, and a covey of mourning doves alighted from the rafters, their wings whistling as they beat them.

"I spent my babyhood here," said Darcy. "You shall think me very poor now, Mr. Brennan."

"I had heard of River Run. Now that I've seen it with my own eyes, I tend to think your father was a prosperous man. And whether poor or rich, Darcy, it makes no difference."

Surprised he thought this way, she cocked her head to one side and narrowed her eyes. "You are not at all what I imagined an Englishman of status to be."

"Status, is it?" he laughed with sarcasm. "Does that really matter either?"

"Not to me, it doesn't. I do not remember much about this place, except for a swing that was attached to that old tree over there. And I remember some of the people who lived here." She lowered her head, and a breath escaped her lips.

"Your parents?"

"Yes, among others, but the images in my mind are vague. My mother died long ago. I imagine my papa is now with her. He left for the frontier when I was a child and has not been heard from since. I was brought to my uncle and aunt very young. They have been the only parents I've known. I do not remember my father's face, nor my mother's. Is that not strange?"

"You were a small child as you said."

"Yes, but you would think I would remember them in that way."

"Sometimes memories come back in later years."

"I do recall my father's hands were large, and my mother had dark hair. She was kind and I believe she loved me." The thought of her mother's affection sparked a painful memory—the day her papa told her Eliza had died and had not been worthy of heaven.

"My mother and father are both gone, and a sister," Ethan said. "I understand your sorrow."

"I am sorry to hear it. I did not know."

Ethan leaned forward. "Is it not an interesting coincidence that we were both motherless at a young age?"

"It is not so uncommon."

"No, I suppose it's not." He lifted his eyes away from hers and scanned the plane of grass before him. "When my mother and sister died, my father and I lived alone in a house he inherited. He was lonely for years until he found me a governess. He was much older than she and she became a good companion to him."

"Oh, that is beautiful." Darcy's eyes softened. "How wonderful that he found her. It is not good for a man to be alone, especially when he is old."

She stared at the empty house. If her mother had not died, life would have been different. Walking on, she spied the cabin. An image sprang to her mind of a girl with red hair standing on the porch, holding a babe in her arms.

"We had a servant who lived there." She pointed in the direction of the abandoned walls that had once been Sarah's cabin. "She had a child and was kind to me. There was a housekeeper also. She was like a doting grandmother." She smiled. "Those are happy memories. I have wondered what happened to those people."

"I wish I could tell you." Ethan looked from her eyes to the cabin. Darcy caught a strange glimmer in his stare, as if he knew something. But how could he?

She proceeded across a field of knee-deep grass. The hem of her dress caught the thorns of a wild rose bush. "Oh, I've ruined my hem for good now."

Ethan reached over to help and yanked her dress free. "It is not torn."

A coy look spread over Darcy's face. "I am sure Miss Roth would never risk her expensive gowns in a place like this. She must be wondering where you have gone."

"Am I intruding upon you?" Ethan asked.

"No. But why you bother with me, when Miss Roth is at Twin Oaks, I do not understand. I'm still trying to figure you out. That's all."

"I would not try."

"Are you saying I am wasting my time, sir?"

"Not at all. Only let me be a mystery a little longer, Darcy."

She paused, gazing at him. "I doubt I could know everything about you in a matter of days, Mr. Brennan. So trust me when I say your secrets are safe from me. "

He made a short bow. "I would trust you with them—when the time was right."

Walking away, Darcy plucked a red clover and held it to her nose. Eyes closed, she drew in the subtle scent. They'd been gone a long while, and as ever, her aunt would begin to worry once she discovered her gone. Dread rippled through her—her guardians would disapprove if they knew she was alone with a man. What was she thinking? She should have told her uncle and gotten his consent before they left. But then, they might feel better knowing he was the man who had brought her home through a rainstorm. They had nothing to worry about with Ethan at her side.

"Speaking of time. Do you not find it intriguing that you were on this side of the river at the precise time I needed help?" Darcy said.

"Yes," Ethan replied. "Call it God's leading that I happened to go out riding when you happened to go wading."

She gave him a sad smile. "I am sorry you put yourself in danger because of me. I feel awful about it."

"That is absurd. What would you have had me do? Let you struggle back on your own and risk drowning?"

Under the quivering sunlight, they strolled at a more sedate pace. Ethan stopped her and touched her hand. "Don't you see I would swim a hundred leagues for you?"

"You would rescue any woman caught in a dangerous situation. There. I have worked out one thing about you."

He smiled. "Which is?"

"That you are brave and not at all afraid of getting wet."

Ethan laughed and shook his head. A lock of his hair fell over his forehead. Darcy reached up and moved it back. Emotion flooded his eyes when she touched him. He leaned down, drew her close, and kissed her. His kiss was the first she had ever known, and she felt herself drifting through the most beautiful sensation. It poured through every inch of her, this feeling of being in love, being captured and rescued all at the same time.

When he drew away, he ran his hand down the curve of her face and pressed his forehead against hers. "I have been wanting to do that for a long time."

"Oh," she breathed. Then, enthralled by the moment, she slid her arms around his neck and touched her lips to his. She dropped her arms and stood back, breathless. Heat rose in her face, and she felt the burn of tears rise in her eyes.

Shocked at what she had done, she hurried from him and ran home between moments of shade and sunlight.

9

*O*n Saturday morning, a carriage grated over the sandy lane leading to the Breese house, and seated within it were two ladies. The brims of their hats concealed their faces, and Darcy wondered who they could be. She emptied the remainder of the cracked corn in her tin to the pair of gray geese her uncle owned, and hurried back inside the house through the side door. She took her time removing the apron she wore, and ran her fingers through the length of her hair to tidy it. Then, after hearing voices, she met Missy out in the hallway when she came looking for her.

"Who is it, Missy?" Darcy asked.

"She did not say, miss," Missy replied in a quiet voice. "But the lady wishes to speak to you and waits in the sitting room." Missy's large brown eyes glanced back to the closed door.

Darcy nodded. "Is it an older lady with hair streaked gray?"

"No, she's young, miss. She has a servant with her who is much older though."

"Hmm. Miss Roth, I wager." Drawing back her shoulders and lifting her chin, she opened the door and walked into the room. It was as she predicted.

Miss Roth and her chaperone had made themselves comfortable in her aunt's best chairs. Dressed in taupe silk with a striped underskirt, she blended with the beige fabric covering the seat. Slipping loose the ribbon tied beneath her chin, she removed her hat and placed it on the table beside her.

Still the same unbecoming hairstyle, thought Darcy. A knot in the back with tight curls framing the pale oval face made her wonder if the severity of it gave Miss Roth headaches.

Darcy turned her eyes to the chaperone who shadowed Miss Roth. How annoying it must be to have someone looking over one's shoulder, not having a moment alone to oneself. Mrs. Mort was a short woman with a full bosom and broad face. Her features were strong and suggested she might have been pretty in her youth. Her air reserved, she sat motionless with her hands folded in her lap when Darcy stepped inside.

Miss Roth lifted her head, and a labored smile raised the corners of her petite mouth. "So, this is the Breese home," she said. "I had wondered what it would look like. It is very quaint and cozy."

"Modest to what you are accustomed to, Miss Roth?" Darcy closed the door behind her.

Miss Roth glanced around the room. "My father's estate in England has a small cottage much like this one where our groundskeeper lives with his wife and children. Our home is very grand, with large rooms and plenty of staff. I had expected to find many servants here, but you have only one that I can tell."

"Missy is all we need." Darcy lowered herself into a chair opposite Miss Roth.

"Still, I do not know how your poor aunt does with just one. It must be laboring for all of you."

"We manage very well. Idleness is not a privilege to us."

"What you refer to as idleness, we refer to as leisure. It is one of the benefits of being wealthy or upper class. I thank my stars for it, for I can do as I please when I please. And my hands are soft and white, whereas I see yours are not. It is such a shame, Miss Darcy. Have you been working in the garden? Is that how your acquired such rough skin?"

Darcy glanced down at her hands, then back at Miss Roth. "Yes, as a matter of fact I have been tending the garden—and feeding our chickens and geese, something I can never imagine you doing, Miss Roth."

Miss Roth looked mortified. "Really? You feed animals?"

"We cannot let them starve. Tell me, Miss Roth, have you any knowledge of gardens, or of chickens or geese?"

"Only that gardens provide flowers, and chickens and geese eggs and meat," she answered. "There is no need for me to know anything other than that. My father's estate has an ample garden, and our cook roasts fowl to perfection."

"I suppose you will be returning home soon."

"Very soon. I confess that I had hoped our journey to Virginia would have been a honeymoon. But it was best to wait and travel with companions. I shall plan a wedding when I return."

Darcy forced herself to speak with courtesy. But her desire to escort Miss Roth out grew to a fevered pitch. Why she had to rub in any details of a wedding was beyond Darcy. "I see. What delayed it?"

"Oh, this and that. I was so pleased Ethan agreed to accompany us to America as our protector, and at the last minute. He assured me his acceptance of Daniel's offer was so he could buy a Virginia mare."

Mrs. Mort choked, pressing a lace handkerchief to her mouth. Her face turned scarlet, and Darcy called for Missy to bring a glass of water. It did some good, but Mrs. Mort looked at her charge with a shake of her head. "I do not believe he meant to imply . . ."

Miss Roth held her hand up to stop her. "Now that Mrs. Mort's interruption is calm, I must tell you I rejected the first mare. But then he chose the prettiest brown mare I have ever seen just to spoil me. It is only ladies of quality who deserve such a fine horse. I daresay there are no horses here that could stand up to my brown mare."

Darcy marked Miss Roth's needling and kept herself composed in the face of insult. "It was kind of him, but I understand Ireland has fine horses and the English prefer them to ours. You could have saved yourself a long journey by going there instead."

"That is indeed true, but after Daniel described his family's horses and the beauty of the Virginia countryside, we could not resist. I shall be the only person in our neighborhood to have a Virginia mare. My dear papa shall be pleased and breed her with the best of his own stock of English stallions, and his opinion of Ethan will certainly broaden."

"Your father had not a great opinion of Mr. Brennan before?"

"Not a great one, but that is his way. He is skeptical of everyone, and would prefer Ethan to be extremely wealthy and titled. But one cannot have everything they desire in a mate. But he does own Fairview, a lovely property. And I have every confidence in Ethan that he shall prosper. Papa thinks he has plenty, but Ethan has told me we shall be poor until he builds up the estate. When we do marry, I shall remove all persons from under his roof who are unnecessary. That will save him a great deal of money."

"It seems odd that your father would agree to you marrying a man he does not particularly like."

"Oh, you interpret my words wrong, Miss Darcy."

Mrs. Mort again coughed, and Darcy glanced over at her. Did Miss Roth have another meaning to her words?

"Then he does have a great opinion of him?"

"More than I have let on."

"Tell me, Miss Roth. Why have you come? You were the last person I expected to see."

"To speak to you to clear the air."

"Well, say on. I am sure you do not wish your time wasted."

"Indeed I do not. It concerns Ethan."

Darcy paused a moment then asked, "He is not sick, is he?"

With a lift of her hand, Miss Roth laughed. "Oh, no. He is very well. I have come to tell you, to assure you, that he and I have had an understanding these last two years, despite what he may have told you."

Her stinging words caused Darcy's heart to sink. A third time, Mrs. Mort coughed into her handkerchief, and Miss Roth glared at her. "Must you do that, Mrs. Mort? It is so disruptive."

Mrs. Mort finished off her water. "I beg your pardon."

Miss Roth turned to Darcy. "I have forgiven him that you, Miss Darcy, distracted him. Though I cannot understand why, except to say that your exotic ways may have tempted him and caused him to be curious. You have no fortune, no family of any consequence, and live in this wild country."

Darcy felt her face flush with the insult. She pushed it back, deep down, and strove not to show it. "Fortunes can fail, Miss Roth. As for my family, we are well respected. My aunt guides the ladies in our church charities. My uncle is a botanist. My cousins are fine young women."

Miss Roth shut her eyes, took in a breath, and opened them again. "Did Ethan make you think he had feelings for you?"

"You have expressed that he could never have feelings for someone like me. The question is insignificant."

"I pray that is so, that he has not made any promises he cannot possibly keep."

"He has made none."

"I am glad to hear it. Ethan is not easily swayed by forward-minded women such as you may be."

"Your accusation is offensive," Darcy said. "Did you come here to wound me, Miss Roth?"

Those insipid eyes looked back at Darcy, masked with cynical concern. "I say this not to hurt you, but to be truthful. This may be the way girls are raised here, so I do not hold you accountable."

Gathering up the fabric of her dress, Darcy squeezed it. "I do not seek your opinion of me, Miss Roth. Your assessment of the kind of person I am is unimportant to me."

"And I care not to offer it any further than I already have," Miss Roth replied. "Yet, we must both agree that Ethan is a man, and being such as his nature may lead him, he may have given over to infatuation which caused him to forget himself. The temptation may have risen out of mere curiosity to compare the two of us."

"If Mr. Brennan has been drawn in by me, and if I have been deceived by him, then you have nothing to fear. But he did say to me that he had no true attachment to you."

With a click of her tongue, Miss Roth shifted in the chair. "Oh, that is simply not true. Tell her, Mrs. Mort."

Mrs. Mort drew her handkerchief away from her mouth. "It is simply not true indeed, miss. A promise is a promise, and Mr. Brennan and Miss Roth are intended for each other."

Miss Roth gave Darcy a haughty smile. "I am sorry, but you must have misunderstood him."

"Then I am sorry you would set your heart upon such a man who would be unclear about his attachments to you, who would allow himself to court another's feelings behind your back."

"Ethan is the most honorable of men. He was drawn away, that is all. You look astonished, Miss Darcy. I suppose you are not acquainted with the ways of the world, not to have known how a man's passions can lead him astray. It happens all the time."

Darcy could not let the comment go by. "Do you love him?"

Miss Roth answered with a long breath. "Of course I do. And I pray you do not come between us."

Darcy looked away. "I have no intention of it."

Miss Roth picked up her hat. "Good. I do not wish to see you heartbroken and for that reason, I urge you to forget him. It is fortunate for you we are leaving Virginia."

All dreams of belonging to Ethan died. Darcy's heart was run through by Miss Roth's sharp words. "You are making this more than it is," she told her. "I have not stolen him from you. You have said he is a man of his word, giving you no reason to fear that he shall come to me. As I reminded you before, you have said I am of no importance in the world."

"We must all accept our place . . . Here, he has penned you a letter and wished me to give it to you." She drew it out of her reticule. "It is the least I can do."

Downcast, Darcy looked at the letter in Miss Roth's hand. "Why did he not come and speak to me himself?"

"He did not have the determination. Men cannot bear women's tears."

Tears? He'd see none from her that day or any day. Darcy took the letter from her rival. "I am not so weak or so smitten that I would cry. You can tell him that, Miss Roth. Tears should not be wasted on insignificant matters."

"Oh, I doubt your words immensely, and I have one last thing to tell you. I have a sizable dowry. I would think you have little to none."

Darcy had had enough, and though she tried to stay composed and a step above this distasteful person, she could no longer abide her. "It would be better if he were poor than marry you. You are selfish and arrogant, Miss Roth, and most certainly you would plague his heart out."

Miss Roth leapt from her seat. "How dare you!"

"I do dare."

"Did you dare to tell him your family history? I did not think so. But then you may not know it yourself. Perhaps it has been kept from you so not to cause you embarrassment."

"I do not know what you mean."

"I mean that Mrs. Rhendon has confided in us. She did not wish to see Ethan make a mistake. Once he was told about your mother's indiscretions it was clear to Ethan he mustn't see you again. If he did, it would bring a great deal of disgrace if others were to discover all this."

"You have been told wrong. My mother was a good woman."

"Good women are not immune from sin. Let us end our talk amiably, and do wish me well, Miss Darcy. I am to be married to a fine man."

"I will go to him and explain. It is a lie."

"You would be wasting your time, and it would be forward of you."

"Ethan will listen to what I have to say, instead of the heartless gossip that has been viciously spread."

"I'm afraid there is no persuading him. It is best you forget. Surely there is a farmer near here who needs a wife."

Darcy stood. "You are cruel, Miss Roth. I knew you hated me the moment we first laid eyes on each other. I am no threat to you."

"I would despise any woman who set her cap for the man I mean to wed. You would want him to break his word."

"If it meant saving him from the likes of you, then yes."

"You care nothing for lineage or status, or that your family has a good name? You care nothing that these events could cause a scandal? You are a disgrace. I hope the same happens to you and you see how it feels."

"It is unbecoming in a lady of your standing to insult me and wish me such ill will, especially in my own house."

"Well, it matters not what you say, think, or do. We are to leave for home tomorrow morning, and when we arrive in England, Ethan and I will be wed." She turned to her chaperone. "Tell her, Mrs. Mort."

Mrs. Mort nodded and leaned forward. "We shall all be happy to put our soles on English soil again." She then turned her eyes away from Darcy's.

"Since you are leaving, why did you bother to come tell me all this? It would have made no difference."

Miss Roth looked at her with fake sympathy. "I always have to have the last word." With not another spoken, the pair walked out. Darcy would not see them to their carriage. She heard it drive away and went out into the hall. The sun streamed through the windows, and she thought of the moment she and Ethan had stood there together. She was hurt that he would play her, hurt that Mrs. Rhendon had gossiped about her family, insulting them, inflaming disgrace. But there was nothing she could undo about what had been said.

Missy came through with a tea tray in hand. "The ladies did not stay, miss?"

"No, they had to go."

"I've never seen an English lady before today, and so finely dressed was she and so elegant in her ways. I suppose she was going to visit one of the plantations and was passing by. Does she know you well?"

"No, Missy. She does not know me at all." Darcy's breath came up in quick gasps as she hurried up the stairs to her room. She leaned back against the door after shutting it, went forward and lay across the bed, brokenhearted and in tears. After a moment of release, she sat up, wiped her eyes, and looked at the letter in her hand. She broke the seal and scanned the bottom to see his name.

Sitting on the edge of the bed near a window where the sunlight gathered, she noticed the date from Twin Oaks and the time he wrote it—ten to midnight. She was not hungry to read his words. Still, she uttered the first line aloud.

"My dear Darcy, I am returning to England first light." Then she tossed the page down.

"How can he leave me?" A hundred reasons rose within her. To begin with, she was not English or elegant or rich like Miss Roth. Her mother's name had been dragged through the mud before him, and he had made a pledge that he was expected to keep, but not noble enough to break when he knew he did not love the lady.

She picked the letter up and decided to finish reading it.

It is with regret, I write to say farewell and to ask that you would forgive me for not delivering this letter into your hand. I could not, for if I had seen your face again, I might have weakened in my decision. I had to consider that to relent would have broken the heart of the lady

I had made a pledge to. I now see the wrong I did her in allowing my affections to traverse elsewhere. Upon learning the truth concerning your family, I was forced to examine what an association with you would have meant. I will not deny I felt something for you, but it was a fleeting infatuation. I am bound by my duty and compelled by honor to do what is expected of me. I wish you well.

Ethan Brennan

Her heart withered. "I must let you go," she whispered. She tossed the missive inside the cold hearth and then set the paper alight. As it caught, her eyes filled. It was not until the letter was lost in the ash that she allowed tears to slip down her cheeks. Outside the door, she heard the tramp of feet on the staircase, the commotion of people downstairs. The Breese clan had arrived home. She wiped her eyes dry and moved away from the fireplace.

Martha hurried through the door. "Darcy, what a day it has been." She slipped loose the ribbons under her chin and removed her hat. Then she paused before the mirror and tidied her hair. "The booths were full of people at the church fair, the weather being as it is. Papa relented and allowed me to buy a novel. Oh, and Miss Roth's carriage passed us as we were coming home." Martha turned to her. "It is odd. Was she here?"

"Yes."

"And without Mr. Brennan and Captain Rhendon?"

"She came with her chaperone to deliver a letter from Mr. Brennan."

Martha stood back and observed her cousin. Darcy could not conceal her feelings from one so observant. "What has happened? Why have you been crying? Did his letter cause this?"

"It is too long to explain. I will tell you later."

"Does it have to do with Mr. Brennan and Miss Roth?"

"Yes. But I am over it."

Together they sat on the edge of the bed. Her cousin gripped Darcy's hand. "You cannot be over something like this in a moment. It takes time to get over love lost. It was love wasn't it?"

A prickle passed over Darcy's skin and she made a swift turn to her cousin. "No, infatuation."

"Perhaps on Mr. Brennan's part. But you?"

Darcy pressed her lips together hard, feeling the swell of anger. "There's no telling what he felt. All I know is he has rejected me and returned his affections to Miss Roth."

"Oh, he was cruel to lead you on," said Martha.

"He did not seem cruel. But I shall not see him again, and now I must forget him. He is only one man, after all." Her chest felt heavy, pricked with needles. How could she ever put him out of her mind?

Martha stood and walked with a thoughtful scowl over to the hearth and looked down into the ash. "You burned it?"

"I could not keep it, read it over and over, allow it to pain me." Darcy lay down with her head cradled in her arms.

Martha went to her and stroked her cousin's head. "Something must have happened to change him. How could he not love you?"

"You mustn't say anything to anyone. He does not love me, and he will not come to me again. Miss Roth told me the most awful things were said about my parents and that Ethan was appalled. How can it be true?"

"I have no doubt Miss Roth made the whole thing up."

"The damage is done whether she did or not. But I believe her. She brought Mrs. Mort with her and she testified that all that Miss Roth said was true."

"Let him go, Darcy. He does not deserve you. Indeed you shall have many beaus. I dare say they shall be lining up outside the door."

Darcy stood, picked up her horsehair brush and brushed out her hair. "I do not care about that now. I have other things on my mind."

"Come downstairs. Mama wants us for supper."

Darcy turned from the mirror. "Promise you will not tell her anything I've told you. I do not want her or anyone else to know. If you do, she will keep at me for days wanting to know all the details. And I would not put it past her to convince Uncle Will to ride over to Twin Oaks and confront Mr. Brennan."

Martha put her hands on Darcy's shoulders. "I shall be quiet. Is there something else you would like to tell me, perhaps what was said about your mother?"

Darcy shook her head. "Miss Roth gave no details. But it was made clear their feelings about where my family stands—too low for their consideration. Perhaps someday I will prove them wrong."

☙

Downstairs the family gathered in the dining room. Dishes clattered as the girls talked among themselves. At the other end of the table, Darcy's aunt unfolded a napkin in her lap. She talked about their journey to town, what had been bought, and how much Darcy had missed out.

"You should not stay at home alone again," Mrs. Breese said. "Oh, and that Miss Roth. What snobbery. Her rudeness not to pause and speak to us is inexcusable. She rolled straight past us without even a nod. I have not raised my girls to be so snobbish."

"A waste of time to dwell on it, Aunt." Darcy lifted her fork and moved the carrots around on her plate.

"Well, I'll tell you this. I cannot deny how glad I was to hear that Miss Roth and her party are departing our shores and returning to England. I say good riddance to that insipid Miss Roth. I do admit, I thought well of Mr. Brennan and am sorry to see him go. Darcy, you were fond of him. Perhaps you can write to him sometime . . . but then his wife might not appreciate that. You best not."

Darcy sat opposite of Martha, with her eyes lowered, her mouth taut, silent while her aunt rambled on. The sound of horse and rider pounding down the drive and halting before their door caused Mrs. Breese to stop talking. Darcy looked up at Martha, and her hopes ran high that it was Ethan.

10

*W*hen the front door opened, and Missy could be heard speaking to the rider, Mari Breese rose from her chair and met her at the dining room doorway. She rushed back in, breathless, waving a letter in front of her, as if to calm her beating heart and abate the warm day. "We've news."

Darcy rose from her chair. "Then . . . it was not Mr. Brennan?"

Mrs. Breese shook her head. "Oh, dear me, no. Why should it be Mr. Brennan? No, a courier has brought two letters from England. Mr. Breese, did you hear me?"

William Breese looked up from his newspaper, then over his spectacles.

Mrs. Breese held the letter out in front of her and studied it. "'Tis strange, but this one is for you, Darcy. Oh, I've been dreading this day, but here it is. I don't know whether it is wonderful or distressing. You may go and read it alone or to us aloud."

"I shall read it alone, Aunt—later." And she set it down on the table in front of her.

"You should read it straightaway for it comes from your grandmamma." Mrs. Breese scooped up the letter and handed it back to Darcy. "Now do you understand why I am so distressed? Or is it excitement? I know not which."

Conceding to her aunt's wishes, Darcy broke the seal and unfolded the page. Her uncle tucked his inside his waistcoat pocket. Her cousins sat in rapt attention, not moving a muscle or saying a word.

"She wishes me to visit her," Darcy said as she read.

Moaning, Mrs. Breese sat down in the chair. "I knew it. Finally she's chosen a time when she is old and ailing to make such a request. Is she ailing, Darcy?"

"She does not say."

"Why does she not ask for your older cousins? They are her granddaughters, too. Will, why has your mother only asked for Darcy?"

Uncle Will pinched his brows. "I do not know, Mari."

"Have you slacked in writing to her?"

"I have written to her often. You know that. And I inform her about the girls and how they are doing. It is difficult being so far apart."

Mari put her hands on her lap. "Perhaps you should have never left England."

"And missed out on marrying you? I would not change that for the world, my dear."

"Then why does she not come here instead and live with us? She could have since the war ended."

"She is old and settled in her home. At her age, to uproot her would be difficult if not disruptive to her health."

Mrs. Breese wiggled nervously in her seat. "Well, go on and read your letter. It may shed more light on the situation."

He drew out the letter, positioned his spectacles and read. "Nothing more to add, other than she hopes we are all well.

She says her joints are full of rheumatism, and that Langbourne is taking care of the estate very well."

"Nothing about sending Martha to her?"

"Not a word."

"Well, I am glad for it. I would worry so if both she and Darcy left home."

"No need to worry on that account," Mr. Breese said, tucking the letter back into his pocket. He drew off his glasses and looked at Darcy. "You are of age, Darcy. The decision is ultimately yours."

"I suppose I should honor her request," Darcy said. She looked down at the letter in her hands and thought of Ethan. She might see him again.

Mouths fell open and Mrs. Breese shifted in her chair. "So quick to decide, Darcy?"

"She knows to do the right thing, Mari. It is only natural she should wish to meet her grandmother," Will Breese said.

"Then I suppose we must send Martha with her. Darcy cannot travel alone. It is too risky."

Martha looked shocked and upset. "I do not want to go. I would be unhappy in a dark house with an old lady. What would I do there but pine away for home?"

Darcy knew to intercede. "Aunt, Martha has an attachment here, and it would be wrong to take her away from him."

Mrs. Breese arched her brows and smiled. "An attachment? Who is it? Give me his name, Martha."

"The new physician, Mama," Martha replied shyly. "Remember, we met him in church. He is very respectable."

Mari Breese sighed. "Oh, him. Yes, Dr. Emerson is well regarded, though I have not spoken to him much or seen him for any ailments. So, I suppose you are right. You should stay home, Martha. But Darcy? I shall worry the whole time she is away."

With a gentle smile, Darcy picked up her aunt's hand. "I would not want that."

"I am astonished. You told me over and over you love this place too much to leave it. Do you even understand what this means?"

"Very much so."

"You would be sailing across the ocean, which is most treacherous and dull."

"I have always wanted to experience the sea."

"You would be landing upon a land foreign to you. You do not know the towns there, and how shall you find your grandmother's house?"

"I speak the language fluently and shall carry a map. Besides, Uncle Will shall give me clear directions—if I decide to go. And there are coaches that take people wherever they need to go."

Her cousins giggled at her comment. Mrs. Breese scowled at them with a severe frown. "You will no doubt get lost," she said, turning back to Darcy.

"I have an excellent sense of direction."

"How does the address read?"

"Havendale, Derbyshire, England."

Darcy's aunt pinched her brows together hard and shook her head. "Surely that is not enough. Will, you cannot let her go."

Darcy rose and embraced her aunt. "If you wish me to stay then I shall."

Mari Breese blinked back tears. "You are good to not worry me." She sighed, looking happy she might keep her charge at home.

But Mr. Breese slapped the newspaper down. "You mustn't decide on your aunt's account, Darcy. Your grandmother has asked for you, and she must have good reasons for doing so."

Mari Breese turned upon her husband with a look of disap-proval. "I cannot imagine the reasons."

"Think, my dear," he replied, folding his paper. He set it aside and looked over at Darcy. "I'd say her life has been lone-some without Hayward. He was her favorite child. I on the other hand was brushed off when I announced my plans to leave for America and study its flora. She thought it a silly idea and that I was too young."

"Oh, if only she could see your watercolors, Papa," said Martha. "Perhaps Darcy could take one to her."

"Perhaps," said Mr. Breese. "And I should think it would bless her soul to see at least one grandchild before she dies."

Mrs. Breese huffed. "She treated you abominably from what you have told me. I would think that enough to object to such a request."

"That was long ago, my dear, and has nothing to do with Darcy."

"Well, perhaps you should go with Darcy, and take Martha anyway just to spite her for not asking for her as well. You can-not let our niece go alone."

"I will consider it. But she did not ask me to come, now did she?"

"No, but why should that matter? You can make up your own mind."

"Indeed I can, and I will. And Darcy can make up hers."

Mrs. Breese bit her lower lip. "Oh, but if you go, then I shall be left here alone with the other girls, and who should protect us?"

"You, my dear, are a bundle of contradictions. You cannot keep your mind settled on one thing. Instead you rush back and forth between this idea and that," said Mr. Breese, his face flushed. "Make up your mind."

Darcy hoped the conversation would end before her uncle made an outburst that would push her aunt to crying.

Darcy cast her eyes down in thought, her throat tightening all the more as her aunt continued to sum up reasons why her uncle should accompany her, why he should not, why Darcy should not go and so on. Once again, the past reared up before her, causing rapids of questions to tumble into her mind.

She glanced over at her uncle. "Uncle Will, you think I should go?"

"You may not ever have another chance. Come with me." He made a swift gesture to his wife that she stay put.

Darcy followed him to the study situated across from the sitting room, where upon his desk were notes and drawings of seeds and plants. He flung open the doors to a bookcase. From it, he took out an old stoneware tankard where he kept a bit of money, out of his wife's sight and without her knowledge. He opened the lid, took out a leather pouch, and placed it into Darcy's hand.

"I have kept this for many a year, knowing someday God would lead you from home. Your father left it for you."

Darcy could not stop her breath from catching. "He did? He cared that much?"

"He thought it would come in handy one day. If you must go to your grandmother, this will help you along the way. Life is too short, Darcy. You must pray to make the right choice. Remember, God has a plan for your life."

"Whatever his plan is for me, this part of it came unexpected." She looked down at the pouch in her hand. "It is exciting and at the same time frightening."

Mr. Breese patted her shoulder. "Adventures always are. I have no doubt this one shall be grand if you decide to embark upon it."

She kissed his cheek. "I would write often and be back home within a year."

"Do not make any such a promise as to time, Darcy. You never know how short or how long a journey may be," he told her, rubbing her chin. "I will look forward to your letters."

"I suppose the idea of you going with me is out of the question. Aunt Mari and the girls need you here."

"Perhaps we can arrange for a chaperone."

"That would cost money. I will be fine without one."

"Yes, they can be troublesome, shadowing your every movement." Mr. Breese lifted her hand and closed her fingers over the pouch. "One way or another, you will need this. If I could afford for the entire family to take a long holiday, I would arrange it. But it isn't possible. My duty is here with my wife and the girls."

Darcy pushed back the tears welling in her eyes. "What was grandmother's letter to you like?"

"Blunt. She did not ask me to visit her."

"I am sorry, Uncle."

"I daresay she has forgotten me for the most part. But I have not forsaken her, Darcy. The Bible says not to despise your mother when she is old. I have written many times and asked her to come live with us. I have even sent money. At times I have felt guilty for being so far away from her now that she is aged."

Darcy wiped her eyes. His words saddened her.

"You're heart has been low these past few days," her uncle said. "What is it?"

Darcy forced a smile. "I think deeply on things, Uncle Will. That's all. Besides all this, I admit I am troubled over Mr. Brennan."

He placed his hands gently on her shoulders. "Hmm, obviously that slip of a girl, Miss Roth, upset you. Is there something I can do?"

"She said, or rather implied, my parents brought shame to our family. Is this true?"

"Tittle-tattle. Your father was a brave patriot, and your mother endured those war years without him. She kept River Run and the mill at Israel Creek running."

"Yes, I have not forgotten what you have told me," said Darcy. "I've always felt proud of them."

"You have every reason to. It was not easy keeping River Run going while he was away. I have always felt sorry for the letter I sent your mother, when I was told the British had hanged your father. She had to live with grief all that time."

"But what joy there must have been when she learned the truth," Darcy said. "I vaguely remember my father's homecoming. Strange, I mostly recall the buttons on his uniform and him carrying me through the hall. He loved my mother, didn't he?"

"As much as any man can love a woman." He crossed the room to his desk, took out a key, and opened a drawer. He showed Darcy a thick, folded parchment. "Your father showed up on my doorstep with you in tow to tell me your mother was dead and handed me the deed to River Run, saying it should be given to you upon your marriage. He said he could not care for you, that you needed a mother, and so left you with us. He never told me more, but I could see his mind was affected."

For a moment, Darcy held the deed in her hands. River Run would be hers one day, but only upon the day she wed. "Such love. Such honor." She looked back at her uncle and handed him the document. "Why would people speak unkind things about them?"

"Do not listen to idle gossip. There is no shame." He tucked the deed back into the drawer and closed it.

"Mr. Brennan stopped calling because he believed their lies. He refused to attach himself to someone like me, according to his letter."

"I shall ride over to Twin Oaks and have a word with Captain Rhendon. I will not stand for it. I'll not have my family spoken ill of. Dear Lord, Eliza is in her grave these many years and they still speak harshly of her. Surely God frowns on such disrespect."

Darcy took a step closer to him. "Uncle, why is there no gravestone for my mother at River Run?"

"I do not know, Darcy."

"It is not right that she should not be remembered in that way. When I return, I will see it is done. And one for Ilene as well."

She kissed his cheek and left for her room. Night swallowed up the twilight, and she sat on her bedside, gazing out the window at the misty land before her, a tumult of emotions flooding her heart.

11

*U*nable to sleep most of the night, Darcy tried to picture her grandmother in her mind. Perhaps she might be an elegant woman, stiff in posture, shoulders back, head high, eyes that spoke of highborn blood. Then again, she could be wrinkled and bent with age, one who regretted the fading bloom of youth.

Tucking her arms beneath her head on the pillow, she watched the shadows cross the ceiling in time with the even rhythm of her breathing. She closed her eyes and thought of Ethan. England—he'd be there. Ah, but would she want to meet him again, endure seeing him with a new wife, one who would flaunt her new name in her face?

She drew the pillow against her and wondered if he had decided not to marry Miss Roth. Did he not say he had no real affection for her? If they were to meet again, how would he react? Would he repent for leaving her high and dry?

In the morning, she went downstairs for breakfast. Fortunately, her aunt was reserved on the subject of her leaving, yet dropped hints as to how fine the riverside was, how lovely the Maryland countryside would be in autumn, how blessed they all were to live in a land of liberty without the burden of monarchy.

"If you choose to leave us, I would be pleased if you would send your uncle a sample of heather pressed in rice paper inside a book of your choosing, Darcy," her aunt said.

Darcy could not bring herself to smile. "I will be happy to, if I can find any. I will see if Uncle Will has a picture of it, to make it easy for me."

She went to his study and found him working. "Aunt Mari wishes for me to send home a sample of heather. Do you have a drawing I may see?"

"No, but I can make one."

"That would be splendid."

He drew out paper and began the sketch. "It is a shrub-like plant, you see." Darcy leaned in. "It blooms bell-shaped purple flowers in summer. By the time you reach England, you will have missed them in all their glory."

"But the leaves are lovely, and perhaps I will find some dried blooms."

"Yes, perhaps." He handed her the sketch and she thanked him. It worried her how weary he seemed.

"What is the matter? I have noticed you seem tired lately."

"Yes, I am more tired than usual, and I have a shortness of breath at times. I suppose it is old age creeping up on me." He placed his hand on her cheek. "Say nothing of this to your aunt. You know how she worries."

She agreed to be quiet, but she wondered if it were the right thing to do. "You must see a doctor, Uncle Will. Promise me."

"I have met with him already. I am to drink plenty of barley water, eat my food warm, and stay out of drafts."

She put her arms around him. "I should not leave, not when you are ill."

"You fear too much for me, Darcy. I am otherwise in good health. I want my heather, and the way I am to have it is if you get it for me."

Stepping outside his study, Will Breese put on his hat. "Wild blackberry leaves are turning and I need samples."

"Would you like me to come along?"

"I would like to have time alone to pray, Darcy. You know how precious quiet is to me, and that it is hard to pray when there is so much activity inside the house. I'll take my dog with me and return for dinner at noon."

By one o'clock he had not returned, and so Darcy and Martha were sent to find him. They walked past the front garden to the road together, to a field opposite the house, lush with knee-high grass that waved in the breeze.

Martha looped her arm through Darcy's. "I think we shall have a gray winter this year, Darcy."

Darcy smiled and lifted her face to feel the sun. "I like winter as much as any season. But when it is cold and dreary, I remember that the wildflowers will return as they always do."

Martha paused and shook out the dust that had gathered on her hem from the road. "I wonder if you shall be here to see them. Your grandmother's invitation to visit her . . ."

"Do not look so sad, Martha. This is my home and I will come back."

With a firm hand, Martha yanked at a head of a clover. "Hmm. You are like the wildflowers, cousin. Gone for a while, but promised to return."

Darcy laughed and shook back her hair.

"Are you worried you might see Mr. Brennan there?"

"Indeed not. I doubt I shall ever see Mr. Brennan again. And even if I do, it shall not be of any consequence to me."

"And if he is wed to that prissy girl, tell him I think him well-deserving of such a thorn in his flesh."

"It is because of me that you would say such a thing, Martha."

"You are right. I would say it of any man who treated my dearest cousin and friend ill."

They walked on, closer to the line of trees that shaded the field.

"You never did say all that was in the letter, Darcy. Were there other reasons for Grandmother asking you to come, other than wishing to see you?"

"That is the sum of it. She said that for many years she has grieved and explained it no further. I imagine not seeing our fathers for all these years caused her much pain, and to know we exist and to never to meet us has been difficult. I do not understand why she only asked for me, and not you or your sisters."

"Perhaps she plans to send for us one at a time, and I shall be next on the list. But I do not ever want to go. I am afraid of strangers and strange places."

"I have thought perhaps there are things I should know, and people I should meet," said Darcy. "I am not afraid."

Martha nodded. "You never are. I admire that about you."

The breeze whispered through the weeping willow they walked under. Darcy drew in the air. "We are young, Martha. Neither of us should spend our days sitting at home. I must find answers, and you must find a husband."

Her cousin laughed. "Have you no such hope in finding a good man, Darcy?"

"I shall desire marriage, if it is for love. If I never find it, than I shall remain as I am."

"I have received two letters from Dr. Emerson," Martha said. "I believe he is sincerely fond of me."

Darcy turned to her cousin. "What is there not to be fond of? You have all the qualities a good man should desire. Beauty.

Wit. Intelligence. And you have excellent taste in books, especially poetry. I hear Dr. Emerson is a deeply spiritual man, in the way Christ would have him be, kind and compassionate. I believe you are fond of him, as well."

Martha blushed and nodded. "I am, indeed. He might stay here in the countryside, or he might carry me away to Baltimore, or even Annapolis."

Darcy blinked in astonishment. "You would prefer the city to the river?"

"I would prefer to be wherever Dr. Emerson chooses to live. But I will admit the river would be my first choice, if I have any say in the matter."

"I am sure he would want your opinion on such an important issue."

"We have not spoken much, or ever been alone. But when I have seen him my heart pounds so hard, I think I should faint."

Darcy felt her smile sweep from her face and a yearning fill her. "I understand. Now, when I think of Ethan, my heart aches. Love is a two-edged sword."

"Yes, Darcy. Oh, we should not be speaking as if I am engaged to Dr. Emerson. I am not."

"It does not hurt to dream."

"What do you dream of?"

Darcy plucked a long blade of grass and then tossed it away. "Me? Well, I dream of growing old beside the two rivers. As you see, my expectations are not too lofty. I will not be disappointed, unless I die young."

Off in the distance, she spied her uncle strolling home and pointed him out to her cousin. A canvas bag hung from his belt, and his dog, Dash, strutted alongside him. He lifted his hand and waved. Darcy pulled Martha's arm, and together they proceeded through the field at a quick pace to meet him.

Dash leapt in front of Mr. Breese, barked, then stood still with a whine. His master staggered forward, gripped his shoulder, and grimaced in pain. When he dropped to his knees, Darcy drew her arm out from Martha's and ran. Martha cried out and followed.

"Uncle Will!"

"Papa!" Martha sprinted past Darcy.

He lifted his face. Fear flushed his skin and shown in his eyes. Then he moaned and fell onto his side. Martha shrieked and threw herself across his chest. "Uncle Will!" Darcy said, dropping beside him. She placed her hand on his cheek, tapping it with her fingers. She pressed her ear against his heart. "Wake, Uncle Will, open your eyes. Martha and I will take you home." But he did not wake.

"It is no good." Heavy with grief, Martha leaned her head against Darcy's shoulder, weeping.

She pulled Martha forward by the shoulders. "He's breathing and his heart is still beating."

Martha's eyes widened and she gripped Darcy. "Hurry home, Darcy. Tell Mama. Tell her to send help."

Jumping to her feet, Darcy lifted her skirts and ran as swiftly as she could toward the house. Her heart pounded and her breath caught in her throat. How was she going to tell her aunt that Uncle Will lay dying in the meadow?

12

The Breese household was the quietest it had been in years. Mr. Breese lay in his four-poster bed upstairs. All the windows were open, and a soft, almost indistinguishable breeze shifted the curtains to and fro. Surrounded by his wife, daughters, and niece, he set his hand atop his dog's head when Dash laid his paw on the bedside and whined.

Missy led a young physician through the door. He set his bag down at the foot of the bed. Dressed in black from his coat to his shoes, he posed a handsome man, with large brown eyes and hair as blonde as the wheat growing in the fields.

"How are you feeling, sir?" he inquired, leaning down to Mr. Breese.

"Everyone is making too much of a fuss. You may want to take my wife's pulse, for she is very upset."

He opened Mr. Breese's shirt and listened to his heart-beat. "Your heart sounds strong and your pulse regular." He straightened up and looked at Mrs. Breese. "Who found him, madam?"

"My daughter Martha, Dr. Emerson." Mrs. Breese extended her hand over to Martha's and lifted it within hers. "And my niece, Darcy. They are good girls, sir, and did all that they could and should do. Darcy ran home for help while Martha stayed with her poor papa. Together with Missy they were able to help my husband home."

It did not escape Darcy's eyes the way Emerson turned his to Martha—a controlled gaze that showed simmering admiration. He turned to Mrs. Breese. "Your husband has suffered a heart seizure, ma'am."

With a cry, Mrs. Breese thrust her handkerchief against her mouth. Then she waved the handkerchief as if to chase the bad news away. "He is to die, I know it."

"No, ma'am. He will not die. But he will need plenty of rest, strong broths, and fresh air. I'm afraid to say he will need to stop working for a time. Nothing strenuous. No exertion. He can no longer venture out alone."

"But his livelihood is partly our bread and butter, sir. And he loves it so dearly."

"I'm sorry. No exertion, ma'am."

"Oh, surely, Doctor, a little water coloring in my portfolio is no harm to me," Mr. Breese said.

"I want you to stay in bed a full week, sir. Then gradually you may do a little work, but again, nothing taxing."

Mrs. Breese slapped her hands on her knees. "Oh, what shall become of us now? We have a small annuity from my father's estate, but it is not enough to keep us all."

"Aunt," Darcy said. "You mustn't think about that now. What is important is Uncle Will's health."

Her aunt shook her head. "It is of the utmost importance, indeed. But we shall have to eat fish from the river the rest of our lives. Washington College commissioned the work, Dr. Emerson, and will not accept an incomplete folio."

Darcy knelt beside her. "We shall write to Dr. Ferguson at the college and inform him of Uncle Will's condition."

"Oh, no, Darcy. It'd be best to delay," insisted her aunt.

"Well, a few weeks to recover will not set him back. He is nearly finished. Later, when he feels strong enough, he can complete it." She looked over at Dr. Emerson for confirmation. "Uncle Will has been collecting flora along the river, sir. He is cataloging them, you see. The work is not difficult."

"In time he can resume his work, as I said. As far as hiking the countryside in search of specimens, he cannot for some time," said Emerson. "No lifting or laboring in the garden."

"We can do any chore Papa needs us to," Rachel said. "That way he will recover quickly. I'm right, aren't I?" A broad smile broke across her face, and she looked over to Darcy. It seemed all the girls depended on Darcy to affirm their hopes.

"I believe you are, Rachel," she replied.

Mrs. Breese huffed. "You are too optimistic, the pair of you. I've seen this kind of thing happen before. My father had a stroke, and we suffered for it. How shall I feed all these mouths now?"

"We shall get by," Lizzy assured her mother.

"Papa will get well, Mama," said Abby.

"You will, won't you, Papa?" Dolley said, kissing her father's cheek.

"I assure you all, I will." Mr. Breese smiled and then shut his eyes. "I have enjoyed the quiet, I must say."

Her aunt arched her brows. "Darcy will need to go to England for certain now. Perhaps your dear grandmamma will help us, Darcy, for I have no doubt she is well off. Your uncle is her son after all."

"Mari, I insist you stop fretting at once." Mr. Breese's tone arrested everyone in the room, including Darcy. She had never before heard him speak to her aunt with such firmness. She looked over at her with concern, for she had all of a sudden gone silent and still, and her face was awash with color.

"I have enough money for you and the girls to continue as things were. You are not to even suggest that Darcy ask my mother for money. And I am not going to die—at least not anytime soon. And when I do, I will thank the Lord for the peace and quiet."

Tears moistened Mrs. Breese's eyes and she set her mouth firm. "All right, my dear. As you say."

With her husband in need of peace and quiet, as well as sleep, Mrs. Breese ushered her daughters and Darcy out of the room. After a brief word with his patient, Dr. Emerson stepped out, closed the door, and met Darcy and Martha in the sitting room. Darcy did not say she was worried over her uncle's situation, but as she tidied up the room, she paused to see that eyes were upon her. Martha stood beside Dr. Emerson, and Darcy wished she could say out loud how fine they looked together.

"It would not be wise to travel alone, Miss Darcy, if that is indeed your course," Dr. Emerson said. "I know a gentleman, a colleague of mine, who is leaving for London with his young wife on business. It would be well for you to journey with them. I'm sure his wife would appreciate the company."

It was happening all too fast. Her mind and her heart churned like the rapids in her river, tumbling with a sudden anxiety of leaving home and the people she loved. And there was the risk that she would meet up with that insufferable Englishman who had tossed her heart to the wind as if it were chaff. She sat still a moment, with her throat tightening, staring at the floor.

"Thank you, sir. It would be a comfort to my aunt if I had someone to travel with, especially someone you know."

"I shall write to them today and help make the arrangements for you to meet them in Annapolis. Dr. Prestwich is a prominent surgeon there, and his wife, Ann, is very pleasant."

"I look forward to meeting them, sir." She curtsied to him, and then when Martha glanced toward the door, Darcy knew to leave the couple alone. She went back into the hallway, heard her aunt fussing out in the kitchen, and sighed deeply. Missy peeked down from the top of the staircase. Her uncle wished to speak to her.

"Do not allow this situation to stop you, Darcy," he said. "I do not want you to worry. I am feeling better already."

"You will take good care of yourself and follow the doctor's instructions?"

"I promise I shall."

"Well, you shall be happy to know that Dr. Emerson has recommended a very nice lady in need of a traveling companion, and he thinks I am just the person. She and her husband are sailing for England in a few days. He is a respected surgeon."

She shifted from her chair to his bedside, lifting his hand in hers. "But how can I leave you now?"

"Must you stay with us until we are in our graves? Are you not entitled to a life of your own? Your grandmother shall not live long, so go to her. I shall have a letter for you to give her. I want you to tell her that I have always loved her, and have prayed for her each day since we parted. If she would leave Havendale and come back with you, I would welcome her to live with us. You go ahead and have your adventure. I have the girls to look after me."

"Are those the only reasons you have to persuade me?"

"You need to find whatever it is God is leading you to, knowing where your roots began and where they must end. From the first moment I saw your curly head at my doorstep,

I saw something in you that I rarely had seen in a child your age. You take everything in as if it were a gift. It would be wrong to keep you here."

Darcy kissed his cheek, and when her uncle had fallen back to sleep, she stepped outside his room and went downstairs. Martha and Dr. Emerson had not been afforded much time together. Darcy's aunt stood beside Martha with her arm around her, looking out the sitting room window. Dr. Emerson mounted his horse, and after he tipped his hat, he made for the main road.

"It is now a certainty, our income is affected." Her aunt spoke in a low but trembling voice, twisting a handkerchief between her hands. "It is enough to keep a roof over our heads for some time, I think, but we shall be reduced to a very low condition if your uncle does not continue his work."

Darcy pressed her lips together and said, "I have faith he shall recover. In this we must be patient, and depend on Dr. Emerson's skill and God's goodness."

Her aunt lowered herself onto the settee. "But if he does not, we shall be forced to live in a small dwelling among the working class. And that is what we shall become—working class."

Martha picked up her mother's hand and squeezed it. "You must have more faith than that, Mama. You will not have to leave your home."

Mari Breese wiped her nose. "Oh, I think I shall. There is little guarantee of anything for me to rely on."

Darcy gazed into her aunt's gaunt face. Worry moved within Mari's expression. There seemed no means to comfort her and waylay her growing anxiety. "Of course there is, Aunt. Remember, *I shall not leave thee, nor forsake thee*"?

"I indeed remember it. And you are good to remind me. I need to put my trust in the Lord and not worry so much. But it is hard for me, Darcy."

"You have your children."

"Yes, and I must release you to your grandmother. You may become so dear to her that when she dies, or perhaps before that, she will provide money that you may send home. I know it is selfish of me to say, but it is a possibility—and if not for us, then for you."

Darcy sighed. "You've worried over me all these years, and now you are settled that I go to England to people who are strangers to me?"

"Not all strangers. Indeed not. There is Mr. Brennan and Miss Roth. They live in the same county as your grandmother. When they hear of your arrival, they will call upon you, and that way you shall be introduced to other families in the area, and have no lack of acquaintances. The English love balls and gatherings, you know. You shall make many friends. Oh, I do envy you in some ways."

The mention of Ethan, his face coming up in her mind, caused her heart to ache. "It does not matter whether I see Mr. Brennan or Miss Roth. We were not friends when they left." She stood and walked over to the window. "I should like to see the house my father was born in, and the land of my ancestors. I should like to see my grandfather's vicarage where my mother grew up, and the church where he preached."

"That is a grand attitude, Darcy. I shall write to Dr. Emerson's friends right away. He told me of his suggestion." She stood and went to her writing desk, rummaging through the middle drawer for paper.

A gentle smile tugged at Darcy's mouth. She stepped from the room, and donning her broad-rimmed hat, headed for the path beside the house that led down to the river. Over roots and stones she went, pausing to pick up pebbles that caught her eye. She placed five smooth stones in her pocket to take on her journey as reminders that she could slay any obstacle that would rise up against her.

At last a reply had come that Darcy would have a pair of travel companions to watch out for her. Their letter emphasized how pleased they would be to have her company. On the day when the wagon was brought around to the front of the house to take Darcy down to the ferry, she put on a brave face. The driver, Mr. George, who had been her uncle's neighbor for fifteen years, put out his hand for her to take in order to step up.

"Good morn to ye, Miss Darcy," he smiled. "'Tis a fine day for travelin'."

"It is a glorious day, Mr. George." Darcy's stomach churned from both fear and excitement. She gripped the handle of her traveling bag and swallowed the lump in her throat. "I will take every inch of it into my mind, so as not to forget home and my river."

"Ah, that will be nice, miss. I was down at the river this morn, and caught a string of fine bass." He reached back and pulled them out of a bucket. Then he handed them to Missy. "You cook them up for the family, Missy. Fish will do them all good." The catch was happily accepted.

Unbidden tears were in Darcy's eyes when she kissed her aunt and cousins goodbye and climbed into the rear of the wagon. Mr. George helped her uncle into the seat beside him. "It is good of you to drive for us, George," he said.

"Your good lady made it clear you can't do much of anythin', Mr. Breese. I am glad to be of help." And he clicked his tongue and the horses walked on.

Mrs. Breese stood out on the lawn, silent and forlorn with her daughters gathered around her. She lifted her handkerchief and waved, then wiped the tears falling down her cheeks and dabbed her eyes. Darcy buried her sorrow over leaving, raising her hand and smiling back at her aunt and the girls, who were more like sisters to her than cousins. She wondered what would become of them while she was away. Would Dr. Emerson and Martha wed? Would Lizzy? And would her dear Uncle Will grow strong again?

Questions about the future swam in her mind. She looked away from the house she had known all her life. It grew smaller and smaller as they turned at a bend toward the river road. The trees stretched overhead in a canopy of green. She drew in a long breath to feel the air fill her lungs, feel the cooling shade, and smell the grass growing alongside the hedgerows.

The flatboat waited at the river's edge. She had thought it was difficult saying farewell to her aunt and cousins, but when she looked into the misty gray eyes of her uncle, her heart swelled into such despair that she threw her arms around his neck and held fast.

"You shall do well, Darcy," he said. "I know it. Now, be off with you. The ferryman waits."

She kissed his cheek and picked up her bag, gave him a smile that spoke of uncertainty, and stepped onto the planks of the riverboat.

"You have the list?" her uncle called to her.

"In my bag." She clutched it against her stomach. "I will not lose it."

"Do not forget—besides the heather, corn, chamomile, mayweed, and charlock. Send them to me when you can."

"I will, Uncle. I won't forget."

Darcy fixed her eyes upon his face. She wanted to sear his image in her mind and hold it firm, so as not to forget the kindness that sparkled in his eyes. With a little effort, he raised his hand, and she waved back.

"Goodbye!" She stretched her arm as high as she could and shouted over the lapping water. "I shall write as soon as I can."

The breeze strengthened, and Darcy watched her uncle flatten his hat over his head and nod to George. A snap of the reins and the horses pulled away. As a chill passed over her, she watched the wagon fade into the line of trees. No turning back now, she drew her eyes away and soaked in the hills and forests, the deer standing at the edge of the river— her river. Waterfowl splashed and skirted the riverbank, and a great heron flew overhead. Sunlight danced over the top of the water.

A pole-man turned his head to her as he plunged his pole into the water. "You comfortable, miss?"

"Yes, thank you." She sat down on a barrel and soaked in the scene around her. She held down the top of her hat, the sunlight catching in her eyes. "This is my first time away from home, my first time to go all the way down the Potomac."

"It will please you, miss. We disembark at the Great Falls. You'll see them in all their glory as you walk along the foot-path. Past them, you'll catch the next flatboat going all the way down to Point Lookout, and what a sight to behold. The river widens as it gets closer to the Bay." Then he lifted his pole and moved in unison with the other men down along the edge of the flatboat to the rear, causing it to cut over the river as if it were greased.

His description caused her heart to pound and her imagi-nation to soar. "Oh, Lord, how I shall miss it," she whispered with her eyes closed. "Please bring me back and let nothing change, not one leaf or flower, not a bend in the bank, not a single stone. Let it remain as it is, forever."

Part 2

Beneath the rose a thorn is found,
Beneath love's smile, a dart,
May Heaven grant, that neither wound
Thy young and guileless heart.
—Unknown, 19th century

13

A breath of sea, earth, heath, and field filled Darcy's lungs. Her hair blew back from her shoulders as she stood at the ship's rail and scanned the horizon. Plymouth Sound's salty breeze filled the sails and cheered the weary travelers gathering around to get a view of England's coastline.

The voyage had been uneventful, save for a few dolphins swimming alongside the ship. Even her companions were dull—Ann Prestwich at least. Dr. Prestwich spent most of his time in the passengers' galley playing Whist. And so Darcy gave herself over to weeks of reading and writing in her journal, in which she tried to make the entries as exciting as possible.

At last, she'd be released from the bonds of boredom, of sea and sky. With eager eyes, she looked out at the town as it came into view with its moored ships and sloops and beautiful Tudor houses. Darcy tried to take it all in. Never had she seen so many vessels settled in one place, nor had she seen houses of this kind and age.

A deep longing poured over her, a hunger that seemed to snatch the breath from her body. This was Ethan's country.

Time had not changed her heart. She loved him still. But she told herself that Miss Roth had hooked her claws into him by now, and he was unhappily married. She felt no sympathy for him on that account. He should not have left her the way he did. His love should have been stronger than his prejudice.

Freed from her companions, who were on their way to London, she hurried to the coach as it filled up with passengers. She had not been afforded a moment's pause for a meal, nor to feel the earth beneath her feet for long. Glad to be by the window, she gathered her cloak about her legs and tried to settle the rapid beating of her heart. The coachman cracked his whip, and Darcy found herself headed for the heart of England. The coach, packed with people, bounced over rough roads and tree-lined byways. To her surprise, no one engaged in conversation, only nodded a *good day* and dozed off to the sway of the coach.

The coach stopped for the night at a carriage inn outside the limits of Bristol. The next morning they moved on, the horses refreshed and rushing over the roads toward Birmingham. Later in the day, she changed coaches at a crossroads in the heart of Derbyshire. Darcy's body ached and she grew tired of the long journey, but at least the coach was empty and she could stretch out.

Later in the afternoon, at a fork in the road, the coachman halted the horses and called back to her. "Here's where you leave off, miss."

She wiped the slumber from her eyes and stepped out. Spears of sunlight fell over a lush green landscape. Granite ledges shadowed the heath where sheltered pairs of fleecy sheep grazed.

Feeling afraid of the lonely surroundings, Darcy looked up at the coachman. "Are you sure this is the place? There is nothing here."

He tipped the edge of his tricorn hat. "You said you were headed for Havendale."

"That's right. But there isn't a house to be seen."

"Follow that road there, and it'll lead you straight to it." He jerked his head in the direction of a byway wide enough for a single horse and rider to travel over. Then he tossed her bag down, and with a thump it landed in the dirt beside her. He tipped his hat again, shook the reins, and the coach rolled on.

Standing alone on the roadside, Darcy watched the coach pass out of view. Her nerves trembled at being left in the middle of nowhere, but she picked up her bag and walked on. The sky was as blue as a robin's egg, the wind soft and scented. She turned her face up to greet the sun, hoping it would comfort her. But the quivering in her breast would not go away. Twilight would soon gather and she could not swallow the thought of treading alone after dark. Tears pooled in her eyes, which she shut tight to push them back. She had to gather her courage.

A weatherworn wooden sign pointed to the east, but the words were so faded and the paint so chipped away that she could not read it. Darcy raised a brave face and went on, past birch woodlands and a monumental stone.

For an hour she traveled without seeing a single soul. As darkness fell, she spotted a ramshackle barn nestled in a grove of trees and decided it would be better to stay there than go on through the dark. The roof, stripped in places to the evening sky, revealed a heaven painted with moonlight. Decaying timbers surrounded her on three sides; the fourth wall was made of stone.

All night she lay in a heap of straw, tormented by hunger and loneliness, wondering if she had made the right decision in coming to a land she knew nothing of, so far from home—

far from Uncle Will, Aunt Mari, and the girls—so far from Dash, the gray geese, and her river.

She put her hands over her face. "What have I done, God? Now I am certainly lost in this desolate place. And the coachman said Havendale was but a short distance away." A heavy sigh slid from her lips, and she drew her skirts about her legs for warmth. "I haven't seen a single person since I alighted from the coach. But you are with me, aren't you, Lord? I shall not be afraid, knowing that."

From her bag she took out a biscuit that she had saved, unwrapped the paper, and bit into the edge. It had hardened but would do. Before she closed the clasp on her bag, she ran her hand across its contents. Two day dresses, linen undergarments, one pair of stockings, brush, comb, and her Bible. A size fitted for a lady's hand while traveling, she opened to the first leaf and saw her mother's fine handwriting and the words, *To my precious Darcy, on the day of her birth*. She scooted over to a shaft of moonlight, turned the pages, and managed to read from the Psalms.

"Here my voice, oh God, in my prayer. Preserve me from fear . . ."

The night in the barn seemed endless and was enough to make her weep a little. She dashed the tears from her eyes, and then lay back and gathered the straw over her. Through an opening in the roof, stars shone and she gazed at them.

"I wonder what Aunt Mari would think if she knew that I was in a rundown barn in the middle of nowhere, all alone in the night?" Then a smile crossed her lips. "Uncle Will would be proud of me."

Shivering, she outlined the star patterns with her eyes, until sleep conquered.

When morning broke, dusty lances of sunlight flowed through the shelter; yet, they did not wake her. A blackbird landed on the roof and sang. Darcy opened her eyes and saw through the hole above her that the sun had climbed in the sky. She brushed her dress down and slipped outside. Heading north, she walked on, happy that the morning rose bright and the birds were singing. Thank God it was not raining. The rays of the sun strengthened and slanted through the trees as if they were welcoming arms.

Her destination was much farther than the coachman had let on, and she walked for hours along the barren road again without seeing anyone. When the sun dipped toward the horizon, her stomach growled for food, and she rummaged in her bag for one last morsel of biscuit.

Before the light retreated behind the gathering clouds, she spotted a house situated upon a grassy hilltop, surrounded by graceful trees. Thick grass covered the yard. Blonde stone darkened in the shadows of the trees. Glass in mullioned windows glistened as if sheets of onyx. She hurried to the lane leading to the house. Etched upon a bronze plaque, embedded in a stone pillar at the entrance, Darcy read the words *Havendale 1682*.

"At last!" Hesitating to go forward, she clutched her bag, gazed at the house, the tall windows, and ivy. She thought of her father and Uncle Will, imagining them as boys running about, climbing these trees, tumbling about the lawn.

Stepping up to the door, she lifted the iron knocker and let it fall. She rapped twice before a servant opened up. A woman of senior years, dressed in a modest brown dress and stark white mobcap, set her hands over ample hips. "Yes? What is it? What do you want?"

Darcy stepped forward. "I have come . . ."

"To see if you can have a meal, is it? Well, go around the back, dear, and I'll have a plate set up for you. But you'll have to work for it. Hope you don't mind scrubbing a kitchen floor." The woman went to shut the door.

Darcy put out her hand and smiled. "I am hungry, and I will gladly help, but I have come to see my grandmother."

The woman's brows arched and a smile spread across her face. "You must be Miss Darcy."

"Yes, I am she." Darcy glanced past her to get a glimpse inside. It appeared dark and lonely, save for the light coming through one of the windows.

The woman laid her hand on Darcy's elbow. "Well, come in quick. 'Tis a wind falling, and you'll catch a chill."

Darcy untied the ribbon beneath her chin and removed her hat, while the servant took her cloak from off her shoulders. She noticed the look of concern when her eyes ran over her clothing. "I walked a long way," she said.

"Hmm. From the fork in the road I expect. I know that's where the coach leaves off, and it is a very long walk."

"Yes. I hope I do not look too untidy."

"Well, you've had a time of it, now haven't you? It's a lonely trek from where they left you, so I imagine you are tired. Brave girl you are to journey all the way from Maryland."

"I am a little weary."

"We've a warm guestroom waiting for you. It has a comfortable bed, and I'll bring up a tray of food."

"You are kind. But I'd prefer to see my grandmother right away if I can."

"Of course, and without delay."

Before going on, Darcy paused to brush down her dress. At least a few wrinkles were smoothed. "By what name shall I call you?" she asked the serving woman.

"Mrs. Burke will do. I'm the housekeeper and cook."

"Have you been with her long?"

"More years than I can count. Follow me, dear. Your grandmother's room is just up these stairs. Oh, she is going to be so pleased to see you."

Darcy picked up her bag and followed. Her hand trembled along the banister. She noticed the simplicity of the house. Not a single portrait hung on the walls, no paintings of any kind, except for one at the top of the staircase of a young woman seated on a bench in a garden.

Her eyes not leaving the painting, Darcy paused. "Such a lovely portrait. Is she an ancestor of mine?"

"Indeed she is." Mrs. Burke turned with a heavy sigh. "That's your grandmother when she was a young girl. You'd never believe she was such a beauty after you meet her, for she is very old and wrinkled."

Downstairs the walls were paneled with dark oak, but the hallway upstairs held a warmer effect, painted pale yellow with large windows that allowed the light to flood inside. Darcy scanned the paintings on the wall and the pattern the sunlight made across it. "This floor is different from downstairs."

Mrs. Burke straightened a crooked landscape on its hook. "My mistress had the old panels ripped out after she married Mr. Morgan. It hasn't changed since, not in fifty years." She moved on with a smile. "What a surprise that you have come sooner than anyone expected, and a fortnight after the dear old soul's eighty-first birthday."

"I pray she is in good health. I would think, with how fresh the air blows here, that she would be."

"Ah, she is a bit forgetful. But she's blessed you know, for not many folk live as long as she, especially when they've had so much heartache."

Heartache? Could her father have caused it? Uncle Will admitted that his leaving England grieved his mother. Yet he told her, *the Lord said for this cause a man shall leave his father and mother and cleave to his wife.* Mari meant more to him than anything. Had her father felt the same way toward her mother, Eliza? Was she the reason he left?

As they headed down the hallway, she made more inquiries. "Does anyone else live here besides my grandmother and you, Mrs. Burke?"

"Mr. Langbourne and his wife, Charlotte, come to stay once in a while," Mrs. Burke replied. "He's your grandmother's nephew and owns this estate. After your father left us, Mr. Morgan changed his will and left Havendale to Mr. Langbourne. Do you know of Mr. Langbourne?"

"I do not. I have never heard of either person." It saddened her that there existed a breach between her father and grandfather. Was it over his decision to settle in America and take its side in the Revolution? Or was it over his choice of wife?

"Well, this family is widely spread, and growing thinner by the year," said Mrs. Burke. "When her sons left for America, I thought my mistress would never get over it. Life has not been the same since."

"Yes, I imagine it was hard to take," Darcy said. "I never imagined Havendale would be such a large house."

"Modestly large, but poor. And many of the rooms are not used."

"Then I am another mouth to feed." Darcy quickened her steps beside Mrs. Burke. "I will work for my keep."

"Work?" Mrs. Burke chuckled. "No need to worry over that. It is not to be expected of you."

When they entered her grandmother's room, Darcy waited just inside the doorway. The scent of rosewater permeated the air. Curtains hung closed over the windows, blocking out the

dull light that had gathered. A fire crackled in a marble fireplace, its radiance dancing across the polished floor and faded
Turkish rug.

In a winged chair sat an elderly woman in a gown Darcy
could tell had once been black, now faded to muddy brown.
The firelight heightened the color of her pale skin from ivory
to rose, and smoothed the lines time had bestowed. She wore
the black veil and cap of a widow, and delicate curls as white
as snow peeked out along the edges. Her hands lay sedate over
the arms of the chair. A golden band with a small pearl glinted
on her finger, and a terrier rested his head on the old woman's
arm.

She shifted in her chair, and her dog leapt off her lap to the
floor and curled up on the hearthrug. "Burke, I am in desperate need of tea. Be sure it is plenty hot, for I am chilled to the
bone today."

"You had tea but an hour ago, ma'am."

"Did I?"

"Yes, ma'am. I shall bring you some broth instead. That'll
warm you up for sure, and it is good nourishment."

Waving her hand, Mrs. Burke made a gesture for Darcy
to come further inside the room. The terrier yapped, and
Mrs. Burke shook a reproving finger at the pup. Darcy held her
hand out to him. He moved to her to be sedated by a gentle
stroke over his pointy ears.

"Quiet, Maxwell," her grandmother ordered. "Hmm. I
rarely hear him bark. Maybe he looked out the window and
saw that man again, poaching my birds no doubt. Where is
Edward? You must tell him straightaway."

With a gentle touch, Mrs. Burke gathered Madeline's shawl
over her sloping shoulders. "Do not fret, ma'am. Perhaps the
man will bring us a plump bird for our supper."

"I will let my husband decide . . ."

"He has, as you know, been dead these last ten years, ma'am."

Madeline shivered and her eyes opened wide, gray and watery. "Dead?"

"Yes, ma'am."

"Ten years you say?"

"Nearly eleven, ma'am."

"Edward. My Edward," Madeline sighed.

Darcy marked how lovingly his name slipped through her grandmother's lips, as if it were the only name on earth, and he the only man she had ever loved. It caused her to whisper *Ethan* in her mind, to feel the tone and cadence of his name spring into her heart.

"Oh, how I loved him." With a lift of her wrinkled hand, Madeline touched Mrs. Burke's arm. "He has left me lonely, you know." Her eyes shifted toward the door when Maxwell whined for another touch from Darcy. "Who is that young woman? Why is she standing on my carpet speechless?"

Darcy stepped forward, and her grandmother looked up at her confused. "Is that you, Eliza Bloome?" Her eyes squinted and she looked alarmed. "Where is Hayward? Where is my son? I demand to know." Half rising from her chair, she dropped back down when her strength gave out.

Darcy approached. "I am Darcy, ma'am, your granddaughter. You wrote to me and asked that I come visit you."

Madeline's lips quivered. Surprise lit her face and she searched for Darcy's hands. "My son Hayward's child?"

"Yes, Grandmother."

"For a moment I thought you were Eliza." She drew her spectacles on and looked up at Darcy. "But I see now you are not. There is no real resemblance. You have taken after Hayward, I see."

"I hope that pleases you, Grandmother."

"Very much so. Such a courageous girl you are to have come all the way across the ocean." Madeline leaned forward as Darcy crouched down to her. "I imagine it was exciting."

Darcy smiled. "At times. But it was mostly dull. I am glad to have my feet back on solid ground."

Madeline pursed her lips. "Strange ground though." With an effort, the old woman leaned her cheek up to Darcy. Darcy kissed it and then sat in the chair opposite. Her grandmother smelled of rice powder, rosewater, and age. Her cheek felt cold, even with the fire blazing in the hearth.

Darcy glanced down at her soiled hem. "I am sorry for my appearance. I wish I had arrived more neatly attired, but I had so far to travel."

Madeline shook her head. "It is to be expected. You came by coach?"

"Part way. They set me down several miles from here where the road forks. The coach route turned north, you see, and so I had to be let out."

A slow breath eased from Madeline's lips. "You mean to say you walked the rest of the way unaccompanied?"

"I enjoy walking, and the countryside is lovely here." She did not tell her that the sun was setting when she got out of the coach, nor that she had to sleep in that old ruin a full night—with a haunting wind and distressing sounds.

Her grandmother's brows shot up. "But you do not know the country here. You were all alone. You could have gotten lost or kidnapped by gypsies."

Darcy smiled. Her grandmother had no idea how free she ran beside the two rivers back home. "God kept me safe, I can assure you."

"Hmm, I see he did. I shall be sure to thank him when I say my prayers tonight. Poor child, you need to refresh yourself."

"Oh, I would welcome that, Grandmother. You are kind." Darcy held her grandmother's hands and stood to leave. As she passed out the door, she looked back at Madeline. She liked her a great deal and looked forward to her time at Havendale. Already her grandmother had dozed off, with Maxwell now curled at her feet.

Mrs. Burke led the way to a modest guestroom. The floor creaked under their footfalls. The walls were plastered, painted dull white. Simple furniture decorated the room—a bed, nightstand, and a green high-back armchair near a small marble fireplace.

Already she had begun to feel at ease, being so warmly welcomed and accepted. Yet, she could not help feeling out of place and homesick for the Potomac and the green fields of home. She felt like a wild thing here, for the people she had met along the way, including Mrs. Burke, were of a more reserved nature. She was more expressive and open about her thoughts and feelings.

She had no idea where she fit in, or how she would adapt. But she had comfort in knowing her stay would be less than a year, even a matter of a few months.

She pulled out clean garments from her bag, shook out the folds of a simple dress of a deep nutmeg hue, and held it in front of her. She stared into the full-length mirror, telling herself she would always be Darcy of the rivers and forests. Then she undressed, washed the dust of the road off her skin, and brushed out her long hair until it felt silky again. A black ribbon lay on the dressing table, and she banded the locks up on her head, allowing some to grace her shoulders.

Carried on the wind that buffeted the house, a sound came to Darcy—a horse whinnied. She approached the latticed window, and peering out at the crest of a hill, she spied a man on horseback riding east at an even gallop. She stared. Her heart beat in her breast, and she glanced away in an effort to calm it. The horseman caused her to think back to the day when she first chanced upon Ethan astride the stallion.

Ethan. She could not forget him, no matter how hard she had worked to get him out of her mind.

An hour later, she went back down the hall to her grandmother's bedchamber. Placing her palm against the door, she eased it open and stepped inside. She drew near her grandmother's canopied bed and touched Madeline's hand with the tips of her fingers. The old woman's eyes opened and glanced over at Darcy.

"You are much improved," said Madeline. "Sit beside me. I imagine you have many questions, but not tonight. Later, when I am feeling stronger. I am old."

It disappointed her, for Darcy's mind rushed with questions. But compassion—for an aged mind and body, and no doubt a heart that had ached many a year—took precedence over her desire for answers.

"I am expecting my nephew and his wife in a day or two."

"Mrs. Burke told me about Mr. Langbourne and his wife. I shall be glad to meet them."

"I do not imagine Charlotte shall be much company to you, Darcy. It is not because she possesses a dignified self-restraint. Something is amiss with her mind, for she is a frail creature and says little about anything that matters. Langbourne tolerates her, I suppose, but does not love her."

"How unfortunate."

Madeline let out a cackle. "She doesn't seem to mind, for she is well cared for. What is love to the upper class but a whim? We are fixed up in England, and that is that. When I first met your grandfather, I felt nothing, no spark of anything. My love for him grew over time. I needed him, you see."

How sad to not have loved from the beginning, to burn and ache for love. And by now, had Ethan entered into a loveless marriage? How her heart grieved to think of it, that he could have had her love instead of shallow regard. God had planted it in her, Darcy knew, a love so deep and virtuous that it could have been born only from the One that was pure, everlasting love.

Her fingers bent, Madeline lifted a gold locket from her chest, opened it, and showed Darcy the miniature portrait within it.

"This is Edward, my second husband and your grandfather. I was a widow with a small boy, your uncle, and Edward took pity on me and brought me to Havendale. I had money, and that helped him decide to wed me. If I'd been penniless, there would have been no hope for my child and me. I hope William is well."

Darcy hesitated to tell her grandmother the truth. "He sends you his well wishes. He would have come with me, but commitments prevented him. I've brought a letter. Should I go get it?"

"I shall read it later." A sad gaze filled her grandmother's eyes. "I do not wish to speak about him anymore today."

"If I may ask, does my father resemble his father?"

"Yes, but he had my eyes. I hope someday they are enlightened to what he has done in hurting me. He left without so much as a goodbye, and the last letter I received from him was many years ago. Not a word since."

"He left for the frontier, so Uncle Will told me. I hope someday he will return."

Madeline paused to drink her broth. "Poor Charlotte. What on earth will she think of your high spirits and open-mindedness, Darcy?"

It seemed as if her grandmother had not heard her remark about meeting her father again. Or had she wished to ignore it?

Maxwell jumped onto the bed and sat down with an anxious stare. Madeline handed him a nibble of cheese from the china plate sitting on the bed beside her. He took it between his teeth and swallowed it down.

"I must say, Darcy, I can see in you your father's determination, and the passion of your mother. Hmm. Perhaps you will draw Charlotte out."

"I shall attempt to engage her by being kind, Grandmother."

"Kind? It may do no good if Langbourne hears your conversations. He keeps a firm hand on his wife's shoulder." Madeline sighed and lay her head back against the pillow propped up behind her.

Darcy paused to study the painting over the fireplace. It portrayed a pair of matched horses and the riders—a lady dressed in a blue velvet riding habit, whose youthful face was one of rich beauty, a gentleman, broad-shouldered and handsome.

"What kind of man is Langbourne?" she asked, the painting posing the question in her mind.

"He lacks all the best virtues one expects in a man—humility, kindness, and a sense of duty. Instead, he can be proud and demanding, and he drinks far too much. Likes rum, you see. Everyone must kowtow to his whims, and he to no one."

"Perhaps disappointing circumstances in life have made him as you say."

"Disappointments? Langbourne has had everything handed to him. You would think his wife would have soothed his overbearing ways, but I fear she has put more oil on the fire than water."

Darcy's interest was piqued. "May I ask how? Would it not be his responsibility and not hers?"

Her grandmother gathered her shawl closer. "Certainly, but a woman can bring out the best or the worst in a man. I imagine Hayward must not have been an easy man to live with."

"I cannot say. But I'd like to think he was."

"Your father had such a strong will. Nothing could change his mind on anything. He was determined to make a life in America, and Eliza chose him over his cousin."

"You mean Mr. Langbourne, your nephew?"

This was something Darcy had never been told. She wondered if her parents' romance had been a tumultuous one, with two men competing for her.

"Yes, that is exactly who I mean. I see a thousand questions are now swimming in your head," Madeline said. "But I shall not answer them today. Too many answers to too many questions can lead a person to places they wish not to go."

Darcy felt sorry for her grandmother. Memories were painful for her. But she wished the conversation could go further. Yet her grandmother would venture only so far on certain subjects, and that left Darcy frustrated with curiosity. So many secrets seemed to permeate Havendale. *Too many answers to too many questions can lead a person to places they wish not to go.* She wondered at the meaning behind those words, and prayed she would understand—if not now, later.

Madeline sighed. "I am weary, Darcy, and need to sleep." Her eyes closed and she slipped off. Darcy stood, drew her grandmother's bedcover up to her chin, blew out the candle, and tiptoed from the room.

After she closed the door, her curiosity got the best of her and she began to explore the old house. She went from room to room, each much the same as the other, clean and void of life. She ascended an oak staircase sleek from years of footfalls tramping over the steps. It led to a third floor. Two chamber doors were there, and after she opened the first and entered the room, she realized it had been her father's bedchamber. Books were stacked on a table near the window. Clothes hung in the sandalwood armoire, a layer of dust on the shoulders of coats and shirts. It was as he had left it. She ran her hands over the fabric, and then closed the doors.

She heard footsteps and turned. Mrs. Burke stood on the threshold with a candlestick in her hand. "I intended to give you a tour of the house, Miss Darcy. But I see you could not wait."

"Forgive me, Mrs. Burke. I could not help myself. I thought perhaps you had gone to bed."

"No, I'm up late every night. There's no need to be sorry."

"This was my father's room, wasn't it?"

"It was."

"It looks as though it has remained just as he left it."

Mrs. Burke touched the stack of books and sighed. "These were his favorites. And over here are his clothes. Everything in this room belonged to him, and he left it all behind for love."

"He must have loved my mother very much to forsake everything for her."

"Do you know the story, Miss Darcy?" Mrs. Burke set the candle down.

"No. But I imagine Grandmother will tell me about it—when she is ready."

Mrs. Burke strode over to the window and drew apart the curtains, allowing the moonlight to come inside. "She has stayed tight-lipped about her feelings ever since your father was disinherited."

"What did my father do to deserve such rejection?"

"Mr. Morgan did not approve of Mr. Hayward's choice for a wife. He said Miss Eliza was below his station, and she had no money to bring to the marriage. Along with this he heard through his connections that Mr. William was in support of the American rebellion."

"I know that to be true. But he was my grandmother's son by her first marriage. Why did his beliefs matter to Mr. Morgan?"

"He would not have his heir attached to a traitor. He believed Mr. Hayward would be influenced, end up supporting the Revolution, and thus bring the family even more shame."

"What happened then?"

"Mr. Hayward defied his father. I remember your grandmother crying as she watched him leave the house with only the clothes on his back."

Darcy sat down on the edge of the bed. "She said he swore she'd never hear from him again. He should not have treated her so badly. It wasn't her fault."

"Yes, well after Mr. Morgan passed away, she tried to find Mr. Hayward, but failed. She gave up all hope that he would ever write to her."

"I am sorry she could not find him. He should have written, regardless of how they fell out."

"Indeed. But Mr. William wrote to her as often as he could, although she did not hear from him through the duration of the war. So few letters ever made it to England or to America those years."

"My parents must have had a passionate affection for each other in order for him to defy his father and leave England. It must have been strong, like a fortress against a storm."

"Hmm, more like a hurricane, Miss Darcy." With a smile, Mrs. Burke picked up her candle, and together they left the forsaken bedchamber.

"We all should be so fortunate as to have a man love us as much as he loved your mother," said Mrs. Burke outside Darcy's door.

Darcy leaned against the jamb before going in. "That he would give up his inheritance for love is a noble thing . . . Good night, Mrs. Burke, and thank you."

After Mrs. Burke stepped away, Darcy went inside the room that had been lovingly prepared for her. Moonlight flowed through the window, spread over the quilt covering the bed, and touched upon the pillows piled against the bolster. She thought of Ethan. Her love for him rose like a crashing, angry sea, gripping her with such longing that she put her hands over her eyes to suppress tears. If only he could have loved her that passionately, given up Miss Roth and her fortune, defied all and stayed with her. No, his was a love that was as fleeting as windswept clouds. But Darcy's was constant. She loved deeply, feverishly, and lived with a broken heart. Ethan would never have the chance to love with such passion, she thought.

She sat at a small writing desk beside the window. She must write home—tell them of her adventure—but not so much as to alarm her aunt. Dipping the quill into the ink, she scrolled the date, and then began to write. *I cannot believe I am sitting in the house where my father grew up, with my grandmother just down the hall . . .*

14

That same night, the sea swept over the shores of Cornwall as it had for centuries. A boat plunged its bow into the choppy waves, leaving behind a sailing ship anchored out in the deeper waters. It made its way into a quiet cove—Cracking-ton Haven in the north of Cornwall. The sea swept over the pebbled beach and poured into rock pools carved out by the tides. Sandstone cliffs cast deep shadows over the waters as a man disembarked and made his way up a serpentine path to the heights above.

His coat would be strange to those living along the shore. Its dark blue color had faded over the years to gray, the silver buttons tarnished. Once there had been gold piping along the scarlet collar and lapels, but no more. It had dry-rotted and torn free long ago. His boots were old, the sheen worn off, and the hat upon his head had gone from black to muddy brown.

His eyes widened and he looked up at the cry of a night-hawk. He felt his face flush, and he looked down at his hands, ruddy under the luminous moon, lined and careworn. Although lean in body, he heaved and struggled up the steep incline. He lifted his legs as if they were leaden, pausing to catch his breath and to look about him. His mind could not absorb the splendor of the land, as if he were blind to it, lost in a colorless world.

Without love, he'd grown sick in body and soul, yet at forty-and-six years he had enough spirit within him to rally a force that drove him to do the thing he must do before his time came to meet his Creator. If he could accomplish the conviction of his conscience, he believed he could leave this world in peace. Without it, he feared a restless eternity.

When he reached the heights above the cove, he glanced down at the ship that had sailed from the mouth of the Chesapeake and out to sea toward England. Before that, he had traveled hard overland, passing through Indian country in the Ohio Territory, into the Alleghenies, through the wilderness of western Maryland, to the Potomac gorge, downriver to the great Bay.

Many hardships he endured on his journey—encounters with Indians, vagabonds, and thieves, hunger and cold in deep winter, and oppressive heat and fatigue in summer. Once a man had met him on the Allegheny trail and recognized his tattered regimental coat, saluted him, and offered a bit of rabbit from his campfire spit. It was the only kindness shown him since he had left his home along the river years before. Those years seemed a dream now, but the face of the one he had wronged never vanished. England, a land he had never thought to see again, would be the place he would find her.

Forgive those who have trespassed against you. As difficult as it seemed, he had to try, and he had to gain her forgiveness before it was too late.

He reached inside his pocket and looked at the two coins in his palm. They would get him by. From his breast pocket, he drew out an old letter, upon it written a name, an estate and its location. Inside, the ink had blurred and faded from the years he had kept it there, along with others he had saved. If he were to die during his journey, someone would find them, tell their author, and ensure him a proper burial.

He turned his eyes away from the sea and walked on—his gait one of a man who had abused drink and left his body wrecked. For days he traveled, trekking toward the heartland of Britain, a few good people driving wagons offering a lift on occasion, food, and often a barn to sleep in.

Once he reached Derbyshire, the wind blew harsh against his face and ruffled his hair, but not his spirit. He set his teeth hard and fixed his eyes forward. Then he went on, through a pass with hills that mounted into the sky like lock-armed sentries and made him feel as small as an ant under their steep shadows. He followed the road, to where he could not tell, for there were no signposts and his memory failed him.

Finally, he stood on the heights where lush green moorland stretched out as far as the eye could see. An unchanged place, he soaked it in, recalled galloping his horse across it and rescuing a lone woman from a pair of ruffians. The sun settled and a gloom fell over the land.

He said aloud, "Darkness will never overcome light." Tonight it was true enough, for a multitude of stars brightened in the heavens as moonlight lit his way.

His throat tightened, and he coughed with such force that his eyes watered. He held his handkerchief up to his mouth and wiped his lips clear of spittle. Blood stained the rag, dark gore that made him shiver with dread. Time would not hold back for him. What he had come to do had to be done quickly.

The north winds strengthened. With them came fog. The chill seeped through his coat and touched his skin beneath it. The cold made him shiver, and he longed to find sanctuary.

"A stranger am I in a strange land," he murmured. "Aid me, Almighty Father. Find me shelter in this place."

He moved on until a frail yellow light flickered in the distance. Making his way toward it, he turned up the collar of his coat and held it tight around his throat—against the harsh wind. Darkness deepened and he put out one hand before him as if blind, searching, reaching ahead, finding his way through bands of moonlight along the road.

The light grew larger and when he realized it was a small lantern set inside the window of a house, he hurried toward it. At the door, he knocked and it creaked open. An old man, candle in hand, nightcap upon his head, peered out. "Who is it? What is it you want?"

The weary traveler dragged off his hat. "I am in need of shelter, sir. May I sleep in your barn?"

The man held the candle higher. "We've but a small stable for our milking cow and horse. You are welcome to it."

"God bless you, sir. A bed of hay shall be a warm comfort." He turned to go.

"Are you hungry?" the man asked.

"I've no want for food. Only a place to lay my head."

"It is no bother if you are. We've bread and cheese to give."

A woman drew up behind the old gentleman and said to the traveler, "Wait here, sir," and hurried away. She returned with a sack and handed it to the sojourner. "I shall fetch a jug of cider, for you, sir, and bring it out to you with a blanket."

"I am grateful," he said, and stepped away to the small stable where he ate his bread and cheese in silence and laid his head into a heap of hay to sleep.

When John Faye stepped inside his humble little barn with his wife Ella trailing behind him, he raised his lantern and saw the stranger in its light. Ella handed him the blanket she carried over her arm. "The man is exhausted and no doubt ill."

"Come, together we must help him inside to a bed and a warm fire."

"I shall not be a burden to you," the traveler said.

"Come now, sir," Faye replied. "No burden is one such as yourself in need. You should have said you were ill. We would never have sent you to spend the night in this drafty place."

He put his arms beneath the traveler's armpits and helped him stand. Through the door they went and he was laid down in a room beside their kitchen. "You are fevered, sir," the woman said. "But just a touch. I'll have you right in no time."

"You need not be so kind to a stranger."

"Strangers may be angels unawares, sir," she replied with a broad smile and kind eyes. "Kind we both shall be, for it is the Lord's commandment. We shall take care of you until you are on your feet and able to go on."

He slipped into sleep. Ella dabbed his forehead with a damp cloth. "I wonder his name," she said to her husband.

"Time will tell." He pulled off his spectacles and wiped his eyes.

"He wears a strange coat, John. I've never seen the likes, have you?"

"A military coat, but not British."

She stared at him with her brows joined together. "You don't suppose he's French, do you?"

"Why would a Frenchman be wandering about the English countryside, my dear?"

She raised her brows. "What would any man wearing a coat like that be doing wandering about the English countryside, my dearest?"

"Exactly. I think I know that coat. American, I think. But he has a slight English accent to his speech."

Ella's eyes widened. "A revolutionary no doubt. Ah, but he is ill, John. He needs a doctor." And she dipped the cloth into the basin of water and wrung it out.

"Not in the night can I go. I'd get lost for certain. We'll have to do our best until morning." John Faye picked up the coat from the foot of the bed and rummaged inside the pockets. "What is this?" He pulled out a packet of letters tied together with a coarse string. "The ink is smudged and I cannot make out the words."

"Let me see." Ella looked over the first one and then handed them back. "Put them back, John. There's no telling why he needs them, and it's none of our business."

"Aye. They may be love letters. For why would a man keep so many in his pocket unless they meant a great deal to him?"

Ella's plump fingers picked up the sojourner's hand and patted it. "Let us pray for him, that his sickness passes and that whatever suffering he has endured the Lord ease his pain."

When dawn rose and entered the windows of the small cottage, Ella woke to find her patient had grown worse. His fever raged on. She roused her husband from his slumber. "He is poorly, John. I am not sure I have the means to bring him out of this."

Faye pulled on his brass-buckle shoes. "I will go for the doctor. It is far, but that is of no matter."

"You are a good man, John. I shall fret for your ride, but pray the Lord watches over you and guards you from highwaymen."

"I shall go carefully, my dear. Expect me back within the hour."

The traveler heard the latch on the bedroom door shut. Tossing aside the covers, he climbed from the bed and drew himself up to the window. John Faye was outside with a saddled horse.

"Back to bed with you, sir," Ella said, coming into the room with a tray. "John will ride to Castleton to fetch a doctor."

Too weary to resist, he obeyed her. The hall clock chimed on the hour when John Faye returned—empty-handed from all the trouble he took. The doctor was away, and so they had to tend to the poor soul as best they could on their own. Ella never left his bedside, spooned strong broth into his mouth, wiped his head with a cool rag, and prayed over him.

By the next morning, the fever had broken, and he felt stronger. They'd been a lonely couple and said they hoped he would stay a little longer. He thanked them for their hospitality and wished them well, and in spite of the couple's urging that he remain with them, the traveler strode out onto the road. Fog lay heavy over the land under a misty sky, and twisted around his boots as he walked off.

Ella watched him go from her doorstep with worry showing in her face, and within seconds the fog blew across the yard and concealed the man.

"And I will lead the blind by a way they know not," he heard her say. "I will lead them in paths that they have not known. I will make darkness light before them, and crooked things straight."

He looked back, and as the fog parted for only a moment, he saw John Faye squeeze Ella's hand and turn back inside the house.

15

The grind of carriage wheels rolled down the hillside and around the bend toward Havendale. Setting down her quill, Darcy leaned toward the window as the carriage rumbled closer. A pair of dapple-gray horses pranced toward the manor, their manes flowing in the breeze, their coats matching shades of moonlight. She slipped around the desk, drew her robe over her shoulders, and peeked back out the window. Down below, a hooded carriage slowed. A man stepped from it, dressed from shoulder to sole in black. He turned and held out his hand to a cloaked woman who hesitated, then set her foot onto the folded step and climbed out.

"Langbourne," Darcy said aloud. "And Charlotte."

He turned and walked ahead of his wife, charging up the steps to the front door. Darcy heard it close with a clamping of its lock. Then the coach rolled away. She waited to hear more—footsteps, voices, a knock on her door from Mrs. Burke to tell her she'd been summoned downstairs to meet the lord and master of Havendale. But none came, and she climbed under the covers of her bed and tried to fall asleep.

She wondered if Langbourne, being her father's cousin, would look anything like her papa, if his appearance could spark some memory of him in her mind. Yet, trepidation at meeting Langbourne overwhelmed her curiosity, for her grandmother had no great opinion of him.

An hour after sunrise, she climbed from bed and set her bare feet onto the floorboards. They felt cool beneath her soles, like the autumn grass back home. She dressed, brushed her hair, and washed her face. Pink sunlight streamed through the windows like the iridescent wings of dragonflies. Motes sparkled within it, floating, twisting with each movement of air. She lifted her hand into the ray to feel its heat, then touched her palm to her heart and prayed that Langbourne and his wife would be kind and accepting of her. Perhaps they could be friends.

She'd learned the custom was to wait until the stroke of nine for breakfast. Upon the final strike of the hall clock, Darcy entered the dining room. A woman, seated alone and dressed in green stiff silk with a gray shawl across her shoulders, glanced up at her. Mrs. Burke poured tea into Charlotte's china cup, then stood back.

"Mrs. Langbourne, this is Miss Darcy."

Charlotte arched her brows. "Is it? I thought you would be taller."

Darcy smiled lightly, lowered her eyes, and curtsied as was expected of her. "I hope I have not disappointed you, Mrs. Langbourne."

Charlotte bit into a slice of toast. "No, not really."

"Mr. and Mrs. Langbourne will be staying at Havendale a few days," Mrs. Burke said, looking over at Darcy.

"Most likely weeks." Charlotte drawled.

"I am pleased to meet you, Charlotte. May I address you as Charlotte? My grandmother has told me . . ."

Charlotte interrupted her with a lazy lift of her hand. "Well now. Just listen to that foreign accent of Miss Darcy's, Mrs. Burke. It grates upon a more refined manner of elocution."

If Darcy could have rolled her eyes without being thought of as rude, she would have. The manner in which Charlotte spoke about her shocked. "Perhaps I should not say another word, if it offends your ears, Charlotte," she said in a quiet tone.

Mrs. Burke stood straight with her hands over her apron, looking at Charlotte displeased. "Miss Darcy's accent is pleasant. She's from Maryland, ma'am."

"I am aware of that," Charlotte replied. "I've never in my whole life met an American, let alone heard one speak." She forced a smile. "So you must forgive my surprise, Darcy. And yes, you may call me Charlotte. We are cousins after all—in a way."

Darcy tried to smile; yet it proved difficult. As she looked at Charlotte, she was reminded of Miss Roth and her haughty ways. But she would not pass judgment. She had no right, and had no idea what kind of life had molded Charlotte into the kind of woman she was purporting herself to be. Perhaps in time, her cold attitude would change as they got to know each other.

"I will admit that an Englishwoman's voice, such as your own, is much smoother than mine," Darcy said. "I tend to speak coarsely in comparison."

Charlotte paused and looked Darcy up and down. "Indeed, that is true." She glanced at the tea and waved it away with a look of disgust. "I prefer coffee."

"I'll have you know, Miss Charlotte, this tea cost forty shillings. It is as good as any coffee can be."

"I do not care how expensive it was. It looks horrible."

"Fine. I shall brew you some coffee. I hope you will not object to having a meat pie for supper."

"Not at all. As long as you do not put onion in it, and we have a bread and butter pudding for dessert."

"Whatever you wish, madam." Mrs. Burke pursed her lips and stormed off with the tray. Back home, Uncle Will and Aunt Mari would have been overjoyed to have such fine tea and a hearty meat pie for supper. Obviously, Charlotte expected more extravagance.

"We had not expected you." Charlotte's expression was cool, absent of a smile. "Why did you not send us word you were coming?"

Darcy lowered herself to a chair and drank her morning tea. "I wrote to my grandmother. If I had known of you, then I would have written to you as well. Please accept my sincere apology."

"Certainly I shall." Charlotte leaned back and shut her eyes. "But I shall not get a word from her majesty upstairs, now that she has you for company. She shall have none of me, though I am so ill."

Charlotte's eyes were large and pale blue, lacking health and vibrancy, within a face so thin her cheekbones extended beyond the corners of her mouth. Her dress hung over her bosom in loose folds for she lacked a feminine form. To Darcy, Charlotte looked sickly, and she wondered if it were self-inflicted or the natural course of things. She hoped she could be of some help to Charlotte. Perhaps spending some time with her might lift her mood and bring her around to eating more than the crust on a piece of toast.

"I am sorry you are not feeling well. Perhaps a walk after breakfast around the grounds would help. I will go with you." Darcy waited for an answer, while Charlotte nibbled on her bread and then set it down, with a heavy sigh, on the edge of a white china plate, edged in gold leaf and blue flowers. Charlotte's setting was different from the others on the table, and Darcy thought this very odd.

Taking the linen napkin from her lap, Charlotte dabbed her mouth. "A walk would only fatigue me, Darcy."

"Fresh air and exercise improves the appetite."

"Yes, I know, and that's all the more reason for me to avoid it. I do not wish to grow fat."

"I doubt you would, if you do not mind my saying so. My grandmother would not mind if we leave the house for an hour or two."

"She forgets that it takes all the strength I have to leave Meadlow, to travel over these weary roads, and sleep in a bed not my own." Lifting her arm as if weights hung from it, Charlotte brushed her hand over her forehead.

"I imagine it would, especially if you are not feeling well," Darcy said.

"You are the first to say so." And Charlotte dropped her arm.

"I'm sure Grandmother is glad for your company. She must be lonely when it is just she and Mrs. Burke."

"I suppose. But who is to say for certain. She seems content with her servant and her dog." Charlotte leaned on the table with her chin resting in her hand. "The day has scarcely begun and already I am weary. I should rest upstairs."

Darcy understood the cool cue. Without another word, Charlotte stood and shambled out of the dining room. The little mantle clock ticked on and Darcy stared at it a moment, then set her cup down on the saucer. She'd waste no more time. She pulled on her cloak, then went outside and breathed in the fresh country air. The urge to explore Havendale excited her, and she walked on toward the open fields. She cared little that she broke with etiquette and did not wait in the house to meet the elusive Mr. Langbourne. He'd meet her soon enough.

Looking about her, she made comparison to her home along the Potomac. Where there had been sunny blue skies, a leaden sky stretched above her. Where the air had been tepid this time of year, here it was moist and brisk. Where the water ran swift over ancient rock ledges jutting up from the river-bed, streams here ran shallow and placid. She had no fear of getting lost and tucked into her memory certain places where stones lay in heaps, where the path turned and left off, where an old willow bent over a brook.

The wind rustled through her unbound hair. Her heart raced and her breath came up short all of a sudden. Ethan had such a hold on her. She paused to lean against a sheep gate, wondered how far his home might be, if she'd ever see him again, if he were in good health.

"Whatever his actions, whatever he may feel toward me now, I pray, oh Lord, help me forgive him."

She hiked over a hillside, down into a ravine where fog drifted. She paused, lifting her eyes to a plateau of limestone and shale a short distance away where shadows struggled. A moment later, she saw a man stagger into view. From where Darcy stood, he looked the vagabond, a forgotten man, a wanderer poor and needy. His clothing, faded and rag-tagged, hung loose over his thin body.

She held back as a horseman galloped up to the man and blocked his way. The fear and urgency on the poor wretch's face startled Darcy. The rider's slouched hat darkened his face. The horse shook its head and reared. It pounded its hooves into the earth, causing the man to stumble backward, raise his arm across his face, and cry out.

Darcy's heart leapt for fear he'd be hurt.

Like a rush of wind, the horseman bore down on the poor wretch, rearing his horse, swerving the beast to and fro around him. Again and again, the vagabond stuck up his arms as a shield and staggered. The horseman shouted and two men ran forward and secured the man's arms. He twisted and strained against them. Dragged away, he collapsed and hung his head; his legs limp now, his feet dragging through the dirt.

Wide-eyed, Darcy covered her mouth to stifle a cry. The horseman turned his head. He'd seen her. Then he urged his horse forward, and bolted down the hill toward her. It seemed her blood froze in her veins, a chill passing over her. She lifted her skirts and ran. The beat of the horse's hooves came up quick behind her. Her hair whipped in front of her eyes and blinded her. She skidded to a halt when the horseman swerved and pulled rein in front of her. She whirled back. He brought the horse around to stop her. She slipped and fell, the ground wet and soaking into her cloak and shoes.

The rider swung off the saddle, his booted feet hitting the turf simultaneously. He reached down and dragged her up. His grip tight, she felt his nails dig through her clothing. She cried out and he shook her.

"Be silent," he ordered.

"I shall not. Let me go or I will shout again!"

His face came within an inch of hers. His breath, hot and smelling of stale rum, brushed over her cheek. "You saw what went on up there. You'll not say a word to anyone, you understand."

She stopped struggling. "Please tell me you meant no harm to that man. At least tell me that, sir, and I will be bound to silence."

He released her. "He was a poacher. Poaching is a crime."

"You cannot hate a man that poaches if his family is starving."

"He has no family to speak of." He called to his dog, a shaggy gray-colored beast, reached for his horse's reins and pulled it forward.

"What will happen to him?" she asked.

"That is no concern of yours." He climbed back into the saddle, his horse sighing under his weight. "At least Havendale is safe from thieves. I know for a fact Madeline Morgan will be content in the knowledge her pheasants are not being eaten by some louse-infested tramp."

Darcy gathered her cloak across her shoulders. "I haven't been at Havendale long, but I think I know enough about my grandmother to say she would not turn away a hungry man."

Silent, he stared down at her from under the brim of his hat. His eyes were piercing, dark like the shale on the hillside. His hair touched his collar, dark and wiry, loose from the binding of crepe ribbon. How rough a man he appeared as the sunlight fell over him.

"Madeline Morgan is your grandmother? Who are you, then?"

"Darcy Morgan . . . from the Potomac, in Maryland."

A deeper frown curved his mouth in an instant, and a startled look flashed in his eyes. "Well, Darcy Morgan. You'll find Havendale to be a cold and lonely place. The sooner you leave it and return home, the better for you."

He squashed his hat down tight and turned his horse. She watched him canter away over the hill, with his cloak fanning out behind him like the wing of a raven. His wolfish dog sprinted after him. Who the man was she did not know, and hoped with all her might she'd not see him again. Could he be her grandmother's groundskeeper? Could she afford such a person?

She headed back to Havendale feeling troubled over the incident. There was nothing she could do for the poacher except whisper a prayer for him. But the horseman—she'd never forget his face, or the rough way he handled her, or the promise that Havendale would prove a *cold and lonely place*. It made her shiver and she quickened her steps.

As she crossed the threshold, Mrs. Burke rounded the corner and bumped into her. "Oh, Miss Darcy. We have had a fright wondering where you had gone. Your grandmother has taken to her bed . . ."

Darcy hurried to remove her cloak and gloves. "Is she ill?"

"Do not be alarmed. She is just tired and asks that she be not disturbed." Mrs. Burke whispered, "When there are people in the house she is rarely up to sitting with them—unless it is you. She asks that you see her later."

"Are you certain? I shall go right up and see her if need be."

"Quite certain. Mrs. Langbourne is in the drawing room with company. Lord knows where Mr. Langbourne is."

Darcy glanced down at her soiled dress. Mud was splattered along the hem and her shoes were quite soaked. "I am not at all presentable by Charlotte's standards, or my own for that matter. I should change."

The urge to tell Mrs. Burke about the encounter with the horseman and what she saw take place grew to an overwhelming proportion. She motioned to Mrs. Burke to follow her upstairs, and once in her room, she shut the door.

"I met a man out on the moors. To say he did not frighten me would be a lie, for he rode very fierce toward me."

"Had he narrow, gray eyes?"

"Yes, I believe so." Darcy slipped out of her soiled dress.

"And a face lined about the mouth?"

"Yes. He was none too handsome, if that is what you mean. He had a dog with him, too."

Mrs. Burke nodded and squared her shoulders. "Well, miss. You just met Mr. Langbourne. I feel sorry for you."

"Why? What have I done wrong?" Darcy pulled tight the laces on her bodice and tied them into a bow. "He chased me down. It is Mr. Langbourne you should feel sad for. He's not a kind man and will reap what he sows."

"Oh, I do not disagree with you on that score. I meant to say, I feel sorry you had to meet him in that way. Let us hope his visit is short. They almost always are."

Darcy stepped over to the mirror, picked up a brush and ran it through her hair. "I saw a vagabond at a distance. He looked very hungry."

"Hmm. He showed up yesterday, and brought a bird to the kitchen door of which I am glad for it. The only time we have a plump pheasant or a quail is when Mr. Langbourne comes to Havendale and goes shooting."

"So you know the man, you know his name?"

"No on both accounts. But he looked at me with a purposeful stare, as if he knew me. I do not recall ever seeing his face, but his eyes were familiar in a way."

Thoughtful, Darcy followed Mrs. Burke downstairs to the sitting room, where a pleasant fire crackled in the hearth. Drifting pale gray clouds swallowed the dusty sunlight that flowed through the windows. A few raindrops spattered the windows.

Seated on the settee was a well-dressed woman of middle years with reddish hair and ivory skin, and next to her, Charlotte. Introductions were made, and when concluded, Charlotte stood and moved to an armchair near the fire.

"This dreary weather will go straight to my bones, and I shall be chilled and sick before long," Charlotte groaned.

Darcy, unsure of what was expected of her, waited.

"I am pleased to meet you, Miss Darcy." Mrs. Brighton patted the seat beside her and Darcy moved to it. "I gather you are enjoying your stay at Havendale?"

"Yes, ma'am, though the journey was long."

"I can only imagine. You are a daring girl to have taken the risk."

"Risk, ma'am?"

"Indeed. For I have no doubt there were many dangers on the way. Thieves on the road, pirates on the sea, and ruffians aboard ship. That is not to say the danger of disease and the appalling food."

Darcy smiled lightly. "You are speaking from your own experience, Mrs. Brighton? I should like to hear of your adventures."

Mrs. Brighton giggled. "Oh, mine? Oh, no. These are things I have read and heard." She paused and looked about the room. "I have been your grandmother's neighbor these past twenty-eight years, and the color of this room has never changed."

"You must know my father."

"Never set eyes upon him, my dear."

"Oh, I see." Darcy looked down at her hands, disappointed.

"You shall be meeting my husband shortly. I think he may have met Hayward once or twice."

Charlotte moaned. "Oh, yes. The prodigal Hayward Morgan and the ever-faithful Mr. Brighton."

Mrs. Brighton's brows arched. "Indeed the faithful friend he is, Mrs. Langbourne. Someone has to do it."

Charlotte shook her head. "It is a waste of his time."

"Not at all." Mrs. Brighton leaned toward Darcy. "My husband inspects your grandmother's mare every other week to give her ease of the animal's well-being."

"That is good of him."

"Yes. She is fond of all her animals, as if they were her children. My husband, Richard, is extremely knowledgeable of horses, and we own several ourselves."

"Only a half-dozen," Charlotte pointed out. "And bought at the fair instead of from one of the breeders. Isn't that right, Mrs. Brighton?"

"Yes, but they are good stock, Mrs. Langbourne. How many does your husband keep at Meadlow?"

Charlotte sighed, Darcy noticing it was her way before answering a question. "I have never bothered to count them, or to ask my husband. It is no business of mine to know, but his."

Darcy thought how unfortunate that Charlotte was not more involved in her husband's estate. Whoever she were to marry, she would want to know everything about him, including the number of horses he owned. To Darcy it was a wife's duty to know all there was to know about the man she'd devote her life to.

Mrs. Brighton picked up where she left off. "Richard has brought along an acquaintance of his who knows a great deal about horses. He was reluctant to come, having never been to Havendale, and no doubt is bored silly by now. Richard can be the talker, you see, and wear people out."

At that precise moment, the door burst open and in spilled two spotted hounds, followed by a gentleman dressed in brown hunting garb, a flop hat, and riding boots.

"Richard, come meet Madeline's granddaughter." Mrs. Brighton stood and pulled Darcy up beside her. "Is she not the picture of what we imagined?"

Mr. Brighton pulled off his hat and bowed. "The very, my dear." He kissed Darcy's hand. "But here, perhaps this gentleman has heard of your arrival as well. Word spreads quickly in these parts."

He turned back to the doorway and opened it wider. And yes, a gentleman of heart-racing good looks and sultry eyes stepped inside the room. At once, his eyes met Darcy's. Her throat tightened, and she froze at the sight of him. Her pulse pounded like a fist against her breast, a painful throb that caused her to gasp.

Ethan!

Shock spread over his face. A look of confusion surfaced like an unexpected storm in his eyes. He stepped further inside, drew off his hat and turned it within his hands. She glanced away. Why should he look so troubled? She was the one crushed—a leaf underfoot, pressed into the mud. He had Miss Roth, or was she now Mrs. Brennan?

Mr. Brighton put a hand over Ethan's shoulder. "Brennan, have you heard of Mrs. Morgan's granddaughter, Darcy, through the grapevine?"

He stared a moment, then bowed. "No, I had not. Welcome to Derbyshire, Miss Darcy."

Lowering her head, she returned his bow with a curtsey. "Sir."

She grew conscious that her breathing quickened. Her throat tightened and she could not swallow the emotions raging through her. Mrs. Brighton had turned again to Charlotte, and the two were engaged in conversation with Mr. Brighton. Their words faded, as if they were in a distant part of the house. She and Ethan were alone, with all else unseen around them, the room empty of things and color. He drew up to her and looked down into her face with such desire that Darcy trembled.

"Darcy," he whispered. She glanced up at him, then away, unable to hold the power of his gaze.

"Darcy, are you not well? You've gone positively pale." It was Charlotte, her voice showing a hint of concern. "Look what you have done to her, Mr. Brennan. You are the cause of this with your good looks and sultry stare."

Ethan stood back, embarrassed. Darcy, feeling the feverous burn rise in her cheeks as well, turned aside and faced Charlotte.

"You must excuse me. I have a headache." She strode from the room, unsure of what to do. She hurried down the hallway, saw the door leading to the garden and taking her cloak, swung it over her shoulders and passed outside. The sky overhead looked stormy and the air smelled of rain. What care did she have if the heavens broke open and soaked her to her bones? She had to get out, away from the others—away from Ethan.

She pulled the hood over her hair and hurried over the stony walkway, onto a dirt path that stretched toward a gazebo on the shore of a small lake. When she reached it, she shoved aside the vines that had grown through the lattice and plunged inside with her breath coming up short. Tears pooled in her eyes and she blinked them back. The surface of the lake turned a muted blue under brooding clouds, dark like Ethan's eyes. Trees shadowed the edge of the water. A flock of starlings crossed the sky, and Darcy followed them with a gaze that ached to let the tears fall, but they would not.

Someone approached, and she moved back into the shadows. The stones in the path crunched under his tread. With nowhere else to go, she turned to face him. What she would say, she did not know. She only knew how confused she felt.

His shadow darkened the vines. His hand moved them back and he drew inside. He gazed at her with sad eyes, and for a moment they stood looking at each other in silence.

"I never doubted your adventurous nature, Darcy. But of all places for you to be, you have come to England?" His eyes had the same warm glow she'd seen before.

"I do not need to explain anything to you."

"You are right. But if I had known you were here, I would not have come."

She turned away. "I imagine not."

"I would not have wished you to feel as you do now."

"Then you must go. Nothing is keeping you here."

"Nothing? *You* are keeping me here, Darcy. You have kept me ever since the day I first saw you."

"Then why . . ." A lump formed in her throat and she steeled herself, thinking his words were meant to tempt her and draw her out. Her eyes closed when he laid his hand on her forearm and drew her close.

"We must talk, Darcy."

"I have nothing to say. Nothing to explain."

She pushed her way past him, her hands clenched, her arms rigid at her sides, tears stinging her eyes. She hurried off, her hood blown back from her face. Getting away from Ethan and his pained look was all she wanted. She could feel him standing outside the gazebo staring after her.

As she approached the door, she regretted not getting into a full-fledged row with him. And she was curious. Had he married Miss Roth and settled for a dull, loveless life with her? And what about the letter he had sent? *The coward!* Her mind screamed as she hugged her arms. He could not tell her to her face? He'd broken her heart, and it all came flooding back. He dared to say he was *kept* by her?

As she passed inside she heard the others in the sitting room conversing, and she paused outside the door.

"Everything has changed now that she is here, Langbourne," she heard Charlotte say. "I doubt you will get a penny more for your troubles. And I shan't get her jewels, if she has any of worth."

For Charlotte to covet her grandmother's jewelry and have no reservations about announcing her desire for it in front of Mr. and Mrs. Brighton repulsed Darcy.

"I already own the house, and it's by my good graces that the old woman has stayed on at Havendale."

"Why, Langbourne." It was Mr. Brighton. "Only a heartless man would throw an old woman out or place her in accommodations below what she deserves. This is her home and her husband's house. You do not mean . . ."

"I mean nothing, except to say Charlotte is my wife and she should have everything in this house, not a girl my aunt knows little of. Where is she anyway?"

"She left a moment ago . . . and so did Mr. Brennan."

"Brennan is here?"

"Upon my request," said Mr. Brighton with a nod. "By your expression, sir, you do not approve. He's a fine authority on horses, and . . ."

"Do not bring him here again, not if you intend to keep your appointments at Havendale." Langbourne sounded bitter. What did he have against Ethan?

Darcy turned her back to the wall and leaned her head against it. The warm welcome she felt vanished. It grew obvious the Langbournes did not want her here.

The shadows in the hallway deepened and cold air whirled around her ankles. Maxwell's nails tapped over the hardwood floor, and he drew up to her, sniffing the tip of her shoes.

"We know nothing of your business, sir, and should not be drawn into it." Mrs. Brighton spoke in a manner that shocked Charlotte. "But I must say, to look at Darcy is to look into the eyes of her mother, though they are of a different shade. She seems shy with us, but I have to believe she is truthful and as spirited as Eliza ever was."

Charlotte laughed. "Oh, that would be a curse upon her."

"Eliza Morgan was a beauty, Charlotte, unlike your sickly, skinny self," said Langbourne. "She was everything a man would want in a woman, and although I hate him for it, I do not blame Hayward for wanting her the way he did."

"The way you also did, Langbourne. Let us not forget . . ."

"Be quiet, Charlotte. Mr. Brighton, what would you do if you had a jealous wife?" A pause followed with no reply to Langbourne's question. "I thought so."

Darcy moved and her shadow fell over the threshold. The dog yapped and whined. They'd seen her, and she had no other choice but to face them. Drawing off her cloak and setting it aside, she wiped her eyes dry and smoothed down the folds of her dress. Gathering her senses, and trying her best to appear as if nothing had happened, she reentered the room. Mrs. Brighton looked over at her, curious. Langbourne, with his boot on the grate of the fireplace, stared at her.

"Ah, there she is, Langbourne." Charlotte tugged his sleeve. "Is she not savage looking? I suppose most of the girls in America are."

Darcy met his eyes, piercing and dark. "*Savage* is not the correct word, Charlotte. Miss Darcy appears civilized, yet . . ." and he pulled away and drew close, "full of tamed fire, I'd say."

Charlotte huffed. "Oh, no, Langbourne. You cannot mean it."

"Emphatically, Charlotte." He kept his eyes fixed upon Darcy, and she looked away. The heat of the fire eased through her gown and warmed her body.

"Had you lost your way, having taken so long to come back?" he said in a lowered voice, drawing her aside.

How he underestimated her. She had a sense of direction born with her. "No, Mr. Langbourne. You have no reason to ever believe I could lose my way. I stepped out before you came inside."

"Everyone loses their way at one time or another. I advise that you not wander too far from Havendale. You saw the kind of people who loiter on the land."

"I do not know what kind of man he is that you caught."

"His actions speak for him. Be wary, Miss Darcy. When I am not here, there is no man to look after the women in this house."

"So I shall, sir."

"And you will keep my business to yourself."

"Of course."

"There is no need to trouble Madeline over such a matter as a poacher. It would frighten and shock her, don't you think?"

A moment's pause, then Darcy nodded. "I would not wish my grandmother to be alarmed." Near the window, she glanced out to see if Ethan had come down the path back to the house. Perhaps her reaction had been too harsh toward him.

"Good." Langbourne gave her a smile from the corner of his mouth. "You look nothing like your father."

"I am told I do."

"You have your mother's face. She was handsome, you know."

"Everyone has told me she was beautiful. You must have known her."

"I loved her."

Astonished at his confession, uneasiness raced through her. How much did he love her mother? Had his feelings remained with him over the years, and would he be kind to Darcy because of Eliza?

A horse whinnied outside in the courtyard. Her head turned, and she glanced back out the window to see Ethan leading a tall horse. "He bought the stallion." She hoped the horse would always remind him of the day they met, how he almost trampled her, but did not avoid crushing her heart.

"What do you mean?" said Langbourne. "Do you know this man?"

"Slightly," she said.

"How?"

"I met him in Virginia, when he visited there with his fiancée, Miss Roth."

"Well, he won't be back, and he is not permitted in this house. You understand?"

"It is your house, as you have said, sir." Questions were on the tip of her tongue. But she dare not ask them.

The others gathered closer to see what was going on, what had caught Darcy's interest.

"Mr. Brennan is leaving," said Mrs. Brighton.

"Without a word?" asked Charlotte. "How rude of him."

"He has other business to attend to," Mr. Brighton said. "He would not divulge the particulars."

Darcy watched Ethan place his boot in the stirrup. The dappled light, made so by the raindrops, glazed the glass and quivered over her face. She glanced over at Langbourne, marking the look of hatred in his eyes at the sight of Ethan.

Langbourne's mouth twisted. "We can do without him."

Oh, but I cannot. Her body trembled with the desire to rush out the door and go to him. *I'd be made a fool if I did. He'd ride off, and everyone would laugh at me. Oh, God, forgive me for my hard heart.*

She fixed her eyes on his form, how he mounted Sanchet, how his thighs hugged the saddle, the way he drew the reins through his hands and held them. Rain dripped from his hat, soaking the tips of his hair. He looked over at her with an expression of regret. He pressed his mouth taut and turned his eyes away. This time she felt as if his horse had trampled over her, her eyes not leaving him until he, and his horse's bronze mane and tail, disappeared over the hilltop.

16

Crossing the border into Fairview, Ethan tapped his heels against Sanchet, and brought the stallion across a stone bridge that arched over a swollen stream. The sound frightened the horse and it reared. The pressure of Ethan's knees against his ribs brought him down, settled him, and Ethan walked him on after a gentle pat of his hand on the neck.

In the distance, shrouded in the gray curtain of rain, he could see the old manor, its windows brightened by a few candles in the casements. A flood of memories rose up in his mind of a happy childhood and a father who taught him both the ways of the world and the precepts of God.

He missed his father a great deal, without a day gone by that he did not think of him. If only he could have an hour to sit and talk to him, to listen to his wise advice on matters he now faced. His father would know what to do.

The scent of moss and heath were heavy in the air as he rode into the courtyard and dismounted. Lacking the wealth to keep a stable-hand, he drew his horse into the stable and removed saddle and bridle on his own. A comforting bucket of oats caused the horse to relax as Ethan brushed down his coat and heaped a mound of fresh hay inside the stall. Then feeling hungry, he left and went through the kitchen entrance. The coals in the hearth were red and smoldering. The scent of fresh bread permeated the room, and a loaf cut in two sat on an oak board atop the table. He pulled a piece free and popped it into his mouth.

"Mr. Ethan, you must be chilled through, sir." Fiona poked her head around the corner of the door and stepped inside. "I've a fire set in your room. Shall I fix you something hot to drink and some supper?"

"No thank you, Fiona. I am fine as I am." He proceeded to go, but she put her hand out to him.

"I see you helped yourself to the bread. If that's all you are to eat, then that is a shame, for I've a stew simmering in that pot over there, and you know how it does me good to see you enjoy anything I've made."

Her expecting eyes could not be refused. "Well, if it is your stew, then by all means stuff me to the gills."

A broad smile swept across Fiona's rosy face, and she bustled over to the pot and ladled a huge helping into a bowl. He told her one was enough, and he inquired after Eliza.

"She is tired, Mr. Ethan." Fiona folded a napkin. "Do not stay long."

"I've news to tell her. Perhaps it will lift her spirits."

"I hope so. She has been very reflective the last few days."

He thanked her for the meal, and once she was convinced he could not eat a morsel more and had cleared the bowl and spoon away, he headed upstairs. In his bedchamber, the fire crackled and hissed, drowning out the clock on the mantelpiece and the steady patter of rain. He undressed, and the fire warmed his body. He went to the window, a high mullioned structure made of leaded glass that went from floor to ceiling.

It faced west, and through it he watched the clouds move above the treetops and cast long shadows over the moorland.

His heart lay heavy in his chest, broken and bruised, but still in love. The passion he felt for Darcy raged within, a storm of emotions spilling out and flooding his soul to its core. Slow and steady, he drew in a deep breath and released it. He reached for his Bible and opened to the Song of Solomon, where the letter, delivered to him by Miss Roth after her visit with Darcy, marked his place.

I cannot accept you, Ethan. [Her words were seared into his mind.] *We are too different, and I would not marry an Englishman for anything in the world, even if you meant to stay. And by no means would I leave my family and home and follow you to England. I will forever be grateful you pulled me from the river, but I do not love you.*

He went to the chair before the fire and sank into it. He prayed that God would remove the love he felt for Darcy if having her was a forlorn hope. Breathing out a final amen, he ran his fingers through his hair and stared at the letter in his hand.

Even if Darcy were to accept him, what would he have to offer her except an old manor with floors that creaked and windows that rattled, on a patch of land just large enough to sustain a garden and a horse?

The idea pained him like a twisting blade. He went down to what was now his study, where the remainder of his father's books stood in neat rows on the bookshelves. As he had studied the accounts and realized the cost of maintaining the old place, he had had to sell some of the old first editions that had been in the family for years. As he remembered them, he grew more convinced that God had set in his heart the desire to start a new life in America—hopefully with Darcy.

"She'll be going back to her home by the river. If I sell Fairview, I'll have enough to settle there and take Eliza and Fiona with me. God will turn Darcy's heart, I know it."

He stood and rubbed his eyes. Then he went upstairs and stood in the doorway to Eliza's room. She sat on a lounge, propped up against a snowy heap of pillows. Her dark hair, streaked with silver, fell in a single braid across her shoulder. A candle illuminated the room, and her face appeared flushed in the quivering light.

He drew up beside her. "Fiona says you are tired tonight. Can I get you anything? Would you like me to read to you?"

"Stay a little while." She touched his hand with hers. "Where did you go today?"

"Havendale."

She drew away from the pillow. "Why would you go there, Ethan?"

"Mr. Brighton asked me to accompany him. As you can imagine, my curiosity was piqued and I had to go. I was hesitant at first, but I felt drawn."

"Did you meet Madeline? I imagine she has grown very old and is not apt to entertain guests anymore."

"She was nowhere to be seen. But I saw Langbourne. Brighton had assured me he was at Meadlow and rarely visits Havendale. He was wrong."

"Did he inquire after me? Did he treat you unkindly?"

"We did not speak."

"I have no doubt his grudge against me and Hayward is as strong as it ever was. I shall not be free of him until I die."

"Do not speak of it," Ethan said. "I must tell you, there is someone else you know visiting Havendale."

"I cannot think who." Eliza settled back and smiled. Her violet eyes were as vivid in color as the first day Ethan met her as a boy. Yet lines had formed at the corners. "Please tell me; it shall make me happy for Madeline. Life can be very lonely for the old. It has been one regret of mine that I have never gone to see her. But I have my reasons for not doing so. Hayward no doubt painted a bleak picture of me in any correspondence he has had with her."

"I am certain it will make you very happy," Ethan said.

Upon his deathbed, Mr. Brennan asked for Ethan's word that he would protect Eliza by honoring her wishes to remain as she was—secluded. He had pledged his word not to speak of her to Darcy in any way other than in the past tense. But now that Darcy was but a few miles from Fairview, he hoped Eliza's mind might change and she would desire to see her daughter, even if by doing so, she risked rejection and having her heart broken all over again.

And so he paced, his hands clasped behind him, his heart heavy within. Finally he turned to Eliza, pausing by the window and praying she would rejoice over the news he was about to unfold.

"When I returned from America, I told you how beautiful Darcy was, how protected by her dutiful uncle, loved by her aunt and cousins. Do you remember?"

A wistful longing sprang into Eliza's eyes for the children she had borne and lost. "How can I forget?"

"Well, I saw Darcy today."

A bewildered look darkened Eliza's face. "You mean you dreamed of her . . . saw her in that way, don't you?"

"At first, I thought it was a dream. But I did see her. She is at Havendale with her grandmother."

After a quick intake of breath, tears glazed Eliza's eyes. She twisted the edge of her shawl between her hands. "Oh! Then—she has . . ." The words stuck in her throat.

"Come to meet Madeline—and you."

Eliza looked up at him with a start. "But she mustn't know about me, Ethan. It would break her heart. Oh, I pray Langbourne does not speak of me to her."

"Is it not time for her to know the truth—that you are alive?"

"It would cause her more pain than you can imagine. For her to learn I have been alive all these years and never tried to see her would give her reason to hate me." She looked up at him, her brows pinched together. "And despise her father for lying to her."

"It is not your fault, Eliza. You must see that, surely."

"It is entirely my fault. One action led to another."

"Yes. But that is not to say a wrong cannot be righted." Ethan went on to tell her about his conversation with Darcy in the gazebo. "I cannot help how I feel. I love her. How am I to express my love for her when I must hold these secrets?"

Eliza stood, her fists clenched at her side as she strode about the room. "I have been selfish. If Darcy loves you, then you mustn't let anything keep you apart—not even me. But please delay a little longer. Promise me."

He could never deny her anything. She'd been a mother to him, and a friend to his father. "I promise, but only for a little while."

"I only ask so that I have time to prepare." Eliza closed her eyes and turned her head to the side. Ethan knew he needed to leave her to her thoughts, and so he kissed her forehead and left. Fiona waited out in the hallway.

"I knew one day God would bring Darcy to us." She stepped ahead of Ethan, holding her handkerchief against her eyes. He realized there were three people in this house who loved Darcy and had been grieved by their separation. He knew he had to trust what Fiona said, and believe that God would bring them all together again, regardless of Eliza's worries.

By late evening, the rain moved off to the east. Ethan sat in his room at his writing desk. He lifted the pen from the inkwell and held it above the paper. After his salutation, he poured his heart out within a single line to Darcy. He had to see her again. He tapped the tip of the quill against the glass lip, when all of a sudden carriage wheels were borne to his hearing. A moment later, Fiona knocked on the door.

"There is a gentleman to see you. I've placed him in the study."

Ethan looked up from the letter. "Who is it?"

"I asked, but he did not give me his name, only said it was important he speak to you. Do not worry. He does not look like a creditor, though he does look clerkish."

Ethan did not go down immediately, but pulled on his boots and drew on his black waistcoat. The visitor stood in front of the fire in the sitting room, warming his hands. He turned with a graceful movement.

"My dear Mr. Brennan." The man bowed his head ever so low with a faint smile. "Forgive me for this late hour."

"I am sorry to have kept you waiting, Mr.——?"

"Hollen, sir." He glanced around the room. "My father owned a house similar to this one. A mite smaller, I might say."

Hollen breathed out each syllable as if his words were of grand importance. His head resembled the shape and features of a greyhound—a long nose and large glassy eyes. His coal-black hair combed flat over his crown hid a receding hairline. His right shoulder hunched forward. His black coat fit snug, his calves covered in wool stockings of the same color, ending with buckled shoes.

"What is your business here, Mr. Hollen?"

"If I may." With a lift of his brows, Hollen bent toward a chair and swept his hand across the seat. Ethan nodded but remained standing. "Allow me, sir, to preface with my deepest sympathies regarding the passing of your father."

Ethan studied Hollen as he spoke. A smooth talker, Ethan surmised, and grew guarded. "Did you know him?"

Hollen inclined his head to the left. "His good name was known by many people. I never had the pleasure to meet him face-to-face or to hear him preach."

"Have we ever met?"

"We have not, sir. I am here on behalf of a client, who does claim to know you."

"His name, Mr. Hollen?"

"He wishes to remain anonymous, sir."

"Is he a coward?"

"Not at all."

"Then why does he not make his identity known to me or come here himself?"

"It is wise he remain unnamed, for the present at least."

"For what reason? Has he committed a crime?"

"You will understand when I explain why he has sent me to speak with you and the lady who resides in this house."

Ethan frowned. "Go on."

"My client has in his possession letters that he believes the lady will be interested in. They are of the most delicate nature, and if the contents were to be broadcast, it would do great harm to the lady's reputation, as well as your father's and your own. And then there is the matter of Darcy Morgan, the lady's daughter. The letters will cause her a great deal of embarrassment."

Ethan fumed. "I assure you, the lady is blameless. There is nothing that could damage her character."

Hollen shook his head and raised one brow. "Apparently she is not, Mr. Brennan. At least according to my client."

Ethan set his mouth. "What could possibly be in a letter that would hurt her?"

"A variety of things, I suppose."

"For instance?"

"Are you aware she had a child with another man while her husband was away fighting in America's revolt, and that she attempted to conceal the child? The child died and she was cast out by her husband."

Ethan stared eye to eye with Hollen. "I know about it, yes."

"He sent her back to England, where she fell into your father's good graces, a man of God who should have forbid a harlot to live under his roof and hide her past."

"Speak another word against my father and I shall throw you out," Ethan warned. "What he did was save her life."

Hollen wiggled his mouth. "Well, sir, whatever else the letters reveal will be worth five hundred pounds for you to possess them. If not, my client is prepared to publicize. And if you decide to alert the constable of this district, he will be sure the lady's indiscretions are exposed."

Ethan jerked Hollen out of the chair by his coat collar. "Blackmail, Mr. Hollen? Extortion? Slander?" He threw him backward. "Get out of my house!"

Eyes wide, Hollen smoothed the front of his coat. His bloodless lips tightened over a set of crooked teeth. "I shall excuse your outburst, Mr. Brennan. I understand it is a shock, compounded by your father's death and this delicate situation. Indeed, it would cause any man to lose his composure." He picked up his hat and glided it onto his head, then stepped to the door. "I must advise you that my client is serious in this matter."

The muscles in Ethan's face twitched. He pointed his finger at Hollen and clenched his teeth. "Warn him, I am serious as well."

Hollen nodded and tapped the tips of his fingers against one another. "As long as he is in possession of these letters, the longer you and the lady will be under his power. I advise you submit to his demands while you can."

Ethan took an abrupt step forward. His shadow crossed over Hollen, and the man looked up at him with dread covering his pasty face. "Unless I see them," Ethan said, "I am unconvinced of anything. It could be a hoax, a forgery, a lie to get money, which I have little of."

Hollen's bony fingers clutched the doorknob. "I shall return in a few days with one letter in hand as proof."

Hollen prepared to step out into the darkness. "I shall not make this easy for your client, Hollen. He won't get a penny. You tell him that."

Hollen grunted and turned. "Hmm. That is your final word on the matter?"

"It is."

"Then prepare for the worst, sir."

Dread rushed through Ethan as he watched Hollen slither out the door and scoot into the rickety carriage that had brought him. Swaying to one side, it rolled off into the foggy night with its sinister passenger hunched inside.

When he could no longer see the grotesque shape passing down the lane from his house, Ethan clenched his jaw and kicked the door shut with the toe of his boot. He thought he was the only one to have ever known anything concerning Eliza's past, aside from his father. Was there something more to her life she had not revealed?

He raked his fingers through his hair, wondering what to do. If letters were revealed, could he protect Darcy? Could he shield Eliza?

From the hearth, the heat of the amber flames climbed his body. He threw his hands against the mantelpiece, shut his eyes, and prayed. "Impart to me the wisdom I need, Lord."

Perhaps ransoming the letters was the only way, for once they were in his hands, he could burn them.

17

That night at Havendale, Darcy dragged a goose-down pillow over her head to block out the ticking of the mantel clock. Turning over on her back, she stared up at the ceiling and watched the shadows quiver across it. "This is torture."

She drew herself out of the covers, lifted the clock from its place, and buried it in a drawer in the armoire, under layers of clothing. "There. Now I can sleep."

She lay back down and watched the moonlight dance over the plastered walls, unable to keep herself from gathering the bedclothes in her hands and squeezing them. Ethan's face full of agony over seeing her again caused her much pain. A tear slipped from the corner of her eye and she brushed it away.

"Oh, God, there must be a reason you have brought us together. Please show me what I must do."

Restless, she got up, slipped on her robe, and sat in the window seat. The moon, touched by airy, fingerlike clouds, met her eyes. The clouds drifted across a vast sea of ebony, and behind them stars appeared. She turned the latch and pushed the window open to feel the breeze that swept over the downs. The earlier rains had ceased, but left the air cool and moist.

Shivering, she ran her hands down her forearms, then reached over and pulled the window closed.

A fox cried in the distance, and an owl hooted in a nearby tree, reminding her of home, the Potomac, and its lush forests. She was more homesick than she had imagined. The days she had spent at Havendale with her grandmother had given them enough time to become acquainted, and they had, but at arm's length. Still, the questions Darcy had concerning her parents went unanswered, and she wanted to tell her grandmother that she wished to return home. But she could not bring herself to do it. Not yet.

A knock fell on her door and it creaked open. Mrs. Burke peeked inside, her cap snug on her head of gray, her nightgown sweeping over the floor above her bare feet. "I saw a light beneath your door, Miss Darcy. I thought you would have blown out your candle by now. Is something troubling you?"

"I cannot sleep," Darcy said. "My mind is restive."

Mrs. Burke stepped in. "Nor can I, and so I went down to the kitchen to have a cup of tea. You can tell me what's troubling you if you wish. I am a good listener."

"I was just thinking how I do not fit in here." Darcy sat up on the corner of the bed. "I am too outspoken, too forward in my ways to be anything like an English lady."

Mrs. Burke cocked her head. "Oh, I think you are a fine young woman."

"Thank you. I miss my family. I suppose they must be sitting down to dinner, and soon all will be going to bed, tucked under their quilts."

"The Breese house sounds like a nice place to live. So little to worry about."

"Oh, there is plenty. I worry about Uncle Will's health and whether he has recovered to his former self."

"I imagine it is a concern that is constant. Letter writing might help."

"Indeed it would, and I shall send another tomorrow. He gave me a list of flowers he wishes me to collect for him. Is there any heather nearby that I could gather?"

"There are plenty of wildflowers along the hedgerows, and heather on the downs in spring," Mrs. Burke replied as she tidied up. "But they have few to no blooms on them now. Is there a bounty of flowers where you are from?"

"The meadows are full of them. And my favorite, lady slippers, grow in the woods."

Darcy's pocket sketchbook sat on her bedside table and she opened it. She already had several pencil drawings to show to the family back home. *God willing, I shall have one of Fairview before I return to my river.*

She hoped she would leave Derbyshire long before spring, in time to see the wildflowers in bloom along the river, the return of the waterfowl, and the newborn fawns. She thought of the dogwoods and their white petals, the snowy blossoms of wild blackberry.

She closed the book and set it back. "Mrs. Burke, do you know if my grandmother has a book of England's flowers in the library?"

"I believe she does. I'll dig it out for you." Mrs. Burke picked up her candle. "Perhaps when Mr. Langbourne returns he could escort you."

"Has he gone?"

"Hmm, but to where I am not sure."

"Charlotte has left as well?"

"She has. I suppose she told you how much she loathes this part of Derbyshire."

"Indeed, she made sure of it. I am sorry for her that she does not love Havendale. It is peaceful place."

"Sometimes too peaceful."

"I cannot bear the city, and my ways are not as refined as Charlotte's. Perhaps it was because of me she left."

"I do not believe so. She never stays long at Havendale and visits but twice a year."

Darcy drew up her legs, wrapping her arms around her knees. "Charlotte seems so sad, and he so removed from her."

"It is his way," sighed Mrs. Burke.

"Do you think it would be all right if I rode Grandmother's mare tomorrow?"

"I do not see why not. Mr. Brighton said she is as fit as a fiddle." She paused before shutting the door and said, "I've heard that Mr. Brennan is a bold rider."

"Yes, I am aware of Mr. Brennan's bold riding," said Darcy.

"You've met him before?"

"Yes, back home. He'd come to stay at a plantation across the river. I do not wish to talk about it." Darcy saw the look of curiosity in the woman's face and smiled. "I've presented a mystery, haven't I? You must excuse me for it."

Mrs. Burke let out a chuckle and shook her head. Her cap shifted and she tucked her stray locks back. "Oh, Havendale has its own mysteries, Miss Darcy. You can be sure of that."

The door closed and Darcy turned to her candle and blew it out. Havendale held an air of secrecy. Secrets that were tucked away in the memories of its living inhabitants, gone to the grave with the rest—she knew she would never know why. When the flame was extinguished, blue moonlight poured through the lattice window and touched upon her face. Shadows crossed the ceiling above her to intrude upon the misty light that washed the room. She closed her eyes, folded her hands, and pressed them to her lips.

"Whatever secrets Havendale holds, whatever mysteries are hidden within its walls, please do not allow curiosity to keep me from returning home, dear Lord."

Long after Mrs. Burke had left, and the quiet in the old house deepened, Darcy heard footsteps in the hall, then another knock on her door. She swung her legs over the side of the bed and drew the robe her grandmother had loaned her over her shoulders. Was she to get no sleep this night?

With candle in hand, she opened the door. In the gloom stood Mr. Langbourne, leaning against the jamb, still in his black greatcoat. Surprised to see him, Darcy stepped back.

"I saw your candle through the window as I came over the hill. I need to speak with you." His stare traveled from her face down her throat. She drew her robe closer.

"Is there something wrong that you need to speak to me about at this hour, Mr. Langbourne? Can it not wait until morning?"

"I would not have bothered to ask if I had no reason. Come downstairs to the library."

Darkness swallowed him up as he drifted away, and Darcy followed him. A low fire crackled in the hearth set in the center of the north wall of the library. The room, paneled in dark walnut, smelled of old books and dust. Langbourne sat in a chair, still booted and mud-spattered from his ride.

"Close the door, Darcy." She hesitated, but obeyed. "Sit down. Here in the chair opposite me."

As Darcy lowered herself into the stiff armchair, Langbourne's eyes locked onto hers. He shifted to one side. "I have not had the opportunity to speak to you alone. You have not told anyone about what you saw, have you?"

She straightened up. "Not really."

He frowned. "What do you mean? Explain yourself."

"Mrs. Burke knows about the tramp, but she doesn't know about what you did to him. I did not tell her."

"It is imperative you do not. Obedience is something I expect in a woman."

"I have said nothing, so as not to worry my grandmother, and I fear if I say anything on the matter, you might have your ruffians injure that man in a worse way if he should come here again."

"Let us hope he does not. I have no tolerance for vagrants."

Darcy pressed her brows together. "I do not understand the aversion I have met here in England toward the less fortunate. The Lord instructs us to help those in need, especially the poor. Please, Mr. Langbourne, have compassion on the man."

He watched her in silence. Then the corner of his mouth lifted. "You are without a doubt Eliza through and through. Your grandfather was a fiery preacher, and charity was something he pounded into her. Perhaps if she had been less sympathetic she would have been wiser."

Darcy longed to escape his cruel eyes, and each time he spoke the name *Eliza* she cringed inwardly. "I wish to go now," she said, and stood.

Langbourne leaned forward. "You are expected to accept the Brightons' invitation to Bentmoor." He handed her an invitation. She took it in hand and opened it. "We have certain social mores here. I detest them, but in this case they are necessary."

"I should be happy to attend." She folded the invitation and turned to go.

"On your own? You have apprehension of very little, don't you, Darcy?"

"There is no reason for me to be uneasy. Mrs. Brighton was kind to me."

"You are not concerned who you might meet at this affair?"

"No, sir. Should I be?"

"It is wise to be cautious, for you will have a swarm of men around you. If anything, they will be enamored by the fact that you are an American girl. I will not be going with you to protect you."

It sounded silly to Darcy. Why should she be guarded of the people Mrs. Brighton would invite to her home? She watched Langbourne stand up from the chair and pour brandy into a glass. Rarely did the Breeses have even a barrel of ale in their home. They were not given to it or any other kind of strong drink. Darcy could see a change come over Langbourne even after one glass. His face grew haggard, his eyes glassy, and his disposition more forceful. She would avoid him.

"I will be gone for a few days on private business," he went on to say.

Suspicion rose in Darcy, and she wondered what Langbourne did when away. "Charlotte must get lonely without you."

"Never mind what I do, or what she feels," he said, turning. "I suppose you will wear your best gown tomorrow night?"

She tried to douse the tension between them by smiling. "I doubt my best gown shall meet with approval."

"Does it matter?" His eyes darkened as the fire in the grate weakened. "Who is it you wish to please?" He swallowed down the amber liquid, went to her, and lifted a lock of her hair from off her shoulder. "So unfortunate you were not born with your mother's hair. It was as dark and very long."

Darcy felt a certain fear of him rise and moved away. Without hesitation, she turned out of the room and ascended the stairs—uneasy at his words, at his touch, and how he made demands on her. At least a visit to Bentmoor would distract her from the weary darkness that permeated Havendale. And upon her return, Langbourne would be gone.

18

*A*lone in her room, Darcy stared at the gown that lay across her bed, doubting it would stand up to the other ladies' dresses in beauty and fashion. With a sigh, she picked it up, held it out in front of her, and smoothed down the folds and creases. The waning light of day caressed the deep ivory color and dark emerald trim. The fabric felt smooth against her palm, and she recalled the day that she and Martha had finished the last bit of stitching on the hem. How she missed her cousin and hoped she would receive a letter from her soon. Had the expectation of a proposal from Dr. Emerson become a reality for Martha?

Darcy smiled at the prospect, and wondered if she would find her cousin a married woman upon her return. She whispered a prayer that, for the sake of Martha's kind heart, it was so. If anyone deserved to be happily married, it was she.

After Darcy had dressed and arranged her hair without assistance, she stepped into her grandmother's room to see if she met her approval.

"It will have to do," said Madeline, glancing the dress over. "I suppose that is the latest fashion in America. It is simple."

"It is the best I have, Grandmother. The trim color is lovely, don't you think? And in candlelight it shall look even richer."

"I suppose. Gloves?"

"I have none. I forgot to pack them."

Shocked, Madeline's brows lifted. "No gloves? Look in my top drawer. There is a pair you may wear. Keep them if you wish."

Darcy opened the drawer, and alongside a few caps and a pair of black lace gloves she found them. They were soft as silk and a gentle cream shade. "These are too expensive for me to keep, Grandmother."

"Pishposh! Where shall I wear them? They have been sitting in the drawer for years. Please take them."

Darcy thanked her with an embrace.

"Enough. Enough. Be off with you, my girl."

A little curtsey and Darcy turned to leave. Maxwell scampered after her. "I will not be late," she said, patting the dog's head and looking back at her grandmother.

"Hmm. You might. If Mr. Brennan is there."

Darcy straightened up. "Well, he shall not delay me."

Madeline smirked. "Prudence and good sense, Darcy. Keep your passions hidden and put your heart in the hands of the One who cares most. 'Trust in the LORD with all your heart, and lean not to your own understanding. But in all your ways acknowledge him. He shall direct your path.'" A peaceful smile lifted her mouth.

Downstairs, Darcy drew her cloak over her shoulders and hurried out to the carriage the Brightons were good enough to send. Once she took her seat inside, her fears turned to excitement. It had been so long since she'd been to any kind of large gathering, the last being at the Rhendons across the river where she'd first set eyes on Ethan.

As she traveled the five-and-one-half miles toward Bentmoor, she soaked in the shades of sunset as it brushed over the landscape. Magenta clouds edged the treetops. Pale purple and blue graced the sky, and flocks of birds made their way to their perches for the night.

The manor house stood atop a hill, twice the size of Havendale, made of red brick and graced with tall windows that caught the hues of dusk. Darcy wondered why anyone would want to live in a house so large when only two people and a few servants lived in it. The footman handed her out, and she looked up at the decorative entrance and the ivy shading it.

A stone-faced manservant dressed in bright red opened the door and stood back to allow her inside, his eyes never meeting hers. It was no life to live, Darcy thought. To serve those who believed they were higher, to show no emotion, to be so mechanical. She felt sorry for him, and spoke. "Good evening. Thank you for opening the door for me."

The footman's eyes blinked, gave her a quick nod, and stepped behind her to draw off her cloak in such a manner that she did not feel his touch. Mrs. Brighton glided forward and moved Darcy toward her drawing room. "Darcy, I am pleased you have come. No escort? Where are Mr. Langbourne and Charlotte?"

"Charlotte returned to Meadlow, and Mr. Langbourne is gone on business."

Mrs. Brighton clicked her tongue. "I should not be surprised. . . . Never mind. There are handsome men aplenty here tonight to watch over you."

"Forgive me for being late," said Darcy, tugging at her gloves. The soft ting of a harpsichord and the voice of a woman singing as sweet as a meadowlark flowed from the drawing room. "How beautiful."

"Do you like it?" Mrs. Brighton walked with her to the open doorway.

"Very much." The music filled her, and she shuddered at the beauty of it.

"It is a piece by Mr. Mozart from *Le nozze di Figaro*—The Marriage of Figaro."

Of course, Darcy had heard of Mozart, but she had never heard his compositions sung. She had not been long in the room when she spotted Ethan on the opposite side. Her breath caught, and she felt a sharp pang seize her heart. She looked about for Miss Roth, or rather, could she be Mrs. Brennan? Not a sign of her.

What did I expect? I knew the possibility of meeting him again. Only this time it would be in a room full of people.

Discreetly, not to show her emotions, she lifted her gaze. Several ladies in finer gowns than hers sat near. He kept his eyes fixed on the singer, and Darcy saw how moved he was by the music. *Can any woman, other than I, see so deeply? He is pained by my attitude toward him. He must feel it as rejection. Help me, God, to mend what I have done to him.*

A brooding look shone in Ethan's expression, as if each note the singer sang had sunk into his being. He was dressed much as he had been the day she met him at Twin Oaks. His hair, cut to his collar, caught the candlelight and wisped over his stark white neckcloth. His coat and breeches were black, his waistcoat dark blue.

When the singer concluded, Darcy heard a woman say to another, "If I did not know any better, I would say an American just entered the room." Eyes turned her way.

"Where? Oh, yes. You can tell by her gown. Such a simple country fashion."

"Madeline Morgan's granddaughter, I suspect."

Darcy gave the women a sidelong glance, and saw that they were the same age as her mother would be, with gray elflocks that flowed over one shoulder, and smiles that feigned sincerity. She turned to face them, inclined her head with a short curtsey, and they, looking impressed, nodded.

She chose to accept their comments as compliments. Yet, she knew then and there that gossip would flow among the company tonight, and she hoped no one would besiege her with questions. Unless, of course, they had something to say that would enlighten her regarding her parents.

Ethan turned his eyes to hers and she felt as if she'd fall to pieces when they met. Mrs. Brighton leaned toward her ear.

"Is not Mr. Brennan dressed fine tonight?"

"Yes, perfectly."

"We invited his boarder—I know nothing else to call her by. But she will not attend. No one ever sees her. I am thinking she is a sickly person and that is the reason she is so secluded."

"His boarder, Mrs. Brighton?"

"Yes, his governess as a child. So do not fear. You have no rival."

"I see," she said, relieved, but searching for the proper words in response.

"You know I have not once met her in all these years we have been in Derbyshire. It is my understanding she does not enjoy social gatherings. But I am glad to see Mr. Brennan has come. It was all very odd at Havendale when he spoke to you. And then you seemed so unnerved. What was it?"

Darcy listened, yet kept her eyes on Ethan's. "Nothing really. We had met once before, when he had come to America with his intended, Miss Roth."

"Miss Roth, you say." Mrs. Brighton laughed. "No need to worry on that account either. I hear he broke off all contact months ago."

"Then they are not married, or to be married?"

"Goodness, no. It is rumored his heart is wrung to another, and Miss Roth, it is said, placed her affections elsewhere."

"She did not deserve him. She did not love him deeply enough. I am glad Mr. Brennan is rid of her."

"Love is all well and good. But without money, how can one live happily?" Mrs. Brighton drew Darcy closer with a tug on her sleeve. "He is coming this way. I shall leave now."

She stepped away, and Darcy swallowed hard as he approached. She had no idea what to say to him. He bowed short. "Miss Darcy. Are you enjoying the music?"

"Yes, thank you, Mr. Brennan. It is my first time." *He is not married. Did she break his heart?* she wondered.

"I imagine you have little of this type of culture along the Potomac."

"You are correct, sir. But the birds make up for the lack of music made by human voices."

The musicians struck up again, and the singer won the attention of all. Enraptured, Darcy hung on to every note, every word, and allowed the music to sink deep within her. The romance of the aria drew her and Ethan nearer, and as the song came to a close, he leaned down and whispered in her ear.

"It ends, *I want to crown you with roses.*"

A rush of heat swept through Darcy, quickening the beat of her heart and the heave of her breath. With her eyes brimming, she stepped back. He was correct. The singer ended with those very words. Were they meant for her when Ethan spoke them to her? Would he crown her with roses?

The audience applauded, and Mrs. Brighton stepped out front. "Ladies and gentlemen, we will have a brief intermission. Please, help yourselves to the refreshment table."

Guests either stood up from their chairs or glided away from their places with laughter and light conversation. Mrs. Brighton waltzed up to Darcy with three gentlemen in tow, all young and dressed to the nines.

"You cannot have our American cousin all to yourself, Mr. Brennan." She waved him back, then took Darcy's hand and moved her forward as the trio gathered around. "May I introduce Mr. Clary, Mr. Hammond, and Mr. Price?"

Darcy lowered her head and curtseyed. Each man bowed and then resumed staring at her. Their gazes were ones of fascination at a new face from a foreign land. But Ethan's—his shifted between his heart and mind. She could tell between the two, for when his eyes grew warm, they were filled with longing. When they grew cold and stern, she saw frustration.

"Miss Darcy." Mr. Hammond's smile revealed a mouth full of crooked teeth. "Welcome to Derbyshire. It is an honor." He bowed, lifted her hand, and kissed the top of it.

"Thank you, sir."

"All of us welcome you, Miss Darcy," Mr. Clary stammered. "It isn't every day we meet an American girl. You must tell us all about yourself."

She heard Ethan sigh, and from the corner of her eye, she saw how he stiffened. He drew his shoulders up and set his jaw. The scowl on his face deepened. He would not look at her, but turned, then strode off. Disappointed, her eyes followed him through the crowd until he disappeared. *Come back.* But she knew he would not as long as she had admirers hovering around her.

"Allow me to fetch a cup of punch for you," said Mr. Price. He looked younger than the others, with a hint of whiskers shadowing his jaw. She nodded and his large brown eyes lit up. Then shouldering his way past the others, he headed with a skip of his heels for the refreshment table.

Darcy felt a tug on her gown, then another, and to her horror it tore. As quickly as she could, she gathered up the fabric against the gap in the seam at her waist. The zealous bungler had stepped on her hem, and when he noticed what he'd done, he tried to free her gown from the brass buckle on his shoe.

"Oh, I am sorry, Miss Darcy." Then the seam tore a bit more, leaving a gap inches wide that broke open beneath her left arm.

"Dear me, Price. Look what you've done," said Mr. Hammond. "What a buffoon you are." Hammond leaned down and freed her dress from Mr. Price's offensive shoe. Darcy's face burned with embarrassment as she attempted to hide the rip with her hand, but the fabric hung so much that her chemise peeked out from behind it.

Fortunately Mrs. Brighton stood nearby. Desperate for help, Darcy darted her eyes her way. Without delay, Mrs. Brighton moved through the crowd, reached her, and drew her away from onlookers to a side room.

"Oh, dear me. What a tragedy. I shall call my maid and have her mend that. Do not worry, Darcy. If anyone should be mortified it should be that bumbling Mr. Price. If he cannot conduct himself in a more gracious and controlled manner, I shall not invite him ever again to Bentmoor."

"So much for my skills at dressmaking." Darcy struggled to make light of the mishap. "I should have made the stitches tighter."

The fine brows of her hostess arched. "You made this gown all by yourself?"

"We have few tailors and seamstresses where I am from. My cousin Martha helped me."

"You are a fascinating creature. No wonder you caught Mr. Brennan's eye. Well, my maid is skilled with a needle, and all shall be repaired quickly." She went to pull the bell cord, but Darcy set her hand on the lady's arm.

"Thank you for the offer, but I'd rather go home."

Mrs. Brighton wiggled a smile. "Ah, that is a pity. The evening is ruined for you. I shall call for the carriage."

At least her cloak hid the damage. But nothing could hide the humiliation she felt, nor the disappointment that she had to leave. How could she stay, with her dress stitched up in haste, with gossip flying around the room? It would be stretched in every direction by the time she heard it. Perhaps if this had not happened, she and Ethan would have had a moment together. Had he heard her gown had been torn and that she was leaving?

She waited by the window until the footman escorted her through another door so she would not be seen. Inside the carriage, she leaned forward and looked out. Beyond the window that faced her, golden candlelight glowed within. Guests settled back into their chairs, and the singer lifted her voice once more as the driver climbed to his perch.

A man's hand grasped the coach door and Ethan's handsome face appeared. "Leaving so soon, Darcy?"

She swallowed the emotion that climbed her throat. "My gown. Mr. Price tore it—by accident, of course. I cannot impose on Mrs. Brighton to have her maid repair it." She rambled on, speaking rapidly. Then checking herself, she met his eyes.

"Yes, I heard," he said.

"I suppose everyone has."

"Is it badly torn?"

"Yes, and it may be ruined for good. How did you know of my retreat?"

"Mrs. Brighton told me," he replied, his eyes firm upon hers.

Darcy shook her head, and a curl fell over her forehead. "Poor Mrs. Brighton. She looked mortified, and I could tell that she regretted introducing Mr. Price to me."

"She should be. Price is known for spoiling young women's evenings."

"Well, I shall salvage my gown somehow."

"It is the one you wore the first time I saw you, isn't it?"

"You remembered."

"How could I forget anything about that day?"

She looked away. "I will not delay you any longer, Mr. Brennan." She put her hand outside the coach window to signal the driver to move on. But Ethan took her fingers within his before she could.

"Must you miss the last of the recital? You may never have another chance to hear such music when you return home. Come back inside. I will stand with you in the back of the room."

She paused to think, then looked back at him. "I can keep my cloak on and then slip out when it is over."

Ethan opened the coach door and held out his hand for her to take. She curled her fingers around his palm. Back inside, she remained near a door for a quick exit. The music, the singing, and Ethan standing next to her in the shadows, escaping the glare of the candles, made the tearing of her gown less important. Through her glove, she felt his hand brush over her fingers and then move away.

When the singer held the last note, applause erupted and she curtseyed low in her blue silk gown, with her silver locks falling over her shoulders. She exited through a door near the musicians, and the guests congratulated Mr. and Mrs. Brighton for the success of their gathering.

Suddenly, the French doors behind Darcy opened. Chilly night air swept over the nape of her neck where she had pulled her hair away to one shoulder. With Ethan, she turned and came face to face with a disheveled man dressed in tattered clothes. Darcy drew in a breath, but fear did not seize her. His dirty eyes lit up when theirs met. Bronzed by reason of his wandering, his face lined by age, he'd no doubt lived a hard life.

His watery eyes enlarged, and he struggled to speak. The shabby jacket he wore over a starved, diseased body made him known to her.

He is the vagabond of the moors.

19

*D*azzled by the candlelight, the drifter's eyes traveled from face to face. He staggered forward and faltered. Aghast, people nearby moved back. The man locked his gaze on Darcy, lowered his head, dragged off his tattered tricorn hat, and with a trembling smile, spoke low and strained.

"It is you. Praise the Almighty, my eyes behold you at last."

Stunned, Darcy remained stark still. Ethan put his arm around her and drew her back. "Who are you?" said Ethan. "What do you want?"

Tears slipped from the man's bloodshot eyes and riveted down the creases of his cheeks. "Do you not know me?" he said to Darcy. "Do you not remember? Did my unforgiving heart drive my memory from your mind?"

Darcy's lips parted, and feeling compassion for the man, she reached over to touch his shoulder. The ladies gasped and the gentlemen warned her. "I am sorry, but I do not know you, sir." Her voice trailed off, and silence pressed in all around them. "I am not the one you seek."

Disappointment contorted his face. His brows pressed into a single line and his mouth curved downward. "I see her face before me. I see her eyes looking back at me." He rushed forward and took her by the arms. Darcy cried out and Ethan flung him back. The crowd gasped.

Gathered into Ethan's arms, she watched the poor wretch's startled face grimace. Confusion filled his eyes. "I am mistaken," he said in a halting voice. "Please . . . forgive me." The wanderer plunged back through the doors, out onto the terrace, where he fled into the dark.

Mr. Brighton, squeezed by curious onlookers, reached the door and locked it. "I apologize, everyone. But all is over. No harm done. Please go back to enjoying yourselves. Cards are in the room." The surge of guests broke apart and Darcy stood alone near Ethan.

"That man . . . " She could not get his face out of her mind, the misty eyes and the look of desperation that contoured his features.

"He is gone," Ethan assured her. "He won't be back."

"Miss Darcy," said Mr. Brighton, his brows knitted with concern. "I am terribly sorry. I have no idea how the man got in without being seen. I will speak to my servants and . . ."

"No harm done." She put her hand to her aching temple. "I pray he will not be hurt by anyone. He is a lost soul who has been mistreated."

"He could be dangerous. And he trespassed. I'll have the constable searching for him within the hour."

"Please, Mr. Brighton, let him go. I do not believe he is a danger to anyone, just a poor soul whose mind is adrift." Darcy stepped away, toward the hall with Ethan. "I wonder who he thought I was."

"A sweetheart from his past perhaps."

"Ah, so he has a broken heart as well as a broken body. If you should see him again, will you help him?"

"Yes, if I happen upon him, I will do what I can." His gaze shifted to her and softened.

Darcy wished to say more, to question him, and hear it from his own lips that he never cared for any other. She drew in a breath. *Force him to tell me his heart, Lord. Do not allow him to torture me any longer.*

A feverish light shone in his eyes, as he slipped one hand behind her, followed the curve of her neck and glided it up into her hair. Tendrils came loose and tumbled between his fingers. He brought his lips close to hers, and whispered, "I have suffered without you, Darcy. Whatever it was that made you despise me, I regret it."

Despise him? She had to explain. But the moment she tried, the footman stepped into the hallway, and they drew apart.

"If you are ready, miss, the carriage is waiting." The footman looked irritated that he had to wait upon her a second time.

Ethan touched her arm. "Darcy, I need to talk to you . . ."

Mrs. Brighton, with a group of ladies, appeared, each looking flustered and concerned. "Darcy, my dear. What a horrible night this has been for you."

"I am fine, Mrs. Brighton. Really." Darcy struggled to smile.

"I thought you had left, due to your dress being ruined."

"I did, but I . . ."

With a shake of her head, Mrs. Brighton drew Darcy away from Ethan toward the door and the footman. "It is best you go home. You may not realize it now, but you have had a shock."

"You might faint any moment, or grow ill," said the lady beside Mrs. Brighton.

"That is so true, Darcy. Now you go on, and do not tell Madeline anything about this . . . except for the dress. But do not mention that man."

Swept down a short flight of stairs to the carriage and the footman and followed by the flood of ladies, Darcy took her seat. And as the carriage rolled away, she looked back and saw Ethan standing outside, watching her leave. Anticipation that he would visit her caused her to smile.

20

The following day, Darcy laced up her walking shoes, slipped on her gloves, and donned her cloak. She could tell, when she glanced out the window, that a chill lingered in the air. The sky hung gray and misty. The birds were silent.

Mrs. Burke met her down the hallway. Maxwell's nails clicked along the floor as he trotted behind her. Darcy peered into Madeline's bedroom before going on, and saw the old woman sitting in her wing-backed chair. She appeared to be asleep. A blanket covered her and her cap concealed her gray hair.

"How is my grandmother today?" Darcy asked Mrs. Burke.

"Weary as always. And growing more so." Maxwell circled around Mrs. Burke's ankles and she shooed him back. "You are going out?"

"I'd like to do a little exploring."

"It is a fine day for it, though cloudy. Take the mare. If you should get lost, that old nag knows her way back."

The moment Darcy stepped outdoors, a sense of release from the shadows and the confinement that was Havendale poured into her. She drew the brisk freshness of the day deep into her lungs. Her breath expelled into a translucent vapor in the morning air. She crossed the lawn to the stable where Madeline's mare was boarded in its stall. The moment she stepped through the door, the heavy scent of hay and animal met her. The horse lifted its head, flicked its ears, and nickered when she ran her hand down its broad neck.

After cinching the saddle, Darcy slipped the bridle over the mare's head, put her foot into the stirrup, and pulled herself up. It would shock most to see her riding astride, instead of seated sidesaddle, the acceptable method of riding for a lady. Astride, she could stay atop the horse and control her without toppling from the saddle at a swift gallop. Back home, Aunt Mari would scold, but her uncle insisted she ride in whatever manner suited her if it meant preventing a fall.

Smiling, she pictured them both in her mind. Aunt Mari with her hands on her hips looking worried, and Uncle Will waving her on in approval. Nudging the horse with her heels, she headed out to the road. Beyond the gate, the mare sprung to a gallop. The moorland lay crisp with dew, and Darcy pushed the horse toward the path that hugged the River Noe. She splashed across the shallows and headed up a hill, her hair whipping back against her shoulders as the pumping of her heart kept pace with the beat of the mare's hooves.

Her eyes filled and burned from the chilly wind—from the anxious churning that rose inside her. *When will he come to Havendale?* She set her teeth and sent the horse over an ancient border. The mare wearied and slowed, and she took pity and soothed it with a *there, there* and a caress of her hand along its glossy coat.

Darcy looked across the vast expanse of land, misty to the north and bright to the south, the heights casting smooth shadows across the lowlands. She could see for miles to the high hills of the west, and the silver ribbons of brooks beneath them in the windswept valley. Stones pitted the fields between gorse grass and thistle, with barren bluffs stretching above them.

A pair of siskins chirped and pranced among the thorny briars in the hedgerows. They reminded her of the goldfinches back home that she had trained to come to the windowsill for the thistle seed she had spread. She longed to return to her river, to stand on the cliffs above the gorge. She yearned for home, for the deep forests, the ferns and rhododendron that grew beneath shady elms, the deer, the birds of the air, and the placid Potomac.

She scanned the land, wondering if Fairview could be seen from where she stood. But there were no houses of any kind in sight. *He must be far. Will I see him again, God? My heart aches so.*

She rode on, down a path to an area where the land smoothed out before her. She had not met a soul along the road, nor had she seen fresh signs of horse and rider in the soft earth. What had been the partitions of a cottage came into view—crumbling divides between stretches of dead weeds, choked by withered vine. Charred remains caused her to wonder what had happened to the family that had once lived there. Had the fire taken their lives, or had they escaped destruction?

At the foot of the hill stood a church made of stone. Even with the cloudy day, the windows sparkled. Light passed across them and created prisms. Then the long gray shadows from the clouds returned. Tall grass waved among the gravestones in the churchyard and flaunted their spiky tips, and several stock doves broke out from among them and took flight.

She swung her legs over the mare's side and slipped off, her feet landing on moist ground. She strode to the wall, sat down upon it, and gazed at the spears of sunlight plunging through turreted clouds. The chill air passed through her cloak as the scent of rain whipped through the breeze.

"I want to go home, God," she said aloud. "I miss my cousins. I miss Uncle Will and Aunt Mari. I miss my river. For what reasons have you sent me to this place? Is there something I must do? Is it Ethan? Am I meant to be his wife?"

The gallop of a horse drew near, and she dashed the tears from off her face. Startled, she turned her head and a horse and rider drew up. The breeze swept her hair across her eyes and she shoved the strands back to see the man's face. When she realized it was Ethan, a shiver passed through her and she drew her cloak closer, her feelings for him rising as he reined in.

"Ethan!" Her breath caught in her throat. She hoped he had not noticed she'd been crying, but by the crease in his brows, she knew he had.

He dismounted and held out a hand to help her down. She chose the opposite side of the wall, creating a barrier between them. They were always meeting in this way—by chance.

"Are you all right?" he asked. "You appear upset."

"I am a little homesick." She folded her arms when he stepped closer. No other words could she find, so fast beat her heart. She fixed her gaze on Sanchet, the stallion's shining eyes flickering in return. "You bought Mr. Rhendon's horse after all. I meant to comment on it before, but it was not convenient."

"Well, I felt an attachment to him, since it was upon him that I first saw you."

Darcy smiled. "Hmm. He is a fine horse. I hold nothing against him."

She held her hand out and Sanchet moved close. She stroked his velvety nose and laid her head against his sleek coat. He smelled of leather and tack, and it made her think of the Virginia plantation where he had been bred and raised, the Maryland bluffs along the river, and the path leading down to the spot where Ethan saved her from drowning. Then it all came back to her again—how she owed him her life.

Sanchet nickered. Darcy patted his neck. "I am not afraid of you. Why, you are gentle as a lamb. What a brave fellow you are to have borne the voyage across the sea."

She turned to look at Ethan. His hair brushed along his coat collar and lifted in the breeze. Beneath the cloudy sky, standing upon the damp grass, he looked more handsome than she ever recalled. He had a careworn look, a windswept expression, and a sorrow that lingered in his stare.

"I saw you as I came up the road. It is a chilly day to be out." His eyes never left her face.

"You're right. I should be heading back." She gathered her hem just above her heels and proceeded toward a break in the wall. The mare stood a ways off munching the grass. Ethan stepped alongside Darcy, on the opposite side of the wall.

"Allow me to escort you back."

"There is no reason to inconvenience yourself."

"It is no inconvenience at all. I was on my way to Havendale to see you anyway."

A weed grew from a crack in the wall and she plucked it out and looked at it. Then she glanced over at him. "Were you?"

He stopped walking and she heard a sigh pass between his lips. "I did not like the way we left things."

Nor had she. Perhaps being cordial would help, and so Darcy decided then and there she must be civil and forgive Ethan. What was done was done. At least they could be friends. *But he had said he wished to be more than that, and I feel the same. Would it be too bold to tell him I love him, Lord?*

She raised her hand, moved her hair back from her face, and fastened her eyes upon the ruins. "Do you know this place?"

"Yes. My father was a minister and we lived here for a short time. I was young and do not remember much. This was also your grandfather's and mother's home. The house was actually a part of the Havendale estate."

Darcy stared at the pile of rubble. "This was the vicarage where she grew up?"

"I am surprised no one told you."

"My Uncle Will said my grandfather preached near Havendale. I saw the church and wondered if this could have been the place. I had no idea this had once been their home—and yours as well."

"Yes," Ethan said. "We have a connection here, do we not?"

Darcy nodded. Pained to look upon the blackened remains, she imagined her mother standing out on the grass, her dark hair blown back by the wind, her young face tilted toward the sun. Had her father ridden up on a blustery day just as Ethan had with her? Did he propose to her by the door, or here by the wall, and had he carried her far away on horseback or in a carriage? Darcy knew she'd never know, but to think they had stood here long ago caused her emotions to rise and fall like the gusts of wind that swept over the land.

She placed her hands atop the wall that separated her from the heaps of charred stone and ash, from the cold remains where there had once been windows and a door. Her mind drifted back to River Run and the empty, decaying house that stood there. Were these evidences of what lives her parents had lived?

"What happened here?" she asked in a grave tone, her brows pinched.

Setting his hat back on his head, Ethan leaned against the wall. "When your grandfather died, your mother was to vacate the house to make room for our family. That is when she left with Hayward Morgan. Shortly after our arrival, a fire destroyed the house, killing both my mother and baby sister."

Troubled, Darcy turned to him. "I am sorry." And truly she was. How could anyone survive such loss, go through life with a tragedy of this kind bound to them? Only God could strengthen such a soul. She realized how strong a man Ethan must really be.

He hung his head. "It was long ago."

"I know how it feels to lose a mother."

"We've lost loved ones in different ways, but it is still a grievous thing, whether they have gone away from us, or passed into God's heaven."

"Yet, God has a way of sending us aid in our time of need."

"His aid came in the form of an inheritance for my father. We had a home to live in. Yet he never preached again from the pulpit, but learned to serve God in other ways. He was kind to the poor and needy. This was his saving grace."

Darcy noticed sorrow flicker in his eyes, along with a light that said secrets were also locked away at Fairview. Neither spoke for a long, tense moment. Presently, with her head low, she laid both her hands over his, and he looked into her eyes.

"I am grieved for you, Ethan." When he did not answer, she drew her hands away and walked on. "Count it a blessing, sir, that you know about your family. I have so little knowledge of my parents."

"Surely you have learned more about your father while staying at Havendale," Ethan offered.

"I am afraid Havendale keeps its secrets under lock and key," Darcy answered.

Ethan answered with a solemn nod. "Some things should be kept hidden and forgotten. But then there are other things that should come to light, if they help in some way."

She turned her head to look at him as she drew through the break in the wall. "You believe that?"

"I do." He took a step closer. "I cannot forget you, Darcy. Can you forgive me? Hurting you was the last thing I would ever do."

"In your letter, you said you never meant for me to think you loved me, that your heart belonged to Miss Roth. I wish you had made that clear in the beginning."

His eyes widened. "I never sent you a letter."

"It was penned in a masculine hand and signed by you."

"No. I never sent it. How did you come by this letter?"

"Miss Roth gave it to me."

He shook his head. "I see. And how did this come about?"

"She came to the house. My family had gone into the village, and I was alone."

"What did Miss Roth tell you?"

"That you and she were to be married upon your return to England."

Ethan huffed and shifted on his feet. "I made no such promise."

"She was emphatic."

"A wicked lie, Darcy. All of it."

"You can see why I believed her. I had no reason not to. I could not stand in the way."

"Miss Roth. She did this. She wrote that letter herself and devised this whole plan to separate us."

"Why would she go to such extremes?"

"Jealousy. Fear. Revenge even."

"But she risked the chance of being found out."

"Indeed. I also was given a letter that said you no longer wanted to see me."

A breath escaped Darcy's mouth. "How cruel of her. Believe me when I say I did not write it."

"How stupid could I have been to believe you had? Forgive me?"

Darcy replied with a look, with a tender glance of her eyes. Ethan faced the ruins. Suddenly he burst forth with passion. "I should have been more of a man. I should have come to you the moment I read that letter."

"Then . . . you were not attached to Miss Roth in any way?"

"Thank God, I was not, nor am I now."

The wind blew keen, and Darcy hugged her arms. Ethan stepped closer, looking concerned. "You are cold. Come, I'll take you back, if you do not mind that we ride together."

She moved on, and reaching the mare, she picked up the reins and turned back to him. He rushed to her, drew her close. "I love you, Darcy. I would live and die for you. Do you believe me?"

She gazed up at him. "I can say—I do."

She hid her head against his breast and held on to the lapels of his coat. He raised her face, and to her lips his melted. He had kissed her once before, but this time it spoke of desperate love, as if the air he breathed depended on her. Tremulous with tears, Darcy put her arms around Ethan and he held her close.

After a moment, he set her back, at arm's length. "There are things I must tell you. I was sworn to secrecy about events that have . . . What I mean to say is, when the opportunity to visit Mr. Rhendon's home in Virginia presented itself, I was urged to accept his invitation with the goal in mind of finding you—to see if you were well cared for and happy."

"My grandmother did this?"

"Madeline knows nothing, asks nothing."

"I should be angry with you, Ethan. But I can tell whatever caused you to swear an oath to be silent, you must have done it out of good intentions."

"With all my heart, Darcy, my intentions were and always will be honorable. Try to understand what I'm about to tell you."

A horse suddenly raced across the fields at breakneck speed toward them, and when its rider crested the slope before them, he drew hard on the reins. The horse reared up and whinnied, then stomped its hooves into the mossy earth.

"Mr. Raverty?" Ethan look surprised. "What brings you out here, sir?"

"I've been sent from Fairview, Mr. Brennan," the breathless rider said. He glanced at Darcy and then gave Ethan a knowing look. "It's urgent you return home without delay. I do not know the reasons, sir."

With haste, Ethan read the note and then shoved it into his pocket. His expression grave, he turned to Darcy. "I must go at once."

"What could be wrong?" Worry swam in the eyes she met.

"I cannot say, but I must hurry." He sprinted to his horse and leaped into the saddle. Then with a swift kick of his heels, he raced off on Sanchet.

Part 3

For nothing is secret that shall not be made manifest; neither any thing hid, that shall not be known and come abroad.
—*Luke 8:17 KJV*

21

$\mathscr{B}$efore Ethan received the urgent message that called him back to Fairview, Eliza sat in her sitting room under the window sketching. She traced from her memory a child's face, then another's, and thought of her two daughters she so loved. Darcy was as close as she would ever be—at Havendale. Ilene, her babe, rested in the arms of God.

A long sigh slipped from her lips and she hung her head within her hands. "Show me, Lord, what I should do. My heart aches to see my child, and you know how I still grieve over Ilene. And Lord, I miss my husband. Wherever he is, please speak into his heart to forgive me."

It was a prayer she had said daily all these years. Waiting for an answer, she lifted her eyes to the scene outside. A carriage lumbered toward the house, halted, and a man dressed in black stepped out. She pressed her brows. Who could he be?

A moment later, Fiona stepped inside the room, her lips pursed, her movements agitated. "A man named Hollen is here, my girl. Should I let him in? I do not like the looks of him." Fiona adjusted her mobcap and waited for Eliza's reply.

Rare to receive a visitor at Fairview. Eliza closed her sketch-book and stood. "What does he want?"

Fiona shrugged. "I do not know. But he says he has business to discuss. He was here once before and spoke to Mr. Ethan."

"Ethan is not here. Send him away."

"I told him Mr. Ethan was not at home, but he insists he will stay until he returns."

"I suppose I will see him." She tidied the crimson throw pillows on the settee, and then smoothed the locks of her hair. Long ago it had been black as midnight, but the years had added silver.

She remained seated when Hollen entered the room, with her hands set on her lap. He paused just inside the door and bowed low to her. He stepped forward, but she stayed him with her hand and then gestured to the chair across from her. Hollen stopped short, stood motionless for a moment, then swayed over to the seat and sat down.

Eliza's hands were clasped, her posture as perfect as a well-bred lady's. "Mr. Brennan is not at home. Is your visit important?"

"It is, madam. Perhaps it is better that I speak to you any-way—privately." He glanced over at Fiona, then back at Eliza. "You see, my visit concerns you."

Curious, Eliza fixed her eyes on the man. "In what way does it concern me, Mr. Hollen? I do not believe we have ever met."

Hollen settled back and drew in a long breath. "We have not, but I have had you described to me." He lifted his finger and made a circular motion with it, directing it to her hair. "I was told you once had raven hair and violet eyes, and that you were very beautiful. May I be so bold as to say you are still to this day?"

Eliza saw the snake lurking behind the warm eyes that stared back at her. "Such comments are reserved for my husband," she said.

"But he is dead. Or should I say separated from you?"

Eliza turned her head aside. She looked over at Fiona, with an expression she knew Fiona would understand. "Fiona, I believe the kettle is whistling. Could you . . ."

Fiona nodded and stepped out. Eliza saw her shadow pause outside the door that she left ajar. *Good. She will listen to every word.*

Hollen went on speaking of things that meant little. Commenting on the room, its arrangement, the furnishings, and then her sketchbook, which he reached over and grasped. He flipped through the pages and praised her drawings. "Ah, this is especially good. Who are these girls? Yours perhaps?"

Shocked by his question, she did not answer. Affronted that he, a total stranger, would look at her drawings without asking, she reached her hand out to him to give it back. When he did so, she set it on her lap, as if to safeguard the memories behind the pictures.

"Why have you come to Fairview, Mr. Hollen?" She would be firm with him. No longer could she abide his flattery—his prying questions and uncomfortable stare.

"I have spoken to young Mr. Brennan, and had hoped to find him at home. But, like I said, it is better that I speak to you, madam. You see," and he leaned forward, a wicked light in his eyes, "I have come to collect payment from him for a number of private letters a client of mine has in his possession—letters written by you, madam, to Hayward Morgan while you lived at Fairview with the late Mr. Brennan."

A cold chill rushed through Eliza. Every muscle in her body stiffened. Her hands tightened around the edge of her sketchbook. "They are forgeries."

"Authentic as the day is long, madam."

"That cannot be. I wrote to my husband in America. How could anyone in England possibly come by them?" *Could Darcy have carried them here? Had Hayward kept them and given them to her? It is not possible.*

"I am here to collect payment for them," said Hollen.

"How much?"

"Six hundred pounds. Five for my client—the rest for my troubles."

She gasped. "We do not have that kind of money. We are poor."

Hollen huffed. "Fairview is a large house. You can come by that amount easily. But do not fear. Perhaps Mr. Brennan has already acquired the money and when he arrives home, he shall give it to me."

She glanced toward the door, saw Fiona's shadow move. "You will excuse me a moment." Avoiding his stare, Eliza went to the door and stepped out. Fiona drew close as she whispered, "Send Mr. Raverty for Ethan. Tell him I am in trouble and need him. He has taken the road leading to Havendale."

Wide-eyed, Fiona touched Eliza's hand. "I fear to leave you alone with that man for a moment, my girl."

"I will be all right. Do not worry."

Eliza turned Fiona toward the front door and the faithful servant hurried away.

When she turned back inside the room, and sat across from Hollen, he looked over at her without an ounce of sympathy. He rose and went to the mirror on the wall. Then he adjusted his neckcloth.

"I'm glad you sent your servant out of the room. But she eavesdropped by the door and should be punished for it." He turned back to her with a proud lift of his head. "Now back to our business."

"How do I know you are not lying to me, Mr. Hollen?" said Eliza. "Your claim is farfetched."

"I have proof." He drew from his coat an uneven stack of yellowed pages, worn at the edges and tied together with coarse brown twine. He flung out his hand and showed her one. She glanced at it and saw the fine handwriting that was her own. With her heart swelling in her breast, she took it in her hand, paused a moment, then unfolded the page. It took her back many years, and she remembered the day she wrote this particular missive. Her eyes drifted down the page.

Forgive me, Hayward, as I have forgiven you. Please allow me to come home. We can begin again with God's help. I know what you did was done in haste and anger. You were hurt and acted on your pain. Do not keep Darcy from me. No matter what I have done, it is wrong to keep her from her mother.

Crushed that Hayward never replied, she refolded the page and fought the burn of tears coming up in her eyes. An old wound had been begun to weep, and she swallowed the hard lump in her throat. There had been no resolution, and she was forced to go these many years without Darcy, forced to hold onto the memory of her face, and the agony of constantly thinking of her, wondering how she fared.

"How did your client come by these?"

"That I do not know."

Bewildered, Eliza gripped the letter until her hand shook. "Is your client Hayward?" *Dear God, let it not be so. Could he add any more salt to this wound I carry?*

"Rest assured he is not. Still, I am not at liberty to reveal his name." Hollen spoke with an air of amusement, but looked as serious as the mission he undertook.

"Whoever he is, he has no right to them. They are my letters. What kind of evil person is your client? And you, for that matter?" Inflamed, Eliza stepped up to Hollen and ripped the letters out of his greasy hand. Then, before he could stop her, she tossed them into the hearth fire. They curled, blackened at the retreating edges.

Hollen's brows shot up and his mouth fell open. "That was pointless, Mrs. Morgan," he shouted. "My client shall be furious."

Eliza put her hands to her breast and glanced at Hollen. "I do not care how he feels."

"You should. He has you in his power to do with you as he pleases."

"The letters are destroyed. He can do nothing to me," she said, trembling.

Hollen muttered under his breath a few harsh words and shook his head. "My client is not an idiot, madam."

"His plan to harm me and extort money from Ethan is over. Now, leave this house at once."

"You think him such a fool as to give me all the letters?"

Shocked, she drew in a breath. "What?"

"There are others in his possession, which he is sure to make known if you do not pay."

"If he is so vile to carry out his threat, he will reap God's judgment for it in the end. I am a woman living in my grief. Has he no sympathy for my despair?"

"The remaining letters shall be given to your daughter, who resides at Havendale for a short while, I am told. It is my understanding you do not wish to make contact with her due to the nature of your sinful life. She would be tainted, no doubt. Since you are refusing my client's offer, she will soon know you are alive, that her father cast you out, and that you have rejected her, knowing she is near. In turn, whatever tender feelings she has had for a mother she thought long in the grave will die. Once she knows the truth, you will be truly and utterly dead to her."

Eliza brushed her hands along the fabric of her gown. Her eyes smarted with tears, and she could find no words to contest Hollen's prediction. The painful cadence that beat in her breast caused her to tremble. From around her throat she freed the tiny gold clasp and handed him her pendant. "This should meet the amount he demands."

She dropped her treasure into Hollen's palm. He glanced down at it, shook his head and handed it back. "What can my client do with this? It would be too inconvenient to find a buyer. You must do that, then give me the money."

She lowered herself to the settee and stared at the fire in a daze, where the flames consumed the letters. She felt light-headed, put her hands to her temples, and pressed into them. She could hear Hollen speaking, as if he were in a tunnel far from her.

"I will wait until Mr. Brennan arrives home," she heard him say. "I have nothing else to do today. Perhaps you should go lie down, madam. You look pale."

Ethan had given Eliza his word that he would not reveal her to Darcy. At one time, while in America, he saw the reasons for it. She used words such as *shame, disgrace*. Eliza believed the childhood memories of a good mother would be shattered and replaced by hate. But now her reasons were no longer valid in Ethan's eyes, and surely not in God's. It would be wrong to keep the truth from Darcy, and he had been prepared to tell her all, until called home on a most urgent matter.

With the emergence of the letters, which Ethan had yet to see, the chance stood firm that Darcy would know the truth sooner or later. Someone possessed the content, and whether he paid for the letters, a threat would exist. What would she then think of him if he concealed the fact her mother resided but a few miles from Havendale?

By the time he reached Fairview, curtains of misty rain swept across the land. Smoke rose from one of the chimneys and vanished before it reached the swift leaden clouds. Outside on the gravel drive stood a rickety carriage drawn by a pair of chestnut nags. They shook their manes and blew vapor from their flaring nostrils. The driver, his coat collar turned up to shield his neck from the drizzle, touched the tip of his tricorn hat to Ethan.

Fiona stood inside the front door wringing her hands. Her brows were drawn down with concern for Eliza. Ethan knew she regretted that she had allowed such a person as Hollen to enter the house in his absence.

"Oh, Mr. Raverty must have raced that old horse of his. You are here so quickly, Mr. Ethan. Good thing you hired him to clean out the stables this season, otherwise I don't know who I would have sent."

"Be sure to give him a double helping tonight." Ethan drew off his hat.

"I will, sir. My girl is in the sitting room with that man," she said, as she followed him inside.

Ethan drew off his coat. "How long has he been here?"

"Too long. I should have told him to go away."

"It is not your fault, Fiona. I am glad you let him in. Now I can deal with him once and for all."

After he patted her hand to comfort her, he headed toward the room where sunrise after sunrise had poured through the windows, painting the walls golden. But on this day, a grim loneliness had entered, and he was determined to slay it.

Ethan's boots stomped over the floor as he pushed open the double doors and walked inside. The curtains were drawn from the windows, and the meager light outside crept in and fell onto Eliza's face. She raised her eyes to meet his. Tears were in them as if all the sorrow of her past had risen up from a silent grave. A festering wound that had long scarred over had been broken open to bleed.

Near her stood Hollen. A smug look on his ignoble face indicated he had had plenty of time to badger poor Eliza into believing her worst days were to come. He had come dressed in the same suit of clothes as before, with his hair flat against his skull. His eyes flickered with false sincerity, while his fleshy, ruddy lips drew tight over yellowed teeth. More repulsive than a snake slithering through tall grass, he rubbed his hands together as if they were cold to the bone.

"Ah, home at last, Mr. Brennan."

"I wasn't expecting you, Hollen—not today. Why are you here?"

"I came to conclude our business," he said, with that scheming grimace that was his smile.

"I should throw you out."

With a tilt forward, Hollen inclined his head. "No need, Mr. Brennan. I was on my way." A triumphant grin passed over Hollen's lips, and he picked up his hat to leave.

Surprised, Ethan glanced at Eliza. "I know everything, Ethan. You need not worry any longer," she said.

"You do not have the money," he said.

"My amethyst necklace can take care of that. You must sell it at once."

"It was a gift from Father."

"Yes, and he would have approved that I use it to remove this burden from us. You understand, do you not?"

Ethan shifted his stare over to the blackmailer. His temper pushed to the brink, he strode over to Hollen and shoved him through the door. "Out, you weasel! Go back to your gutless client."

Hollen turned back to Eliza, bowed, and tipped his hat. "Good day, madam." Then he passed through the door with his shoulders squared, but at a quicker pace. Concerned for Eliza, Ethan called Fiona into the room.

"Strong tea, Fiona, if you please. Eliza is unwell."

She grasped his hand. "Sell my necklace, Ethan. It is to safeguard Darcy. I do not care what they do to me."

"I have just come from her. I was about to tell her everything when I received your message." He sat down beside her.

"Darcy . . ." She looked up at Ethan with a searching gaze. "Is she all right?"

"She grieves for you and her father. I found her at the ruins."

Eliza sighed. "Ah, it must have saddened her."

"She is searching for answers, Eliza. Did you not teach me that the truth sets us free?"

She touched his cheek with her fingertips, smiled, and dropped her hand in her lap. "I have been so wrong—and you so right. During my morning devotions I read this verse in the book of Lamentations. It has stayed with me all morning, and now I know why. "*I am in torment within, and in my heart I am disturbed.*" God help me, Ethan. I must make things right with Darcy."

Ethan kissed her cheek. "Tomorrow morning I will ride to Havendale and bring her back with me. Prepare yourself to meet with her. She is to be my wife."

22

After Darcy watched Ethan ride off, she made her way back to Havendale at a slow pace under a turbulent sky. Her heart overflowed with emotion and her thoughts brimmed with joy. Ethan loved her, adored and cherished her. His heart had been as broken as hers, and now healed, they could love again. So filled with elation, she could have fallen on her knees there in the grass and praised God that the truth behind their misfortune had come to light.

After she settled the mare, she passed inside the house unseen. Quiet prevailed in every room. The only sound within came from the clocks ticking on the mantelpieces. Upstairs she passed her grandmother's room and peeked inside the door. Just as she had left her, Madeline sat in her chair asleep. Not wishing to disturb her, Darcy went on to her room.

She penned a letter to Martha about the events of the day and imagined the excitement her cousin would feel while reading her letter. Darcy pictured her seated alongside the rest of the family in the cozy sitting room reading it out loud. They'd all pay rapt attention. Darcy smiled and set the quill down, sealed the letter, and set it beside another to her Aunt Mari and Uncle Will.

"I wonder if they miss me as much as I miss them." She placed the letters on a silver dish at the edge of the desk. Mrs. Burke would take them to be posted later. At suppertime, she went downstairs, entered the kitchen, and inhaled the comforting scent of apples, nutmeg, and cinnamon. Mrs. Burke was preparing a tray for Madeline.

"She says she hasn't the strength to come down the stairs." Her brow wrinkled, and she shook her head.

Darcy picked up a napkin from the table. "Shall I go up and sit with her?"

"No need. Stay here by the fire. I need you to watch that pie for me. Can't let the crust burn." Taking a plate down from the rack, Mrs. Burke heaved a breath. "How was your outing?"

"Wonderful." Darcy popped an apple slice Mrs. Burke had missed into her mouth.

"On a day like today? So dreary and you say wonderful? You are full of life, Miss Darcy. Most would not venture out on the moors in this weather. It must be the adventurous spirit you inherited from your father."

And my mother.

Darcy's stomach gurgled with hunger. She sat in the chair before the fire and pulled bits of bread from a loaf and dipped them into the butter dish. The butter had melted from the heat, and tasted sweet on her tongue. Mrs. Burke set a plate of roast beef and braised carrots in front of her.

"I won't see you waste away. Now eat up."

Darcy had more than the desire for food tonight. Her mind raced with thoughts of Ethan—Ethan and his sultry eyes, his loving kiss, his warm embrace.

Mrs. Burke smiled. "It does me good to see you eat so well. Not like Mr. Langbourne, who hasn't a care, neither the courtesy to inform me when he will be home. His rule is that meals always be ready for him in case he does arrive."

"But that could be days," said Darcy.

"Days? Often weeks or months. And then I don't know if Miss Charlotte will be returning with him or not."

"He was just here, and he has left again?"

Mrs. Burke pressed her mouth hard and narrowed her eyes. Her stiff gestures told Darcy she did not care for Langbourne or approve of his behavior. Although she was in Madeline's employ, Langbourne was lord over Havendale. She had to obey him, whether she liked it or not. He had the power to throw any servant out if he pleased, and she wondered how long he would tolerate her visit. Would he command her to leave?

"He came home while you were out. He looked angry. Stomped about, shoving past me as if I were not to be considered. He questioned me about the tramp I've seen, asked if he'd been around. I dare not say. I avoid him when he is that way, and so should you. He left the house again with those men that do only the Almighty God knows what kind of business."

The vinegary housekeeper pushed through the kitchen door with the tray, while Darcy stared out the window and watched the clouds drift apart. A misty sky surrounded Havendale, pale blue, muted gray on the horizon. Would it bring snow, or would the wind shove the clouds off and leave the sky cold and barren?

Cupping her chin in hand, she wondered where Langbourne had gone. What kind of business drew him away? How could he stay so long apart from Charlotte? Not once had Darcy seen Charlotte smile. Perhaps he kept a mistress somewhere and Charlotte suspected it. Obviously, he did not love his wife, and Darcy felt sorry for Charlotte.

Her thoughts turned to Ethan. He had looked so troubled when he rode off. It must have been something of great importance that drew him away. And so she spoke a quiet prayer for him—and for those in his household. She felt the urge to go to her grandmother's room and tell her where she had been and that Ethan had declared his feelings for her. But Mrs. Burke returned.

"Madeline's tired tonight, more than usual." Mrs. Burke set the tray down on the table. The small china plate that had slices of cheese on it was missing.

Darcy shoved her plate aside. "Did she ask for me?"

"She did, but only that she wondered where you had been all day."

As Mrs. Burke spoke, a zephyr whipped up outside and rattled the windows in the kitchen. She paused, then said, "I did see that man again today—the tramp. I beckoned him from the window to come near. I'd given the poor soul food through the window, but he turned and walked away."

"I believe he is the same man I have seen." She went on to tell Mrs. Burke about the day on the moors, and then the Brightons' affair. "Mr. Langbourne made me promise not to say anything. But since you have already seen him, I had to tell you."

"I'm glad you did, miss. Perhaps we can help him together."

"At the Brightons', I was close enough to him to see he is sick and starving."

"Dear me," said Mrs. Burke. "You must have been frightened."

"He did not hurt me or anyone else. But he thought he knew me, or that I looked like someone he knew."

With a start, Mrs. Burke's brows shot up. "He did? That is indeed strange. From now on you should not go out alone."

Darcy smiled a little. "I am not afraid. If I should see him again, I'll urge him to accept some food from us. It would be the right thing to do."

"But there are others who would fear for you, miss. You should not cause any to worry. So, if you should see him again, do not approach."

How could she do such a thing? If the man were hungry, she should feed him. If he were cold, she should give him warmth. Would it be so dangerous to give a cup of cold water to one so thirsty?

As she pondered all this, the fire in the hearth flickered against the gusts that raced down the flue. Gray ash scattered out onto the flagstone floor. The wind whispered and moaned through crack and crevice as night fell. She walked down the hallway with a candle to light her way. Loneliness for Ethan and home weighed heavy upon her, as the cold darkness swallowed the remnants of the day.

The golden flame of her candle caught Darcy's eyes. It reminded her that hope lived as long as it had an open heart to beat in. Past a large window, she approached her grandmother's bedroom. Weak candlelight edged the threshold in a thread of amber. She smelled the age-old scent of rosewater, heard her speaking to Maxwell as if he were her child.

After a quiet tap, Darcy turned the brass handle and moved the door in. Madeline lay in bed with her Bible in hand, spectacles poised on the tip of her nose, and Maxwell curled up at her feet. The dog lifted its head and pricked its ears when he saw Darcy, then whimpered. Madeline looked over at Darcy and gave her a weak smile.

"May I come in, Grandmother? Mrs. Burke said you are tired. But I wanted to see you before I retire to my room."

"I thought you had forgotten me, Darcy."

"I could never do that," Darcy said, shutting the door behind her.

"I have not seen you since you went to Bentmoor. Tell me about it. Was it a pleasant evening? Did you meet a lot of people?"

"I enjoyed the music immensely." She sat on the edge of the bed. "But a gentleman stepped on my hem and tore it." She could smile at it now.

Madeline huffed. "How dreadful. How unfortunate. You left, of course."

"Shortly afterwards, yes." Darcy decided not to mention the poor sojourner. It would alarm her grandmother, cause uneasiness, and Madeline would be against Darcy accepting any more invitations to Bentmoor. She worried whenever Darcy ventured out alone. To be kept inside four walls and a patch of ground could not be borne. Her adventuresome spirit would suffer and she'd go mad with boredom. Silence regarding the wanderer meant her freedom. So she held her tongue.

As far as Ethan, she would inform her grandmother that they were in love. What her reaction would be Darcy was uncertain.

"So that is all there is to tell?" Madeline closed her Bible and set it aside.

"I'm afraid the rest would bore you."

"I see. Well, then. Tell me where you went today. When I asked Burke she said you were out exploring, not a soul knew where to."

"I went to St. Anthony's. You know, the little church on the moor where my grandfather preached."

A strange color washed over Madeline's face. Her eyes blinked, and her spectacles fell off her nose onto her lap. "Oh? I suppose you saw the burned-down vicarage."

"I did. I think it must have been a lovely home at one time. I imagine it was welcoming and many people came to visit, to be encouraged and prayed for."

Madeline sighed. "My late husband should have had the ruins cleared away years ago and the house rebuilt. But he had no interest in doing so. Neither has Langbourne."

"I know the story of the young vicar, his wife, and daughter," Darcy said.

Surprise lit up Madeline's gray eyes. "How? No one speaks of it."

"Ethan Brennan of Fairview came riding along while I stood by the wall. He said the vicar had been his father, and that it was his mother and sister who perished. He also told me my mother grew up in that house."

Shutting her eyes, Madeline turned away. "I cannot remember much of the past, especially the people in it. It is like a fog in my mind most days."

Darcy paused a moment and gazed at her grandmother's face. By her features, Darcy knew Madeline had been a beauty in her prime. She watched her raise her hand to her temple and with her fingertips move a lock of hoary hair back from her face. She pulled down the white mobcap that covered her crown. Dressed in a white nightgown, a wrap of white wool she wore around her shoulders. Even her bedcovers and sheets were white, her pillows and the curtains that hung from the canopy. It was as if she were wrapped in snow. Or was it a symbol of purity?

"Some things are better forgotten." Madeline said. "Better left in the past where they belong. I think God made it that way so we would not be so sad when we age. For it seems he made us to remember happier times, don't you think?"

Darcy nodded. "I believe so."

"And when you get as old as I, you feel you have known all you are capable of knowing, depending on how keen a mind God gave you. Remembering to get through life is what matters." A smile brightened Madeline's face and she chuckled. "You must think I am on the edge of madness, Darcy."

"Not at all. You are wise, Grandmother."

"Hmm, perhaps, but not enough. There are things I should have done differently. But that is the way of things. We leap before we look." She laid her hand across Darcy's. "I pray you never do that, my girl. Always think carefully before making a decision."

"I try to use both my head and heart."

Madeline pressed her lips firm. "Ah, the heart. That seems to be an American notion. Here in England, we upper class strive to use our logic in situations of the heart. I hear that in America, class matters not and people marry whomever they please. Do you understand what I mean?"

"I do. But in America the rich are not apt to marry a person of lower distinction—unless they are madly in love and cannot help themselves."

Madeline laughed. "My, my. What things must go on. But seriously, Darcy, you mustn't go to the ruins again. It is too sad a place, and as for Ethan Brennan—I can see you love him by the mere mention of his name. He just may be the one for you."

"Have you met him?" Darcy asked quietly.

"Not in person."

"Then how do you know whether he is a good match for me?"

"I knew his parents. I met them at church when they arrived. She was a charming woman. Her death was tragic."

Darcy cocked her head. "Ethan told me his father found good company later in life. She soothed his grief by being his companion and a governess to Ethan."

"You think her noble, do you?"

"Indeed, I think she must be."

"I shall say this much. I recall there was a great deal of insipid tongue wagging. I cannot remember why, or even her name. . . . I remember so little of the whole event. Yet, I have a feeling Ethan told you too much."

"He told me he loves me."

"Loves you? Oh, my."

"We met last summer, in Virginia." Darcy told Madeline the details about the gathering at Twin Oaks, how he almost ran over her with Sanchet, how he saved her from a near drowning, and that they both believed God had brought them together again. Madeline looked confused and fussed with the trim on her wrap. Her brows pinched and she worked her mouth to find the words to reply.

Darcy squeezed her grandmother's hand. "Do not worry."

Madeline's eyes grew misty. "It is not that. I refuse to worry, for you are to leave for home soon and Mr. Brennan shall remain at Fairview. Unless . . ."

"He has not asked me."

"But he might. And what will you do then?"

"I will accept."

"Buy your wedding clothes, Darcy." Madeline wiped her eyes. "I think I shall pass on soon."

"Oh, please, do not say that. Do not cry."

"I am tired, Darcy. I miss my husband. I prayed to see you before I leave this world because you were my Hayward's only child. I am happy to have had that prayer answered. But

Hayward—how I longed to have seen him again. But I doubt I ever shall."

Though flattered, Darcy felt sad that Madeline had no interest in the other girls or in seeing Uncle Will. She could not understand the reasons. "I wish with all my heart you could meet your other granddaughters and see Uncle Will again. I think you would like Aunt Mari, his wife."

"I was so young when I had William, and having not seen him these many years has practically erased his face in my mind."

Her words pricked Darcy. "That is something I shall pray returns."

"I loved William, but your father—he was my favorite child, and I asked for you because you are a part of him. He left without saying good-bye. He knew we would not approve of him marrying Eliza. She was beneath him, you see. So he was gone. My husband sought him out, found him, but it was too late. They had taken their vows."

Darcy embraced her. The old woman trembled in her arms, then pulled away. Such expressions of affection were not normal at Havendale.

Madeline patted down her coverlet. "Why did he not come with you?"

Her memory slipped again, but Darcy was patient. "My father journeyed west, Grandmother. No one has seen or heard from him since—not even Uncle Will."

"And that has pained you, hasn't it, Darcy?"

"Yes. I cannot understand why he abandoned me, and why he left River Run to decay. Uncle Will lives close by, but why he did not take it over I do not understand."

"Perhaps Hayward asked him not to."

"That may be. I want to believe what I've been told, that my father could not bear the loss of my mother, nor take care of me alone."

Madeline straightened her back. "I am glad Hayward left you with William. No doubt he has been a father to you, Mari a mother, and your cousins sisters."

"They are my family in every sense of the word."

"You miss them?"

"Yes, very much."

"Thank the Lord, Hayward did not take you with him. Think of the hardships you would have suffered."

"I fear I would have become even more savage than what Charlotte said I was."

A burst of understanding came to Darcy, and she pondered her grandmother's words. All these years she had felt unwanted, unloved, and forgotten. But now she realized that her father loved her so much, he left her with the Breeses. She had a roof over her head, food to eat, and a family. Although the world beyond River Run fascinated her, Hayward had done the right thing in leaving her behind. But that he ran from his troubles by losing himself in the backwoods worried her.

She picked up her grandmother's hands, cupping hers around the crooked fingers. They were cold. "I am sorry he hurt you by leaving the way he did. I'm sure he never meant to."

"His love for the place you call River Run was stronger than his attachment to me," Madeline said. "Do you care about that place?"

Drawn back to the land and river she loved, Darcy felt a yearning so deep within her soul, a summons to return, that a long, deep breath slipped from her lips. Would Ethan go with her, back to the place where they first fell in love?

"I care as if it were my life," she answered.

Madeline laid her hand on Darcy's shoulder. "Then you must go back to the place you love most, and remember me as you saw me—alive, and happy to have seen you, for I have seen my lost son in your eyes. Havendale is not for you. It is depressing, full of ill, and Langbourne is its master."

23

*S*trong gusts of wind shook Darcy awake, rattling the windows, causing the walls of her room to shudder, and hurling across Havendale like the waves of a boiling sea. She sat up in bed. Goosebumps bristled over her skin, and she glanced about the room. It had been a dream, but so real.

She began to remember—how her palm pressed against window glass, how the frost outlined her fingers, the tree with its heavy branches casting long shadows over patches of stiff brown grass, a silent sentinel on a winter's night. Her swing glided back and forth on thick ropes encrusted with ice. Darkness and moonlight. A woman's figure crossing the yard. Her cloak fanning out in the wind, flying forward around her legs. Gusts blew back her hood. Flaming red hair, illuminated like tongues of fire by the flame that flickered in a lantern near a hitching post.

She remembered creeping to the door in a pair of scratchy woolen stockings. Voices were outside in the hallway. Footsteps clattered up the staircase. Shadows moved on the wall. Muddy footprints marred the polished floor. Two figures disappeared into a room at the end of a passage. A shaft of candlelight spread out across the Turkish runner. She walked toward it.

Inching around the door, she saw her mother, her ebony hair, rich as the night sky, cascading past lean shoulders. Long strands covered her face as she grimaced in pain. Brilliant white teeth clenched, her eyes shut tight, her hands tearing at the bed sheets. That night, fear rose in Darcy and she remembered how she inched back after covering her ears to block out her mother's cries. And there was another woman who stood by, holding Eliza's hand, with a white mobcap over her hair.

A mist filled Darcy's eyes, and when she blinked them back she saw an infant, wet and coated, squirming in the gentle arms of the cloaked woman. Her name was Sarah—the woman who bent down to her, her face like an angel's. Darcy stepped down the hallway toward the staircase. Moonlight streamed through a side window and spread over the floor. Darcy called to Sarah and waited.

"Little miss. You should be abed," Sarah scolded. "Is it the wind? Has it frightened you?"

"I'm not scared."

She gazed up at the bundle in Sarah's arms. "Can I see?"

Sarah moved the blanket aside. Damp soft curls clung to the baby's head and a mew passed through the bow mouth. "She's pretty, isn't she? Skin the color of cream and cheeks rosy as dawn."

She remembered how bewildered the event had made her feel, how in her innocent way she had asked, "Is this Mama's baby?"

How she could have forgotten the sad look in Sarah's face she did not know, nor the reply to her question. "This is my babe," Sarah had told her. "Her name is Ilene. You understand?"

The answer had confused Darcy. "Then where is Mama's baby?"

Red spirals tumbled over Sarah's shoulders. "You ask your mother when you are older. But she'll tell you, she has no babe except you."

In all these years, Darcy had not forgotten the little girl with the bubbly giggle and shining eyes. She had not understood why Ilene had left the world so young—why she had left her. She remembered Fiona and her motherly ways and Sarah's kindness as well as the wistful gaze in her eyes. Her mother's face she could not recall, only the flowing hair and a voice that soothed her when she was afraid.

Fully awake, her heart ached with the visions. She clutched the front of her nightdress and yearned for Ethan—longed for home where her memories were born. Unable to sleep, she rose and dressed. Second best, the olive-green linen flowed past her waist. She slipped on her stockings and shoes. Then she brushed her hair back so it flowed down to her waist. *He'll come today—Ethan.*

She crossed the floor to her window and gazed out at the moon hanging behind drifting clouds. A few hours and the sun would rise. Then a frantic voice called to her out in the hallway and Mrs. Burke opened the door. "Dear me," she huffed and puffed her cheeks in and out. "Come quick. 'Tis your grandmother."

When Darcy hurried into Madeline's room, it lay in darkness save for a little light from the vermillion coals in the grate. Darcy groped her way to her, her bare feet not making a sound along the old rug. Maxwell sat by the hearth and looked up. Madeline opened her eyes and a soft cry poured from her lips.

"Hayward. Oh, my son, Hayward."

Darcy leaned over. "Grandmother. I am here. What is it?"

Madeline searched for Darcy's hand. Once she found it she gripped it with what Darcy knew was all the strength she could muster. "I have seen him. I have seen Hayward."

Troubled, Darcy touched Madeline's cheek. "A dream, Grandmother. Papa is far away in America."

"No. No. I saw him, I tell you. I saw him as real as I see you. He spoke to me, told me he was sorry for hurting me. He asked if I would forgive him."

A chill passed through Darcy and she glanced at Mrs. Burke as she stood near the bed wringing her hands in her robe. "Please bring a glass of port, Mrs. Burke." And off the serving woman went.

"Darcy, please. You must believe me," Madeline said.

"Tell me what happened. I am listening."

"I was asleep, and the wind woke me. I looked over and saw the curtains at the terrace doors flutter, and then he stepped into the room. I did not know him at first and was so frightened I could not call out. He then said to me 'Mother, it is I, Hayward.' When he drew closer, I saw his face. It was Hayward. How could I forget my child's eyes?"

"He told you his name?" Darcy's hand trembled in her grandmother's. From head to toe her body surged with both fear and elation. Could it be true? Could it really be him?

"He called me *Mother*, Darcy. Is that not enough for me to know? And his voice—it was the same, yet older. And yes, he said he was Hayward. As I beheld him, he lifted me gently by my shoulders and spoke. I scarce heard what he was saying, for I was so alarmed. I went to throw my arms about him, but when he heard Burke's footsteps, he staggered back, and as she entered he slipped out the doors into the dark. He is ill, Darcy. What shall we do?"

"I shall find him."

"How? Tell me. You cannot go out on the moors at night."

"Do not worry."

As if a seam in the clouds had split open, rain beat down on the house. Moments ago the moon had shone. Now a swift-moving storm overtook it, and the room chilled with the wind flying through Madeline's terrace doors. The curtains rose as if arms flung them to the ceiling. Darcy hurried to them, shut and latched the doors tight. But before she did, she peered out across the terrace and to the steps that led down to the lawn. Beyond it stood the stable. No one was in sight. But when she moved back, there on the floor were muddy footprints. Her heart swelled in her throat.

"Perhaps he is close by," said Madeline, growing more desperate. She twisted the edge of her sheet between her aged hands. "He may have found shelter in the stable and is afraid to come back to the house for fear we will not believe him. And he knows what Langbourne would do to him if he did. That is why he came through to my room, and not the front door."

Darcy moved back to the bedside. "But Langbourne is not here."

Mrs. Burke returned with the glass of port. As she guided the glass into Madeline's hand, she spoke calmly to her. "There, there. All shall be well."

The port moistened Madeline's lips. "I saw my son, Burke. You believe me, don't you? Not William. No, it was Hayward."

"Of course I believe you. Rest now." And she drew the blankets up closer to Madeline's chin. Darcy drew her aside and gave her a questioning look.

Mrs. Burke shook her head. "There was no one."

"But the doors were still open when I came in, and there are muddy footprints on the floor. Go look."

"The wind, Miss Darcy. The latch has never been too secure. And those prints could be made from the dust on the floor and the rain coming inside."

Darcy looked back at the doors. She knew Mrs. Burke to be wrong. "Poor Grandmamma."

"I hear you!" Madeline threw her hands to her face and broke into tears. "You both think I am mad. Or that I was dreaming."

"A dream perhaps," Mrs. Burke said. "But not mad."

Darcy gathered the old woman in her arms to calm her. Madeline's frail body trembled as if all the emotions of a lifetime had broken forth. She drew back from Darcy. "Go find him, Darcy. He cannot be far."

Maxwell leapt up from his spot and with a growl scampered out the door. Darcy looked after him as he raced down the hallway to the staircase. Something drew him, alerted him to a presence.

She stepped out into the hallway and took up her candle. Worried that the man who could be her father had gone out into the storm, she hurried down the hallway to the staircase. Downstairs she hastened to don her cloak, slipped on her leather walking shoes, lit a tin lantern from the candlewick, and took from a hook on the wall a flintlock pistol in case she was wrong. With her heart pounding, she drew her hood over her hair, then lifted the bar over the door and pulled it open.

If it is true he is my father, God help me find him. Rain and a hungry wind struck her as she walked out into the torrential night rain.

24

Ahead, Maxwell barked and darted forward. Darcy raised the lantern and watched the dog run to and fro. Frantic, he sniffed the ground, then pricked his sharp ears and growled without showing barred teeth. Darcy moved forward, her shoes sinking into the rainwater pooling in the grass. Rain pelted her face and dripped from her lashes.

Maxwell circled, then sprinted toward the stable, stopped, and barked. Darcy froze when a dark form moved near the door. He backed up, his knees buckled and his body shook violently. She held the lantern high to see his face, brown as the mud that splattered his worn boots. His hair lay matted against his head, dripping and soaked.

Darcy stared. *The man from Bentmoor.*

He raised his hand before his eyes against the glare of the lantern's light.

"I will not hurt you," Darcy said over the din of rain. "Are you Hayward Morgan?"

"I am. Please . . . I have come a long way."

It could not be helped, the tears, the pain of seeing him again, of trying to remember. Her breath hurried as she gazed into her father's troubled eyes. She hurried to him, took hold of his arm and guided him toward the house. "You are ill. Come inside." He stiffened and hesitated. "Come. You cannot stay out here."

Through mud and puddles, they reached the door. Mrs. Burke stopped short midway on the stairs, her face one of shock. "Lord, have mercy. She was right."

"Mrs. Burke . . ." Darcy feared her father would collapse in her arms.

"Thank the Almighty, Miss Darcy. If he had wandered out on the moor in this weather, the Lord only knows what could have become of him, the poor soul."

Darcy looked at the face of a man ravaged by the years. "He needs a warm fire, a bed, and medicine. We must take him to one of the rooms upstairs."

Mrs. Burke's feet tramped down the stairs as quick as they could carry her. She shut the door to the wind and rain, and helped Darcy bring Hayward up the staircase. So weak, the toe of his boots bumped against the edges of one step, then the next.

"We must take him to the east wing, Miss Darcy, on the uppermost floor." Mrs. Burke slipped her arm beneath Hayward's. "It is closed off. No one goes there. The farthest room would be best, in case Mr. Langbourne should return. He will not know Mr. Hayward is there as long as we keep him quiet."

When they reached the upper floor, Madeline met them. She shivered in her nightclothes and cap. Her gray eyes glistened bright with tears as she beheld her prodigal son.

Darcy looked at her. "I have him, Grandmother. Do not be afraid. Mrs. Burke and I will take good care of him."

With outstretched arms, Madeline stepped forward, and once she reached her son, she placed her hands around his face and lifted it. "Hayward, 'tis you." She kissed his forehead, then his cheeks. "Oh, my son, my son."

The room they brought Hayward to had not been slept in, in many a year. Heavy curtains hung over the windows. Dust lay thick on the furnishings. Darcy helped her father to a chair and drew off his wet coat. A fire soon roared to a great red mound in the fireplace, and heat chased the deep chill from the room.

Mrs. Burke shoveled a few hot coals into a bed warmer and placed it beneath the bedcovers. "Thank goodness we kept some of Mr. Hayward's clothes. I will get them."

Madeline stood beside her son's chair, and while they waited for Mrs. Burke to return, Darcy knelt down and drew off her father's boots. His feet were cold and pale. She rubbed them between her hands. Then she took up his hands and chafed each until his skin blushed. These she remembered. They had changed little—still strong and manly—large enough to cover hers.

Her eyes beheld Madeline's and understood the need for silence, to listen to the quiet murmur of Hayward's breathing and the crackle of the fire. Within minutes, Mrs. Burke returned with an armload of clothing. Among them, Darcy found a warm nightshirt and a pair of woolen socks.

Madeline touched her son's cheek. "His hair has grayed." And she brushed it away from his forehead. After so long, after years of living with an aching heart, her mother's love for Hayward remained steadfast. It touched Darcy, and a light smile crept over her lips.

With Mrs. Burke's help, Darcy removed her father's tattered clothes. So filthy were they, that Mrs. Burke burned them. His skin had molted beneath his shirt, and a thick scar crossed his left shoulder. "He fought in the Revolution," she told her grandmother and Mrs. Burke when their mouths fell open at the sight.

"Oh, he was wounded." Madeline's fingers trembled as she touched her son. "I have seen such wounds before. It is a wonder he survived at all."

Darcy washed away the grime that had hardened into his wrinkles. His eyes opened and found hers. A light broadened within them.

"I saw you before—at another place. Many people were there. You were dressed like an angel, Eliza." His voice, weak and raspy, stunned her as if it were the first time she had ever heard him speak.

"I am Darcy, your daughter."

"Darcy? Darcy, my little girl?"

"Yes, Papa."

He grabbed her hand, pressed her fingers to his lips, and kissed them. "I left you with William. I hoped you'd understand why."

Darcy leaned in. "You did what was best for me. For that, I should be thanking you. Uncle Will and Aunt Mari have taken good care of me, as if I were their own. And my cousins are my sisters."

He touched her cheek. "God has led me to you. I have thought of you day and night ever since I left River Run. My heart has ached being apart from you."

"Then why did you leave me? Why did you not stay? I needed you."

"My heart was crushed within me. I retreated, tried to lose myself in the wilderness. Forgive me if you can."

Darcy gave no reply. Her heart wanted to forgive and forget. But her mind could not let go—not yet. There were so many unanswered questions. Her soul called out to the One who could help her. Forgiving would be hard, and she needed strength to do it.

Hayward looked at Madeline. "Mother, I am sorry for the pain I caused you. It was long ago. But no doubt you still remember."

"Shh. Lie still," she said.

"I loved Eliza. I had to leave her. She was a good wife, until . . ." He trailed off and looked back at Darcy. "You shall despise me for what I've done, Darcy."

"Enough talk, Papa. You must rest."

"Please, you must let me tell you."

She paused, saw the plea in his eyes, and could not forbid him. "All right, I am listening. But no matter what you say, I cannot hate you, Papa. It isn't in me to despise anyone."

"You call your cousins your sisters. You had another, you know."

Surprised by this, she stood back. "I do not remember a sister. I only remember Ilene—a little."

"Ilene was your mother's child. But not mine. Now do you see?"

Shock rippled through Darcy. "Ilene? I remember I loved her, Papa. But you say she was not yours?"

"I went away to war," Hayward said. "I was captured and sentenced to a prison ship. My brother was told I had been hanged. Will wrote to your mother, and in her grief another man comforted her—led her astray. She thought I was dead."

"How awful. Poor mother." Darcy fought the tight feeling in her throat.

"She had a girl living at River Run. Sarah was her name. She tried to guard the child, tried to protect Eliza and you. But I found out the truth and hated her for it, her and Eliza."

Darcy lowered her head and tried to absorb what he told her. She could not speak, but when Madeline laid a gentle hand over her shoulder, she reached up and held the aged hand. They would pass through this storm together, and Darcy felt comforted to have the support of her grandmother.

"I never told Will and Mari about this, Darcy. So do not wonder why they never spoke of it. I deceived them, as I have deceived everyone."

She looked at him, dread sinking into her. "What happened to my mother? Why did you not put a stone over her grave?"

Hayward moaned and wiped his eyes. "Your mother did not die, as I led you and others to believe."

"But—later? She died later?"

"No. I sent her away."

"Why would you do that? What could she have done to deserve such rejection?"

"I could not bear her betrayal."

"Where did you send her?"

"Back to England. That is why I am here. I want to find her."

"Why did she not reach out to me?"

"Her shame prevented her, my child. And you were so young . . ."

"Where is she?"

"The last I knew, at a place called Fairview."

"Fairview?" The name fell from her lips bittersweet.

Hayward struggled to rise. "Please—let me tell you everything. There is more."

"More?" Darcy clenched her hands. "How could you have lied to me?"

Her grandmother stepped up to her. "Darcy, please, try to hear your father out. It is the only way to know what has happened."

"I was bitter, but did not want to hurt you," Hayward said.

"How could you have left me to grow up believing Mother was dead? I have lived with that image of her lying still on the bed and you telling me she would not go to heaven. Did she deserve such condemnation from you? Did I deserve to have that planted in my mind?"

"As God is my witness, no. She was no harlot, no man's mistress. She fell, and I should have forgiven her when she pleaded for forgiveness." He hung his head. "I should have never said what I said to you. It was wrong—cruel."

Darcy stared at him, wishing she could cry. But the pain cut so deep she could not. "Did I deserve to be torn from my mother?"

"I meant to hurt her, not you. I wanted to protect you."

"But I was injured by it. To have lived all this time without her . . ."

"She wrote to you."

"When?"

"You were little. I kept your letters along with the letters she wrote to me. When I arrived in Derbyshire, I had the misfortune of running into Langbourne. He threw me from Havendale, took the letters, and said he would kill me if I ever set foot here again."

"Then he must have hidden them somewhere in the house—downstairs in his study."

"Or burned them," Mrs. Burke interjected. "I've seen him do that often enough. He has a mistress in Castleton, and whenever she sends him word to come to her, he burns her messages."

So that is where he had been, instead of in Meadlow with Charlotte. How sad for her that her husband gave himself to another. She wondered if Charlotte felt abandoned. Did she know of Langbourne's betrayal? She looked at her father, and realized he had been through the same thing as Charlotte, except it had not been when he was with Eliza, but away. Charlotte had no children, and only God knew if Langbourne had any. Her mother had brought a child into the world. It was a pity her father could not have forgiven her and had compassion for her.

Hayward called to her when she headed for the door. "The letters are lost to me, but her words are seared in my mind."

She turned back. "Words that begged for forgiveness, no doubt."

"Yes. In the wilderness, I prayed for you and for the wife I wronged. I met God there. He cast down my hard heart. I have repented, Darcy, of what I did to my mother here, to my wife, to you. You believe me, don't you?"

Her heart swelled when she saw the sorrow within his eyes. "I do, Papa."

"It has been my hope to return to River Run with your mother and begin our lives over again as a family."

"How can you expect her to go back with you?"

Hard as the truth was to accept, the penance in her father's gaze and the heartrending plea in his voice scored Darcy to the quick. Tears stung and the pain of being lied to, of secrets kept from her, crawled up her throat in a ragged sigh. She strode back to the door.

Hayward called to her, "Darcy, forgive your mother and me." She turned and looked at him.

"I have many things to think about." She walked out and closed the door behind her.

At the end of the corridor stood a latticed window. She hurried to it, shook and pulled at the latch until it opened. A rush of bitter air blew against her. She drew it into her lungs in deep gulps. Gripping the sill, she stared out at the land and saw veils of mist twist across the lawn, around the bases of trees. The rain had ended and a frigid line of purple clouds skimmed the horizon.

Did Ethan know that the woman living in his father's house was her mother? Did her mother know she had come to England? Had Ethan told her? Darcy balled her fists. She stared forward, her breath heaving. On the moor, near the charred ruins, he said he had something important to tell her. Then he was called away—back to Fairview.

Darcy's emotions overwhelmed her, and she grasped the latch to close the window. But the wind fought against her. Finally able to shove the latch in place, she stepped away and turned. Her grandmother stood in the doorway beside Mrs. Burke. Both women looked concerned, shaken by the event. They stepped aside and Darcy passed back into the room. Hayward looked over at her, forlorn.

She stood at the edge of the bed, her mind drifting toward the vague images of the past. "If there is anything else you need to tell me, speak now. You may not have another chance, Papa. Do your best to gain my forgiveness, for it is a hard thing for me to do at the moment."

She remained silent, and listened to every stutter, every bumbling word, and every explanation he made. Strange as it seemed, despite her heartache, a burden lifted within her as the minutes went by, one that had been there all her life.

25

$\mathscr{S}$unrise came without rain, and like most mornings with birds singing and fog drifting across the land in sheer ribbons. But for Darcy, when she looked over at her father as he slept, the new day had become a new start. She did not think he would make it through the night. But color had returned to his face and his chest moved up and down evenly. She stood from the chair, and with one hand rubbed the back of her neck. Soundless, she stepped from the room, and went down the hall. Mrs. Burke was coming up the staircase.

"A package arrived a moment ago for you, miss. 'Tis here on the corner of my tray."

Darcy lifted the small package wrapped in brown paper and twine and looked at the handwriting. Ethan. Recent events had not distracted her longing for him. A gift from him caused her to smile and she wondered what it could be.

"Do you think your father can manage a dish of soft eggs and a cup of savory broth?" Mrs. Burke asked.

"I hope so. Whatever you can do to build his strength will help, Mrs. Burke."

"Well, I'll sit with him a while. You take a pause." Down the corridor to his room she trudged, with her tray of eggs and beef broth.

Darcy sat on a step and pulled loose the twine and paper. "A book. *Wildflowers of England.* He remembered. How lovely." Her mind drifted back to that day in the field along the Potomac, where she gathered specimens for her uncle. He had gone with her, and it was there, beneath the shadows of the trees, he kissed her for the first time.

She poised the book, bound in royal blue leather, the pages edged in gold leaf, in her palm. A note attached read, "*I cannot endure the hours without you. My heart is, and forever will be, yours. Ethan.*"

She pressed the book and note to her breast and felt the beat of her heart. "So much to think about, Lord," she whispered. "But oh, I am thankful he loves me."

Patter grew louder behind her. She turned on the step. Maxwell panted at the landing, looked down at her with his glossy black eyes, and wagged his tale. When she stood, he whined and scampered away. She followed him to her grandmother's room, where he scratched on the door.

Madeline sat in an armchair in front of the window. Sunlight bathed her face and sparkled through the scent bottles on her dressing table. A wool blanket covered her lap and legs. With a slight smile, she looked over at Darcy and motioned for her to come near. Darcy saw a change in Madeline—her gaze brighter, happier. Not the usual forlorn stare.

"Come draw up a chair and sit with me, Darcy."

"Are you well today, Grandmother?"

"I am. Yet my body is tired—so tired." Wincing, Madeline shifted in her seat. The blanket slipped, and Darcy adjusted it for her.

From a corner, she drew forward a chair covered in olive green fabric. "Did you not sleep well?"

"I dreamed much." Madeline sighed. "I saw my husband."

"Mr. Morgan?"

Madeline smiled, eyes shut. "No. My first love . . . William's father. He told me he has waited for me a long time. Then I saw Mr. Morgan. He was young and looked happy. Perhaps he is content that Hayward has come home. How is my son?"

"He is doing the best we can hope for. Mrs. Burke is with him."

"Ah, Mrs. Burke is the best of servants. I do not know what I would have done without her all these years."

"I have appreciated her warm regard toward me," Darcy said.

"Yes, she has told me how much she likes you. I suppose Hayward has managed to tell you as much about himself and Eliza as he is able."

"He has, but illness causes his mind to struggle."

"Take pity on him, Darcy. You must forgive him, and your mother as well."

"I have tried to picture myself in their places, struggled to understand their broken hearts. But I could never reject the one I marry."

"Even if he were to love another woman?"

"I could not hate him and leave him for good. We would go on for better or for worse."

"I know, being a mother myself, that people who love their children will do all in their power to protect them."

Darcy thought a moment and then nodded. "I understand."

"Do you? You have no children yet, my dear. When you do, that is when you will know what lengths you will go to shield them from harm. But you will not always be able to do so. Your heart will break many times over, and you will cry a river of tears—as I have."

Struck by Madeline's confession to have felt such sorrow over her sons convicted Darcy. She moved from the chair and wrapped her arms around her grandmother's shoulders. "Oh, I am sorry."

"Do not be. God has comforted me through it. I have prayed for Hayward and William since the days they were born. At least William's life has been good. An excellent wife and all those daughters . . . and he raised you, Darcy."

Darcy made no comment, but leaned down to stroke Maxwell's ears. Life promised sorrow and joy, she knew, and children would be a blessing from the Lord. She hoped she and Ethan would someday have their quiver full, but with that blessing would come trials.

"Uncle Will has been a father to me, Grandmother. You would be proud to see his home, how his girls have turned out, and the life he leads. His career is well-respected."

"He told me so in a letter. William never gave me a moment's grief, except when he left for America. It has been difficult not seeing him all these years." Madeline tugged at the blanket and her eyes grew misty. "I knew Hayward was stealing away that night with Eliza. I could have tried to stop him. But I did not, knowing it would make no difference."

"Why?"

"Because I knew he needed a wife, wanted a wife. Eliza was not afraid to follow him to America. I remained silent until my husband argued with me over Hayward's choice. I urged him to accept it, but he followed them, enraged that Hayward would defy him. Your father stood up to him and refused to annul his new bride."

"But he denounced her later. She believed he had died, and I have thought she must have wallowed in such deep grief that is why she fell prey to another man. Papa could have gone on loving her."

"Yes. And you see how he loves her still." Madeline touched Darcy's hand. "I am content now. My prayers were answered. I have seen you and Hayward. Tell me you will not grieve if God takes me home."

Darcy breathed out. "I will not be able to help myself. But that is long in coming. We must all go back to America together. You could be with both your sons that way, and all your grandchildren."

"No, Darcy. It is not meant to be."

"Why not, Grandmother?"

"I can sense my time is near. Do you know the hymn by Mr. Charles Wesley, 'Father, I Stretch My Hands to Thee'?"

"I know it well."

"Then you must sing it to me." Madeline leaned her head back and closed her eyes. "It will comfort me, Darcy. Go on."

Pausing a moment, Darcy gathered the beginning words in her mind. Then she took her grandmother's hand in hers and sang:

> Father, I stretch my hands to thee;
> No other help I know;
> If thou withdraw thyself from me,
> Ah! whither shall I go?
> What did thine only Son endure,
> Before I drew my breath!
> What pain, what labor, to secure
> My soul from endless death!
> Surely thou canst not let me die;
> O speak, and I shall live;
> And here I will unwearied lie,
> Till thou thy Spirit give.
> Author of faith! to thee I lift
> My weary, longing eyes;

O let me now receive that gift!
My soul without it dies.

It surprised her to see tears form in the corners of Madeline's eyes. And when she opened them, she blinked them away and smiled. "You have a beautiful voice, my girl. Thank you for comforting an old woman."

"I would do anything to give you ease, Grandmother."

"Good. Then you do realize what you must do for your parents?"

"I am not sure. My mind is torn."

"You must do what is right. I expect Langbourne to return soon. He despises Hayward and if he knows he is here under this roof, he will cast him out and you with him. Not only that, but Hayward must see Eliza. You must see to it that he gets away to Fairview before it is too late. Promise me you will."

Darcy squeezed her grandmother's hand. "I promise."

Madeline leaned her head back against the chair. "'Tis well, Darcy. Now you will see how God mends the breaches."

26

*B*ack in the lonely wing, inside the neglected room, Darcy approached her father's bedside. Propped up on pillows, he made short, quick efforts to breathe, his flesh moist. She laid her ear against his chest and listened. Soft gurgles of liquid infected his lungs. Earlier in the morning, he seemed better, but now he had returned to the struggle.

Mrs. Burke drew up behind her. "He has not improved, miss."

"When I woke this morning, he seemed better." That he could regress so quickly worried Darcy. She laid her hand across her father's brow. His skin felt cool to the touch, yet perspiration beaded on his skin. "He needs a doctor. Tell me where to go and I'll bring him back."

"The closest I imagine is hours from here. I haven't known a doctor in these parts since I was a young girl. There isn't enough time to find one."

Darcy bit her lower lip. "I need to send word to Fairview and ask my mother and Mr. Brennan to come."

Mrs. Burke stepped back to Darcy, her hands folded over her breast. "Oh, no, miss. Mr. Langbourne will be returning."

"How can you be sure?" Darcy asked.

Mrs. Burke hesitated. "He told me so. I know him well enough to say he would do your father harm. He hates him that much, and Eliza as well."

"But he is too ill to travel, and how would I get him there? I need Mr. Brennan."

"I will go to Reverend Reed." Mrs. Burke stepped through the door. "He is close by and will help us."

Darcy nodded in agreement. "Please, hurry and bring him back."

"I'll go right away, Darcy. Now don't you worry. We will see your father through," Mrs. Burke said, as she hastened out the door.

Hayward lifted himself and reached out to touch Darcy's arm. "I must get to Eliza. No more waiting."

"No, Papa. You are not well enough."

He reached for his boots. "Help me with these, child."

She snatched them up and put them behind her back. "You must wait. The vicar is coming, and with his aid we will leave for Fairview."

He looked up at her, his eyes glistening with hope. "I will see your mother at last? You swear it?"

She touched his cheek. "Yes."

Mrs. Burke had not been gone a quarter of an hour when Darcy heard the beat of a horse coming down the drive. Her heart swelled, hoping it were Ethan. She rushed to the window and looked down. Disappointed, and fearing for her father, she drew back when she saw Langbourne swing down from his saddle. Mrs. Burke had been right.

The front door slammed shut. The sound reverberated throughout the old house, and the anxious churning in Darcy's chest trembled through her limbs. She hurried away from the window and to her father.

"Papa." She placed her hands on his shoulders. He looked at her. "Langbourne has returned. You must stay quiet. Do not attempt to move from the room."

"I do not care if he finds me. He took my letters and I want them back."

"Please, Papa. Stay here until I return. You shall have your letters one way or the other."

Faint as it were, she heard Langbourne call out for Mrs. Burke, then for her. He deserved to wait. He had taken her mother's letters, treated her father cruelly, and she would not hurry to his beck and call. The urge to confront him brimmed over as her hand gripped the door handle.

She went out into the narrow hallway and down the servant's stairs at the rear of the house. Her steps soundless, she approached the landing. Down to the next floor she went and within reach of the broad staircase that led down to the first floor a shadow crossed the wall below. With a catch of her breath, she froze. Dread prickled over her skin. A blast of winter, a heartless soul, had returned to the house. His shadow grew larger and Langbourne halted a few steps below when their eyes met.

Hatless, his hair looked uncombed, wisps curling about the edge of his neckcloth. His eyes were weary and he narrowed them upon sight of her. "Confound it, Darcy. This house is like a tomb. Where is everyone? Why did you take so long?"

"I did not hear you at first."

"I called for Burke. She should have met me at the door."

"I sent Mrs. Burke on an errand."

The skepticism in his gaze did not escape her, and she feared he would ask what kind of errand. Then what excuse would she make to satisfy him? "An errand?"

"Yes. To post a letter."

"She should be in the kitchen preparing supper."

Lowering her eyes, Darcy moved on. He followed and made his way ahead of her, causing her to stop short. It unnerved Darcy, the way his eyes scanned her face.

"I have not told you, Darcy, how pretty I think you are—with the way your hair falls over your shoulders, how the light catches it. It is enough to drive any man mad."

She felt her face burn, at once stung with anger. How dare he treat her in this way, bar her from going on, speak to her with such unbridled lack of inhibition. "You should not say such things." She moved. He stopped her. She had to keep her head, think how to escape without causing alarm. Defiant, she folded her arms and stared at him.

"Do not be so offended," he said.

She glared. "Your compliments should be reserved for your wife—or your mistress."

He laughed. "Charlotte is not pretty. Why should I lie to her? As for my mistress, she is, and she knows how to please me."

Darcy frowned. "How can you live as you do? How can you have no conscience that it is wrong to betray Charlotte? Did you not mean the vows you made before God?"

"Ah, now you would preach at me? Charlotte is as cold as death and always complaining of illness. If you would see her beneath her chemise, you would be shocked at how frail a woman she is. She has given me no heir. And does she care? Not a whit."

"Let me pass."

He circled his fingers around her wrist. "You should meet Rowena. Some call her a harlot. But she is a kind and gentle soul, and faithful. She is the only woman I willingly provide for. Without me she would starve, or be enslaved to another man."

"Why are you telling me these things?"

"I would have taken care of your mother if she had let me. I hope she lived to regret it."

Darcy jerked away and breathed out a sigh of frustration. She hated his words, the manner in which he looked at her, the smell of wine on his breath. If only Ethan would walk through the door.

Langbourne inched forward, and she would have tripped back if she had not put her hand on the banister to steady herself. "I do not wish to hear any more of this. Let me by."

"You are frightened of me, aren't you?" he said.

"Not at all."

"Then why are you trembling?"

"I am cold."

"Why do you withdraw from me?"

"You are too close . . ."

"Not close enough, I'd say."

"I wish to go to my room and you are preventing me."

"Only because I have news to tell." Langbourne leaned back against the wall and put one boot upon the step in front of Darcy. "I have decided to close the house. I may even sell it. Everyone is to leave and settle at Meadlow."

Darcy's throat tightened. She supposed he believed it was generous of him. "Not I, Mr. Langbourne."

He pulled away from the wall. "You will do as I say."

"I will do as I wish. You have no authority over me."

"I am your only male relation while you are here, and you are under my roof. You will obey me. Besides, you might enjoy Meadlow before you return to America. Unless, that is, you are prepared to go now. Have you enough to pay for return passage?"

She had not thought of this. She'd come with so little money, and the coachman who took her overland charged her more than what the ticket was worth. One gold coin would not buy her way home. But it did not matter. She'd marry Ethan.

"I'll give you what you need," Langbourne said, "as long as you take Madeline's care into your hands and accompany her, with Mrs. Burke of course. I can use a new housekeeper."

"Grandmother is too frail to leave Havendale. She has lived here most of her life and it would kill her to leave."

"Nonsense. She will have Charlotte for company, and I plan to move Rowena to a residence near Meadlow to keep me company."

Shocked, Darcy's mouth fell open. "That would be deplorable. How could you?"

"Gentlemen do it all the time. Charlotte will not care. What is important to her is to live in a fine house, have pretty clothes, and money to spend. She would be glad to be free of her wifely duties."

Disgusted, Darcy looked away. For a moment that seemed forever, he stood over her—a menacing shadow of a man. She had to control herself, and if she made the appearance that she would submit to him, he'd leave her alone. As soon as they could get away, she would be far from his demands.

Madeline's call saved her. "Grandmother needs me."

She hoisted her hem and tried to pass him. He bowed short, then stepped aside. With a sweep of his hand, he gave her leave. She went on and thought of her father suffering upstairs. What would Langbourne do if he knew his old rival had defied his warning to stay away, and instead lay sick and dying in an unused room?

She prayed Langbourne would retire, that he would not hear the minister's arrival. If there were a way, some plan she could use to keep him from seeing the vicar with Mrs. Burke, she would use it.

Darcy wondered what risks she would take, what danger she would face to defeat Langbourne's plans for her. For in his eyes burned lust unfulfilled, and in his heart were rooted jealousy and resentment. She knew he hated both her parents, and realized that she had become the object of his revenge. He would hurt them through her if he could.

She had to hurry to her grandmother, explain what the hours ahead held for both of them. Madeline's eyes were wet with tears as Darcy gripped her hands. "I cannot go to Fairview with you, Darcy," she said. "I cannot go anywhere."

"But if you do not come with us, Grandmother, Langbourne will move you to Meadlow."

"You mustn't worry, dear. It was in my husband's will that I live here for the remainder of my days. Langbourne cannot force me. Now, you must do what you can for your father. Besides, you and Mr. Brennan have an understanding. You love him and he loves you. That is where you belong."

Darcy kissed her grandmother's cheek, wishing she could convince her to leave with her. She heard the grind of wheels approach, looked out Madeline's window, and watched the minister's wagon draw up at the rear of the house. A man alighted from the driver's seat and handed down Mrs. Burke, who hurried through a servants' back door.

She turned back to Madeline. "The vicar has come, Grandmother. I don't want to leave you."

"Must I order you, child? Be off with you."

"I shall kiss Papa for you."

Madeline touched Darcy's cheek. "God bless you, Darcy."

In a burst of emotion, Darcy threw her arms around Madeline and held tight. Madeline drew her back and kissed her forehead. "Go now," she said, patting Darcy's cheek. "I shall pray for your safe journey."

27

$\mathcal{D}$arcy stepped through the door and made her way to the servants' stairs. First Mrs. Burke appeared, followed by Reverend Reed, a man of middle age. His verger stood behind him, a head taller and broad-shouldered. He was dressed in the traditional black garb, and a shock of gray hair touched his coat collar. She'd seen him standing at his pulpit, the same one her grandfather and Ethan's father had preached from, his eyes aglow with the good news of the Gospel. Now that he had come to aid her father, hope came alive in Darcy. Before her stood a man who lived what he preached, and his kind eyes met hers.

"I am here, Miss Darcy, to help in any way I can," Reed said.

Darcy felt a draught on her neck from the window and thought how cold her father's room must be if the fire had died. "You have my thanks, sir." She glanced down the hall. "Mr. Langbourne has returned home. We must be as quiet as we can. If he discovers us . . ."

"Do not fear, my child. Mrs. Burke has told us everything, and we will get him safely away to Fairview without making a sound. He can make the journey you think?"

"I pray he can, sir."

"Then we must waste no time."

The fire in the hearth had indeed died down to a heap of red coals. Even in the chill, sweat glistened over Hayward's brow. Darcy picked up a cloth and wiped his face.

"Thank you for your help, Mrs. Burke. I think it would be best if you look in on my grandmother now."

"Of course, and if Mr. Langbourne should ask where you are, I will delay him. Godspeed, Miss Darcy." She left, shutting the door behind her.

Reverend Reed leaned over Hayward. "Mr. Morgan? Can you hear me, sir?"

Hayward's eyes opened. "I can. Where is Darcy?"

"I am here, Papa." She picked up his hand. "This is Reverend Reed and his verger, Mr. Snead."

"You have come to pray for me, sir?" said Hayward. "Last rites, is it?"

"If you wish it, I will."

"I have confessed Jesus as my Savior and repented of my sins. Though they were scarlet, He has made them white as snow."

"Yes, and you may rest easy."

"Papa, we must get you up," said Darcy. "I will help you with your boots." She retrieved them, and kneeling down she slipped them on. Then she wrapped him in his coat. "Not a sound, Papa, as we slip away."

The men lifted Hayward and held him up beneath his arms. They led him down the stairs to the passageway, to an outer courtyard. The horses sighed and flicked their ears as Hayward was placed in the rear, and a blanket thrown over him to keep him warm. Darcy wrapped her cloak closer and glanced up at the window that belonged to Madeline. A figure passed across it, and she turned away to board the cart. But when the rapid thud of footsteps approached, she froze.

From the gloom of the opening Langbourne stepped out.

Impatience had banked a fire inside Ethan. His time had been spent dealing with Hollen and the conspiracy the seedy little man had brought to their doorstep. Now that he had resolved the loose ends to a difficult situation, he would ride to Havendale and claim her.

He'd ridden all night, through the rain, then by the guidance of a full moon, anxious to reach home. The roads were mire and the horse's flanks were mud-caked. As he rode into Fairview, he studied the old place where he had spent most of his childhood, first under Eliza's tutelage, then beneath her motherly hand. To all things, he thought, an end comes, and he felt no sorrow to let the estate go. And how much more content would Darcy be to accept his proposal if it meant living along the Potomac, near the family she loved?

He drew up, wondering what Eliza would say. Surely she'd be happy as well to leave this place of grim solitude with her daughter. The idea of restoring River Run raced through Ethan's veins as much as it had with Hayward. He would rebuild, start a new legacy, and at last bring Darcy and her mother together again.

When he came through the door, Fiona met him with a broad smile. "Dear me, you are a sight, Mr. Brennan. Give me your coat and I'll clean and dry it by the fire."

"I hoped you wouldn't have noticed, Fiona. You have gotten too old to wait on me."

Fiona put her hands over her hips and huffed. "No, I am not, sir. Age is in the mind, and I'm young inside mine. Besides I would be unhappy if I was retired from taking care of you and Eliza, don't you know."

Ethan slipped off his coat and handed it over. "How is she?"

"Worried over you, and anxious about Darcy. You know I am too, sir, but full of joy that I shall see her again. That child meant the world to me. She was so bright and sprightly when little. You say she is the same even now. Pretty too, I imagine, just like her mother."

With a sigh, she laid his coat over the back of a chair and turned it toward the fire. Ethan thought about what she had said, how loved Darcy was.

"She is all that you say, Fiona. And she is the most beautiful woman I have ever laid eyes on—inside and out. There is no reason to worry."

"Well, Eliza cannot help herself. She fretted over you traveling in this foul weather, that you might catch cold. I can tell you, we both long for summer days at River Run."

He drew his neckcloth away from his throat. "After Darcy and I are married, we will be leaving England to start a new life there."

Fiona's eyes lit up and she yelped. "All of us, sir?"

"All of us, Fiona."

He nudged the old servant's chin, and went upstairs where at the landing he met Eliza. A change had come over her, as if a dark cloud had lifted and a golden dawn had risen over her. No longer were her eyes forlorn. No longer did she wear her hair tucked beneath a mobcap. It hung clean and fixed in soft ringlets, pulled back from her face by a satin ribbon. Today her eyes were bright as the amethyst at her throat.

Eliza's fingertips touched the pear-shaped gem and smiled. "I will give this to Darcy when I see her, Ethan. Hayward said the color matched my eyes."

"She will treasure it, I'm sure."

"Still, I wish you would use this to pay Hollen."

He kissed her cheek. "No."

"But if it will help . . ."

"It isn't necessary."

They went together into the small sitting room to talk. Eliza sat down close to the window. Ethan noticed how she glanced outside, as if she were expecting someone. He sat down in an overstuffed chair across from her.

"Hollen handed over the remaining letters and promised to quit his association with the person who hired him on pains of arrest." He drew the letters from his inside pocket and handed them over.

Her eyes filled. "Praise God."

"Yes, an answer to prayer. Hollen was pleased with the amount I offered, that it was enough for him to leave Derbyshire, hopefully never to return."

"I had written them so long ago. That they even remain to this day is a miracle." Eliza looked over at Ethan. "I will be able to give them to Darcy from my own hand. Then she will see after reading them how much I loved her, how much I missed her."

Ethan went on to tell Eliza about his ride over to the inn where he discovered Hollen was staying, an ancient place made of stone, pitted windows, thatched roof, that smelled of rum and ale, tobacco smoke, and English cookery.

"There is an inn of that kind along the Potomac trail. I wonder if it is still there."

"Most likely it is." He stood when Fiona stepped into the room. "Is my coat dry?"

"That it is, sir. And I brushed it down. You will look fine for Miss Darcy."

"You are going to Havendale today?" Eliza said, her eyes bright.

"Yes, and I will be bring Darcy back with me." He bent down and picked up her hands. "Do not worry. She will love you as before."

Fiona laughed and smacked her hands. "Eliza, my girl. God has answered all our prayers." Eliza wiped her eyes. Fiona's smile fled and she scanned the room. "Oh, I best get into the kitchen and make a huge supper for us all."

As Fiona bustled to the door, Eliza called to her. "We must have apple tansy. It is Darcy's favorite."

"I will make the best apple tansy this side of the continent, my girl."

Eliza proceeded to the door ahead of Fiona. "Not without my help. I shall not sit idle knowing I am soon to see my Darcy again. Everything must be perfect."

A smile he had not seen in Eliza since his father had passed away lit her face. Grates and jangles could be heard coming down the drive. The sound drew Ethan to the window. "Surely Hollen has not changed his mind and dared to return with more demands. I'll thrash the little beggar," he said.

Eliza paused at the door. She laid her hand against the jamb and listened. Then she turned. A feeling seized her heart. It seemed familiar, like the moment she saw Hayward riding his horse down River Run's dusty lane toward her after the war. He'd come back to her battle-scarred, starved, his face worn but shining bright as the noonday. She joined Ethan at the window to see a pair of men alight from a wagon and then move to the rear and aid another from it.

Islands of gray parted in the sky. Mist clung to the earth, and she wiped her eyes thinking it were her vision. But the mist remained and strengthened as tears welled. Scarcely breathing, without motion, she watched on. With great care the two men held the one who struggled to find his footing. She could not see his face, for it was bowed against his chest.

But something within said she knew the man. His hair, aged silver, hung loose about broad shoulders, broad shoulders that reminded her of . . .

He looked up, caught her gaze, and Eliza's heart throbbed. She gripped the windowsill, and it rushed through her the identity of the man she beheld. To cry out, to shout his name, stuck in her throat. Her feet became weights and she could not move. Tears escaped her eyes, drifted down her cheeks. Every sunrise, every scarlet dawn, every starlit night that had come and gone gathered together. Time had passed quickly since the last moment she saw him retreating from her, as she stood at the rail of a ship.

He wished her no more, stopped loving her, and banished her to an unknown fate that promised ill. Darcy, their child, was the property of her father, and she would be denied her, forced to live a secluded, lonely life.

She whispered, "I came to you long ago. Now you come to me. How sad it is—the years that have separated us."

Ethan touched her on the shoulder. "Who is it, Eliza? What is it you say?"

Her hand covered her trembling mouth. "Oh, sweet Lord."

"You know those men?"

"I know one man." She nodded. "It is Hayward."

A surge of strength passed through her and she dashed from the room, down the staircase with her hand sliding along the railing. She reached the door, Ethan behind her, and flung it open. She stepped out and stood still upon the threshold. Hayward lifted his head and freed from his guardians, fell to his knees before her. The wind swept back her hair, and she stared down into his eyes with all the old feelings of rejection rising to the surface. How painful it still remained that he had not forgiven her for succumbing to another man's affections and by it bearing a child—a daughter lost so young.

Ethan stood beside her, and when overcome by the sight before her, Eliza's knees buckled. He held her up and laid her head against his shoulder.

"Eliza is not able to face this, sir. Perhaps you should leave. Return later when she has recovered."

Hayward's eyes filled and sorrow covered his face. "Please, young sir. I have come so far."

Reverend Reed stepped forward. "And he is not long for this world."

Eliza's heart plunged to a deeper depth of sorrow. She could not turn her face to look at him and allowed tears to burn her eyes as they had so many times before. "He rejected me and may have had no heart to forgive me. But mine remains true to my husband. Yet, I cannot speak to him now."

Reed stepped closer. The verger helped Hayward to his feet. "Madam, Mr. Morgan has made great pains to seek you out. He is an ill man as you can see by his countenance. Will you not allow us to bring him inside? He has no other place to go."

Eliza drew away from Ethan, and took in a deep breath. She moved forward and Hayward reached out, gripped her hand, and kissed it with ardent fervor. Slowly she drew it away.

Ethan helped Hayward stand. "Of course, sir. Bring the gentleman inside." He aided Hayward through the doorway, while Eliza stood aside.

In the foyer, Fiona stood back with her hand at her throat and her eyes round as saucers. "I cannot believe my eyes. 'Tis Mr. Hayward."

"A posset, Fiona," said Eliza. "And anything else you can think of that might give Mr. Hayward comfort."

Fiona hurried away, muttering beneath her breath and glancing back over her shoulder.

Ethan regarded Eliza with a great deal of anxiety. "Eliza?"

She nodded. "I am shaken, Ethan. I never expected he would come to me. I thought I'd been long forgotten."

"Obviously not. And this explains the letters."

"He must have had them with him, and then they were stolen. Do you think that?"

"I do, and you can see he has suffered." He turned and saw the verger help Hayward to the settee. Reverend Reed crossed the room and drew Ethan aside. Eliza went to Hayward, and picking up a throw that lay across the settee, tucked it over his body.

"Where did you find him?" Ethan asked.

"We were called to Havendale, sir."

"Then Miss Darcy—why did she not come with you?"

"It is urgent I unfold to you the sequence of events that have occurred this day, sir," Reed said. "For I believe Miss Darcy to be in a most desperate situation."

A tremor shot through Ethan. "Tell me, sir."

"I was requested at Havendale after she sent Mrs. Burke, who told me of Mr. Morgan's unexpected arrival and condition. Seeing the moment was not to lose, I traveled to Havendale with my verger, Mr. Snead. Miss Darcy would have sent word to Fairview for you and the lady to come, but she feared Mr. Langbourne would not allow you entrance, and do harm to her father."

"But why has Darcy not come with you?" Ethan asked once more.

"She was prevented."

"By whom?"

"Mr. Langbourne."

Ethan drew in a breath. "By force?"

"You might say that. It was a most startling situation."

Ethan glanced over at Eliza. Still she had her face turned to the window. There was need for their conversation to be quiet, and so Ethan lowered his voice. "What happened?"

"As we laid Mr. Morgan into the rear of my wagon, with Miss Darcy about to board, Mr. Langbourne burst out into the courtyard with a pistol in hand and with eyes like live coals. I told him to stand down, but he raised his weapon at me and ordered Miss Darcy away. He recognized Mr. Morgan, and as a man of God I cannot repeat the foul words he spoke. With his weapon turned upon the poor man, Darcy hurried to her father and put her body between them."

Fear rippled cold through Ethan's body. *Darcy.* No, Langbourne would never have fired his pistol. He looked at Reed with a plea. "She is . . ."

"Unharmed, sir."

"Why would he be so cruel and prevent her from leaving? She has done nothing to incite his anger."

"She has indeed—by harboring Mr. Morgan, whom he despises. Langbourne has set out to reap vengeance upon Hayward and Eliza by keeping Darcy from them. And you, sir, are also on his list of enemies. He said he would do all in his power to dissuade her from you. And, if I may repeat the words, he swore to shoot you like a dog if you were to set foot at Havendale."

Ethan set his mouth firm, clenched his jaw and fists. "He cannot keep her against her will. I will go to her."

Reed placed his hand on Ethan's shoulder. "I wish you god-speed, sir."

28

$\mathscr{E}$than raced Sanchet across the moors. The smooth mounds ascending above the valley shadowed the rocky edges of bluffs on the hillsides. His hands grew slick inside his leather gloves, and the wind cut through his hair, almost blinding him. Sanchet kicked up clots of earth and heaved his girth with the pace of his hooves.

In the distance, Havendale came into view and Ethan's brow furrowed as his conviction surged through his body. Sunlight flashed over the glass in the windows that faced him and a host of sparrows flew above the chimneys. He'd find her, loose her from Langbourne's hold, and return to Fairview with her.

Sanchet flared his nostrils, snorted, and flicked his ears. Suddenly a horse and rider plunged around a bend, followed by one other man on a smaller horse. The rider jerked hard on the reins and skidded the black roan to an uneasy halt in front of Ethan. His crony waited beside him. Langbourne stared hard at Ethan, all color washed from his pinched face. The sky grew darker—an ominous sign that came with the breeze and roughened his hair. His large horse snorted at the flap of wings alighting out of the trees behind Ethan.

"Turn back, Brennan. You are not welcomed on my land."

A muscle in Ethan's cheek jerked. "How will you prevent me from going on? I am here for Darcy."

Langbourne sneered as his horse sidestepped. "I forbid you to trespass, and the law says I can shoot any man who does."

"The law also says a man may hang for kidnapping."

"You speak nonsense."

"You deny you are keeping her here against her will?"

"Certainly I do."

"I have been told what you did, how you kept her back on threat of murdering her father in cold blood."

"Whoever told you that is an utter fool. Darcy made the choice to stay. She has not resigned herself to a reunion with either parent."

"I was told differently."

"She has grown close to her grandmother and will not leave her."

"Yes, but not at the expense of her parents."

"Her father is nothing more than a stranger to her. And her mother? Well, Darcy has so little recollection of Eliza. There is no attachment."

"Is it not time you stop punishing Eliza? You have a wife and owe it to her to let the past die."

Langbourne steadied his restless horse and laughed. "You know nothing of my wife."

"I know that she is unfortunate. It is broadly known you have a mistress."

"You have reminded me, Brennan, the tongue is the weapon of women, cowards, and fools."

"Truth is the weapon against evil, sir."

Scarlet rage rose in Langbourne's face. "You will not turn your horse and leave my property?"

Ethan moved his horse a pace forward. "Let me pass."

"No, sir!" With angry stares, the other drew up beside Langbourne and widened the barrier between the two men.

"Let Darcy tell me to my face she will not leave with me," Ethan said.

Langbourne made no movement to stand down. Instead, he stared at Ethan and moved his hand close to his pistol. Ethan knew he was serious and would carry out his threat. It would be better to live for Darcy than to die.

"I will not allow you to go any further," said Langbourne. "Even so, you would find her gone for all your efforts."

Ethan clenched his jaw. "What do you mean?"

"I have sent her away."

"You are a liar, sir. Darcy knew I would be coming for her."

"Did she? Well, she told me she believes you to be a scoundrel for not telling her about her mother and wants nothing to do with you or her. Can you not see, Brennan? She did not send Hayward to Fairview out of the kindness of her heart. She threw him out, no matter what that vicar may have told you."

The urge to pull Langbourne off his horse and strike him down raged through Ethan. Was it not time someone humbled him and sent him to wallow in a mud hole, his fine suit of clothes ruined, his pride spoiled?

"And there is another issue." As if to test Ethan's restraint, Langbourne narrowed his eyes and said, "You know Hollen was employed by me?"

Ethan smirked. "I do. That is over too."

"It will never be over." Langbourne leaned forward, his eyes spiteful. "Darcy will be the blade to twist in their hearts, and in yours—when I have ruined her."

With those words, Ethan spurred his horse forward and threw his grip onto Langbourne's coat. Langbourne raised his arm and pushed him back. His servant hurried to his aid. The horses reared, stomped the ground, and twisted. Langbourne's hand flew to the grip of his flintlock pistol.

Then without hesitation, with no second thought flickering over his chiseled face, Langbourne ordered his man to move away and leveled the pistol at Ethan.

29

A tap, tap on the window stirred Darcy from a restless slumber. No harsh wind, no rain—only a sighing through the eaves of the house. She lay quiet, struggling against weary emotion, aware of the stillness in the house. She sat up, and though the chill in the room struck her, she threw back the blanket from her legs, swung them over the side of the bed, and stood. Despair lingered in her breast and she folded her hands against her heart to pray.

Running her hands across her eyes, she worried about her father and estranged mother, aching for Ethan as her vision cleared, for she had cried herself to sleep. "When he is told what has happened to me, he will come," she said aloud.

She could not escape the image of Langbourne trudging out into the courtyard with his fists clenched. Hate burned in his eyes as he raised his pistol and swore to shoot her father. *Intruder, trespasser, fiend,* he had called him.

When Darcy stepped between them, Langbourne shoved her aside. Her father cried out and struggled to rise. He shouted to Langbourne not to harm her. Reverend Reed's verger shielded her father, and Reed rebuked Langbourne for his cruelty while trying to reach Darcy. Langbourne demanded Reverend Reed to remove Hayward, himself, and his verger, off his land. But no amount of stern words could sway him from keeping Darcy back.

The room stood at a high point of the house, on a floor of rooms that had gone unoccupied for years, with only Madeline's and hers lived in on the eastern wing. Cold and with little furniture, and one window made of rows of diamond-shaped glass laced with black leaded seams, it felt detached from the rest of Havendale.

She rubbed her bruised wrist. In an iron-like grip, Langbourne had pulled her back into the house and up three flights of stairs, thus injuring her. At least he relented, con-victed by Reverend Reed's stern words, and let her father go. But what good did it do to keep her from leaving with him? He railed it was for her own good—and for Madeline. He would not allow her to abandon her grandmother. She had to do her duty. Her obligation was to her—not to the parents who had abandoned her. And how dare she bring into his house a dirty ragtag prodigal, a man who defied the family, who stole Langbourne's choice, and ran off like a felon to a foreign country?

"I do not care who he claims to be," Langbourne told her. "He has no connection to this family—not anymore—and is not welcomed. You, on the other hand, are Madeline's grand-daughter, and you will do your duty by her by obeying me. You will accompany her to Meadlow, and what you do afterwards I care not. But I will not have you abandon her like her sons did. Only know this: you will have no help from me if you decide to leave Meadlow."

Langbourne seemed one man with two minds. He had sympathy in one regard, for Madeline—that she would not leave Havendale alone, that her granddaughter would be the greatest comfort for her during this transition. But at the same time, he had no compassion whatsoever on poor Darcy or her father, and showed such ire toward Ethan that it caused Darcy to tremble inwardly.

To punish her disloyalty, he ordered her to stay put. One of his men would keep an eye out if she dared to leave. Darcy did not argue. The mad gaze in his eyes, the harsh tone of his voice, the clenching of his teeth frightened her.

"You may leave your room when it is time to leave," he said. As he stepped out the door, Darcy caught a glimpse of a man waiting in the hall. His head closely shaved, his eyes small and close-set, he nodded to Langbourne. He closed the door for his master, and Darcy set her ear against it and listened to Langbourne's footsteps fade away.

In an attempt to brush away the muck that covered the diamond-shaped panes, she nicked her finger on a crack in the glass. It stung and she put it into her mouth to soothe the wound. Her hem would have to do. She picked it up and rubbed a few panes until the muted day shone through—the sky slate, windswept mist crossing the land. She could not see the courtyard below, for the window stood too high. Shifting her gaze to the grassy plains beyond and to the lane that led to the house, she anticipated Ethan would appear mounted on Sanchet, spurring him toward her. For several anxious minutes she kept her hopeful eyes fixed upon the gate, and soon her expectation turned into anxiety.

Her stomach ached from nerves and a lack of food, and she hugged her arms to endure it. But her thirst caused her to crave water and she wished some were in the old white pitcher that sat on the table beside the bed. Running her hands over the sleek curved handle, she looked down into it. It was empty.

The room grew airless, and she tried to unlatch the window. Rust had sealed it tight and it would not budge no matter how much she struggled. Her need for air drove her to keep trying. If only she could feel the relief of the wind against her.

The hoofbeats of a horse came faintly to her, and she hurried back to the window, where she saw men on horseback moving toward each other at a brisk trot. "Ethan," she breathed out in a hopeful sigh. The other man she realized was Langbourne, along with one of his cronies. "Oh, Lord. Do not let Langbourne forbid him."

Desperation welled inside as she watched the scene outside in the misty distance. She gripped the edge of the window, as Ethan pushed Sanchet forward and grabbed Langbourne. Langbourne twisted away, moved back, and aimed his pistol. She gasped, and fear struck her cold that he would fire.

"No, Langbourne! Do not do it!" she cried, tears rising in her eyes.

With his life in danger, Ethan relented to whatever Langbourne ordered him to do, turned his horse, and galloped off.

"Come back," she whispered. Her hopes dashed, her heart sunk in her breast. She slipped to the floor, covering her face with her hands, cried a little, then dashed the tears from her face.

After a wait, she scrambled to her feet, hurried to the door, and opened it. The hallway, silent and empty, stretched before her, and the light from a far window beckoned. Langbourne's henchman already snored in a chair, leaning back against the wall. She hesitated, afraid she might wake him, pressed her hands behind her on the wall, and slipped away.

If she were to go down the main staircase, she might face Langbourne. She could not allow him to control her like this, to force her to obey his will and be a pawn in his quest to hurt her parents. She had to escape Havendale and make the trek to Fairview no matter the conditions.

She could see the servants' stairwell but a few yards away. In desperate haste, she made for it, and stepped down the first few steps without making a sound. Then they creaked beneath her footfalls at a place where there were neither windows nor light to guide her. Placing her hands against the plastered walls, she slowly made her way down, taking care not to trip. The plaster, chipped away in places, scratched her palms as she felt her way through the dark, down to the kitchen—a flagstone-floored room with a huge stone fireplace where the coals had long turned to gray ash.

An empty copper kettle hung from an iron hook, and the table was swept clean of dishes and crockery. Something scurried across it and caught her eye. She gasped, her throat tightened, and she drew back. On its hind legs, a small brown mouse stared at her with black eyes. It nibbled a crumb between its hairless pink paws, blinked, and then hopped to the other end of the table, leapt to the floor and scampered under a cupboard. It poked its whiskery head out from beneath it and wiggled its nose. Darcy crept past the little creature and dipped a ladle into a barrel beside the door. She drank, and the water soothed her parched tongue.

She looked out the window at the vast fields. Her cloak lay near the front door, and she thought if she could retrieve it without Langbourne seeing her, she'd slip out. But there she was, so close to another door where she could go at once. She moved toward it. Considering how cold it would be to cross the moors without a covering, she hesitated.

Then a presence fell behind her and she froze. A chill raced up her back and prickled over her skin. Setting the ladle back down in the water, she turned to see Langbourne.

"A keen wind blows." He jerked open the rear door, moved just outside it. "Come, breathe it in. Look out at the moors in the distance. If you wander across them you'll meet with danger—even death. You are a stranger here and do not know the ways of the moors."

Darcy lifted her head. "I am a Morgan. I have my father's blood in my veins. I am no stranger to such a place."

"So you were planning to leave and take the risk? That would have been foolish, Darcy. You have no idea how many souls have gotten lost on these moors and frozen to death in the night. Some have gone missing and were never found."

"You have no trouble."

"I grew up here and know it better than most."

She did not answer. Instead she moved to the door. Langbourne stepped closer and she backed up against the table. "Why must you be so troublesome, Darcy? I demanded you remain upstairs for your own good."

"Your henchman is more troublesome than I, sir. He could not stay awake long enough to notice I slipped out. He forgot to lock the door."

"Yes, and I have sent the incompetent fool on his way without his pay." He paused and leaned back against the table. "You have a sharp tongue, Darcy."

"My tongue was parched, sir. For you left me without water. That is one reason I left my room."

He grunted. "I dare not ask what the others were. Is there a reason we cannot be friendly to each other?"

"Friendly? You expect my friendship after what you did to my father?"

"We see things differently, but I should hope you will think on my actions. I only meant to protect you."

"I do not need your protection, for I was in no danger. He is my father no matter what he has done. I am to honor him."

"Once you are at Meadlow, and have time, you will come to realize I am right and you are wrong." Langbourne ran his fingernail over the edge of the table. "You should not have left your room. I had planned to come to you and sort out our differences."

It grew in his eyes again—that wanton look of desire. She despised it, for his gaze should have been for Charlotte. She wanted to run. He snatched her arm, tightened his grip, and drew her close. Fear trembled through her body. His eyes, sharp as daggers, grew enflamed.

"I saw Mr. Brennan from the window," she said, twisting free, stepping back and meeting him stare for stare. "Why did you turn him away? Why did you pull your pistol on him?"

Langbourne shrugged. "That is my affair. Not yours. All I can tell you is you won't be seeing him again—at least not any time soon."

His words cut deep, and she clenched the folds of her dress. "Why are you so bitter, so without compassion and forgiveness? Why must you control everyone around you?"

"Because I am lord and master of Havendale. It is my duty."

Mrs. Burke walked into the kitchen. She paused and raised her brows, gave Darcy a glance, and looked over at Langbourne. "I'm sorry if I have interrupted, sir."

"What do you want, Mrs. Burke?" He spoke low and harsh, but with a hint of leniency.

"I've come for the hamper of food for the journey, Mr. Langbourne. Perhaps Miss Darcy can help me? I'm glad to see she is out of her room at last."

Langbourne glowered. "You should have had that ready hours ago. Darcy is not a servant, and you should know better than to ask such a question or make such comments."

"Beg your pardon, Mr. Langbourne." She narrowed her eyes and looked at him ready to exchange verbal blows. "I just needed help carrying it. But I'll manage on my own." She dragged a wicker hamper out from beneath the table. Darcy reached down to help, but Langbourne pulled her back.

"You heard what I said, Darcy. You are not a servant."

She looked at him, drawing in a breath, and feeling confused by his endless cycle of contradictions. "She needs help. Why shouldn't I give it?" Then she drew the basket up by the side handle. But Mrs. Burke gave her a little smile and a gentle touch of her hand.

"I have it, miss. Thank you anyway." And she stepped from the kitchen out into the hallway. Darcy could hear banging above her now—Madeline pounding her cane on the floor and calling to her, Maxwell barking. She did not wait for Langbourne's permission, but squeezed past him and hurried upstairs, relieved he did not stop her.

The brass knob on Madeline's door felt as smooth as oil from all the hands that had turned it through the years. The room had the feel of emptiness, as if no one had lived in it. The bottles and trinkets on Madeline's dressing table were packed away. Her powder box, jewel box, horsehair brush and ivory comb were inside her trunk. All that remained were the furniture and the made bed. Darcy recalled the first day she met her grandmother in this room, how it smelled sweet with rosewater. Now only a hint lingered.

Madeline stretched out her arms and Darcy hurried to her. "Grandmother, I am here."

"Where is Hayward? What has happened?"

"He is safely away at Fairview."

A little worry went from her eyes. "Oh, I am glad. He is to see Eliza, and she will make him well."

"Yes, everything shall be all right."

"You are the only one who understands what I am feeling, Darcy."

She gave Madeline a cheerful smile, hoping to lighten her burden. "Charlotte will grow weary of us and Maxwell. Then she will insist we return to Havendale. Have you ever been to Meadlow?"

"Never. I have not been away from Havendale in twenty odd years. I found no reason to venture anywhere else." She began to tremble. "Oh, dear. London—the city of vice. I do not wish to go there."

"No, no, Grandmother. We are not going to London. Meadlow is here in Derbyshire not too far from Havendale."

Madeline sighed. "'Tis no better, my girl. Home is where the heart is, and here in this house is mine. I raised my boys here, loved and lost my second husband here. And the churchyard on the hill is where he lies near to my first. The first was so young, you know. I hardly remember Harrison's face, it was so long ago."

The sadness in Madeline's voice brought tears to Darcy's eyes. What a sorrowful life the woman had lived. She held her grandmother's hand. Her veins were raised and blue, her skin cold and clammy. Each breath seemed labored, pained, and in her eyes swam fear.

"I wish I could take you to my home along the river," Darcy told her. "It is peaceful there, and we have godly neighbors who'd do anything for a person in need." Madeline asked her to describe it again, and as she did Mrs. Burke opened the door and waited on the threshold.

"They are ready for us to come down, miss. What can I do to help ease my mistress? She is so distressed."

"Stay with her a while, will you?" Darcy said. She kissed her grandmother's forehead and stepped out of the room determined and persuaded she must change Langbourne's mind. Her grandmother was too ill, too distraught to leave her home, let alone handle the journey.

Downstairs in the foyer, Langbourne handed over the keys to a man in drab work clothes. Short and barrel-chested, he glanced up at her, and walked away after tipping the brim of his hat to his employer. Langbourne turned.

"What is the delay?" he said, with his voice rising. "Go back upstairs and tell your grandmother to hurry up."

Darcy took a step down, her hand firm on the balustrade. "You mustn't do this to her. I beg you, sir. Have pity and let her stay."

He pinched his brows. "Pity her? I am doing what I feel is best for her. I want that understood, and I will not repeat it again."

"She is too frail to travel."

"I will listen no longer to your unwarranted objections, Darcy. Perhaps I was wrong. I should have let you leave with that beggarly rogue or let Brennan have you. But it's too late now. Madeline needs you to accompany her. Just think what it would do to her if you walked out that door without her."

"I am not like you. I am not without feeling, or compassion for another. I will stand by her."

The clack of Maxwell's nails came down the stairs behind her. Darcy looked back. Madeline appeared at the floor above dressed in her faded gown and widow's cap, her shawl over her shoulders, her arm looped in Mrs. Burke's. A single twist of her gray hair lay over her right shoulder. Her stare chilly, she glanced down at Langbourne with a proud lift to her head.

Langbourne crossed his arms. "Darcy says you are ill. I will have Charlotte send for her doctor once you arrive. He lives but a short distance from Meadlow." He then dropped his arms. "So, you see. You shall be better off at Meadlow after all."

She made no reply. Instead Madeline met Darcy's eyes with a soft smile. "Do not worry over me, Darcy. I know what I must do. God has shown me my illness shall pass as easily as a south wind."

Closer to Mrs. Burke, the grand lady proceeded down the stairs one slow step at a time. When she reached Darcy, she placed her hand through her arm and the three women went on together toward the front door.

From the back of the chair next to the door, Mrs. Burke lifted her mistress's gray cloak and placed it over Madeline's shoulders. Darcy tied the tassels into a bow. She fought the lump that grew in her throat as she looked into her grandmother's face, so calm now and resigned. Maxwell rushed ahead, jumped inside the carriage, and stuck his head out the window.

And although the sky whirled with stormy clouds in a deepening sky, Darcy wished she could kiss her grandmother's cheek farewell and walk off in the direction of Fairview—to the man she loved, and the parents she longed to know. But she could not bring herself to part from her frail grandmother as she held her close to her side.

30

*O*utside the gates of Havendale, Darcy drew the hood of her cloak over her hair, and leaned outside the carriage window. She called up to the driver, and he slowed the horses to a stop and looked down at her from his perch.

"What is it, miss?" Irritation marred his face and the yellow glow from the coach lamps barely colored it.

"You are to change course."

"The only course I'm takin' is to Meadlow as I was paid to do."

"No, you must take us on to Fairview."

He wiggled his head. "I cannot do that. Mr. Langbourne's orders are to take you and the ladies to Meadlow. He warned me you would try to persuade me to go another way. But he pays me well enough for obeying his orders and not listening to the whim of a batty woman."

"Batty?" she stormed, then calmed herself. "We can pay you more," she smiled. "There is nothing batty in that, is there?"

"The answer is no. If you wish to go to Fairview, then you will have to wait until after we reach Meadlow." Turning aside he shook the reins and the horses carried on down the rutted road.

Darcy leaned back with a deep sigh of disappointment. "I tried."

The carriage dipped and swayed, jostling the passengers seated inside it. Darcy scooped Maxwell up from the floor and set him between Madeline and Mrs. Burke, where he nuzzled down into the creases of their cloaks.

"Do not be distressed." Madeline stroked Maxwell's ears with a gloved hand. "Once we are at Meadlow, I shall be settled, and you can make your journey. Better yet, let us send for Mr. Brennan."

"'Tis a good idea, mistress," Mrs. Burke agreed. "We shall send for Mr. Brennan the moment we arrive. Surely he will come, Miss Darcy, and without any delay. He will be glad to know you have not thrown him off. For I have no doubt Mr. Langbourne told him a pack of lies to make him think you did."

Madeline's eyes lit up. "Write to him and tell him to come straightaway, Darcy."

"I shall write the moment we arrive, Grandmother."

"If there are any persons he wishes to bring, tell him to do so. You and Ethan can marry in the nearby church. I should like a little wedding. A wedding would most please me."

Darcy looked over at her grandmother. Her mention of "any persons he wishes to bring" made her realize she had forgotten her father and she had no memory at the moment of her mother being at Fairview. Madeline's eyes were glazed, as if she were somewhere between the past and the future.

"I wonder how long it will take for us to arrive at Meadlow." Darcy drew her cloak closer. "It grows chilly and I am afraid for you, Grandmother. Are you cold?"

"I have Maxwell to keep me warm," Madeline said.

Darcy gave her a little smile. "He is your best friend."

Madeline shook her head. "My best animal friend. You and Mrs. Burke are my best friends. Oh! What will become of my mare? We left her behind, Burke!"

"I'm sure she is fine," said Mrs. Burke. "No ill shall come to her. She's safe and sound in her stall, I am sure."

Her lips trembling, Madeline slapped her hand on her lap. "I want Mr. Brighton to go to Havendale first thing and fetch my little horse. He's the only one I trust to care for her."

"Mr. Langbourne may not allow it," Mrs. Burke said.

Madeline huffed.

Darcy touched her grandmother's shoulder to calm her anxiety. "We will write to him as well, Grandmother."

"That will give me ease, Darcy. You do it for me. I'm afraid I shall be too weary to put a pen to paper when we arrive."

"I promise I shall. Do not worry."

"Why are we traveling so late?" Madeline said, her tone one of growing fear. "I have no doubt there shall be highwaymen out on the road."

"Maxwell will stave them off with his bared teeth and ferocious growl," Darcy told her. Madeline chuckled. "Try to sleep. I'm sure Mrs. Burke has a comfortable shoulder for you to lean on."

"Always has," said Madeline.

Madeline leaned on Mrs. Burke's shoulder. After a moment she fell to sleep, and the clouds broke away to reveal a full moon rising along the horizon. Darcy stared out the window at the quiet fields, wondering what Ethan was feeling, what he was thinking after being forced from Havendale? Oh, but she was glad he did not challenge Langbourne any further by testing his threat. For she had no doubt he would have shot Ethan—a thought too horrible to consider.

Ethan paced the floor of his room and raked his fingers through his hair. Darcy would not leave without sending him a letter. Something was not right, and he felt it. It clawed deep within his belly and moved up his throat, caused his hands to shake and his heartbeat to race.

Moonlight broke through the windows, brightening the room as he drew his boots over his calves. Hayward lay in a sickroom upstairs, Eliza watching over him. Ethan knocked on the door and stepped inside. He waited and watched, for the pair were troubled with amends to be made and Ethan did not want to burden them.

Eliza had not spoken a word as she sat on the bedside and listened to Hayward. Often his sentences were broken, incoherent. Other times he stared into her eyes and spoke tenderly, always ending with *please forgive me for sending you away.*

He drew near, saw that Hayward passed in and out of sleep. "How is he?"

"Worse, I am afraid. He is sleeping now. I listened to his pleas, to his explanations. He has lived all these years out in the wilderness among the tribes. He told me he met God there and was shown the errors of his ways."

"I do not doubt it. Many a man has met the Almighty in the wilderness."

"I see the regret in his eyes, and he has seen mine. I told him about your father, and it appeared to give him some relief to know I was kindly treated these many years."

"I remember."

"He was a good man. I miss him. You know that, don't you?"

"Yes. There hasn't been a day gone by that I have not seen it in you."

She dipped a cloth into water, wrung it, and bathed Hayward's face. "We have forgiven each other. He can rest now. It won't be long before he is gone, too. You must call Darcy and bring her to him. And I must reconcile with my daughter."

As Eliza spoke, and while he observed her tender care for Hayward and the urgency in her face to see Darcy, his worry for his beloved nagged him. And how would Eliza react when he told her what had happened at Havendale and that Darcy had gone?

He touched Eliza's shoulder and turned her to him. "You should rest awhile."

"I cannot." Eliza's eyes glinted with tears. "Reverend Reed gave Hayward last rites."

"I am sorry."

A light smile touched her lips as she brushed the tears from off her cheeks. "It is all right, Ethan. I realize he has loved me despite his anger toward me. He would not have bothered to make the journey and seek me out if he did not."

"My father would have thought well of Mr. Morgan's efforts, as well as your compassion for him."

"Yes. He would have urged me to forgive him." She paused, and then looked up with sudden concern. "I am anxious about Darcy." She stood. "Would it be better if I were to go to her alone? Which room is she in?"

He stopped her with a touch of his hand on hers. "She is not here."

Eliza grabbed his sleeve. "Not here? Why? What has happened?"

"I rode to Havendale. Langbourne met me outside. He said she went away."

"Away! To where?"

"He would not tell me."

"You must find out."

"I intend to." He raked his fingers through his loose hair and paced. Then he explained to Eliza how he insisted Langbourne allow him inside to see for himself Darcy had gone, and how in reply, Langbourne drew his pistol and threatened to shoot him. "If I had not removed myself, I am certain he would have made good on his threat."

Eliza's eyes were wide. "He is lying."

Ethan paused. "She would have come out to me if she were there, unless . . ."

"He prevented her somehow."

"I should have resisted." Ethan shook his head, feeling ashamed. "I have to go back. But I cannot leave you now in such a desperate time. What can I do to help? I can find the doctor."

"A doctor cannot help my husband now." Eliza reached up and touched his cheek. "Hayward hasn't much time. He needs his daughter. You must leave first thing in the morning and find her."

31

*W*ind drove across the moors and ruffled the gorse grass. Clouds swept in from the east, their long shadows crossing the land, embracing the moon, and darkening the streams into deep blue ribbons. Havendale was far behind them, and the carriage rolled past hamlets, crumbling walls of stone, and square-towered churches. Darcy wished the driver would stop so she could go inside one of those sanctuaries, kneel in a pew and pray. But the whip lashed and the horses plodded on.

She looked over at her grandmother and worried how much Madeline could take. And for this reason, she told herself again and again, she could not have let her make the journey alone, even with Mrs. Burke to accompany her, who was also aged and frail. Darcy had no idea what kind of place Meadlow was or how Madeline would be treated there. She had to see to it she'd be well cared for before taking the next step of getting away to Fairview.

She turned her eyes to the window. The landscape seemed to blur together now with little change. Her hood lay across her shoulders, and she drew it up over her hair with gloved hands, remembering a time when her locks were soaked with the river and how Ethan caressed them back from her face.

The carriage dipped and sprung back to the road. The jolt woke Madeline and she let out a little moan. Darcy knew her grandmother's inner strength to endure had crumbled. If only Langbourne had listened to her and considered how a move would distress Madeline body and mind. But he would not. His word was law and his mind closed to what he called *the foolish whims of women*.

"Do not weep, Grandmother. We will be at Meadlow soon, and there you can have a hot cup of tea and a warm bed."

"Will be better than the cold attacking me, and this horrible swaying and bumping." Madeline pressed a handkerchief against her eyes. "But even as that shall be over, I feel a little afraid of this change."

"At least we are together." Darcy adjusted a heavy wool blanket over Madeline's knees.

"I am grateful for it, Darcy. But you are not here by your own free will." She leaned her head back and shut her eyes. "Langbourne forced you."

Darcy tried to be reassuring. "By my own free will I chose to come with you."

"A difficult decision to choose between your parents and me. You should honor them over me."

"I will see them once I know you are settled."

"How dare Langbourne send Hayward away?" At last Madeline remembered, but for how long? "My son had no strength to argue, did he?"

"He is in good hands now that he is with my mother and Mr. Brennan."

"Yes. I have no doubt of that."

"Ethan will bring them to Meadlow after he receives my letter."

"Indeed they shall," said Mrs. Burke. "Mr. Hayward shall be right as rain by then."

Madeline's eyes glistened. "You think so, Burke?"

"I know so," Mrs. Burke nodded. "All he needed was some tender nursing and his wife to improve."

Darcy waited to speak, thinking back on how she had broached the subject of Madeline staying with the family before. To think of her living with Charlotte in an unfamiliar place pressed severely on Darcy. It would have made things easier if the driver had been willing to change direction. She felt like a prisoner inside the dismal carriage.

"Grandmother, return with us to Fairview when Ethan comes. I know it would mean another journey for you, but you could live with us, you and Mrs. Burke."

Madeline stroked Maxwell's ears and sighed. "I do not know, child. I am so weary. But that is not to say I don't want to. I do."

"Then it is settled. We will all leave together."

"Well," said Mrs. Burke with a smug look and a wiggle of her head. "That will certainly put Mr. Langbourne in his place."

The carriage turned at a bend in the road and climbed a hill. Madeline laid her hand over her heart. "Tell the driver to stop. I do not feel well."

Panicked, Darcy opened her window, stuck her head out and called up. "Stop at once. My grandmother is ill." The driver slowed the horses and pulled to the side of the road. He jumped down and appeared at the window.

"What now, miss?"

"My grandmother is not feeling well."

"Is she? Well, there's not much I can do about that. We will be at Meadlow shortly."

"Fairview is closer, is it not? We will pay you for your trouble. Now turn and take us there at once."

"You are wrong, miss. Meadlow is closer, not even a mile away. Fairview is back that way and I'll not turn." He eyed her and drew in a deep breath. "I have my orders."

Darcy balled her fist and groaned. She heard the snap of the coachman's whip, and the carriage rocked and creaked past a scattering of poor hamlets, houses with thatched roofs, small windows where few faces passed behind sullied glass. The horses turned at a sharp bend in the road. A chill rushed through Darcy at the site of a gibbet swinging from a tall post, within the iron cage tattered ribbons of rotting clothing, over the exposed bones of a highwayman. She looked away, disgusted at the scene, and prayed for the soul that met his end in this barbaric way.

Madeline had drifted back to sleep against Mrs. Burke's shoulder, and stirred when the driver called out, "Meadlow, ladies!"

The carriage entered through the gates and swept along to a circular drive, the gravel crunching beneath the spinning wheels, until the horses slowed and came to an easy halt. Darcy leaned forward to look out the window at the grand house that stood on a flat span of deep green lawn. Two stories were graced with large mullioned windows set within a façade of blushed brick, offset by a black lacquered French door with bright brass fixtures. Two chimneys climbed against the racing clouds and spewed smoke. Gnarled ivy grew over the facade, leaves quivering in the wind.

Darcy watched the front door open and Charlotte step outside dressed in pale gray silk, looking as lifeless as the Grecian statue that stood at the foot of the steps. She felt frozen to her seat, wishing she did not have to go in.

With a forced smile, Charlotte gathered her lace shawl over her narrow shoulders. "Welcome to Meadlow." She spoke in an elegant tone, yet her eyes told Darcy she had no joy in their arrival, no anticipation of having female company to fill her lonely days. They were intruders.

Once Mrs. Burke set her feet firm, Maxwell jumped out and sniffed the ground. Two female servants stood behind Charlotte and she motioned for them to help Madeline. They hurried down the steps as the driver guided her out, and with cane in hand, and the two maids supporting her, Madeline was led up the steps and into the house.

Darcy watched Charlotte pat her hair back and wondered why she wore it so severe. Tight and combed into a stiff chignon, a thin nimbus of brown encircling her face, giving her a stern, aged look. Perhaps if she wore it loose and in twists she would look more feminine, thought Darcy.

Handed out, she gathered up her hem, walked up the steps and stood in front of the forlorn mistress of Meadlow. She held her hand out to Charlotte. But Charlotte ignored the gesture and looked down the lane. "My husband did not accompany you?"

Compassion for this abandoned wife filled Darcy. "He did not."

A crestfallen look fell over Charlotte's face and she looked away. "Then he comes on horseback. Did he say when I should expect him?"

Darcy paused in front of Charlotte. "I am sorry. He made no mention of it."

"Did he say what business keeps him away?"

"I only know he was closing the house. Perhaps when he is finished he will make his journey home." Darcy hoped her words gave some hope to Charlotte.

A weary sigh escaped Charlotte and she glanced at Darcy. "If I have no expectations, I shall not be disappointed, shall I? I pray, Miss Darcy, you will never know the pain of being trapped in a loveless marriage."

Darcy's smile faded, and she ached for poor Charlotte, who jerked away and turned back inside the house. Her mind continued to stir with empathy. To be neglected and betrayed seemed an overwhelming blow. Did Charlotte know about Langbourne's mistress? Darcy would not tell her. It would hurt Charlotte, and even if she did know of his infidelity, to speak of it would open her wound.

When Darcy entered the foyer, she drew off her cloak. "I need to send a message, Charlotte. May I have ink and paper, please?"

"On the table over there." Charlotte pointed it out with her eyes.

As quick as her feet would carry her, being stiff from the long ride, Darcy gathered the quill in hand, dipped it into the inkwell and wrote '*Come to me, my love. I need you. I am at Meadlow north of Havendale. Kiss my father and mother for me*' and tell them I am praying for them.

She folded the note and handed it to Charlotte's servant who stood closest to the door. "Please see this is sent to Fairview without delay. It is urgent." The girl nodded and took it from Darcy's hand.

With Mrs. Burke on one side, and Darcy on the other, they aided Madeline to an upstairs bedroom. Not at all what Darcy expected, the room had a warm feel to it, the furnishing lavish, a gray marble mantelpiece framing the hearth. Maxwell jumped onto the bed and laid himself down with his eyes intent upon his mistress.

"I hope you will be comfortable here, Madeline." Charlotte stood by the door.

Without turning, Madeline said, "'Tis a pretty room, Charlotte. I should like to go to bed."

Mrs. Burke hurried to open a trunk and take out Madeline's nightclothes. Darcy helped by removing her grandmother's shoes. When she glanced back, Charlotte was closing the door. She looked up at her grandmother, noticing the faraway gaze glistening in her eyes.

"When you see your Uncle Will again, please tell him how fondly I spoke of him . . . that I love him and have missed him."

"I will, Grandmother. But you may be able to do that yourself one day soon."

"You know he wrote to me faithfully, that is until that revolution happened and then few letters ever made it into the country. I was glad when they resumed again."

"Uncle Will and Aunt Mari are both avid letter writers," Darcy said, setting the shoes in front of the fire. "We will write to them and tell them all that has happened."

This made Madeline smile, though faintly. "Describe each of the girls to me again."

Darcy began with Martha, and painted a picture of each of her cousins as vividly as she could, their beauty, their likes and dislikes, their talents and endowments. And she told Madeline about the different flowers her uncle collected and how he painted them in his portfolio. For the moment, the conversation was a great distraction to their present troubles and seemed to help Madeline rest easy.

"I am proud of my son." Madeline folded her hands across her chest. "What wonderful young ladies my granddaughters must be. If God sees fit that I should live longer and go to Fairview with you, then I shall go to America, Darcy. There is nothing left for me here."

32

$\mathcal{E}$arly the next morning, just as the sun rose, Ethan saddled his horse and set out for Havendale. He would have traveled there through the night, but Eliza persuaded him not to. Too many dangers were on the moors to cross them in the dark. She would have worried to the point of sleeplessness if he had gone with only the glare of the moon to guide him.

Prepared to meet opposition, he carried in his belt his flintlock pistol. No one came out to meet him. Not a sound came from the house or the stable. He jumped down from his horse and stepped up to the door. Mrs. Burke would answer, he thought, but after several tries no one came. He knocked loudly with his fist. "Open up! Open up, someone!"

He tried the handle and found it locked. He went around to the back, to the servants' entrance. The door handle turned, but the door stuck when he pushed upon it. Pressing his shoulder to it, he rammed it until it broke open. Now in the kitchen, he called out Darcy's name. Silence followed. He went through to the hall, found the furnishings in the rooms covered in white sheets, all the drapes drawn shut, the house empty and lifeless.

"Darcy! Darcy!" Ethan called. He bounded up the staircase, two steps at a time, his hand fixed firm over the handle of his pistol. Each room he searched, every door he opened. The bedrooms were empty. Darcy was gone, and so were the others. But to where?

"Help me find her, God," he whispered, and walked out into the sunlight. Thank the Lord the clouds had parted and a blue sky appeared. A brisk wind blew against his face and brushed the loose strands of his hair along his shoulders. Pushing them back, he strode toward the stables. All the stalls were empty, except for one. Madeline's mare shook her shaggy head and went back to chewing the oats in her trough.

Frustrated, Ethan stomped out, his boots sloshing through a mud puddle in the yard. Sanchet lifted his head and snorted when Ethan whistled to him, and as he picked up the reins a man in work clothes came around the corner of the house. He stopped short when he saw Ethan.

"No one is home, sir. Who are you and what do you want?"

"Ethan Brennan of Fairview. I am here for Miss Darcy Morgan."

"Not here."

"Do you know where she has gone?"

"Don't know. The ladies left last night. Mr. Langbourne on horseback. The house is closed up."

"And you are?"

"The caretaker newly hired by Mr. Langbourne. I live in a room above the stables." He moved on. Ethan stepped up to him.

"Surely you must have heard where Miss Darcy was sent to."

"I don't know why you'd think that. I'm nobody." The man paused, dragged off his slouch hat and scratched his head. "You attached to the young lady?"

"She's to be my wife."

The man raised his brows. "Ah. Well, you bein' in such a lather to find her makes sense now."

"Her father is dying. I need to bring her to him. If you know anything that might help me, please tell me what you know."

"Well, I can say when Mr. Langbourne handed me the keys, I saw the young woman standing on the staircase. She did not look happy, and I heard Mr. Langbourne speak unkindly to her as I left the house. He mentioned Meadlow. Perhaps the Brightons know the place. They're the closest neighbors. Go ask them, sir."

Of course—the Brightons. Surely they would know. And so, Ethan vaulted in his saddle and turned Sanchet out onto the road toward Bentmoor. He pushed the horse to a gallop over the high road above Havendale, kicking up mud beneath its hoofs. The Brightons would direct him to Meadlow and, with God's help and his swift horse, he'd rescue Darcy from what the powers of darkness had planned for her life.

Not long after leaving Havendale, he stood on the Brighton's carpet in their sitting room, in his mud-splattered boots, anxiously turning his hat in his hands and shifting on his feet.

"Yes, Mr. Brennan, we visited Charlotte one year at her country house," said Mrs. Brighton, as she sat on her blue settee. "It had been a dreadful journey over poor roads that rattled my bones, and upon arrival Mr. Brighton and I were stiff and sore from head to toe. Weren't we, my love?"

"Yes, indeed," Mr. Brighton responded. "Even worse, the house was cold. Not a very friendly place, I recall. Couldn't wait to leave."

Mrs. Brighton went on, Ethan wishing they would quickly answer his question as to where Meadlow was located. "I was bored to death sitting with that despondent Charlotte two whole days. I promised never again to visit such a gloomy place and be subject to freezing nights with no fire. She read no poetry, played no music. All she could do is play cards, and how can one stand that day after day?"

Mr. Brighton perked up. "And don't forget the bland food, my dear. Why are you interested in going to Meadlow, Mr. Brennan?"

"The woman I love is there, sir. Miss Darcy Morgan."

"Miss Darcy," exclaimed Mrs. Brighton. "A visit?"

"I do not know. But she has gone. I believe that is where she is, with her grandmother."

"Oh, Madeline will not like that place. It isn't far, is it, Richard?"

"Oh, not far at all. Let me direct you, Mr. Brennan. It is quite easy." And so Mr. Brighton proceeded to give him precise directions and a landmark, being the old gibbet, and finally the look of the old house.

Ethan thanked them both and, without another word, quickly departed.

✍

Morning tea was brought up on a tray. Charlotte sent word she could not join at table with her guests. Her limbs did not allow for her to sit in the stiff chairs without growing fatigued. It was just as well. Darcy wished to write letters. To sit with Charlotte would have stretched her nerves.

Darcy hated being in a strange place—especially in Langbourne's house. A sad feeling lingered, perhaps since the only people living there were Charlotte and her servants. There were no children, no sound of pattering feet or laughter. Charlotte hadn't even a dog or cat to keep her company. And so, the house held an old, friendless air that permeated every room. To shut it out, she closed her eyes and imagined in her mind her river—the sparkle of sunlight atop the ripples and pools, the dark cliffs, the birds and deer, the green forests, and the abundant wildflowers. She pictured her family and the old house at River Run. She and Ethan had stood in a field there not long ago, where he first kissed her.

"Oh, Ethan," she sighed. "One day, we will restore the house to its former beauty, and fill it with a brigade of children. Sanchet will graze alongside my mare. And God willing, mother and father will be there again."

Anxious for her letter to reach him and for his arrival, she listened to the sighing wind and the call of rock doves nestled in the eaves. She heard movement outside her door, and stepping out into the hallway, she saw Charlotte and a servant standing outside Madeline's room. The maid had her head down and spoke rapidly, as if she were trying to explain something to her mistress. Her eyes darted toward Darcy and her sad expression deepened. Charlotte turned and looked at Darcy with expressionless eyes.

"My grandmother? Is she awake?"

Charlotte cleared her throat. "No . . . She . . ."

Fear spun within Darcy. She hurried toward the door, but Charlotte's voice, raised more than usual, arrested her. "Before you go in," Charlotte said, "you must know, no one knew until the maid went in to bring her breakfast. Such things happen with the aged. It was to be expected."

"Knew what, Charlotte? What do you mean such things are to be expected?"

Charlotte glanced away, and then looked back at Darcy. "Madeline was old, and her health none too well. My husband must have been aware of it. So why did he send her to me? Now I have to deal with this."

Without waiting, Darcy rushed through the bedroom door. Inside she found the other maid, the one she had given the note to, changing the linens on the bed.

"Where is she? Where is my grandmother?"

The maid set a pillow down and looked over at her.

"Why are you not speaking?" Darcy asked.

Charlotte drew up beside her. "She passed on, Darcy, while you slept. I thought you were capable of understanding my words."

"She died in the night?" Darcy asked, shocked. Tears burned her eyes.

"You did say she was ill when you arrived."

"Why didn't you send for me?"

"Dear lord, Darcy! No one could determine the hour the old lady would decide to leave this world. We were all asleep."

"I just wish you had come and told me as soon as you knew."

Charlotte clapped her eyes shut. "I wish you had expressed with more force that Madeline was this close to dying. I am put out that you did not, and angry with my husband. He should not have sent her to Meadlow."

"Where is she?"

"My servants moved the body to another room. This is a guestroom and I would hate for anyone in my circle of friends, if they were to visit, to sleep in a bed where a deceased person had lain for too long. They'd be appalled. No one likes to sleep in a bed someone passed away in."

Frustration rose in Darcy and she shook her arm free from Charlotte's hand. "Be quiet, Charlotte!"

Eyes widening, Charlotte gasped. "What? How dare you speak to me in that manner? I am just as upset as you are."

"How can you treat this event with such coldness and think only of yourself and your inconvenience? I wish we had never come here."

"Well, no one forced you. You may leave at any time."

"I was forced. Grandmother was forced. She should have died in her own bed at Havendale, not suddenly taken from the home she lived in for decades and placed with strangers."

As if a dagger struck through to her core, Darcy dashed from the room. At first, she stifled the want to cry. But she could not prevent the tears from welling. She covered her face with her hands and allowed them to fall. She had not realized how much she had grown to love Madeline.

Charlotte swept out into the hallway. In a forced show of sympathy, she caught up with Darcy. "Is there something a servant can bring you? Wine, or perhaps some sweets? They always lift my spirits."

Darcy stood still and silent.

"Well," huffed Charlotte. "I did not think you cared so much for the old woman."

Darcy looked at her. "She was my grandmother, Charlotte. Is there no sorrow in you at all, no sadness at least for me?"

Charlotte lifted her brows. "Please mind yourself while you are in my house, Darcy. I will send for the undertaker. I suppose she would want to be buried beside her—let me see—two husbands?"

"She would. And you need not worry yourself. I will take care of everything."

"My husband would not approve. I've sent for him."

"You knew where to find him?"

"Of course. I know where he goes when he is away from me."

Darcy wiped her eyes dry. "Where is Mrs. Burke?"

"Oh, I meant to tell you about that. Seeing I have enough staff at Meadlow, I will find her a new situation."

"She will stay with me. I have an obligation to her."

Charlotte gave Darcy a mocking smile. "I daresay I do not understand you. You have no duty to a servant. The best thing for her is to be placed in a household where she will work and be cared for. Is this the view in America, that you treat servants like family members?"

Darcy drew in a long, slow breath, turned away and left Charlotte in the gloomy hallway with her maid standing behind her. There was no consoling poor Mrs. Burke. Darcy found her weeping in an upstairs bedroom, so small it could only fit a single bed and dresser. Darcy poured her a glass of water and made her drink it.

Mrs. Burke drew out a handkerchief and blew her nose. "I knew it were coming. God rest her soul."

"You were good to her, and I thank you for that, Mrs. Burke. Now Charlotte tells me she will find you a new position. But I would be happy if you came with me back to America."

Mrs. Burke smiled a moment. "You are sweet to offer, miss. But my home is England. I have family in the north, a rather large one actually. I am at an age where I can retire in peace and be near them."

"But how shall you live?" Darcy asked.

"I set money aside over the years—for a rainy day—and that day has come. My sister is a spinster, and she will allow me to live with her. My brothers are farmers with wives, children, and grandchildren. The good Lord knows I shall be happy."

On the floor, at the foot of the bed, Maxwell whined. Darcy picked him up and set him in Mrs. Burke's lap. "He is yours now. You will take care of him, won't you?"

Mrs. Burke cuddled the little dog close. "Oh, I shall. Thank you, Darcy."

"My grandmother would have wanted you to have him." She ran her hand over the dog's head, and then heard a horse gallop down the drive. Her heart skipped. Had Ethan received her note? It had to be him. She rose and rushed over to the window, threw back the curtains and peered down into the courtyard.

"Is it Mr. Brennan?" Mrs. Burke said.

Darcy's hopes were dashed when she saw Langbourne swing down from the saddle in his black cloak, the pale morning light showing on his angry face. "No. It is Mr. Langbourne."

"Dear, Lord." Mrs. Burke set her handkerchief aside and joined Darcy at the window. "We shall surely have an unpleasant time now."

Disappointed, Darcy stood back, squeezed Mrs. Burke's hand, and went downstairs to meet him.

33

By the time Darcy stepped off the last step into the foyer, Langbourne had cast off his hat and cloak. A cold draft blew against her as a servant closed the front door, but did not abate the fever racing through her nerves. She fixed her eyes on Langbourne as he removed his gloves.

"Where is my wife?" His voice sounded raspy, his tone irritable.

Darcy faced him. "Upstairs, I believe. She hoped you would come."

"A most inconvenient time for Madeline to have passed on. I suppose you shall blame me."

Darcy said nothing, only looked him straight in the eye. With an uneasy gait, Langbourne turned to the maid. "Bring me something to drink. I don't care what it is as long as it will soothe my throat. There was a hard wind riding here."

When the maid gave her curtsey and was gone, he approached Darcy. She felt a shiver wash over her, but remained where she stood. He drew her hair between his fingers. "You, at least, made it to Meadlow in good health. I have no doubt Charlotte will grow jealous of you, but do not mind her cold ways. She never interferes."

Darcy recoiled. "You go too far, sir."

"Not far enough." He looked up the staircase at the sound of footsteps. Charlotte appeared and Darcy observed with perplexity the genteel smile that graced her mouth upon sight of her wayward husband. *She loves him. Why?*

"You came so quickly," Charlotte said.

"Well, when someone dies in one's house, one should take care of the details. I could not leave it up to you to deal with. You do not have the head for it or the fortitude. It was, however, ill-timed."

"As if this could have been marked on a calendar," Darcy said. "It is not Charlotte's fault. Perhaps if you had left Madeline at Havendale, she would still be with us, and you sir, would not have been so put out. I told you she was ill and could not travel."

He sneered. "There's that bold tongue again."

For a moment, they stared into each other's eyes. The contention between them flared. Coupled with the grief she felt, her loathing of him grew to unbearable proportions. She drew her skirts around and rushed back up the staircase to the room given her. She locked it, then threw herself across the bed and wept.

A funeral carriage drew up to a rear door at Meadlow. Two men dressed in black carried the body of Madeline Morgan away. Darcy asked to accompany them back, but they shook their heads at her and said it was something just not done.

Charlotte knocked on Darcy's door and spoke to her through it. "Everything is settled. You should stop weeping,

Darcy. You must make plans as to what you will do now that Madeline is gone."

"I wish to go to Fairview and then home," Darcy answered back.

"Then go. I will not stop you."

She listened to Charlotte step away. Neither she nor Langbourne cared what happened to her, and they had sent Mrs. Burke away the moment the funeral carriage left. Still, she wept, until her heart grew calm and her tears dried. Ethan had not come and she yearned for him. When the maid came to her room with a fresh pitcher of water, Darcy questioned her.

"You gave the note to the coachman?"

"Yes, miss. He said he'd post it the first chance he had, which I think would be either at Castleton or even Manchester. It will take time."

"There is no one here who could have delivered it?"

"No, miss. Sorry."

After the maid left, Darcy looked over at her cloak lying across the back of a chair. The mantelpiece clock ticked as she paced the floor. "I can do this. I've hiked the river paths and climbed the cliffs. I sailed across the ocean to England alone, and walked to Havendale. I do not need to fear." Then she got down on her knees and bent her head in her hands. "Help me, Lord. I cannot stay here another minute. Show me the way. For thou art my rock and my fortress; therefore, for thy name's sake lead me, and guide me."

She had to travel light, and so she placed only one set of clothes in her bag and closed the latch. Picking up her cloak, she drew it over her body, and fastened the tassels at her throat. Then she slipped out the door, went down the staircase with her head held high, and walked away from Meadlow without a look back.

34

$\mathcal{D}$ew lay on the grass and crackled beneath Darcy's shoes. Walking at a steady pace, she had no worry for rain. The joy of knowing she was headed for Fairview, for the warm embrace of Ethan, drenched her soul. She'd see her mother, her poor lost father. And finally, they'd sail away across a blue welcoming ocean back to America, to the Potomac and the home she loved.

After passing through the gates, she stood a moment looking down the road. If they had come from Havendale that way, then the logical thing was to head in that direction. Yes, to the south, and then beyond Havendale she'd come to Fairview. On she went, keeping to the road where a marker pointed the way toward the villages nestled in the Hope Valley. Prints from horse and wagon were deep in the mud; trees sparse, and old Roman walls lined the road.

She found herself walking on a hill overlooking a vale. The wind bore through her cloak and fought its way in to chill her limbs. She wrapped it closer against her body and shivered. Reaching an outcropping of stone, she climbed it to see farther into the valley. She stood on a rise of rock that jutted up from the earth in layers of gray limestone. It came faintly to her at first, the sound of a horse pounding over the mossy turf. She turned and when her eyes fixed on the rider heading her way, she cried out, "Ethan! Ethan!"

He slowed Sanchet, stopped and looked toward the sound of her voice, then urging his mount with his heels, he raced the horse up the slope toward her. Anxious to meet him, Darcy took a step down, then another.

"Ethan!" she called to him. "I am here!" She watched him spur his horse to a quicker pace and her heart raced with each beat of Sanchet's hooves.

Halfway down the cliff the rocks began to slip. Then they gave way. She cried out, reached and grabbed for something to keep her from falling. As she slid down the ledge, the rocks cut into her hands and arms. With nothing to hold her, she felt only space about her, as if time had slowed. Her cloak spread out like the wings of a bird, her arms outstretched. Then the air within her lungs was forced out when she landed on the ground several feet below. The world went black, then returned in a daze. She heard a horse halt near her, heard it blow out its nostrils. Hurried steps came to her; Ethan's voice was so anxious and alarmed.

Opening her eyes, she beheld him kneeling over her, his eyes flooded with worry. "Darcy. Are you badly hurt?" he asked breathless.

"I have had a bad fall. When I saw you, I wanted to climb down to you. I have never had such a bad fall before."

"Tragic as it is, something like this was bound to happen. What were you thinking to climb way up there?"

"You know . . . I am naturally curious." She found it difficult to inhale, to speak.

He arranged her hands around his neck and went to lift her. Pain shot through her body and she felt the blood rush from her face and pressure pulse through her temples. "It hurts to move. My legs feel numb." Alarmed at this, she felt tears well. She forced them back when she saw the great distress that sprang in Ethan's eyes.

"We must hurry." His arms went beneath her and he gathered her close against his breast and carried her. Before them was a grassy ascent beside the broken line of rocks. Up the hill he went with her pressing against him, shielding her face from the wind. Reaching Sanchet, Ethan wished he could plunge his boot into the stirrup and swing up.

"Keep your arms about me if you can, my love, and hold tight."

Darcy locked her fingers. "I shall try."

"We have a long walk ahead, but we will make it."

He hurried on with her in his arms, descending the hill to more level ground. Sanchet followed, shook his mane and snorted. Though pain coursed through her body, and her legs seemed weightless, she felt safe with her arms around his neck, and his arms holding her close against him.

✍❧

The next things Darcy was aware of when she opened her eyes were the flame of a candle and the darkness of night through the windows in the room where she lay. She heard a small clock ding the hour of nine. Figures moved about the room and she heard them whisper. Someone lifted her hand and pressed kisses against her fingers.

"Ethan?" She gazed up at him. His eyes were warm for her.

"I am here, Darcy."

"Am I at Fairview?"

"Yes, darling."

"What happened?"

"You fell. Lie still."

"Yes, I fell. Stupid of me, wasn't it? How many times does this make that you have come to my rescue?"

"A few. But that is why God put me here—to watch over you—to love you."

Darcy could feel the glow in her eyes as she gazed at him. He was her guardian, her protector, planned from the beginning of time.

She tried to sit up. When she could not, fear shot through her. "My legs." Frightened, she reached down. "I cannot feel them. I cannot move them."

Another person approached, a face she did not know, a man with great white whiskers lining his jaw, and a shock of gray hair neat about a round face. "Miss Darcy, I am Doctor Viers. You have had a terrible injury. Lie as still as you can."

Darcy ceased struggling and looked up at him with questioning eyes.

"You can thank Mr. Brennan for carrying you all the way to Fairview and then riding several miles to bring me back. I am rarely called to this part of Derbyshire, for it is a long way for me to travel, but he explained how urgent it was that I come."

Darcy looked over at Ethan. "Thank you," she said quietly.

The doctor lifted her wrist and timed her pulse with his watch. "The fall has caused paralysis to your legs. Now, in time, if you are careful, you may recover. But there is the chance you may be permanently crippled. It all depends on the extent of the injury you incurred."

No. It could not happen to her. She had to return home, walk the river paths, and climb the bluffs. She had to ride and fish, dance at country balls, and sit in her favorite spot in the little church near River Run. How could she be any kind of a wife to Ethan as a cripple?

"You are wrong. I can walk. See, let me show you." And she threw back the sheets and covers, and pushed her legs over the side of the bed.

"Darcy, no." Ethan stopped her.

She waited, looking into his eyes, trembling.

He asked Doctor Viers to leave the room, and when the door closed, Ethan cupped his hands around Darcy's face. "You must be patient."

"I am damaged." She lowered her eyes and began to cry. "I do not expect anything from you. I release you."

"You think I love you any less? You think I would abandon you? I love you, Darcy." He drew her into his arms and embraced her hard. "You are the dearest thing to me and you are to be my wife."

"A crippled wife. No, Ethan."

"And as my wife," he went on, "I expect you to listen to me." He said this with a quick smile. "I know how hard that will be for you to do, but I insist upon it. We will post the banns, be married in a fortnight, and then leave for Maryland. Your father left us River Run, and with what money I acquire from the sale of Fairview, we will restore the house and buy anything you wish to fill it with. Not only that, your mother and Fiona are coming with us."

"My mother and Fiona? I remember Fiona. She was good to me." A strange memory ran through Darcy's mind. She saw herself in Fiona's arms beneath a floor hugging a doll, looking up at the light seeping through the crack. "There was a time she protected me."

"Yes, and she and your mother cannot wait to talk to you. They are just outside the door." He rose to call them.

Darcy held out her hand. "First, what has happened to my father?"

Ethan's smile left his handsome face. "His suffering ended the hour before I returned with you."

Darcy let out a long breath, grieved he had gone, sorry she had not been there to hold his hand. "And so did Madeline's. She passed in her sleep at Meadlow."

Ethan lowered his head. "I am sorry over both. But glad they are in heaven together, Darcy. Try not to grieve too hard."

"And my mother? Is she well?"

"In body, but her heart is broken that you are hurt. She wants to talk to you. May I call her in?"

Darcy's heart lightened. Would her mother look the way she remembered, her hair dark, with motherly hands that held her, and a voice tender and sweet? Now to be reconciled seemed to vanquish the former pain, the losses she had endured, the trial she faced.

She pressed Ethan's hand against her cheek. "Please, Ethan. Call her. Tell her I need her now more than ever."

35

$\mathcal{T}$wo weeks after the Reverend Reed read the banns in church, Darcy and Ethan took their vows. Darcy marveled at the stained-glass windows and thought about her grandfather, wondering how many couples he had married in the course of his ministry. Although she loved Fairview, Ethan let the estate go and sold it for a fair sum, the new owner swearing he would pull the old house down and replace it with a larger one.

Eliza and Fiona accompanied them on the voyage home aboard a pretty sailing ship called *The Dove*, reminiscent of that first vessel that had dropped anchor in the St. Mary's River a century before. As in the days of Noah, the dove returned with an olive branch in its beak. They were returning to River Run with peace and joy in their hearts.

Upon arrival at Point Lookout, Ethan paid for a post chaise, and after miles and miles of bumpy, dusty roads, they reached the end of the lane that led to the Breese house. Ethan called up to the driver to stop, and once the horses were settled, he lifted Darcy out and carried her down the sunny path toward the house and the welcoming arms of her dear cousins.

Martha was the first to embrace Darcy as she lay in Ethan's arms. "Darcy, I have missed you." She kissed her cheek.

"I have been bored to death without you, Darcy," said Lizzy.

"You have brought Mr. Brennan back with you." Martha's eyes beamed as she looked at him. "So good to see you again, sir. And carrying my cousin once more."

"We are married," he said.

The girls squealed at the news and chattered on like magpies. Mr. Breese stepped out the door with his wife and his dog. "My lord, it is Darcy and Mr. Brennan." They rushed to her, kissed her. "Why are you carrying her, sir?" Mr. Brennan asked.

Once the explanation was given, Mrs. Breese collapsed back against her husband. "Please tell us it is not to be, Darcy," and much sorrow was expressed. The girls gathered round and Martha wept against Darcy's shoulder.

"No, no. Do not cry. I shall recover. I know it."

"It cannot be helped," cried Mrs. Breese. "I knew it. Darcy, why did you not take care where you trekked? It pains my heart to see you have been crippled."

"I intend to overcome my condition. I am determined."

"How? You see your uncle. He still walks breathless. I have watched over him every minute since you left."

Martha wiped her eyes dry. "We have a very good doctor, Darcy. You remember Dr. Emerson? He can help, surely."

"How is he, Martha?"

"Very well. We are engaged." She turned to her parents. "And Darcy and Mr. Brennan are married, Mama, Papa."

Mrs. Breese threw up her hands and joy overtook her tears. Mr. Breese looked down the lane. "And who is this you have brought home with you?"

"My mother, sir, and Fiona, her best friend in all the world."

Dismayed, Mr. Breese shook his head. "What? How can that be? We were told Eliza was dead."

"It was never true, sir," Ethan said. "She had lived with me these many years. We have a lot to discuss."

"Indeed we do. But what fantastic news this is!"

The whole crew rushed down the lane toward Eliza and Fiona. Darcy and Ethan waited, and when everyone was introduced Mari Breese threw her arms around Eliza, and embraced her with more tears.

"My daughter is strong, Mari." Eliza took up Darcy's hand. "And so happy to be home, as I am. I had lost all hope of ever seeing the river again. But God found a way."

"It is good of you to say so, Eliza." Mari Breese smiled and moved back her girls. "Please come inside. We have so much to talk about."

Before going in, Eliza turned to William Breese. "I have sad news to tell you. But it does not come without good."

He looped her arm through his. "Then let us go into the sitting room and sit a while, Eliza."

Darcy, Ethan, Eliza, and Fiona stayed with the Breeses while the house at River Run was being rebuilt, Ethan partaking in the labor, Mr. Breese sitting in a chair in the shade observing all the goings-on. He had not returned to himself after his stroke and took his ease beneath the shade of an ancient tree, with his dog lounging at his feet.

Along a country path that bordered the land sat the cemetery where Addison and Ilene were buried. Darcy saw the sorrow in her mother's face over her loss, but also because her husband could not be laid there in the ground he so loved.

Later that spring, upon Ilene's gravestone, were etched the words *It is well with my child*, and on the day it was erected,

Eliza wept and placed blue forget-me-nots beneath it. For the remainder of her life, she did so every spring, until she too lay next to her child, waiting for that promised day of jubilation *when God shall wipe away all tears from their eyes; and there shall be no more death, neither sorrow, nor crying, neither shall there be any more pain: for the former things are passed away.*

And on warm days, Ethan took Darcy down to the river and waded with her into the water, holding her in his arms, her head resting on his shoulder. There in the deeper currents the river caressed her legs and brought healing and strength to her body.

Finally, on the day when all was complete at River Run, Ethan gathered the family together. Mr. and Mrs. Breese and their unwed daughters sat in the wagon with the painted red rims, the girls dressed in their Sunday best. Martha and her new husband, Dr. Emerson, rode on horseback alongside them. Eliza, Fiona, and Darcy rode in the carriage with the hood down, and Ethan drove the horses down the river path beneath the shade of the ancient elms.

He looked over his shoulder at Darcy and smiled. Dressed in white, a broad-brimmed hat decorated with white silk flowers shading her face, a broad blue ribbon tied under her chin, she looked more beautiful to him than ever and he made a point of telling her so. She laid her hand softly over her stomach and smiled, roses in her cheeks. A son would be born to them by Christmas, who would pass on River Run's legacy to his son, his grandson, and each generation for the next two hundred years.

Now, when they came upon the house, everyone cheered. Its windows sparkled in the sunshine, and its green lawn swept alongside the sandy lane. Potted plants sat on the porch, and the old tree—that sentinel through time—guarded a swing. Eliza wiped her eyes and Fiona put her arms around her. Mrs.

Breese declared it was the finest house beside the two rivers. Darcy stared at it, absorbing every inch.

"Do you like it?" Ethan asked, lifting her down from the carriage, cradling her in his arms. "Is it as you remember?"

"Yes. Thank you." Darcy kissed his cheek. "It is more beautiful than I could ever have imagined."

With Eliza and the family walking behind them, Ethan carried Darcy over the threshold, set her feet down on the smooth oak floor, and helped her walk inside. Darcy's gait was unsteady, but her heart was finally home.

This is my rest forever: here will I dwell;
for I have desired it.

—*Psalm 132:14 KJV*

Discussion Questions

1. Who do you feel Darcy turned out to be most like, her father, Hayward, or her mother, Eliza, and why?

2. What was Darcy searching for?

3. What were Darcy's strong points?

4. What were her weaknesses?

5. What kind of impact did it have on Darcy when she was told her mother was dead and that her father had abandoned her?

6. Name three things about Ethan Brennan you admired the most.

7. Do you feel Darcy was able to accept the past and forgive others?

8. Which character did you most closely identify with?

9. Who was your favorite character in the book, and why?

10. What was your favorite scene in the story, and why?

11. Why is it admirable that Hayward made the journey to England in order to find Eliza and ask for her forgiveness?

12. Why is it important that we forgive each other?

Apple Tansey

Take three pippins, slice them round in thin slices,
and fry them with butter; then beat four eggs,
with six spoonfuls of cream, a little rosewater,
nutmeg, and sugar; stir them together, and pour over
the apples; let it fry a little, and turn it with a pye-plate.
Garnish with lemon and sugar strew'd over it.

from *The Compleat Housewife* by Eliza Smith, 1727

Bonus Chapter from Book 3 of
The Daughters of the Potomac Series

Beyond the Valley

Cornwall, England

Autumn 1778

Sarah Carr would never look at the sea the same way again,
or listen the same way to the waves sweeping across the shore.
And never would she embrace her first love again. Drawing
in the briny air, feeling the wind rush through her unbound
hair, now spoke of danger and loss. Basking in blue moonlight
under the stars and having Jamie point out the constellations
had now become a thing of the past that could never, in her
mind, be repeated.

Tonight a hunter's moon stood behind bands of dark purple
clouds as if it were the milky eye of evil. Along the bronze sand,
deep green seaweed entwined with rotted gray driftwood. The
scent of salt blew heavy in the air, deepening the sting of tears
in her eyes, and tasting bitter on her tongue.

She had pleaded with Jamie not to go down to the shore
with the others when they beat on the door and called out
that a ship had wrecked in the harbor. But an empty pocket
and a growling stomach influenced him to go. For over an
hour, she waited for him to return and then she could bear the
anxiety no longer. Sarah slipped on her worn leather boots
and hurried down to the beach, working through the tangle of
frenzied scavengers in hopes she would find him.

People rushed about her, some with torches, others carrying glowing tin lanterns. There were calls and shouts over the howl of the wind and the noise of the sea. They carried sacks, barrels, and crates, tossed in the surf and washed ashore, others taken perilously from the sinking vessel. The groan of its timbers caused Sarah to shiver, as she thought of the poor souls trapped aboard. She could make out its black hulk in the moonlight, its main mast shooting up through the boil of waves like a spear.

"Have mercy on those left behind, O Lord." She shoved back her tangle of hair and watched the hapless ship go down into the dark depths of an angry sea.

A bonfire threw sparks over the sand. The foamy edge along the surf seemed a ribbon of gold near her feet. The few sailors who had survived looked on wide-eyed and drenched to the bone. They shivered in the cold, with no weapons to fend off the looting.

A firm hand moved Sarah back, and she gasped. "Come on, girl. This is no place for ye to be." She turned to a man in untidy clothes. His wet hair corkscrewed around his ears and hung over his forehead. He turned up his collar against the drizzle and wind. She recognized him as one of the villagers, a fisherman by trade, but did not know his name.

"You must leave this place before it gets too rough, Sarah. We'll take Jamie to the chapel with the others. Come with me."

She shook her head at his meaning. "Jamie? Where is he?" she shouted over the blast of wind as she glanced at the chaos around her. "Why must we go to the chapel?"

The man did not answer. Instead he shifted on his feet, frowned, and glanced away. Then, with no answer, he took her by the arm again and led her across the sand. Her hair, the color of burnt umber, floated about her eyes, where the mist blurred her vision.

"Are we gathering there to pray?" she asked. "We need to pray for those poor souls caught in the sea." She lifted her skirts and stepped unsteadily. Her limp made it difficult to navigate the beach.

"Ah, let me help you." The man threw his arm across her back. "Over this way. Watch your step. Steady now."

He took her to a place where the rocks made a barrier between the village and the sea. In the orange firelight, Sarah saw bodies stretched out on the sand in a row, their clothes soaked and splattered with sand. Faces were ashen in the torchlight. Their arms were crossed over their chests. The worst of her fears exploded into reality. She trembled and felt her knees weaken.

Upon a blanket lay the body of her husband, Jamie, his youthful face whiter than the wet shirt that clung to his lifeless body. His eyes were closed. His dark hair was soaked and clinging to his throat. Sarah gasped. "Jamie!"

She shivered from the cold wind that shoved against her, that pounded the waves upon the beach, from the grief that pounded a merciless fist against a breast once content with love, thinking it would last forever.

"No!" She fell beside him, threw her arms across his chest, wherein lay a silent heart. "Lord God, do not take him from me. Bring him back!" She shook with weeping, and someone pulled her away.

Four men wrapped her lad in the blanket and lifted him. She followed. Her skirts twisted around her limbs as the wind gusts grew stronger. A storm had battered the Cornish coast, and another whisked across sea and land behind it. Within moments, clouds smothered the moon and stars—the bonfire and a few lanterns the only lights to guide their steps up to the centuries-old stone church.

To rally her strength, she took in a deep lungful of air. Instead of relieving her, its mix of smoke from the bonfire and the brackish wind choked her. Behind her, she heard the waves break over the rocks, rush over the sand and pebbles, and suck at the shipwreck. A few lights in the cottages afar off glimmered in the darkness. She stumbled, regained her footing, and brushed away the tears that stung her eyes.

Fifteen sailors from the shipwreck and five villagers were laid to rest in the parish churchyard the next morning. Four somber widows walked away in silence along with their fatherless children, made poorer by their loss.

Sarah drew her shoulders back, determined to rise above her grief and face what life had just thrown at her. But her heart ached, and she knew no amount of fortitude could hide it. She tipped the brim of her hat downward to hide her tears.

"What is done cannot be undone," she said to the woman who walked beside her. "God asks of me to go on. And I shall for my child's sake."

Her neighbor, Mercy Banks, placed her hand over Sarah's shoulder. She was as tall as Sarah, lean with a pleasant countenance and large brown eyes. Known for her kindness to those in need, Mercy comforted Sarah with her touch.

"You must come home with me, Sarah. The least we can do is give you a warm meal and a bed for the night. It would be too lonely in your little cottage without Jamie."

Sarah glanced down at the three children as they walked alongside their mother. Their heads were as blond as sand, their eyes like Mercy's. Two clung to Mercy's skirts. The oldest boy walked ahead and swung a stick at the geese in the road.

"Thank you, Mercy. But I am leaving Bassets Cove." She could not impose on her neighbors who had young mouths to feed. "My landlord is not a rich man. I can expect sympathy, but not charity. He and his wife need a paying tenant. So I've told them I am leaving."

Mercy's face crinkled with worry. "You are leaving this minute? Let me speak to my husband."

Sarah touched her friend's shoulder. "Do not worry. I will be all right."

"But where will you go, Sarah? You have no family, no parents, no brothers or sisters. Have you a distant relative who would take you in all of a sudden?"

"I am going to Jamie's sister Mary and her husband. November is around the corner and the cold weather will be here. I must go while I have the chance."

Mercy pressed her mouth, then let out a long breath. "To the Lockes? It is said Lem Locke is a smuggler, that he will stop anyone by any means if they get in his way. It isn't as if he is helping any of the poor in Cornwall, for it is also said that he hoards his goods in the caves along the coast, and sells rum and brandy at a high price to the gentry. You should reconsider."

"I have nothing to fear, and nowhere else to go. I am sure it is only a rumor you have heard about Lem. Jamie told me if I should ever need help to go to them. Why would he say that if they were bad people?"

"Perhaps Jamie did not know Lem Locke as well as he should have. Not only that, they must have heard the unfortunate news by now, and they should have come for you, if they have any Christian charity in them at all. Why are they not here?"

"I had no way of sending word. Paper is so precious, and I had none. But I imagine they may hear from others before I reach them, but only of the wreck."

Mercy cocked her head. "Have you met them before?"

"Only Mary. It was a few days before Jamie and I were wed. She was quiet but not completely cold. Yet, I do not think she approved of our marriage, and would rather have seen her brother marry a fit woman. She never said where Lem was."

"Away smuggling, no doubt. I pray he is kind to you, Sarah. It is what you need right now."

Once they reached her cottage door, Mercy kissed Sarah's cheek. "I wish you well, and will keep you and your child in my prayers. If you should need to return, come to my door before anyone else's. Understand?"

"Yes, thank you." Sarah hugged Mercy, then watched her go, with the children in tow, down the sandy lane that led into the heart of the village.

Before stepping inside, Sarah glanced up at the gray sky that swirled above. "If only you would clear the clouds away, Lord. I might feel better if I were to see the sun. But if not today, then tomorrow."

Pushing the door in, she stepped over the threshold and paused. The sparse little room seemed neglected, as if no living soul lived there anymore. They owned little, and few things were left of Jamie's—his pipe, and Bible, and one change of clothes. She packed them in a sack with her own scant possessions—brush, comb, and one pair of stockings. The rest she owned was on her back.

Determined to be strong, she wiped away a tear and heaved the bag into her arms. After she shut the door behind her, she took the path to the rear of the cottage and slowly climbed the grassy slopes. It would take her longer than the average person to reach the moorland above, for having been born with one leg slightly shorter than the other hindered her gait, enough to cause her stride to be uneven. It had been the source of ridicule when she was growing up, orphaned and living in a workhouse for children. Told her mother was dead, her father unknown, she wondered if she were an abandoned child, an embarrassment to some gentry family for being flawed and possibly illegitimate.

Abused and starved, she kept to herself, and barely spoke to anyone, until a good-looking young man came down the lane that bordered the field she worked in. The wheat had been scythed and she, along with other able bodies, stood in a line to gather the sheaves into bundles. He leaned on the fence rail and watched her. The next day, he offered her water from his canteen. On the third day, he approached her during her ten-minute rest time, sat beside her and told her his likes and dislikes.

"I hate the smell of wheat," he told her. "It makes me sneeze." She remembered how his comment had made her giggle. "I'm a net maker, but I hate eating fish. Don't like the bones."

"What *do* you like?" she asked in a quiet voice.

"Bread and butter . . . and pretty girls like you."

She had hidden her face in the sleeve of her dress, for she felt the burn of a blush rush over her.

By the fourth day, he suggested she leave with him. "I live in Bassets Cove, not far from here," he told her. "It's a beautiful place. The sea air is good for one's health, you know. I am alone. You are alone. I could use a wife."

Sarah stood and brushed the bits of chaff off her dress. "You could not possibly want me."

"Why not? You're very pretty, Sarah. And I like the way you think."

"Hmm, haven't you noticed my way of walking?"

"Yes, what of it?"

"I am crippled." She leaned down, emphasizing the words.

He jumped up and put his hands on her shoulders. "I do not care. Marry me."

He had been the first man to ask, the first not to care about her *imperfection*. He was a means of escape and the start of a new life, a net maker by trade. She reasoned he would protect her, take care of her, and she understood they would never rise above a humble existence. If not Jamie, who on God's green earth would have her?

"Well," she had told him while looking into his blue eyes, "I suppose the Lord has brought us together. You need a wife, and I need a protector. I accept you as you are, not a rich man, if you will accept me as I am—a cripple."

She never forgot the expression on Jamie's face, how his eyes lit up as he gazed into hers. "You may limp, Sarah, but you are healthy. You and I shall not be alone. Not for the rest of our lives. We will have lots of children and grow very old together. And I shall become a wealthy man one day. You will see." And he leaned down and kissed her cheek.

Inside the little cottage, life seemed abundant. Jamie wove the finest nets and mended others for the local fishermen. There was food on the table and rent paid most of the time. But after only a few months wed, his lack of affection, his never saying he loved her, began to disappoint Sarah. She never mentioned it to him, deciding she would sacrifice romance for a roof over her head, food in her belly, and companionship.

And so, at age seventeen, she had left the wheat fields, with him strolling alongside her as the sun went down. Married nearly six months, she now found herself alone in the world again.

She came to the little church that overlooked the sea. Sunlight glimmered in the windows. But the gray stone gave it a cold appearance. She stepped over the thick grass, and drew near Jamie's marker, a small, narrow stone with his name and date. She stood in front of it and sighed, while her cloak fanned behind her in the wind.

"You did not kiss me good-bye, Jamie. You spoke not a word to me, but rushed out the door without a second thought. How I wish you had listened when I warned you not to go. But it was not your way. You showed little attention to my pleas. You made it clear your business was your own and I need not be concerned, only be happy when you would return home with a sack full of goods. I shall miss you."

She closed her eyes, spoke a prayer for his soul, and moved on. Once she reached the crossroads, she headed south along the coastal road, and tried not to think of how hungry she was. Her last full meal was the night Jamie left to plunder the shipwreck. She thought about how he had gulped down the humble potato stew, grabbed his hat, and rushed out the door at the urging of his mates.

The bag slipped in Sarah's arms. She pulled it up, held it tighter, and glanced back. Leaving the village and the blue cove caused a wave of sadness to ripple through her. She wished some of her long-time neighbors, besides Mercy, had followed, begged her to stay, urged her not to go, and gave her all the reasons why, offered her work, some kind of position to keep her from starving. Then she hoped to see a wagon or coach heading in her direction. But the road remained lonely and windswept.

She was dressed in a homespun dress open at the front, and her beige striped petticoat fluttered about her slim legs. The hem was a bit tattered and soiled from wear. Her straw hat lay between her shoulder blades. The blue ribbon, faded gray, looped around her throat. No point wearing it upon her head, for the wind would blow it off or worsen the wear on the brim.

Six miles later, she set the sack down on the roadside, then gathered her hair in her hands and twisted it into a braid. Her dress felt tight against her waist. She loosened the stays before going on.

A half-mile further, misty sunbeams shot through the clouds and plunged toward earth and sea. Sarah gazed with awe at the heaven-like spears and the distant patches of blue. For a moment, it raised her soul and soothed the pain that lingered in her heart.

She watched sparrows dart across the sky and land afar off. Then she moved on down the sandy road. This time she strove to walk with ladylike grace. But this proved, as it had many times before, a task too difficult and wearisome to do.

Want to learn more about author
Rita Gerlach and check out other great fiction
from Abingdon Press?

Sign up for our fiction newsletter at
www.AbingdonPress.com/Fiction
to read interviews with your favorite authors, find tips
for starting a reading group, and stay posted on what
new titles are on the horizon. It's a place to connect
with other fiction readers or post a
comment about this book.

Be sure to visit Rita online!

http://ritagerlach.blogspot.com
www.inspire-writer.blogspot.com